ONE LAST KILL

A CALLAHAN BOYLE THRILLER

SPENSER WARREN

Cover design by: Dane Low
Formatted by: Vellum

Version1

Will a hit man meet his end? Discover how to read your next Cal Boyle thriller — FREE!

Find out how to get your FREE copy of the Callahan Boyle prequel novella, *Marked For Murder*!

Read until the end to discover how to get your free copy of *Marked For Murder*, a book available only to my readers. *Marked For Murder* is an action-packed thriller that showcases one of Cal's first kills as a hit man in the Chicago mafia. I'm confident you'll love every page.

What happens when Cal kills the wrong man? From ferocious fist fights to careening car crashes, read as Cal navigates a burgeoning drug war between the Chicago mafia and a rival gang, whose leader is hellbent on ensuring Cal never sees another day. Will Cal find a way to take down his never-ending list of enemies?

Stay tuned for your exclusive offer to receive your FREE copy of *Marked For Murder.* Not only will you get your hands on a great read, you'll also be among the first to be notified of new releases by signing up for my "hit list." I'll keep the emails fast, friendly, and fun, and you can unsubscribe at any time.

Until then, I hope you enjoy *One Last Kill.*

To Mom and Dad. Thanks for always believing in my dreams.

C allahan Boyle sat in the back row of Chicago's CIBC Theatre trying to get comfortable, which was tough given the complete lack of legroom for a man of his height. He was there for *The Book of Mormon*'s evening show, yet he wasn't interested in the performance— he'd already seen the play ten times. The target of his interest was his next victim, who was sitting in the front row on stage right.

He'd been following George MacErlean for weeks and figured the show's final performance was his best and last chance to make his move. With MacErlean's girlfriend cast as Nabulungi, the female lead, Cal had repeatedly shown up to stake out the man in a setting where he knew MacErlean couldn't weasel away.

Unlike his other trips to the theater, Cal wasn't alone this time. As the most ruthless and efficient of the Chicago mafia's hit men, Cal rarely needed backup. Yet during the previous performance, Cal had felt several eyes glued to him, suggesting MacErlean had watchdogs. Cal had brought his good buddy Alfonso "Fonzie" Benetti to help take out

MacErlean's men should they interfere. Fonzie was waiting to do his part in the car with Cal's driver, Tony Fregosi.

Intermission was in a few minutes, and Cal couldn't wait. He was anxious to get this over with. Weeks of tailing and hard work would manifest itself in a brief moment of perfect execution. He only hoped it went according to plan.

Fonzie's voice sounded in the Bluetooth earpiece. "What's up, my brother? We're still circling the block. Should be back on Monroe in no time."

Cal coughed his acknowledgment. The last song of the first act was almost finished, then he'd be free to speak. Until then, he had to listen to the smacking of Fonzie's gum through the earpiece.

"Tony, turn up the goddamned air-conditioning," Fonzie said between chomps. "I'm sweating my black ass off."

Even though Tony, the driver, was only eighteen and Cal preferred not to drag him into such a critical mission, he'd come to trust the boy over the last several months. Tony's ambition and fire reminded Cal of himself when he was younger, when Cal had actually wanted something more out of life than an easy paycheck.

The curtains closed and the lights lifted, springing Cal into action. He rose from his seat and beelined for the hallway before a crowd could form. He wanted to make sure MacErlean came outside, as was his custom, and to see if any of his goons were staying close to him.

MacErlean was quite the conversationalist. He enjoyed glad-handing with the audience, trying to prove how good of an actor he could be. Cal hadn't known much about MacErlean prior to being asked to tail him, but he had heard the man was the classic definition of a struggling actor, failing time after time to land a role of significance.

Must live through his girlfriend's success, Cal thought.

Once MacErlean grew tired of bragging about his girl-friend and cracking wise, he often moseyed out the theater entrance for a smoke. Today, Cal was hoping to catch him before his cigarette transformed into a pile of ashes.

"True to script so far," Cal said into his microphone. "I can't wait until we find out what this jerk has to say and can end this."

"Don't get too excited. This motherfucker is mine to grab. Time to show the boss what I can do."

"You'll be able to get your hands all over him, Fonzie. Just let me be the bait to get him outside."

"Why the hell are we grabbing this guy anyway?"

Tony's voice was audible through Fonzie's mic. Cal felt annoyed at the boy's question but figured it was best to explain the situation.

"MacErlean had a meeting with the mayor. At least that's what Alfredo's been made to believe. Remember the mayor's State of Chicago press conference a few months ago? He specifically cited the mafia's activities in his speech. Alfredo thinks he's onto us and that MacErlean was the one to spill the beans."

Cal had to lower his voice as he ended his explanation. A large crowd of theatergoers flooded the lobby and headed outside, despite the sweltering late-August heat.

Fonzie exhaled into the mic, creating a harsh sound in Cal's earpiece. "I still don't think it's a great idea grabbing him in public, even at night. He hasn't been one of us for a while, right? What could he know that could rattle Fredo's old bones?"

"I'm not sure, but if he's giving dirt to the mayor, it could be dangerous."

"How do they know it was MacErlean? Could've been anybody."

Cal sighed and kept his eye on his mark. MacErlean was visible from Cal's vantage point in the lobby. Any minute now and the target would be acquired.

"They all insist it was him. There are a lot of people on the payroll in City Hall, and any of them could be leaking stuff back to Alfredo."

Tony's voice sounded over the mic again. "When you say this guy was one of us, you mean he was a flunky?"

"You may be an errand boy, but I ain't no flunky," Fonzie said. "I may not be made yet, but I've killed more men than you ever will."

Cal tuned out the arguing and watched as MacErlean drew closer. There were no signs of the men Cal had previously seen protecting the potential informant.

Out of the corner of his eye, two men in brown tweed jackets and matching slacks began charging up the aisle inside the auditorium, arousing his suspicion.

MacErlean was only feet away from Cal, his jacket brushing against a short old lady. Cal watched him exit and turn to the left for his usual smoke break. All according to plan.

"Are you guys out front? He just left, heading right for you," Cal said into the mic. "Let him light up first. When his back is turned, make the grab."

Cal thought he saw the old lady's eyebrow rise. He matched her gesture and turned his head to the left. The men in the tweed jackets were trying to push their way through the crowded lobby, both pairs of eyes fixated on the exit doors.

Cal knew he had to step in. The taller of the two men, bearded and donning Ray-Ban sunglasses, brushed against a poised, slender woman conversing with the eyebrow-raising dame. Cal dashed around the old lady, much faster than he probably should have, and stopped the two men in their tracks.

"What do you want?" the shorter man asked in a thick Eastern European accent. Cal couldn't tell whether it was Ukrainian, Romanian, or perhaps Russian.

"Yeah, out of the way," Bearded Man said.

Cal wasn't the best at creating distractions with words. He was a man of action. On instinct, his fingers reached inside the pocket of his black dress slacks, grasping his jack-knife. The men's eyes were like daggers attempting to tear through Cal's pocket. Cal met their gaze with a steely glare of his own. A loud, feminine scream pierced the air behind them.

The shorter man charged forward, attempting to pass Cal and get outside. Cal decked him with a sharp punch in the stomach. The man slumped forward, and Cal threw him back into the crowd, eliciting more shrieks inside the theater lobby.

Bearded Man clubbed Cal in the back of the head and attempted to follow with a punch to the gut, but Cal blocked him and threw a hard right hook at his assailant's face, knocking the man's sunglasses off in the process.

Cal heard honking outside. *Time to go.*

He dashed out of the lobby, unconcerned about the panic-stricken eyes trailing him outside.

The first thing Cal saw was Fonzie holding his Glock 9mm in his left hand. In plain view of a large crowd of theatergoers, he was dragging a petrified MacErlean, who had his hands raised like a police suspect, into the back of Tony's black Hyundai Sonata. This was not how MacErlean's pickup was supposed to go.

Cal rushed through the crowd, drew his Beretta from his inside-waistband holster, and held it in the air. He wanted to scare the crowd back indoors and prevent the goons he'd encountered from following.

"Everyone back inside. This man is a crook and he is being brought to justice."

Before anyone could whip out their cell phone to record the incident, Cal jumped inside the passenger seat while Fonzie tackled MacErlean into the back seat.

Cal's plan to use the scared theatergoers as a shield was dashed as the short goon came racing through the crowd. Cal saw him reach inside his jacket. He was pulling out a gun.

"Punch it, Tony!"

The kid put the car into drive and sped away from the curb. Screams pierced the air. Cal ducked when Bearded Man ran out, gun drawn, and joined his friend shooting at the car.

"Holy hell, Cal. I didn't think anyone would be shooting at us."

"Dodge this traffic, we can't have our tires shot out."

Tony swerved between two cars after making it through the Monroe and State intersection. They sped down the street before turning right onto South Wabash Avenue. Cal let out a deep exhale from his closely held breath once they were headed south.

That was close. Too close.

2
_____

Smoke wafted above the heads of the four mafia leaders seated on the black leather sectional in the great room of Alfredo Petrocelli's Gold Coast penthouse. Other than the stirring of a drink or the exhale of cigar smoke, none of the members of the mafia leadership had made a sound since a phone call beckoned Alfredo to his office.

"If one of you guys don't say something, I'm gonna shit my pants."

Al Meransky, the North Side caporegime, wrinkled his brow and shifted in his seat. The movement of his pants against the leather sounded like a loud fart. The other leaders' eyebrows rose in disgust.

"When you're done ripping ass over there, we've gotta figure out how to calm Alfredo down. This isn't good." Frankie Ramone, Meransky's equal for the South Side of the city, always had a way of starting a serious conversation with a joke. It was his humor that Vinnie appreciated most about the fat caporegime.

Seated to Vinnie's right was the consigliera of the

Chicago mafia, Melissa Ranieri. She relaxed her entire body into the cushion behind her, her long tan right leg crossed over her left, her black skirt barely halfway down her thighs. She smoked a thin black cigar. It seemed fake, like something from the movies. Even though she was Vinnie's cousin, he had to admit she looked good smoking it.

"Relax, boys," she said. "Uncle Alfredo's a little nervous, that's all. We still don't know what the mayor knows."

Meransky broke in. "Yeah, what's all of this hoopla with the mayor? How come I ain't heard about it?"

"'Cuz it's not your business. Cal is handling it. Cal works for me," Frankie said.

"Oh really? Last time I checked, fatso, Cal wasn't a soldier. He's our best hit man. That means he works on both sides of the city. Not just the South Side, though you sure as hell could use him down there. How do you get any business done with all the murders?"

Frankie rose off the couch and shook his fists, ready to challenge his fellow capo. Vinnie rolled his eyes and stood up to set his empty glass down on the counter. Melissa didn't miss a beat and gave Vinnie a knowing wink before rising to her feet.

"Fresh drink for the gentleman?"

Vinnie shrugged his shoulders and watched as his cousin grabbed his empty glass. It was exactly like Melissa to observe the next item that needed attention. No wonder she'd been so effective leading the mafia's prostitution ring as the top madam before being picked for consigliera.

As business savvy as she was, Vinnie was upset that he hadn't been chosen for the mafia's top advisory position. It was enough that his father risked putting a family member in the position and made them vulnerable to attack by rival gangs, police, and politicians alike for anyone who wanted an easy way to get to Alfredo. Vinnie could handle any such threat, whereas he didn't think Melissa could. But it was also a discredit to all of the work he'd done behind the scenes over the years to learn the family business and think of the best way to take advantage of new business opportunities to secure their future.

Vinnie shook away the thought and set his gaze on Frankie and Meransky, willing them to get their acts together. As underboss of the family, both men answered to him. In turn, Vinnie only answered to his father. Yet he knew Alfredo took Melissa's feedback more seriously than his own.

He took the band holding his ponytail together and removed it with his fingers before running them through his brown hair. The capos watched this ritual with puzzled looks on their faces before Vinnie shook his hair out and let it hang long to dust the tops of his shoulders.

"Can we get serious for a minute? Save your arguing for later."

Frankie looked at Vinnie like he'd been caught with his hand in the cookie jar. Meransky waved his hand forward as if it were nothing, and Melissa tiptoed carefully back to the couch with a fresh martini for her and a vodka soda for Vinnie.

"What, you don't bother to get me nothing?" Frankie asked.

"Enough," Vinnie said. "You all saw my father's mood before he took that phone call. Imagine what he's going to be like if it's bad news. Frankie's right, we have to find a way to keep him calm."

"I've never seen him like that in all our years together," Frankie said, returning to his seat. "Yelling, screaming. I've seen that. I've never seen him do the damage he just did, though."

Vinnie glanced over at what remained of the small circular wooden table between the great room and the kitchen. A substantial bronze sculpture sat atop the table, most of which had been driven into the floor. Even for being expensive decor, the fancy table wasn't able to withstand the impact of the decorative sculpture.

Vinnie wondered where the chairs had gone before remembering they'd been flung across the room. Wood pieces lay scattered from the visible portion of the foyer to the door of Alfredo's office. It had been a temper tantrum for the ages. Vinnie hoped that, unlike many of his father's bursts of outrage, his next action wouldn't lead to a rash and faulty business decision.

"I mean, what can this possibly be about? I feel like I should know what's going on with the mayor. C'mon, somebody hit me."

Vinnie glared hard at Meransky, and the capo wilted like overcooked kale into his seat. Vinnie smiled inside, knowing he had Meransky under his thumb. Frankie looked at Vinnie and shrugged his shoulders. Vinnie nodded, allowing Frankie to share what exactly was going on.

"Cal's going after a guy who used to work for us. Some guy I don't remember. It was probably three or four years back. Maybe he was one of yours."

Meransky jumped forward, lifting his backbone off of the cushion with an authority that Alfredo would be proud of. "One of mine? One of my guys would never cause Alfredo to flip his shit like that."

"We don't know for sure whose guy he was," Melissa said. Her eyes were as icy as the cubes rising in Frankie's scotch glass.

Meransky sank back into the seat again. "Go ahead."

"Anyway," Frankie continued, "one of the aldermen was at City Hall a few months back. Guy's a good friend of ours. Has been tight with us for years. Says he saw this shady character heading to Mayor Caruso's office. Superintendent Walker was going in with him."

"Wait, what? The chief of police was chumming around with an ex-mobster? Walker doesn't like us one bit. He's one fucker who can't be bought," Meransky said.

"No shit, Al," Melissa said. "Let Frankie finish the story."

Frankie picked up his empty glass and tilted it back, swirling some melting ice cubes into his mouth. Melissa slinked off the couch and grabbed the glass when Frankie put it down, giving him a pout as she walked away with it.

"Aw, thank you, dear. I knew you were a good girl." Frankie turned away from Melissa and back to Meransky. "Again, I'll reiterate what the hell is going on. This guy and Walker go into the mayor's office, and our alderman buddy starts chatting it up with the receptionist at the front of the office. They're real good friends. Walker leaves after a few minutes, but the guy stays in there. It's a half hour, then an hour, then an hour and a half."

"The alderman was chatting with the secretary that whole time?" Meransky asked.

"No, numb nuts. He got her to call him when the guy left. Found out the name of the guy. George MacErlean. He called Alfredo and said he looked like a guido, might be one of ours. What's a guido doing with Mayor Caruso? A guy who hates our guts despite all we've done for the bastard."

Vinnie nodded along with the story. It was a story his father had told him many times before. Why Meransky felt the need to know all the details when they had it under control was beyond him, but he knew it was his job as underboss to put everyone on the same page to talk some sense into his father.

"Only it's not a coincidence," Vinnie said. "The mayor gave his state of the city speech and mentioned how organized crime, aka us, is responsible for the increased violent crime rate. He placed a target on our backs."

"Ah," Meransky said. "And that's when you knew that MacErlean tipped the mayor off."

"Precisely," Vinnie said. "Only we aren't sure what he told the mayor. My father's been nervous about it for a long time. That's why we met with Frankie and sent Cal on surveillance."

Meransky scratched behind his ear and jerked his thumb toward the office. "Okay. *Something* must have happened to cause him to go berserk. What do you think it was?"

Vinnie shook his mane of hair again and tapped his palms on his thighs. "I'm not sure. Cal was going to grab him today. Maybe something went wrong."

"Cal went to find out what the little rat knows," Frankie said, smiling as Melissa returned with his drink. "Let's hope our man delivered."

"Cal's the best. Of course he delivered." Melissa tucked her legs beneath her and flipped her bleached-blonde hair in place behind her head. She batted her eyelashes, then rolled her eyes as the men stared at her. "Trust me, I know a stud when I see one. I've met a lot of big shots since taking on this gig, including spending more time with you boys. Outside of Cal, I haven't seen too many studs."

A loud bang caused all four of them to jump out of their seats. Alfredo's office door opened. The clanking sound of leather soles pounded the hardwood floor like a horse trotting on a cobblestone courtyard, riding to victory at the command of a king's knight.

"What is it?" Al Meransky asked. Even seated behind him, Vinnie could see Meransky's scrambled-eggs-and-bacon expression, eyes and lips running down his face in all directions.

Alfredo smiled like he'd won the Illinois Lottery. The room took a collective deep breath; even the broken furniture was able to exhale.

"Good news, lady and gents. We've got him."

3

After battling the evening traffic for half an hour, Tony Fregosi drove slowly down Mackinaw Avenue. The street was a dead end, and a brick wall stood off the corner of the vacant lot where Frankie Ramone had suggested they take MacErlean. An old cinder-block shed that hadn't been used in years was barely visible from the dark street. It would be the perfect spot for Cal to get to work.

Tony shut off the engine and opened the driver's-side door.

"Don't even think about going in with us," Cal said to Tony. "Stay with the car. You can take my gun just in case. Between my knife and Fonzie's gun, I don't think we'll need it."

Tony's confident posture slumped back in his seat before he could exit the vehicle. "C'mon, Cal. When am I going to finally be a part of some real action?"

Cal placed his hand on Tony's shoulder and stared into his eyes. "Look, kid, you're not ready for this kind of stuff.

Torturing and killing people isn't for fun. You've already done more than enough."

Fonzie stood at the back of the car and struggled to pull MacErlean's stiff body out of the back seat. He'd pistol-whipped MacErlean when he wouldn't shut up on the drive over.

Cal handed Tony his gun, a Beretta M9, and moved to help Fonzie with MacErlean. They needed to get him inside before he regained consciousness.

Cal picked up MacErlean's limp form and slung him over his shoulder. Fonzie's mouth was agape at the display.

"You lift, bruh?"

"Something like that."

Cal carried MacErlean toward the small shed. It resembled a public park restroom rather than the small toolshed it had been. A house under construction on the lot had burned down, but the shed had survived the fire.

"Could this place be any more revolting?" Cal asked once they were inside.

The smell of the place was horrid. Broken vials of crack littered the floor and half-eaten McDonald's hamburgers rotted around them. A rather large rat skirted the perimeter of the room toward a Big Gulp cup.

"Beggars can't be choosers. Let's tie this knucklehead up before he comes to."

Fonzie started tying MacErlean to one of two metal folding chairs left in the shed. Cal meandered over to join him as he recalled his first kill. He was only twelve years old. His father had just been murdered, and his beautiful, loving mother had died a few months later.

While Cal hadn't mourned his father's death, due to his drunken abuse of him and his mother, he discovered that day that he'd inherited his father's rage. Rage that was blind enough to cause him to do something unthinkable, something he realized few people seriously contemplate doing—taking another human life. That kill was the event that had set his life as a hit man in motion.

Cal blinked and forced the memory to evaporate as MacErlean began to stir. He saw the same terror in his eyes that Cal had seen in the young boy seventeen years earlier.

"Help! I'm in here with two crazy bastards!"

"Damn right you are," Fonzie said. "And we don't have time for any of your shit."

Cal watched as MacErlean tried to shake free of the ropes that bound him. It would prove useless. Fonzie and Cal weren't Boy Scouts, but they knew how to tie a solid knot.

"What do you people want? They don't pay me nearly enough for this shit. Let me go, and I'll tell you everything."

Great. A man without a backbone who'll tell you anything you want to hear just to save his own ass.

Cal pulled his jackknife from the pocket of his slacks and released the blade. Better to show off the weapons early and prove he meant business.

Cal strode toward MacErlean and held the blade against the side of his face. MacErlean's entire body shook. Sweat trickled from his forehead, joining the dried blood caked under his nose and around his mouth from Fonzie's pistol-whipping. Cal could smell the fear on his breath. He'd killed enough men to know that, even when someone knew death was imminent, they couldn't fight their body's own evolutionary instincts for survival.

He made a small incision above MacErlean's cheekbone. Just enough to leave a gentle cut. MacErlean screamed and would've jumped out of his skin had the ropes not been holding him down.

"My friend Fonzie has told you that I'm one of the best. When the shit hits the fan, I'm the guy Alfredo Petrocelli calls to clean up. So, here's what we're going to do. I'm going to ask you a few questions. How you answer those questions determines whether you walk out of here alive or not. Got it?"

MacErlean's voice trembled. "Yeah, I got it."

Fonzie smiled and shifted his head to the left. Cal took the cue and backed off from MacErlean, closing the blade and putting the knife back in his pocket. MacErlean exhaled a sigh of relief and closed his eyes. Cal stepped forward and fired a hard right hook into MacErlean's cheek.

The force of the blow was so strong, MacErlean would've hurtled backward had Fonzie not been there to hold the chair in place. Cal backed off again and paced in front of the chair. Fonzie had moved to the other side so Cal could strike the left cheek. Cal struck again, this time in the same spot Fonzie had nailed him in the car. MacErlean let out a shrieking cry that nearly pierced Cal's eardrums.

Fonzie pulled a second chair next to MacErlean. Cal walked toward it. He preferred dealing with his victims at eye level. It made it so they were on the same playing field.

"MacErlean, you've seen I don't play games. If I don't like what I hear from you, there's plenty more where those punches came from. Even if you do manage to get out of here alive, your face will be so bruised and battered that you're gonna wish I'd killed you."

MacErlean sobbed. Cal wondered if MacErlean thought it was worth it to sell out the Petrocelli family to the mayor and break the law of omertà.

"You said you weren't paid enough to deal with this shit earlier. Who's paying you? Who are you working for?"

MacErlean sniffled and stared at the ground below.

"Security guys. They work for the mayor. That's all I know, I swear."

Fonzie eyed Cal. Cal shook his head. Fonzie liked to occasionally get in on the action and add his own brand of violence, but that wasn't needed. Not now.

"Are those the guys who tried to gun us down outside the theater?"

MacErlean nodded. He fixated his gaze on Cal and his sobs ceased. "Those two protect the mayor. They're his bodyguards."

"So why were they protecting you, dipshit?" Fonzie asked.

Cal glared at Fonzie, unappreciative of the interruption. He looked back at MacErlean.

"Answer the question."

MacErlean closed his eyes. "The mayor wanted to keep me around. He wanted to make sure nothing happened to me."

"Why would the mayor work so hard to keep you around? You're a bad actor who couldn't hack it driving cars for the mafia back in the day."

MacErlean appeared to hesitate. This was the point in the altercation where Cal knew he'd have to press harder. He knew MacErlean wouldn't give up what he'd said to the mayor that easily.

Cal decided to try one last time. He knew Fonzie had a knife on him in addition to the gun. He nodded at Fonzie and mentally prepared himself for the scream as Fonzie pulled out his knife and slashed MacErlean across the throat. It wasn't a particularly deep cut—Fonzie was sure not to cut the carotid artery—but it would do the job just as well. MacErlean's eyes bulged in horror as blood rushed down his neck, staining his white dress shirt even further.

Only air escaped MacErlean's throat as he tried to scream. It was time to make him spill his guts before his imminent death. Cal readied his own knife, preparing to make one last cut should MacErlean remain silent or deny the truth.

"MacErlean, you are going to die. I'm going to ask you nicely before I cut you in a more sensitive place. Why was the mayor protecting you?"

MacErlean gurgled as more blood spurted from his throat. Cal felt like ending it now and putting him out of his misery.

"I...I spoke to the mayor. Told him...told him." MacErlean coughed some more, so violently that Cal was sure he would pass out before he faded into death.

"Told him what?" Cal's voice growled in anger. He should've taken more time to think this through. Despite MacErlean's admission of the mayor's bodyguards, Cal had nothing to go back to Alfredo with. It could cost him.

MacErlean fought the pain and spoke up again. His words were softer, and Cal and Fonzie had to lean closer to hear him. "I shared Alfredo Petrocelli's grandest secret with the mayor. It wasn't about business. It wasn't about the drugs, the prostitution, the loan-sharking...Caruso doesn't give a shit about that."

MacErlean kept coughing. "The mayor knows...he knows how to put an end to Alfredo Petrocelli once and for all. And it's all because of me."

The informant started laughing now. Blood continued to pour out of his throat. He was transforming from a man doomed for death to a man filled with life.

Cal couldn't let MacErlean laugh at him like he had won. It reminded him of the young boy talking shit about his father after his death. Anger welled up in Cal and he began to move the knife toward MacErlean.

One final look from MacErlean caused him to stop. This look was much more serious, almost sympathetic.

Maybe he's slipping into death after all.

"I know a few secrets about you."

The color drained from MacErlean's face. It was only a matter of time.

"Oh yeah, dead man? What's that?"

MacErlean coughed profusely. His eyes were beginning to roll to the back of his head. How he'd made it this long, Cal didn't know.

"It's your mother... Died in a car accident, right? Well, her...death...wasn't...an...accident."

4

The next morning, Cal and Fonzie were called in for a meeting with Alfredo. The fact Alfredo had called Cal, and not Vinnie or one of the capos, told Cal that this meeting was serious business. Cal wondered if the MacErlean hit was too messy for his liking or if a video clip of him and Fonzie grabbing MacErlean at the theater had surfaced on the news. The mob boss gave no indication and just said he would see him soon.

Cal and Fonzie arrived at the Petrocelli compound in the northern suburb of Evanston. It was a large redbrick house with a driveway that circled around a giant oak tree and was packed with black vehicles of varying makes, all shimmering as if freshly washed. Perpendicular to the circle drive was a longer driveway that led to a garage farther back on the property.

Fonzie parked at the back of the drive, blocking in the cars ahead. Bruno, one of the low-level soldiers who guarded the house, was standing on the front lawn smoking a cigarette. Cal couldn't understand why people enjoyed those cancer sticks. They stepped out of the car, and Bruno nodded as they walked toward the front entrance. Fonzie stopped midstride to turn back toward the soldier.

"You out here washing all these cars, Bruno?"

Bruno removed the cigarette from his mouth and exhaled smoke with a huff.

"Hell no. That's what those hood rat kids like Fregosi are for."

"Hood rat? You talking shit about Tony?" Fonzie reached toward his belt.

Bruno dropped his cigarette butt and jumped back. "I didn't mean Tony, but kids like Tony. They're all the same anyway."

Cal glared at Fonzie. It was best not to stand outside and make small talk while Alfredo was waiting for them.

"Nice catchin' up with you, Bruno," Fonzie said as he followed Cal through the front door.

"A real pleasant character, that Bruno," Cal said.

"How long you think he lasts?"

"Maybe a few months. He's been here longer than some of the others."

Cal walked through the foyer and into the living room. As he passed, he couldn't help but notice the portraits of the last five Chicago mafia bosses on the wall to his right, with Alfredo and his father and grandfather among them. Though Cal had lived in the Petrocelli house from the age of twelve to twenty, the portraits always stood out to him among the impressive decor of the home.

When they reached the living room, a young man with a longish mop of hair pointed toward the open study door, revealing a massive amount of books along the far wall. Cal led the way without a word and forced a smile as he made eye contact first with Alfredo and then Vinnie.

The pale-blue Oxford dress shirt Vinnie wore appeared

out of place underneath a black suit jacket and tucked into a pair of white khaki shorts. A pair of Maui Jim sunglasses tinted his eyes from view, but Cal could still make them out.

His adoptive brother wasn't a big guy; he was more wiry than bulky. Cal knew it bothered Vinnie that Cal had grown into a muscular and imposing figure whereas Vinnie had stayed lean and presented a less intimidating presence.

"Cal, my brotha!"

Vinnie wrapped one arm around Cal and embraced him in what could only be described as a bro hug.

Fonzie stepped into the room and shook Vinnie's hand as Cal made his way toward the large oak desk Alfredo was seated behind.

"Cal, it's good to see you."

Alfredo's stiff gaze suggested he wasn't in the mood for small talk. His thick and wavy graying-brown hair stood atop his head, revealing a forehead creased with wrinkles. If he wore clown makeup and dyed his hair red, he'd be a fine impersonation of Ronald McDonald.

Unlike his son, Alfredo was strongly built. He used to be a hit man and enforcer as Cal now was, except he'd done it with the knowledge that he would be a made man for his efforts. He only stood an inch taller than his six-foot-tall son but, at around 230 pounds, was much heavier. Most of it was muscle from his days of roughing up those who opposed his father when he'd been boss. Yet, a slight belly protruded above his belt.

Alfredo sat and motioned toward the two leather chairs across from him. From the corner of the room, Vinnie stared down at his fingernails a little too long for Cal's liking, as if he knew the next few moments would be filled with tension.

Alfredo peered at them while pouring a glass of brandy for himself. He tipped the bottle toward Fonzie and then

Cal. Fonzie grabbed a nearby glass. Cal thought it was too early for drinking.

"Tell me about the MacErlean grab," Alfredo said. "I heard business was taken care of."

Fonzie smiled and looked at Cal. He was normally extra talkative, but Cal knew Fonzie was just as scared of Alfredo as anyone else.

"Yes, MacErlean is dead," Cal said.

Alfredo and Vinnie stared at Cal, unblinking.

"Go on," Alfredo urged. "Tell us exactly what happened."

Cal told Alfredo everything. From the men in tweed jackets approaching him in the theater lobby, to the screaming people outside as they saw MacErlean being forced into the vehicle, to the gunshots, to the fatal stab to the heart that Cal delivered to end the night. The only detail Cal left out was what MacErlean had said about his mother's accident.

Alfredo leaned back in his chair, arms crossed. "I assume you asked MacErlean what he told the mayor."

Cal nodded. "He said he told the mayor about what he called your 'grandest secret.'"

Alfredo raised his brow again, drank a swig of brandy, and tapped his fingers on the desk. He glanced at Vinnie, who shrugged and brushed his bangs out of the way of his sunglasses.

"What sort of secret did MacErlean say I had?"

This was the part Cal was afraid of. MacErlean hadn't provided any details, and Cal had been too quick to kill him after the information he had revealed about his mother.

"I got a little impatient before we whacked him. He mentioned the mayor was very interested in protecting him.

I figured that was enough to confirm your suspicions that the mayor may be a dangerous party."

Alfredo rose from his chair and pointed at Cal like a dog owner yelling at his new puppy for peeing on the carpet.

"Goddamnit, Callahan! You're the best fucking soldier I've got, and you can't get some basic details out of some punk actor?"

"You're right, I should've investigated further. I wanted to respect your privacy since I know I'll never be a made man and there's certain things I shouldn't know."

Alfredo looked at Cal like he wanted to explode. It reminded him of his father yelling at his mother when the dinner was cold, despite him getting home from work late.

"Damnit, Cal, do you think I give a shit about that right now? Who cares if you're not Sicilian? You've been a part of the family for seventeen years. A lot longer than your own family. Benetti isn't made either, and I trust even him with this business."

Alfredo stopped huffing and paced toward the front of the room. Cal and Fonzie sat in silence before Vinnie spoke up.

"The important thing is we know that MacErlean really was an informant for the mayor and that the mayor has highly armed security working for him. Now, let's think about how this ties back to us, Dad. MacErlean used to be a lackey for Al Meransky, is that right?"

Alfredo nodded and walked toward the desk.

"MacErlean was a driver for us, probably four years ago, a slick young guy with greased back hair. I must have seen some sort of potential in the kid. Anyway, I knew he was a rat when some of Meransky's guys got picked up by the cops for drinking and driving. Instead of piling everyone in his car or calling a cab, he let the guys drive home and called the police. Un-fucking-believable."

Fonzie laughed. "The guy sounds like a lowlife snitch."

Alfredo sat back down at the desk and leered at Fonzie as if this were the first time he'd seen him that day.

He turned his attention back to Vinnie. "Yeah, that's why you shoulda whacked him when you gave him the boot."

"My point was," Vinnie pressed on, "if we knew what MacErlean found out from his time with us, then we could use that to determine how seriously we take a potential threat from the mayor."

"He couldn't have learned much," Cal offered. He felt like he could use that glass of brandy now. "If he was nothing more than a driver, he wouldn't have been included in any big conversations."

"What if somebody talked? Al's got a big mouth," Alfredo said.

Vinnie rose from his chair in the corner. "What did Al know that might cause Caruso to come down on us in his speech?"

"Could be nothing," Fonzie said. "Crime in general has picked up in the city. People are tired of it. He could've just been rattling off names."

Alfredo shook his head. "If MacErlean was tight with the mayor, he had to know something."

"C'mon, Dad, aren't we grasping at straws here? We have no way of knowing what it is. It could be anything."

Alfredo finished his brandy and poured another glass. He didn't offer Fonzie a refill.

"Alright, Vinnie. I want you to think on this one. Find out from Al what MacErlean might have picked up on."

He pointed toward Cal. "I want you to follow Caruso around for a while. Just like you did with MacErlean. Find out his habits and how many men he's got. If you discover anything useful, I'll set up a meeting to see what kind of trouble we're in."

Cal wanted to roll his eyes at the prospect of another surveillance assignment. They were boring, but Cal knew Alfredo trusted him to be discreet without tipping off the target. Still, tailing Caruso was a risk, especially since his men might recognize him. He'd have to think of a way around that one.

"I'll get started right away."

Alfredo tipped some more brandy down his throat. Cal wondered how many he'd had already.

"Good, now get out of here. I've got a lot of people to see. Let's try not to have any messes this time, huh?"

Vinnie nodded at Cal and Fonzie as they stood up. "You boys behave yourselves. Let's hope we can bide some time before the mayor finds out what happened to MacErlean."

Cal and Fonzie walked out of the study and back into the living room. Vinnie followed them and closed the door behind them.

"What's up with Fredo?" Fonzie asked. "He basically acted like I didn't exist."

Cal shrugged. "Hopefully he didn't hear you call him Fredo. You know how much he loves that."

"Man, fuck Fredo," Fonzie said in a whisper. "Let's hurry up and get out of here. I'm getting hungry."

They stepped outside and headed for the car. Fonzie's next question alarmed Cal.

"Man, have you ever thought about why it is we do what we do?"

Cal raised a brow in shock. He wasn't used to thinking about such philosophical questions. He liked to focus on getting the job done. Anything else was a distraction.

"I guess I haven't considered it. It's something I'm good at, and it makes me pretty good money. Isn't that what a job is supposed to do?"

They arrived at the car and got in. Fonzie turned the key and backed out of the driveway and into the street.

"No, I mean it. Killing people, chasing after thugs, beating people up, doing other shit you don't want to do? Is that how you want to spend your life?"

Cal couldn't believe what he was hearing. Everything he knew about Fonzie indicated he loved working in the mafia more than anything. It wasn't often that a black man was accepted into the mafia, even if his mother was Italian. Perhaps he didn't know his friend as well as he thought.

"I don't know. What else would I be able to do? At least you can sing—maybe your mom can get you on the right track in Hollywood."

Fonzie laughed and drummed the steering wheel along to a Drake song. "I don't want nothing to do with Hollywood, man. Or my mama. What's she ever done for me?"

The rest of the ride passed in silence. The question lingered in Cal's mind, right next to the question of his mother's accident. He let them roll around his brain for a moment before falling asleep.

5

A lfredo had told Vinnie to leave the room and not allow any visitors for a while. He needed more time to review the Caruso situation. It was starting to become a pain in the ass.

Cal may have taken out Caruso's slimy informant, but it was time to prepare for the next step. Alfredo had kept things low-key since the mayor's promise to snuff out crime. He'd ordered his men to go easy on drug sales, prostitution, loan-sharking, and sketchy union contracts. The dial-back had done a real number on the business, and revenues kept going south. Even though he was running an organized crime outfit, they were like any other major corporation—you always had to keep an eye on the profits.

Alfredo knocked his knuckles on the desk and opened a drawer. He kept especially secret business dealings locked away in a location only known to Melissa. The manila folder he pulled out of the drawer was filled with information on Ross Caruso. Inside, every detail of every campaign dona-tion and favor the mafia had pulled to get him elected was documented. Not only for the mayoral seat, but the Illinois State Senate seat he used to hold as well.

Alfredo already knew what MacErlean had told Caruso —he just needed to put on a good show in front of everyone else. How MacErlean found out, he didn't know. Sending Cal to investigate the mayor was nothing more than a wild-goose chase. If he got lucky, maybe Cal would take out some of the mayor's men along the way. It was yet another reason he was glad he made the decision to adopt him seventeen years ago.

* * *

CAL'S FATHER had been a complete wreck. Tom Boyle worked in a warehouse on the South Side where the mafia kept imported heroin from South America, among other legitimate holdings. In his days as underboss, Alfredo paid special attention to that very profitable line of business.

One day, Alfredo realized the money wasn't pouring in as usual. He suspected someone was skimming the profits. The arrangement was that the guys doing the dealing got a percentage, then the capo got a bigger percentage, and the warehouse manager at the time, Gustavo Mariucci, got a slightly larger percentage to keep things running smoothly. The largest percentage, over 50 percent of the proceeds, fed up the chain to the boss, Alfredo's father.

Word got to Alfredo that Mariucci was taking a larger share than he was entitled to, and it was up to him to teach the warehouse manager a lesson. It wasn't the kind of lesson where he would ask Mariucci nicely to stop taking money— it was one that would be taught at the end of a shotgun barrel.

On the day he planned to kill Mariucci, Alfredo mistook

Tom Boyle for the warehouse manager and killed him instead. None of the other workers batted an eye when they found out that old Tom, a roaring drunk who treated everyone rotten, had been shot. The death had even scared Mariucci straight—to the point where he offered to reduce his take on the heroin business. It had worked out better than planned.

After Tom's death, Vinnie begged Alfredo to do something about Cal, a real quiet kid who hung around with Vinnie when they were both at the warehouse. It wasn't the best environment for a kid to be around, but Alfredo had to keep an eye on things, and the boys enjoyed playing together after school.

Since Vinnie was smart for his age, he knew that Cal and his mother weren't doing well financially. His mom was a waitress who didn't make a lot of money, so they relied on the meager amount of government assistance they could get while she scraped around for a second job.

Like any naive child, Vinnie asked his parents, Alfredo and Susan, to take Cal in because they were good buddies and Vinnie thought Cal's situation would improve as part of their family. Family was a strong pillar in the Petrocelli house of values, but Alfredo initially felt taking Cal from his mother would contradict his own belief about the importance of family. He didn't want to take Cal in when he had a loving mother to watch over him, even if living with her wouldn't provide the best life for the young boy.

His thinking changed one day at the warehouse when he saw Cal standing on the catwalk above the shop floor talking with another boy. It sounded like the boy was laying into Cal real good, telling him what an awful man his father was. The other boy's father often complained about Tom's abusive habits at the warehouse.

No matter how terrible a man was, the worst thing you could do was tell his son how awful his father was after his death. The boy's speech made even Alfredo queasy, and he was the one who'd killed the bastard.

The boy wouldn't let up. Alfredo saw the anger written all over Cal's face. He saw his body shake and knew it was pure adrenaline assaulting his veins. The second Cal pushed the boy over the edge and glared at him as he fell to the ground, his head splattering open like a dropped beer bottle, Alfredo saw something in him. Something that could serve him well down the road. He couldn't put his finger on it then, but he knew he had to protect the boy.

He ran down the stairs and grabbed Cal. Cal's mother, Mary, Mariucci, and the other warehouse workers came running in the direction of the shop floor. Alfredo pulled Cal into a closet to keep him hidden. He wanted it to appear like an accident. There were no cameras. No one else would be the wiser.

He remembered the lack of fear he'd witnessed in Cal's face. Instead of seeing the tears he would have expected from someone so young who had just committed murder, Cal was expressionless.

"Hey, kid, what the hell's the matter with you? You killed that boy, you know that?"

Cal stared at Alfredo. Even back then, the boy's eyes were like ice.

"He made me angry. He kept saying mean things about my dad. I didn't want to do it, but I couldn't stop myself."

Alfredo wondered how remorseful the boy had felt. All of the best soldiers and hit men had no remorse, or rarely showed any emotions. Good soldiers were difficult to come by, even back then.

"Now that boy is dead and his mommy and daddy won't have their little boy anymore, how does that make you feel?"

Cal wiped his nose on his sleeve as if to signal he could only be bothered with his own needs at that moment. Alfredo shook the boy, hoping for an answer. Part of him wanted the boy to cry in shame and ask for forgiveness. Another part of him hoped Cal would brush it off as if the small boy meant nothing to him.

"I don't have my dad anymore," Cal said. "Sometimes things don't turn out the way you want them to."

Alfredo smiled at the boy. He knew then, under the right guidance, that the boy could be highly useful to him. He thought back to what Vinnie had said. Vinnie had begged him to take Cal in while his mother got back on her feet.

Would it be worth it for him to take out the boy's mother for an outside shot at raising a future top-notch hit man? Alfredo figured since he'd already buried the father, what harm was it to bury the mother?

She could never provide Cal the life Alfredo and Susan could. He'd have a brother in Vinnie to look out for him, and he'd go a long way to filling the emotional void left when Alfredo's youngest son, Luca, died. He was committed to Cal right then.

"Listen, kid. I'm not gonna say anything. We're going to play this off like an accident. When the police come in to question things, I'm going to say I wasn't around when it happened and discovered the body after everyone else did. You think you can stick with that story?"

Cal nodded and Alfredo saw the boy relax.

"Good. You're gonna go places, boy."

* * *

ALFREDO TOOK another sip of brandy as he recalled that day. The risk he had taken by having Cal's mother killed in a car "accident" had paid off. Cal was initially devastated but was able to grow up in a loving home and never had to wonder where his next meal would come from.

Over the years, Alfredo had more than benefitted from Cal's presence. He would've had him made by now had tradition not been such a stickler on reserving the made distinction for men with Italian ancestry.

Maybe the Commission would go for it this time, seeing all the good that Cal did for the Chicago family. But that would require Alfredo revealing Cal's greatest kill of all, the very kill he didn't want Caruso to hang over his head to blackmail him and destroy the powerful crime syndicate he had worked so long to build.

This is my empire, Caruso. If you want a piece, you're gonna have to wait in line.

6

After a light lunch with Fonzie, Cal went back to his apartment, thinking about the events of the last several hours. He was glad to get the MacErlean business over with and was ready to start tailing Mayor Caruso. Though surveillance wasn't his favorite job, he enjoyed the feeling of being on the hunt and ensuring the mafia's enemies were dealt with properly. Cal couldn't think of a more exciting profession for his skill set, even after Fonzie's philosophical question following their meeting with Alfredo.

Later that afternoon, Cal received a call from his girlfriend, Maria, inviting him over for dinner. Maria was a PhD student at the University of Chicago, studying psychology. Even though she was often busy with a rigorous study and research schedule, she knew how to let loose and enjoy life, which was Cal's favorite part about her. She reminded him that life could be more than tailing enemies and killing them.

As they reached the end of their conversation, Maria told Cal that she loved him. Cal hung up before Maria could ask him why he failed to add "I love" to Cal's utterance of "you too." The word "love" had such a strong meaning, and it was something Cal didn't want to throw around lightly. Other than the love he felt for his mother growing up, Cal wasn't sure if he'd truly loved anyone. He could say he liked the Petrocellis and appreciated what they'd done for him by taking him in, but he never felt like he loved them.

He really liked Maria, maybe he even loved her, but acknowledging that love and putting his heart on the line was something he couldn't bring himself to do. As a hit man, he wondered if he even had a heart.

Around four o'clock, Cal walked to the store for a bottle of Maria's favorite chardonnay and took an Uber to her apartment.

Once he reached Maria's building, Cal pushed the buzzer for Maria Espinoza and heard a click, signaling he could come up. Sometimes, Maria got so excited for Cal's visits that she ran down the stairs from her third-floor apartment just to hug him a few seconds earlier. It felt nice to have that effect on someone.

The gentle patter of Maria's footsteps was inaudible this time, so he assumed she was busy putting the finishing touches on her tamales. He was curious how she managed to cook and assemble them in her small studio.

"Mr. Wino is here," Cal said after opening the apartment door. Maria's back was to him while she placed some bagged tamales in the freezer. She turned around to smile at him; he couldn't help but smile back. There was something different about her that made life seem worth living.

Maybe the missing "I love you" hadn't pissed her off after all?

Maria walked toward Cal and melted into his arms. He held her tightly and reveled in her scent as their lips met.

She smelled like a mixture of vanilla and seasoned beef from the cooking. They kissed once more before Cal broke away to soak up her beauty.

Maria's tan skin shone brightly, even under her white T-shirt and Daisy Duke–style jean shorts. Her black hair was as thick as a horse's mane and hung down past her waist, hugging her hips in the way Cal's hands would if they were on a nightclub dance floor. She sometimes threatened to cut it and donate the severed locks to charity, but she hadn't as of yet.

Even though he couldn't bring himself to say the L-word after a year of semiserious dating, Cal wouldn't change a thing about her. From the curves of her body in all the right places, to her ambition in completing her PhD program, to her smarts, to her cooking, and even her occasional fiery argumentative style, Cal couldn't imagine his life without her.

"Dinner's ready. I hope you're hungry."

Cal coughed, clearing his throat. "Ahem, I think you've failed to notice my great taste in wine with this wonderful chardonnay selection."

Maria eyed the wine, then darted her eyes toward Cal's. "Wow, I'm impressed. You know that's my favorite, right?"

"That's why I bought it."

Cal tilted the bottle toward her, the label facing up as the bottle rested on his palm. "Unoaked, just how you like it."

Maria gave Cal a peck on the lips and touched the side of his face with her fingertips. The touch was light, but it caused Cal to flinch. Though a childhood scar had faded, its memory was fresh in his mind.

"Oh, I'm sorry. Let's eat, shall we?"

Cal's stomach rumbled as he followed her.

"What did you make for sides?"

Maria gestured toward the kitchenette where the tamales were sitting in a baking pan on the stove, still warm from the steamer. A large pot of yellow Mexican rice sat on one burner and a saucepan filled with refried beans on another. On the tiny bit of counter space Maria had placed a bowl of guacamole salad.

"This looks great. How did you find the time to make all of this?"

"It took a lot of bribes. My friends from my program heard I make mean tamales, so they were over here bright and early to help out before we hit the books for the afternoon. Those bags in the freezer are their reward."

Cal wrapped his arms around her and snuggled against her from behind, placing kisses against her neck.

"What do you say I savor something else before we devour these tamales?"

She winked at him over her shoulder and stuck out her tongue. "Let's eat, mister. I know you've got your mind elsewhere."

Maria grabbed a plate from the cupboard and fixed a plate for Cal. She put two large tamales covered in a mole sauce and Chihuahua cheese on the plate, along with a helping of the rice, beans, and salad. Cal grabbed his plate while Maria prepared one for herself.

"My mind is completely on these tamales. I've been dying for you to make these for months, and you do it on a whim for your school friends."

Maria joined a smiling Cal at the small table next to the entrance. Cal was tempted to dig in before she sat down— the tamales looked that appetizing—but he patiently waited while she set her plate down and brought over two wineglasses.

"Allow me," Cal offered as he took the bottle from her,

uncorked it, and poured the chardonnay into their glasses. They raised their glasses and toasted each other, smiling at the clinking noise. After taking a sip of the wine, Cal tore into the tamales, loving the sweet and salty tastes on his tongue.

"This is absolutely delicious. How did you learn to make these?"

"It's an old family secret. My father learned how to make them from his mom in Mexico. We prepare the mole sauce the day of too. Most restaurants don't know how to make them right."

Cal savored another bite of the tamales and agreed that Maria's rendition was the best he'd ever eaten. He needed to sample the rice, beans, and salad before he completely wolfed down the tamales.

"How do you like the rest of it?"

Cal could only nod, as his mouth was too full to respond. He took a drink of the wine before telling her how delicious it was. The rest of their meal carried on in relative silence as they enjoyed the taste of the dishes. Eventually they'd cleaned their plates, and Cal helped himself to a few more tamales while Maria poured more wine. Her gaze on Cal was cooler than it had been at any other point that evening.

"So earlier today when we talked—"

"I know what this is about," Cal interrupted. He felt a flash of anger fill his insides. Hot waves of venom blew upward from his stomach, tickled his ribs, and made their way into his heart, where he felt the fury roar further into his esophagus.

Maria looked taken aback and placed her hand atop her breast. "What do you think this is about?"

The venom in Cal's body leapt up his throat and exited

in his words. "The end of the phone call. You're insecure because I didn't say that magic word."

Maria's eyes bugged out at him. "Me? Insecure? We've been dating for over a year, and you can't say one simple word? Just one."

"Technically, it was two. I forgot the 'I.'"

"Oh, fine. You forgot the 'I.' I'm glad you could say one of the words. Now, where's the other one?"

Cal took another bite of the tamales. If he was going to get lectured, he wanted to enjoy some of the food on his plate. Maria glared in response.

"You have some nerve eating while we're trying to have a serious conversation."

Cal slammed his fork down on his plate in another outburst. He remembered his father doing the same thing when his mother told him not to go to Indiana to gamble away money they didn't have. Cal hated that. Why was he doing the same thing now?

"You're wrong. We're not having a serious conversation here. You're lecturing me. You know how much that pisses me off, Maria."

Maria shook her head and frowned at her empty plate. Cal was surprised by how calm she seemed. Maria loved to argue until she was talking a hundred miles an hour and mixing in as many swear words as a soldier in combat. She tilted her glass of wine toward her mouth, took a long swig, and then set the glass down, her arm stiff with tension.

"I know how you feel about me, Callahan. Why is it so hard for you to reveal anything about yourself? You still haven't told me what you really do for a living. I've been to your apartment a hundred times. You can't afford to live there as a bouncer."

Cal had underestimated her. It wouldn't be dishonest to

tell her that he loved her, because he thought he did. Many years of killing made him forget what love might feel like, even if it was right in front of him.

They stared at each other in silence. Many times when they got mad at each other, the yelling and screaming would only last for a few minutes. Then they would proceed to rip each other's clothes off and make passionate love. Cal didn't see her giving in this time. He wasn't giving in either.

"I've told you before, I'm not just a bouncer. People pay me good money to protect their interests and solve their problems. Powerful people."

"Are we really going to go on with this schtick?"

"What schtick?"

"Where you just 'protect people.' Let me ask you this, Callahan. Do you do any work for your father? I know all about Alfredo Petrocelli. He's nothing but a goombah. A MacDaddy mobster."

Cal couldn't help but let out a laugh. *What the hell is a "MacDaddy"?*

"Alfredo isn't my father. My father was murdered when I was twelve years old. My mother died in a car accident two months later. You don't need to remind me."

Maria pushed her hands away from the table and held them up in mock surrender. "Oh, I'm sorry. Except that I'm not sorry because I know how much you hated your father, and I really don't know how you could've loved your mother because you certainly don't love me."

Maria finished her wine and picked up her plate. She threw the plate in the sink where it clanged against other dishes. Cal was surprised it didn't break. He'd never seen her this violent before.

"That's not true."

Now he was on the defensive. It would go a long way for

him to apologize and admit he had a tough time being vulnerable about his feelings. But Cal didn't do therapy, and he wasn't about to be treated like one of her research subjects. He'd really hoped to enjoy a nice evening of dinner and sex with Maria, but instead he held an inflated sense of pride leading to this fight.

"Really? Maybe you should think about that next time I see you. If I want to see you. I can't believe I whipped up my papa's tamales for you. You should go."

Cal saw little point in arguing. He knew where this was headed. Like all of his old relationships, this was going straight down the drain.

7

C al exited the Dunkin' Donuts on a warm and rainy Monday morning. It was time to begin his surveillance work to determine if Mayor Caruso really was going to cause trouble for the Petrocellis.

As if the early-morning surveillance mission wasn't enough to ensure Cal wouldn't get a full night's sleep, he had spent the night tossing and turning with Maria's words pounding in his brain, making him feel lower than at any other point in his life. Stealing the lives of others paled in comparison to the misery he felt at how he'd treated Maria after all the effort she'd put in to prepare a fancy dinner for him. Yelling at her like his father had screamed at his mother, and how Alfredo barked at anyone around him, caused Cal to rethink his priorities.

Since he hadn't slept well, Cal got an early start to the morning and thought about how he might make it up to Maria. He remembered an afternoon they'd spent together earlier that summer, before Cal had to worry about tailing MacErlean and could relax a bit. They started their day together at Navy Pier, riding the Ferris wheel, checking out the small stores, and eating pizza before they walked to Michigan Avenue so Maria could check out the shops.

They'd walked past Saks Fifth Avenue, and Maria had let go of Cal's hand and looked at the window with excitement. A beautiful cream-colored ruffle dress was displayed on one of the mannequins in the storefront window. Cal saw Maria's eyes glow with wonder. He knew right then that she wanted it. While Maria ended up buying a different dress at a different store that day, Cal wondered if he should've taken her back to Saks and purchased the dress for her.

The minute he made the decision to get out of bed, Cal flipped open his laptop. He went on the Saks website and immediately purchased the dress for her. The immense price of the dress didn't concern him. For good measure, he found a matching pair of heels and threw them into his online shopping cart. Maria was worth every penny.

This is what it meant to love someone, he thought. Feeling good about giving them a present they deeply desired and not expecting anything in return. It caused a warmth in his heart that he'd never felt before.

Cal arrived at Tony's car, complete with new license plates after the MacErlean grab, with two large coffees. As exhausted as he was from the lack of sleep, he felt he could drink both of them himself.

He was reluctant to use Tony for this particular task—he'd much rather have Fonzie along with him—but Fonzie was occupied keeping watch on some of the lower-level drug dealers in the South Shore neighborhood. Frankie Ramone had passed along Alfredo's orders not to target new customers in case any narcs were around cracking down on business. Cal knew how the reduction in profits hurt Alfredo, but that was nothing compared to the sense of helplessness he must have felt at having to operate his business in reaction mode. The Caruso situation was stomping on the throat of not only the mafia's business but Alfredo's freedom. The sooner Cal figured out what was going on, the easier his boss's nights would become.

Cal handed Tony the iced coffee, and the boy gulped down the liquid. Cal wasn't sure how he wasn't getting a brain freeze. He took a sip of his own straight black bitter liquid, reveling in the burning sensation running down his throat.

"I'm glad we picked up coffee on the way. Otherwise, I'd never be able to wake up," Tony said.

"As Ben Franklin said, 'Early to bed, early to rise, makes a man healthy, wealthy, and wise.'"

Tony glanced at Cal with a perplexed look on his face. He shrugged, then smiled with a slight hesitation before pulling away from the curb. They decided to head to City Hall and park as far away as possible while maintaining a view of the front of the building to see if they could spot the mayor outside. Cal wanted to see if he could determine which entrance the mayor took into the building and if he had any security with him. If he ever had to have a physical confrontation with the mayor, he wanted to know what he was up against.

"I think you're pretty wise," Tony said. "Fonzie totally messed up with MacErlean, but I know you wouldn't have. You would've knocked that guy out, and no one would've seen a thing."

When Cal didn't respond, Tony began talking again. When he got to talking, he didn't stop. Cal focused on the task at hand while pretending to listen.

"How long are we going to be out here? What happens if someone suspicious goes in? Are we going inside?"

"Hold it, Tony. One question at a time. This is only day

one of surveillance. We have to establish Caruso's pattern before we do anything. It would be foolish to do otherwise."

"You're right. I see why the boss wants you on this one. I knew you were wise."

Cal glared at the boy. He was starting to get on his nerves.

"Look, don't patronize me, kid. This life may seem glamorous from the outside, but it isn't."

Tony kept driving. They would be in position in about five minutes, right when traffic started getting thick. "Are you alright? You look kind of out of it."

Cal's mind was reeling after his argument with Maria the previous night. He'd texted her to apologize, to let her know that there was something special arriving for her soon, but she hadn't answered. His worry must have been showing.

"Isn't this how I normally look? Like I've always got my game face on?"

Tony chuckled and took another sip of his coffee. "Yeah, you usually look like a tough bastard. I wouldn't want to mess with you. I've been meaning to ask you something, though. What's that stuff in the back?"

Tony pointed to a briefcase Cal had placed in the back seat containing various surveillance equipment: small microphones, transmitters, earpieces, cameras. Cal rarely used the stuff but had it around in case he needed it. When he told Tony, he gasped, as if he were in James Bond's presence.

"I thought you said we weren't doing any of that kind of stuff?"

"We're not. But if the need arises, we'll be glad we have it. A good Boy Scout is always prepared."

They arrived at LaSalle Street, and Tony did a U-turn to

park on the opposite side, facing the main entrance of City Hall. It was a little before seven, and Cal wasn't sure when the mayor would get there. It was a good thing the 7-Eleven was nearby in case they needed more coffee.

"How long are we gonna wait for?"

"You have to be patient. You know how many hours I've spent staking guys out in my career?"

Cal noticed Tony had already finished his iced coffee in the time it had taken to drive to their destination.

"Man, this will be a long day," Tony said. "I had plans with my girl today. Hopefully this won't take too long."

"I didn't know you had a girlfriend."

"Yeah, her name's Teri. She's a real pretty girl. A dime piece, you might say."

Dime piece? Between Maria and now Tony, Cal couldn't keep up with all the slang being thrown around.

Tony turned to Cal when he didn't respond.

"What about you? You have time for a girl when you're not out here stalking or killing people?"

The question caused Cal to clench his jaw. "I don't talk about my personal life."

The tone of Cal's voice closed off any further conversation. He didn't mean to get snappy with Tony, but the argument with Maria continued to hang over his head. He knew he needed to go over and apologize, but he wasn't sure how. Empathy wasn't in his nature.

A half hour later, Cal spotted a tall figure in a gray-and-black pin-striped suit walking toward the building with a briefcase in one hand and a newspaper under his arm. He smiled as he walked past the throngs of people on their commute. He appeared confident and even slightly arrogant. Cal and Tony glanced at each other. They knew it was Caruso.

"Looks like he goes in the same way anyone else does," Tony said. "Nobody with him. Does that mean we're done?"

"No. The mayor's office is on the fifth floor; we can't draw any types of conclusions on who might be visiting him."

"Damn, that's right. What if I go up there? I'll pretend I'm driving for someone who has an appointment with him and say the guy's in the can. Maybe that buys me some time to use that equipment back there and we can place it in the mayor's office."

Cal saw where Tony was going with this and was intrigued, despite the plan's hasty nature. The biggest issue was they had no idea who might be on the mayor's calendar for the day.

"What are you doing?" Tony asked as Cal pulled his cell phone out of his pocket.

"I'll call some officials in the building to see if I can set up an appointment. Alfredo knows a lot of aldermen. I'm hoping to get a secretary to say one of them has an appointment with the mayor at the time I try to set the appointment for. It's not the greatest plan, but it might give us an idea."

"I think we should wait to see if someone else goes in the building who might arouse suspicions. Like the superintendent of police or something like that."

Cal was impressed with Tony's instincts. He was a little disturbed that he wasn't thinking along the same lines as the kid, given his many years following and snuffing out targets.

"That means we could be here awhile. Are you sure you can handle that?"

"Hell yeah I can. I'm gonna need some more coffee first."

Tony got the coffee and they waited for a while. No one interesting showed up until around nine o'clock, when two Chicago Police cars and an unmarked Crown Victoria pulled up to the curb. A burly man with a bushy mustache stepped out of the back of the Crown Victoria. He wore a police uniform adorned with stars along the trim and a matching cap.

Cal recognized him from the papers as Lawrence Walker, superintendent of police. Two officers got out of each of the cop cars, stood next to Walker, and waited. It was the two other men who exited the unmarked car that captured Cal's attention.

They were both over six feet tall and wore dark tweed jackets and matching dress slacks. Their sunglasses hid their facial features well, but Cal noticed one of them had a beard. They resembled the men he'd had a run-in with at the theater.

"Are those the same guys who tried to follow us?" Tony asked.

"Yep, that's them. I wonder why Superintendent Walker's with them."

It could only mean one thing—Lawrence Walker was planning on meeting with the mayor, especially if he was being escorted by two of the mayor's goons. Cal watched as Walker, the goons, and the police officers entered the building.

It was in that instant that Tony sprung out of the driver's seat of the car and dashed across the street, his feet kicking up puddles of rain as he ran.

What the hell is he doing?

Cal wanted to yell back but saw Tony stick out a thumbs-up sign as he raced for the front of the building.

He knew if he didn't rush in after him that the kid would be in for a world of trouble.

8

C al sat in the passenger seat longer than he should have. He felt so enraged that he didn't want to move. Not only would he have rather had Fonzie for this mission than Tony, but now the kid had put both of their lives in danger by running into City Hall on a whim.

Cal pounded his fist into the back of his seat and glimpsed toward the back, where his briefcase was opened and one of his small transmitter sets was missing, just as he'd suspected. He let out a deep exhale and his head fell back against the seat's headrest. He tried to imagine what Tony was thinking, what exactly he planned to do with the device.

That's when it hit him. *He's going to try to plant the device on the mayor.*

It seemed like an incredibly stupid idea. As far as Cal knew, the only dangerous thing Tony had done in his life was to serve as a wheelman for the mafia. Their encounter with MacErlean the other day was likely the most action the kid had ever seen outside of a Hollywood action flick. Tony had no idea what he was getting into entering the lion's den with Caruso's thugs and Walker's vengeful police force waiting. Cal had to admit the move was bold. If successful, they could learn more from this one surveillance mission than what Cal often discovered from ten rounds of stakeouts.

Cal reached back toward the briefcase and grabbed the small listening device corresponding to the equipment Tony had taken. He switched it on and put the earpiece in his right ear.

The sound of something crashing against the floor caused Cal to jolt in his seat. He wasn't sure what it was, but it didn't exactly signal good fortune.

Cal put the listening device closer to his ear when he heard no further noises. Had the noise been the device crashing to the ground and breaking? It was too small to create *that* big of a noise.

"What on earth are you doing? You shouldn't be running in a building like this."

Cal knew immediately who the gruff voice belonged to. It was a voice he'd heard one too many times on television. Superintendent Lawrence Walker.

"If you're looking for your phone, it's over there."

So that's what the noise was. Cal wondered how Tony had lost his phone and how he'd run into Superintendent Walker. The fact that there was another voice, one that resembled a voice from one of the men in the tweed jackets at the theater, told Cal that Tony might be in danger.

Cal felt at the pockets of his jeans, feeling the bulge of his cell phone in one pocket and his jackknife in the other. His Beretta was comfortably tucked in the back of his jeans. He was ready to go and see just how much trouble Tony was in. He adjusted the earpiece, trying to pick up any additional details from the transmitting device.

"Go take care of that little shit," Walker said. "He's up to no good."

Cal's heart pounded as he crossed the street. There was no way Tony could contend with the mayor's goons. Cal had no doubt he could take them out, but he figured they'd be stiff competition for the Average Joe, which Tony certainly was in his mind. He couldn't let anything happen to his young friend. They were too close to finding answers.

The cavernous lobby was packed upon his entry to City Hall. He scanned the stairwells and never-ending main hallway lined with elevators, wondering how he would find Tony. Given the amount of people circulating throughout the building, he figured he had a chance of blending in, even in a T-shirt and jeans. He knew the mayor's office was on the fifth floor, so his first thought was to head there. A security guard's sharp gaze froze him in his tracks as he made his move toward the nearest stairwell.

The guard squawked something into his walkie-talkie and booked it toward Cal. Running up the stairwell suddenly seemed like an appealing option. If he did that, Cal knew that he'd be assumed guilty of whatever the security guard was marching over to accuse him of.

Cal couldn't decide whether he should play it cool or run. The guard was gaining fast and Cal heard more activity in the earpiece.

"Good morning, Superintendent," a soft feminine voice said over the receiver. "I'll phone Mayor Caruso that you've arrived. He'll meet with you shortly."

The guard was only feet away, and Cal had no choice but to step to the right to avoid the man's head of steam. He turned his head, but the guard kept walking past and up the stairs Cal was planning to escape to.

What's going on?

Cal wanted to keep listening but wondered where Tony was. Had he escaped undetected? Listening to Walker's activities wasn't going to help him. He forced himself to switch off his earpiece.

Thunder-like footsteps pounded the marble floor behind him. Cal saw the security guard freeze at the first landing of the stairwell opposite him. They both turned around and saw what Cal was afraid he would find—Tony racing down the stairs and a man in a tweed jacket hot on his heels.

A crowd had formed, bunched in front of Cal and the stairs the goon had just descended from. There were so many of them that Cal could hardly see Tony run through the front doors of the building and into the street. Thankfully, his pursuer had a slight drag to his back leg as he ran, causing him to fall farther behind.

Cal shoved through two men in beige raincoats and ran toward the exit. If Tony really was in trouble, he had to stop the goon before he could do any damage. Cal heard the shouts of the security guard behind him as he ran, but he couldn't care less about being pursued by the round man.

The horns of several cars blared as the goon ran into the street with reckless abandon. He nearly tripped when he got to the median as he waited for the cars heading south. The ruckus gave Cal enough time to leave the building and keep the man in sight before he ducked into an alley, near Tony's parked car.

The gentle pitter-patter of rain dripped on Cal's head as he crossed the street in front of the northbound traffic. He saw the man he was pursuing standing alongside a white Ford Focus parked in the alley.

The man began shouting, and the other goon emerged from a crouch behind the Focus. They turned their attention to something on the ground and started stomping at it. That's when Cal heard the cries of pain. Tony's cries.

Cal charged toward the men, hoping to make enough noise for them to stop their assault of Tony and confront him instead. Sure enough, the goons turned in his direction. The man who'd been crouching reached into his jacket to pull out a gun.

Cal reached the gunman just as he was attempting to fire and tackled him to the ground, sending the gun flying, both men groaning as they collided with the cement. He felt the other man jump onto his back, trying to pull him off.

Cal shot a quick elbow at the man's head and hit pay dirt when he felt the sharp bone of the man's jaw against his elbow. Cal jumped to his feet and threw a right hook to send him to the ground. Just as quickly, the gunman was at his back, trying to strangle him. He thought of his Beretta tucked in the back of his jeans, and went to reach for it, but knew he wouldn't have enough time with the recovery speed of the two men.

Cal slipped away, narrowly avoided the man's follow-up punch, and threw a left jab at the gunman's ribs. The gunman staggered but came back at Cal with another jab. Cal blocked the attempt with his forearm and prepared his own counter when a sharp kick slammed into his back, nearly sending him stumbling to his knees.

The other man was back on his feet now and his kick gave the gunman enough time to recover. Even though Cal was pretty seasoned at hand-to-hand combat, he knew from the size of both of the men that they would be formidable challengers and wouldn't go down without a fight.

The gunman got off a right hook that struck Cal square in the cheekbone. The gunman followed with another kick to the back and a jab to his jaw, the pain causing Cal to finally fall to his knees. Once the kicker locked a tight grip around his neck, he knew he was in deep trouble.

To further weaken him, the gunman kicked him in the ribs. The kick was painful, but it was better to get kicked than locked into a sleeper hold and have no chance of saving Tony.

"Who are you? Why were you at the theater?"

The gunman stood tall over Cal and glared at him with his sharp gray eyes. The accent was definitely Eastern European. The other man spat on Cal's head in disgust. Cal knew he only had a small window in which to escape. The men would question him and then kill him, either in the alley if they were courageous enough, or somewhere else.

Cal saw Tony lying motionless against the wall but noted the gun that he'd knocked out of the gunman's hands was only a few feet away.

"Are you working with this boy? You should've let us kill him. Perhaps you could've saved your own life."

Cal remained silent. His ribs ached and he knew he'd have a bruise on his face later, but he didn't want to draw any more attention to Tony.

This was Cal's best chance to make use of his Beretta if he could distract the goons long enough. He was surprised his captor hadn't seen or felt it. If he could snake his hand into his pants, he could escape the situation himself.

"Fine, be quiet," the gunman said. "But know this. If you don't talk, we'll kill the boy and take you to be tortured. We'll chop your fingers and toes off one by one until you tell us where MacErlean is."

"I don't think that's necessary," Cal said, trying to buy time. Time where Tony could revive and recover the gunman's weapon and turn the tide against the goons.

"Bullshit. You attacked us on your way out of the theater. What did you do with MacErlean?"

The grip tightened around Cal's neck. They clearly expected him to talk. He noticed Tony gently stir out of the corner of his eye, the only movement his hand extending for the gun.

"Let me ask you the same question," Cal said. "I know you're working for the mayor. Why would he want to protect a known criminal? It seems awfully suspicious to me." Cal inched his left hand closer to his gun. He had to be ready to strike when the opportunity presented itself.

The gunman laughed and shook his head. "What makes you think we're working for the mayor? Is that what MacErlean told you? Are you going to believe that rat?"

"Enough with this nonsense," said the other man. "Let's kill this guy and finish off the kid. Who gives a shit about MacErlean?"

The gunman snarled. "Fine, Phillip. But first, I'll give him one more chance to tell us where MacErlean is. I can't say I won't kill you, but maybe we'll let the boy go."

Cal knew that was a lie. He saw Tony's hand close around the gun. He moved his own hand to the small of his back, feeling his weapon in the process. Neither of the goons seemed to notice. After a brief silence, Phillip spoke up again.

"He doesn't want to talk, Marco. Let me break this fucker's neck and end this."

Marco shrugged his shoulders and nodded. Just as Cal felt Phillip move his forearms to crush Cal's neck, he saw the muzzle flash as Tony fired. The bullet struck Phillip in the side. Phillip's grip loosened completely as he fell to the ground.

Marco dashed toward Tony and kicked the gun loose

from the boy's grip. Now that Cal was free, he pulled the gun from his jeans and fired at Marco, hitting him square in the chest.

The silver in Marco's eyes faded to white as he slumped to the ground. Cal knew he'd shot him in the heart. He wasn't sure where Tony had shot Phillip. He turned around and saw the goon roll over onto his side, groaning in pain. Unfortunately, he would survive.

Tony looked at Cal with fear in his eyes, perhaps surprised he'd survived the attack. Cal glimpsed at the street and saw pedestrians gazing into the alley. It would only be a matter of time before the police arrived and Cal and Tony would be questioned.

"Let's get out of here."

9

Vinnie toyed with the bangs of his long brown hair, contemplating whether he should cut it. With the recent scaling back of business due to increased police scrutiny, there were less day-to-day operations for him to direct. That was fine with him. A *Tech Insider* magazine lay on the coffee table in front of him, and Vinnie had nearly devoured the entire periodical already.

A knock at the door startled him. Vinnie was staying at his luxury suite in the Gold Coast neighborhood. The fact that someone was knocking meant they had come from the inside. Out of habit, Vinnie checked the peephole and felt relief once he saw his father's burly frame standing outside. His own suite was a few floors up.

"I was hoping you'd be here," Alfredo said as he walked in wearing one of his custom-made suits and Brunello Cucinelli wingtip shoes. He took a cigar out of his breast pocket and lit it as Vinnie closed the door.

"Hey, don't smoke in here. The place will reek for days."

"What are you gonna do about it? All of you were lighting up in my place the other night."

Vinnie scowled and sat down on the couch in the open living room. Sometimes he grew tired of being in his father's shadow and longed for the day when he'd be boss.

Alfredo remained focused on the old way of making money. Bribing politicians and cops to turn a blind eye to drugs, prostitution, loan-sharking, contracts, and all of the other traditional areas of the mafia business was only so effective. His temper often didn't do him many favors with the people he needed to buy off. Vinnie was already several steps ahead of his father, thinking about the next frontier for the mafia to make a killing. His *Tech Insider* magazine talked about the next wave of technology; articles on cryptocurrencies, virtual reality, and cyber security got his brain thinking. He hadn't figured everything out yet, but he knew he'd be the one to lead the mafia into the twenty-first century.

Alfredo sat across from him and retrohaled his cigar, letting the smoke waft from his nostrils like a dragon. He looked at Vinnie as if he was waiting for something. Vinnie stood in recognition and poured drinks for the two of them. Once they'd taken a sip of their drinks, Alfredo set down his cigar on a coaster on the glass coffee table.

"You talk with Meransky?"

"Yeah, we talked. He didn't have much to say about MacErlean, though. Other than the fact that he was a nosy prick. Says he drove Al around a few times."

"Let's hope he didn't hear nothing important. He was with us, what, four years ago?"

Vinnie thought hard on when MacErlean had worked for them. There were so many names and faces over the years that he couldn't recall. "Maybe. It's hard to say for sure."

"Let's just say four years. You remember what happened the year before that?"

Vinnie didn't need any more prompting. It was four years ago that his grandpa Louie, the last boss before his father, was poisoned. The autopsy said it was a drug overdose from pain medication, but Vinnie was convinced it was intentional. Anyone who was closely tied to his grandfather in his final hours, including the nurses and soldiers guarding his bedroom, were killed off for their incompetence. There were a lot of hot missing persons cases back then. Fortunately, no one had linked them to the mafia.

"Anyway, that's what I wanted to talk to you about," Alfredo continued. "About your grandpa's death."

Vinnie shrugged. "Are you suggesting MacErlean knew about the poisoning?"

"I have no clue, but that's not the point. What I'm about to tell you, you can't tell anyone else. Not your mother, not anybody. You understand?"

Vinnie gripped his drink tighter. The expression on his father's face was frightening. He'd seen his father kill other men and yell at them so hard his face would turn purple. He wasn't sure if he was prepared to hear what his father had to say.

"If MacErlean told the mayor what I think he told him, then we could be in some serious trouble."

"What kind of trouble?"

"Big fucking trouble. You know every major mafia family makes up the Commission, right? Chicago, New York, LA, Detroit, Miami, all of us. It's like a big board of directors for organized crime. Me and all the New York families are the leaders, but we all have each other's backs, even though we run our own thing."

Vinnie nodded. He knew about the Commission. He still

wasn't sure what this had to do with MacErlean and Ross Caruso.

"Any time someone has a problem with a boss, you've got to go to the Commission first. We talk it out for a while and then make a decision about what to do. You can't just take out a boss without permission. That's asking for death. So, what would you do if you wanted a boss dead?"

Vinnie raised his brow. "Why are you asking me this? You think I'm out to get you or something?"

Alfredo laughed and took a drink, slamming the empty glass down on the coffee table as he finished. "I'm not talking about me. Though I'm glad to hear you're not thinking of taking your old man out anytime soon. I'm talking about your grandpa."

"What? You mean someone wanted Grandpa dead? And the Commission didn't know about it?"

Alfredo pointed a finger at Vinnie. "Bingo."

Vinnie remembered his grandpa had been extremely ill, even before his death, and that his father was already making a lot of the decisions as underboss. But who would have wanted him dead?

"Did someone want you to be the boss? It's not like anyone would've opposed you."

Alfredo smiled again before setting his face as firm as stone. Vinnie could tell something was wrong. His father appeared uncomfortable yet seemed too happy, considering he was discussing his father's death. Vinnie couldn't think of anyone who would've wanted his grandfather murdered, until he saw Alfredo look down at his hands in shame.

"Don't tell me you ordered a hit on your own father."

Vinnie knew as soon as he said it that it was true. But why?

Alfredo could only nod as he continued to stare at his

hands. "You know how hard it is to acknowledge that? That I ordered the death of my eighty-year-old father?"

Anger overtook Vinnie. His head was swimming in denial. He couldn't believe a man they'd both loved had been senselessly killed. "But why? Why did you do it?"

"It was just his time to go. He wasn't about to retire, not while he held such a powerful position. I was the one doing most of the boss work, but he got all the glory. Heck, I was already in my fifties and had been underboss for over a decade. It was time for a new direction. Time for me to take over. Believe me, son, when it's your turn, I'll know when to get out of the way."

Vinnie stood up and threw his full glass of vodka soda across the room, the glass shattering on the floor.

"Are you fucking kidding me? You couldn't have waited a few more years to take power and let Grandpa die in peace? I thought you were all about family. How could you kill your own father?"

Vinnie bent down, his face only inches away from Alfredo's. He'd never been angrier in his life. He'd inherited his mother's sense of calm and preferred to negotiate conflict with peaceful discourse. Yelling at his father, he knew how the other half lived.

Alfredo's expression was blank. Vinnie swore he could see a tear making its way out of his father's eye. Before he could react, his father's massive hand struck the side of his face, staggering him. Alfredo stood up and loomed over Vinnie, his face shifting from sadness to rage.

"You listen to me, goddamnit. If you weren't my son, I'd have you strung up by the balls and killed right now. I wasn't the one who killed your grandpa. I may have had it done, but I'm not the one losing sleep for killing a senior citizen."

Vinnie shook so violently he thought he would enter a

shivering frenzy. Part of him wanted to stand up to his father, but he knew that would end poorly. Alfredo had a few inches and over forty pounds on him. He'd never survive a fight against the old man.

Alfredo took a deep breath and put his hand on Vinnie's shoulder. "Look, if Caruso knows about this, not only does he hold this secret over us, which could shut down our operations, but he can use it to go to the Commission. Imagine if the Commission knew I ordered a hit on my own father. You know what that would mean for both of us? We'd be fucking dead. Now get your head on straight for a second."

Vinnie backed away from his father and went to the kitchen. He grabbed another glass from the cupboard and poured himself a fresh drink, straight whiskey. He took a long drink of the sweet liquid and poured another. Returning to the living room, he sat back down on the sofa.

"So why are you having Cal do surveillance?" Vinnie asked. "If you know what MacErlean told the mayor, we're gonna have to take Caruso out anyway."

"I want this to appear civil at first, provide some misdirection. Besides, this affects Cal too."

Vinnie took another drink, wondering what his father meant. How could his adopted brother be involved?

"Why? Why does this affect him?"

Alfredo frowned. "Cal killed Grandpa Louie."

10

Cal and Tony took off down the alley, running even as the shouts of pedestrians echoed behind them. Cal needed to find a good hiding spot until they could escape. Going back to the car wasn't an option.

They emerged from the alley onto Wells Street and entered a public parking garage. They ascended the stairs to the top floor and stood near a parked Prius, panting from the rapid escape.

"What the hell were you thinking?" Cal shouted. Tony bent forward, placing both hands on his knees. "You could've gotten us both killed back there. If Alfredo hears about this, it'll be both of our asses."

Tony remained still, breathing heavily. After a minute, Tony lifted his head to face Cal, fighting back tears. "Are you kidding? I just saved your ass. Plus, I planted that bug onto Superintendent Walker's shoe. We can hear whatever he's saying to the mayor right now."

Cal couldn't care less what Walker and the mayor were discussing. He wanted to scold Tony for his actions and the trouble they'd caused. Though Cal was incensed inside, they were probably fine as long as they laid low.

"Do you have the receiver?" Tony asked. "Have a listen. I know it will be worth it."

Cal reached for the earpiece and switched it on.

"Crime is a major issue in this city. Always has been. We've got to do our part to nip this in the bud before it affects people's perceptions of the city. Companies won't want to do business here, people will stop moving here. It'll be bad for the economy."

Superintendent Walker gave a gruff laugh. "Alright, Mayor. How do you suppose the Chicago PD gets the funding to shut down all this crime? My men are working too much overtime as it is. We've got to hire more officers, it's as simple as that."

"Don't worry, I'll make sure you get the funding," Caruso said. "Besides, I think it's time we put a clamp on a particular sector of crime. Crime will always be around, but it's the organized sort we need to stop. Send the mafia to their graves."

"I wondered why you mentioned them in your speech a few months ago. Have an extra vendetta against the mafia?"

"I sure do. Don't repeat this, Walker, but my grandfather used to be in the mob. He wanted to be a legitimate businessman and run his little bakeshop, but those bastards sucked him in. They wanted the shop as a front for cocaine back in the early seventies when they were experimenting with the drug trade. That led to heroin and all the bad stuff. It was awful business, and my grandpa saw the effect it was having on the neighborhood."

"So, what did he do?"

"He went to Alfredo Petrocelli's old man and said enough is enough. They wouldn't be able to use his bakery as a front for drugs anymore. The allure of the money to keep the place afloat and provide the life he wanted wasn't enough. Business was so good that he could keep the place open without their help. They eventually beat him so bad that he couldn't run the business anymore. He ended up losing everything, got dementia, Parkinson's, the whole nine yards. He was never the same after that."

"So you want revenge for Gramps? Even though the Chicago mafia is as weak and underground as it's ever been?"

"I'm sure Alfredo Petrocelli would deny that, but yes, that's what I want. Imagine this, Walker, if we could reduce our crime rate the way New York was able to in the early part of the century, what do you think that would do for the both of us, huh? We'd be fucking heroes."

"Yeah, you've got that right. You've already got your eye on the next gig?"

Caruso laughed. "Don't worry about that yet. For now, just have all your best officers in every area where we think the mob is doing business. If we can't get 'em all behind bars, at least we'll dwindle their bank accounts. We'll make 'em so weak that we'll eventually eliminate all of the power they have. I can see poor Alfredo quaking in his boots."

Cal switched off the earpiece and handed it to Tony. He didn't want to be caught with the device if the police managed to corner him. It sounded like Caruso was out for revenge. But the police had always been after the mafia. Maybe not with this kind of vengeance, but the threat of incarceration and death was ever-present for every mobster.

Why was Alfredo cracking beneath the pressure this time? Why was he having Cal follow MacErlean and now Caruso? What was he so worried about?

"Alright, kid, good work," Cal said to Tony. "I'm sure

Alfredo will be pleased to know he was right about Caruso being a threat. Next time, though, don't run off. We can't have close calls like this again."

"I won't. What do we do now?"

"Get out of here and ditch that earpiece. You can worry about the car later. Get home and stay out of sight for a while. I'll have to tell Frankie about what Caruso said, but for now, I need to clear up a few things."

Tony protested, wanting to follow Cal around some more, until Cal warned him off. Something about Caruso's story bothered Cal, but he couldn't quite figure it out. Maybe Fonzie would be able to shed some light on it.

A few minutes after Tony left the parking garage, Cal followed, ensuring he exited in a different location in case anyone was following and wanted to connect them.

Cal pulled out his cell and called Fonzie. While Cal knew he wasn't a made man and would never be let in the inner circle of the mafia's activities, Cal found Alfredo's recent behavior rather peculiar and inconsistent with his typical calculated planning.

Fonzie answered on the second ring. "What's shakin'?"

Cal told him about the run-in with the mayor's men and his suspicions of Alfredo's motives after listening in on Caruso and Walker's conversation.

"What makes you so suspicious?"

"I get why Caruso wants to crack down on crime. He's got constituents to worry about, and he wants to prove popular since he's freshly elected. Cleaning up the streets of Chicago would go a long way to secure his future political ambitions. But why protect a rat like MacErlean? Why is Alfredo so worried about some extra police pressure?"

"Man, what makes you think I'm gonna know anything about that shit?"

"Get downtown and have a drink with me. I sure could use one after this morning."

They hung up and Cal kept walking. He dialed Maria's number. He felt even worse about their argument and unresolved apology after his close call with the mayor's goons. Cal wondered if he was still cut out for this kind of work. His last two jobs had been far too messy for his liking. The excitement was there, but the execution was lacking.

"What? I'm off to class," Maria snapped.

Cal was surprised she'd even picked up. He wanted to yell in response to her hasty reaction but knew that wasn't the way to go.

"I promise I'll make this quick. I realize how big of a jerk I was at dinner. You deserve someone who isn't afraid to tell you that they love you and share the most intimate details about their life. I love you, Maria. I can't believe it's taken me a year to say those words, but I needed to tell you."

The silence on the other end of the phone was louder than the pounding in his heart as he waited for Maria to respond.

Had he gone too far? Or not far enough? Should he mention the dress he'd bought her? Was she even in the mood to reconcile right now?

"Maria, say something."

"Cal, this is completely unlike you. What's going on?"

"I feel really bad about last night. I can't stop thinking about how upset you looked when I left. Nearly getting shot sort of puts things in perspective."

"Oh my God, are you okay?"

"I'm fine." He didn't want to tell her that it wasn't the first time. Eventually, he wanted to explain everything. She deserved to know. Even if it meant he'd lose her.

11

———

C al had intended to cook for Maria that night, but Susan Petrocelli called to invite him for dinner. When Cal initially declined, Susan, ever the inquisitive one, asked if his plans involved the girlfriend that she had heard about but hadn't met. As much as he tried, Cal couldn't refuse Susan, and she urged him to invite Maria to dinner as well, after she insisted Alfredo wouldn't talk about the business.

They arrived at the Petrocelli compound a little after six. Only one other car was in the driveway, a shiny new olive-green Mercedes-Benz. Melissa Ranieri and her husband, Paul, stepped out.

"Callahan! Who's the lovely lady?"

Cal's heart drummed in fury and he felt a jabbing pain in his chest as he introduced Maria to Melissa. He hoped the happiness that came from finally acknowledging his true feelings for Maria would last and wouldn't be destroyed by the family.

"Well, aren't you one of the most beautiful women I've

ever met?" Melissa said. "I must say, that's such a lovely dress. Where did you get it?"

Maria blushed and glanced down at her new dress. She looked absolutely ravishing in it. Cal was extra pleased that he'd called the store and promised a fat tip after his run-in with the mayor's goons to have them personally deliver the dress to Maria late that afternoon.

She'd jumped into his arms and cried when he'd picked her up, telling him how much she loved the dress and what it meant to her and their relationship.

"Oh, thank you. Cal got this for me from Saks."

"Oh my," Melissa said. She began fanning herself and batted her eyes at Cal. "Looks like someone's a high roller. You know, that purse is an interesting color. Coach isn't quite Saks, but it looks great on you."

Melissa laughed and flipped her bleached-blonde hair back over her shoulder and adjusted her fake breasts beneath her dress. Cal could smell vodka on her breath.

Cal saw Maria's eyes flash and her fists clench as Melissa turned her back and reached for her husband's arm. He reached over to his girlfriend and grabbed her hand, assuring her it would be alright. He suddenly felt inadequate for buying Maria a less-luxurious purse as a present a few months ago. He could only hope that the family wouldn't do anything else that pissed Maria off.

Paul Ranieri was a highly successful day trader in the city and supported the mafia when business was tough. Given Mayor Caruso's pressure, Cal wasn't surprised Melissa had brought her husband to dinner. Alfredo would probably squeeze the poor man for as much money as he could after Susan served some of her famous dessert.

Paul gave Cal a manly nod, linked arms with his wife, and lumbered slowly toward the house. Cal gathered Maria in a similar fashion and they followed the couple inside where they were greeted by Vinnie and his girlfriend, Stephanie, serving as host and hostess while Susan finished the meal preparations.

"Who is this fine young lady?"

"This is my girlfriend, Maria. Maria, this is Vinnie."

Maria and Vinnie shook hands before Vinnie raised her hand to his lips and kissed it. Maria flinched and drew back toward Cal. Vinnie flashed his trademark smile at her and she exhaled in relief.

"I hope you don't mind the intrusion. It's a greeting I use with all beautiful women."

"Not at all," Maria said through a strained smile. She scratched the back of her head and looked around the foyer. Vinnie introduced Maria to Stephanie and followed Cal into the living room. Cal was pleasantly surprised to see Frankie Ramone and Al Meransky sitting in the living room talking to the Ranieris.

Frankie waddled his way from the couch to where Cal was standing and wrapped him in a bear hug. Frankie was on the shorter side and had a hefty stomach that bulged over his gray slacks. What little hair he had left was dark and parted to the right. Despite his flabby appearance, Frankie was as tough as nails, a quality that served him well leading the mafia's operations on the South Side.

"You made it all the way out here? I thought you hated coming this far north," Cal joked. Frankie was notorious for going years at a time without leaving the city limits.

"Ha ha, very funny. You brought this fox with you?"

Cal wanted to roll his eyes at the comment as he introduced Maria for the third time that evening. After their brief meeting, Frankie stepped out to help Susan in the kitchen. Frankie had been the Petrocelli family chef when he was younger before rising up the ranks as an enforcer with Alfredo and often helped out with the meal preparations whenever members of the family cooked a fancy meal.

Meransky jumped up from the couch to take Frankie's place. Cal noticed him ogle Maria's body. Cal shot him a menacing look when his eyes fixated on Maria's cleavage, which rose gently above her dress. The North Side capo flinched before regaining his composure. "Cal, I heard what happened with MacErlean. Nice job, mate."

"Al, not now. I'd rather not talk business in front of Maria."

Maria poked Cal in the arm. "No, I want to know about business. You're so secretive as it is."

Meransky's lips closed tightly as if he wasn't sure what to say. He knew he'd slipped and broken one of the long-standing rules of life in the mob—don't talk about business around those who don't know anything about the business.

"Well, Cal is a quiet guy. That's why we love him."

Cal was relieved when Susan and Frankie emerged from the kitchen and asked everyone to take their places in the dining room. Dinner would be served shortly.

With the precision of a military company, everyone took their seats at the large ten-person table. Each plate was set with some of the fanciest china that Cal had ever seen. He knew Susan only brought it out for special occasions. The plates were porcelain white with an ocean-blue trim with vine and floral patterns. There were matching coffee cups on saucers and dessert plates. Full glasses of water and red wine were at each plate.

Susan tugged on Cal's shirt before he and Maria could take their seats and wrapped him in a motherly embrace, squeezing far too tight, like she hadn't seen him in years.

"I'm glad you finally brought a girl home to meet the family. She must be quite special."

Cal gazed lovingly at Maria and realized how right his adoptive mother was. His heart was filled with a warmth from having her at his side again, no longer fighting. He only hoped Alfredo wouldn't find a way to use Maria against him and that she still saw some good in him after spending an evening with the mafia's finest.

"Yes, this is my girlfriend, Maria. Maria, my mother, Susan."

Susan's smile was as bright as Cal had ever seen it. He could tell Susan wanted to hug her, but she instead reached to shake Maria's hand before stepping back to gaze upon the couple with adoration.

"It's so good to meet you, Maria. I always hoped Cal would find someone to share his life with. You look absolutely perfect."

Cal noticed the other guests staring at him as Susan and Maria finished their greeting and Susan ran back to the kitchen.

An aroma of freshly baked bread filled the room as Frankie brought in a basket of bread for each end of the table. Susan balanced a large tureen of Italian wedding soup and placed it in the center of the table. Frankie returned with two large bowls of salad, and Susan followed behind carrying a giant platter of pasta. Even after many years of large family meals, Cal was amazed at how so much food could fit on one table.

"Shall we dig in?" Alfredo asked.

In the midst of worrying what everyone's impressions were of Maria, Cal hadn't seen the boss enter the room. Everyone sprang into action with the food item closest to them as if hypnotized by his authoritative voice.

Susan started with the soup, pouring a sizable portion into her bowl before passing the tureen to the right until it finished with Alfredo. The remaining dishes made their way around the table in a similar fashion until everyone was enjoying the hearty meal. Cal especially loved the pasta choice, a linguine Bolognese with Italian sausage. Susan had a gift for making sauces, and the Bolognese had the perfect blend of sweetness and tomato flavor.

"Cal, it's so wonderful that Maria is here with us," Susan said between bites. "She's more beautiful than I could've imagined."

Maria smiled and rubbed Cal's arm. "Stop, you're making us both blush."

The table broke out in a soft laughter. Cal felt everyone's eyes on him. He didn't like being the center of attention.

"So, what does your girlfriend do?"

Susan had a tendency to think it was the man's duty to speak for his woman when presented with the opportunity. She continued to allow Alfredo to speak on her behalf after nearly forty years of marriage.

"She's a PhD student at U of Chicago. She's studying psychology."

"I'm into industrial organizational psychology," Maria said.

Susan had a blank expression on her face and turned to Alfredo in confusion before flicking her eyes in Cal's direction.

"What does she want to do with that?"

Cal looked to Maria, hoping Susan would take the hint and ask her the questions from now on.

"I'm still deciding. Part of me wants to do research and pursue academia, but I might want to open up my own practice or work in companies doing talent development work. I'll see where things go."

"Interesting," Susan said. She nodded her head for a few moments until Alfredo tapped her arm.

"You know, Maria," Alfredo began, "Cal may look rough, but he's a great guy. I'm sure he takes extra-special care of you." He peered directly into Cal's eyes, as if he was reading exactly what Cal was thinking.

It was the *fuck with me and she dies* look Cal had seen many times before. But why would Alfredo be upset with Cal? Even with the messy pickup of MacErlean, Cal was doing his job, a job that, while he still enjoyed doing it, he suddenly felt at odds with, as if what Fonzie had asked him yesterday was a sign.

He looked at Maria and saw that her face glowed with happiness. For the first time, he imagined that, someday, he and Maria would be sitting at a large table gathered around a home-cooked meal with their own family.

The pleasant thought left Cal as soon as it arrived. Ever since lunch with Fonzie earlier that afternoon, Cal kept wondering what secret Alfredo was worried about the mayor revealing. They'd exhausted all possibilities in their discussion from the revenge angle of Caruso against the mob, to the squashing of the mafia's business interests, to wanting to see Alfredo thrown in jail. None of them made enough sense.

The loud clanging sound of Vinnie's spoon stirring his soup against the bowl gave him a clue. He remembered arguably the worst kill he'd been asked to perform in his time as a hit man. Killing then-boss and Alfredo's father, Louie Petrocelli.

Even for a man with loose morals, Cal had been opposed to killing the old man. Killing a boss meant nothing less than death, unless such a hit was sanctioned by the Commission. Only Alfredo's threat of throwing Cal off the payroll coerced him into executing the hit. It wasn't hard to do. The old man was on so many medications for various illnesses that all Cal had to do was crush several of his pills into a powder and mix them into his soup. Within a half hour, the old man was dead.

Frankie slammed a large piece of Susan's tiramisu down on the table in front of him, driving Cal's thoughts away from the old boss's hit. But once he'd recalled it, he knew it was the secret Alfredo was dying to protect.

"This is delicious," Maria said. "I need to get the recipe."

"Well, that's a family secret," Susan said. "But if Cal smartens up and marries you, we can keep it all in the family."

"I don't know about that, Susan," Cal said. "Maria makes the most amazing tamales, so you might want to give up that closely guarded secret now."

Cal glared at Alfredo as he said "closely guarded secret" and swore he saw a flash of terror in the boss's eyes.

"Vinnie, Cal, meet me in the study," Alfredo said. "I've got something to discuss with both of you."

"Oh, dear, can't talk about business wait?" Susan asked. "We're enjoying each other's company."

"Oh, it's not business. We've got a special present for you." Alfredo got up from the table and kissed his wife's forehead. He flared his nostrils at Cal before leaving the room.

Vinnie and Cal got up from the table and kissed their own significant others as they followed Alfredo into the study. Vinnie took his familiar seat in the back corner next to the window. Alfredo sat at his desk and Cal remained standing.

Surprisingly, Vinnie started the conversation. "Have a run-in at City Hall today?"

Cal felt like a pig trapped in a corner, ready to be slaughtered. The tiramisu he'd eaten was starting to do backflips in his stomach. Vinnie and Alfredo both had looks of dissatisfaction on their faces, and Cal wondered how much they knew.

"It was the men who were protecting MacErlean. They weren't too happy about running into me. I took care of them."

Cal kept his answer short and sweet on purpose. He didn't want to bring up Tony's involvement in the affair. If he could play the whole thing off as his idea, he would probably suffer, but at least he'd keep the kid out of it.

"Oh yeah?" Vinnie asked. "I heard one of them is still in the hospital. He could talk."

Cal nodded. He'd expected Phillip's wound hadn't been fatal. Alfredo poured himself a brandy and tilted it toward Cal.

"I take it you started surveillance on Caruso?"

Cal nodded and told Alfredo everything that had happened, without mentioning Tony's involvement or going into exact detail about how the transmitter was placed on Superintendent Walker. Cal explained that the mayor's interest in going after Alfredo was because of what was done to his grandfather.

"It's clearly a revenge ploy, but the mayor has his own interests as well," Vinnie said after a pause. "You think it's time to set up a meeting?"

"That might not be a bad idea. If I think we need to whack Caruso, Cal, you'll have to make this one a lot cleaner. You better get that second guy before he's out of the hospital and thinks about talking. Hopefully Walker or

Caruso haven't gone to see him already. It would make my meeting with him less effective."

"Yes, sir." Cal was hesitant to take out Phillip. Suddenly everything Alfredo or Vinnie said made him feel queasy, like killing for their interests wasn't such a good idea anymore.

"Are we done here?" Vinnie asked. "Mom will worry about what we're up to."

Alfredo stood from his chair and reached for his bottle of brandy, before flinching and pulling his hand away. "Yeah, I'll see if I can meet with Caruso this week. Cal, you better get out of here. I'll have a car take Maria home, tell her you had to cover bouncing duty at one of the clubs downtown."

Alfredo made a move to exit the study but then turned to face Cal.

"You've been off lately. I hope this doesn't become a regular thing. I need you, son. More than ever."

Son. Alfredo had no right to call him that. The last seventeen years, Cal had been more than grateful Alfredo had taken him in after his parents' deaths. He considered the Petrocellis a real family. After tonight, Alfredo was nothing more than a boss hell-bent on achieving his own goals.

12

C al left the Petrocelli house in the same car he and Maria had been picked up in. He sat in the back seat, not wanting to be bothered with small talk with Alfredo's driver while he plotted out his mission for the night. He'd need to text his hospital contact to find out where they were keeping Phillip. He realized he hadn't brought his gun with him to the Petrocelli house, but he did have his jackknife in his pocket. He hoped he wouldn't have to use it and could instead rely on a more "accidental" method of killing.

Cal told the driver to head downtown, saying that he'd give him more precise directions once he knew which hospital Phillip was at. He got on his phone and sent a text to his contact, Forrest. Forrest could tell you anything you needed to know about any shady character in Chicago. Cal assumed he would know about Phillip's whereabouts so he didn't have to do all the digging on his own.

I need to find someone. A man who got shot in the ribs near City Hall this morning. Still alive.

Forrest responded to the text almost immediately.

I had a feeling you would ask. He's at Rush, 10th floor.

Cal hadn't expected Phillip to be at Rush, since it wasn't the closest hospital to the shooting. Yet, he trusted Forrest and instructed the driver to head there.

Less than a half hour later, the car stopped alongside the curb and dropped Cal off. He saw a young woman walking out of the hospital. She looked to be in her midtwenties, around Maria's age. She was carrying a small child in her arms. Cal noticed they both smiled at him on their way out.

People don't smile at you, Callahan. You're a killer, for crying out loud.

Cal watched as the woman walked farther up the street, stopping as a car pulled to the curb to pick them up. Again, Cal thought of Maria. He imagined picking her up from the hospital to take her child home. *Their child.* Having children was something he'd never thought about before. If there was anyone he imagined creating life with, it was Maria.

Cal found himself pausing just inside the hospital doors. The smells of the warm outdoor air called to him from one end, and the unpleasant odors of death and decay beckoned from the other. One direction signaled life and possibility of a new world if he acted on his subconscious. The other would keep him down the same path of murder and evil.

He turned around and exited through the doors, much to the delight of the person behind him who was trying to sneak past. Cal didn't know where he was going, but he couldn't go in there and kill Phillip. At least not with the image of the woman and her child fresh in his mind. Maybe he would go somewhere and get a quick drink. That would do it.

Cal turned left and took a few steps down the street. A tap on his shoulder caused him to turn with the fright of a person who'd seen a ghost. Whoever had touched him had more than startled him.

"Going someplace?"

"Fonzie, what are you doing here?"

"Just here in case you need some backup, brotha. Frankie told me that Fredo sent you down here to kill the man Tony couldn't quite kill. It's a shame, isn't it? You could've stayed and enjoyed dinner."

Cal was shocked. Yesterday, Fonzie was questioning whether the mob life was worth it. Here he was checking up on Cal, almost as if he could sense his newfound hesitation at carrying out Alfredo's orders.

"Yeah. Just staking out the area. You never know if the mayor has any more guys. Could be waiting for me." It was the only thing he could think to say that would explain why he was walking away from his mission.

Fonzie nodded. "Good to see your instincts haven't gone away. Don't worry about that. I'll handle any guys out here while you go in and take care of business."

Cal shook his head and walked through the hospital doors once again. It was exactly the wake-up call he'd needed. The trip to the elevator was free of hassle from hospital staff. He'd have no trouble reaching Phillip's room.

Cal rode the elevator to the tenth floor where Forrest said Phillip would be. He shook his head at his foolish fantasies of having a family with Maria. He couldn't have a family. He couldn't keep being a hit man and have children; it wouldn't be safe. Besides, he wasn't sure if he and Maria would work out. He didn't know if he could keep his promise of revealing more intimate information about himself. It was too painful.

When the elevator doors opened, Cal stepped into the hallway. All Forrest had told him was which floor Phillip was on. Now he'd have to find the actual room. Cal decided to start with the hall to his left. He walked down the hall as quietly as he could. He peered into the first three rooms, but all he saw were elderly patients hooked up to various machines. Those rooms smelled the worst of all.

A nurse started walking down the hall toward him, her clogs galloping with the speed of a dozen horses.

Crap.

He'd have to make up a good story about why he was hanging around the hallway at eight o'clock.

"Hi, sir? We're closing this floor to visitors for the rest of the night."

"Really?" Cal asked. "My sister is here visiting her husband. He was shot today, but I hear he's gonna pull through. I parked the car while she found the room. Can you tell me where it is?"

The nurse eyed him with empathy, as opposed to the suspicious look Cal had been sure he would receive. "Oh, Mr. Kowalski? Poor thing. He's in the last room on the right."

Poor Phil.

"Thanks a lot. Have a good night."

"Thanks, you too."

Cal walked down the hall and felt for the knife in his pocket. Satisfied it was there, he pushed the partially opened door ajar and entered the room. It must have been meant for two people, because the bed nearest the door was empty, while a curtain was drawn around a second bed.

Cal closed the door behind him and strode over to the curtain. He wondered what state the man was in. Was he awake or in a medically induced coma?

Cal grabbed the edge of the curtain and slowly pulled it open. He didn't have a chance to see what was behind it before a large hand shielded his eyes and an arm clamped tightly around his collarbone from behind. He realized he'd been careless and hadn't checked the bathroom or the closet to see if anyone was hiding when he entered.

The person holding him removed their hand from Cal's eyes and secured their grip beneath his arm. It allowed Cal to see that Phillip's throat had been slashed. Fresh blood soaked the man's hospital gown and the bedsheets. Next to Phillip's bed, sitting in a straight-backed chair, was the last person Cal expected to see—Mayor Ross Caruso.

"Hello, Mr. Boyle. Such a pleasure to meet you."

13

The smile on Caruso's face was wide, and from what Cal could tell, fake. Despite having seen him many times on television, and earlier that day walking into City Hall, Cal hadn't realized how confidently Caruso carried himself in person.

Even seated, Cal knew Caruso stood taller than his own height of six feet three inches. Everything else about Caruso's appearance screamed phony politician. His hair was dyed an inky black, and his smile revealed unnaturally white teeth.

"You want me to take this guy out, boss?"

Caruso shook his head at the man holding Cal. "Not yet. Let's see how Mr. Boyle answers our questions."

Cal recalled the encounter with Marco and Phillip earlier that morning. It had been difficult, but he'd managed to escape. He'd been lucky to have Tony with him. He'd have to find a way out on his own now.

"I have a question for you, Caruso," Cal said. He would play the mayor's game and wait for his opening, when the man holding him let his guard down. "Why kill Phillip? If you wanted him to die anyway, why not let me do it like I was supposed to?"

"Ah. Like you were supposed to? Who told you that you were supposed to kill Phillip?"

"No one," Cal lied. "I knew he was going to live after what happened in the alley. I came back to kill him before he talked. I guess I was too late."

"Yes, you were. Phillip said that you and the kid you were with were the ones who picked up MacErlean the other day. Is that right?"

Cal didn't answer. He knew that part would get out.

"Did you kill him?"

Cal refused to answer. Caruso lifted a finger at the man behind him. Cal's captor responded by trying to rip his right shoulder out of its socket, sending a wave of pain coursing through his body.

"Answer the question, asshole," the man said.

When Cal refused to speak again, he felt another squeeze of the shoulder joint, and he couldn't help but groan in pain. Caruso flashed his teeth again.

"Mr. Boyle, we can make this very easy or very hard. Before Phillip's untimely death, he told me all about you and that young driver you had with you. I know you're working for Alfredo Petrocelli. Otherwise, why would you have taken MacErlean?"

"Yeah, I killed him. So what?" Cal answered, his voice rising in irritation and pain.

"Then you know why we were interested in protecting him. For someone so low on the totem pole, he knew quite a bit about you and Mr. Petrocelli. What he told us doesn't just concern Alfredo. It concerns you as well. I think you know what we're talking about."

Caruso gestured at the man behind Cal. The putrid odor

of sweat permeated the room as the man lifted his arms off of Cal and held a gun to his back. He patted Cal down, searching for a weapon. He reached Cal's pockets and pulled out the jackknife. Satisfied Cal had no other weapons, the man pointed to a chair for Cal to sit in. He reluctantly obliged.

"Isn't it great that we can talk like gentlemen now? I don't have to worry about you trying to escape. Not that you would if you want what's best for that boy you were with. I'd love nothing more than to go eye for an eye by taking him in."

Caruso smiled that phony politician smile once again. Cal swore he saw the corner of one of his pearly white teeth sparkle as he talked. Cal could see why Alfredo hated Caruso's guts.

"Alright, I'm listening. What do you want?"

"I think I'll be asking the questions around here, Mr. Boyle, not you. Before you killed poor Mr. MacErlean, did you find out what he told me?"

"Not specifically, no. But I have a pretty good idea of what it is, as you hinted at earlier."

Caruso didn't laugh, his smile only grew broader. Cal wondered how he could sustain such a smile for immense lengths of time. How many dinner parties, fund-raisers, meetings, and speeches required such a cheap grin?

"Ah yes. Justice is finally being done, my friend. Do you know how much pain my grandfather's demise caused me? If the Petrocellis would've let my grandfather legitimize his business the way he wanted and not beaten him half to death, maybe he would've been more than a mere vegetable in the final years of his life and I could've had much better memories of him. Alas, Alfredo doesn't care much about family, does he? If he did, he wouldn't have ordered the death of his own father."

Cal kept his face still, refusing to signal any recognition of the hit. He realized he'd been right in thinking that was the secret Alfredo was dying to protect. How MacErlean found out about the hit was beyond him. As far as Cal knew, only he and Alfredo knew the true circumstances behind Louie Petrocelli's death.

"You already knew that was what MacErlean told me. But did he also tell you that I know it was you who did it? Jesus, you really are a sick bastard, Boyle. Letting your new father kill his old man? You basically ordered the death of your grandfather. I'm sorry, but that's cold. Ain't that right, Bernie?"

The man with the gun could only grunt. Cal hadn't realized how big the man was until he observed him head-on. His head resembled two bowling balls squashed together with dark-black hair along the sides. He sported a trimmed goatee and had a falcon tattoo atop his chest, beneath his wrinkly neck.

After more silence, Caruso stood from the chair and walked toward Cal's seat. Cal stood to meet him. He didn't want Caruso to think he had any power over him, or that he inspired any fear. If Bernie didn't have the gun pointed on Cal, he would've taken Caruso down right there. Maybe then things would go back to normal. But he knew it was too late for that.

"I think you can see the gravity of the situation for the both of you. If I were to tell the Commission that Alfredo ordered a hit on his own father and there was no good reason for him to do so, they'll come after him, his kid, and you. You'd be as good as dead.

"But I'd hate to see that. I've heard all about you, Mr. Boyle. For years, you've been behind some of the most well-executed killings of the mafia's enemies. You could prove quite useful. What would you think about joining forces with me? You could finally leave that rotten liar Petrocelli behind and be fighting for good. I want to clean up the crime in this city, and with a man like you by my side, I really think we could be going places."

Cal was shocked at the request. He was being asked to leave one power-hungry person only to join forces with another. It didn't sit well with him. Besides, why trust Caruso? Alfredo and the mafia were "family," even if he was beginning to imagine a future without them.

"I understand it's a difficult choice. Let me make it a little easier for you. See Phillip over there? Remember Marco? I'll instruct Superintendent Walker to charge you with their murders. I've also recorded your statement admitting you killed George MacErlean. That's three murders on top of dozens of others I'm sure I could link back to you, with proper police attention. Either you stay with Alfredo and the Commission kills you, or you spend your life in prison, if I have some mercy. Or you join forces with me and you stay alive and free. I can promise you greater riches than whatever the mafia is paying you."

Caruso's smile widened, and Bernie laughed behind him. This wasn't the outcome Cal had expected when he'd arrived at the hospital. Why had Fonzie shown up and prevented him from leaving? If there was one thing Cal knew at that moment, it was that he wanted to be done with this life. Killing and doing dirty work for men like Alfredo, men like Caruso—it was something he could no longer justify.

"You'll never tie me to those murders," Cal said. "What would people think if they knew the mayor of Chicago was associated with common criminals? It certainly wouldn't look good for your promise to reduce crime. I'm sure we could also dig up the records of the Petrocellis supporting your ascension in the Illinois State Senate with donations. Heck, they bought you the mayoral seat with all of their financial backing."

Caruso's smile faded and his cheeks turned a deeper shade of tan. After taking a deep breath, Caruso flashed the trademark smile again.

"I guess I underestimated you, Boyle. You're smarter than I thought. But let me give you something else to consider. I'm sure MacErlean told you about your mother's death. I'm sure Alfredo Petrocelli saw your potential as a killer from a young age. What makes you think he wouldn't have had your mother killed in order to take you in and use that to his advantage once you were older?" Caruso stepped past Cal and drew the curtains back around the bed where Phillip lay before heading for the door. He motioned to Bernie, who tossed Cal his jackknife, with the gun trained on Cal as he shuffled toward the door.

"That actually happened, didn't it?" Caruso asked. He looked to the door and took a deep breath. "The offer is open until I tell the Commission as planned. After that, you're on your own."

Caruso made a move to open the door. Even though Cal realized he wanted to end his days as a hit man, especially considering what Caruso had told him about his mother, a tiny piece of his brain was still loyal to Alfredo, still loyal to the mafia that had been such a big part of his life.

"Knowing what kind of man you are, there's something Alfredo can do to change your mind about telling the Commission. Isn't there?" Cal said.

Caruso flashed his annoying smile again.

"Good night, Mr. Boyle. As I said, the offer stands. For now."

Cal watched as Caruso and Bernie exited the room. He'd have to quickly follow before any nurses came in to check on dead Phillip. There was no doubt about it now: Cal was stuck between a rock and a hard place.

Either join forces with the mayor or side with the Petrocellis even longer.

lfredo Petrocelli took the Purple Line to the Red Line for his trip into the city on a steaming-hot Thursday morning. He planned to meet with Mayor Caruso to see if he could knock some sense into him. As a powerful mobster, Alfredo never relied on public transportation, yet he felt like living among the everyday citizens of Chicago for one day. With his disguise, no one would recognize him for who he really was.

A salt-and-pepper wig was fit securely over his thick graying-brown mane. A similarly colored mustache with adhesive backing was stuck above his upper lip, and fake stubble was sprinkled on the sides of his cheeks. It was a little overboard, but he was appreciative of Melissa's efforts at his disguise. He would only remove the phony facial hair once he was in Caruso's office, and not a moment before.

He was somewhat nervous about meeting with Caruso, and a dull throbbing sensation in his head added to his discomfort. When Cal said he'd run into Caruso on his way to eliminate the second of the mayor's goons at the hospital, Alfredo was intrigued. His intrigue turned into fear the moment Cal told him the mayor planned to go to the Commission with the news that he had ordered a hit on his own father.

Once his suspicions of what the mayor knew were confirmed, he knew something had to be done about it, which was why he had a meeting set up with Caruso right away. His intention was simple—get Caruso to back off. He wanted to show him that, despite being backed into a corner, he was still a powerful and dangerous man who couldn't be fucked with.

Alfredo got off at Lake and walked to City Hall. After being directed upstairs by a security guard, Alfredo entered the reception area of the mayor's office and told the receptionist that Joe Lewis had arrived to see the mayor. That was the name he and Caruso had agreed upon to prevent anyone from knowing the boss of the Chicago mafia was meeting with the mayor.

Instead of being escorted back by a staffer, Alfredo was surprised to see Caruso himself walk down the hall to greet him. What a piece of work: dyed hair, whitened teeth, freshly pressed suit. The tan was probably fake too.

"Mr. Lewis. How are ya?" Caruso asked in the loudest and phoniest possible way.

Alfredo extended his hand and squeezed extra tight when Caruso shook it. He kept his grip in place, hoping to hear the crunch of the mayor's bones. Caruso's smile remained but was less prominent as he gritted his teeth in pain.

"Very well, Mr. Lewis. Let's head to my office, shall we?"

Alfredo followed Caruso back to his office. He was dying to take off the ridiculous wig and mustache as soon as he got inside. Several eyes followed as he walked down the main corridor. Beige cubicles filled the entirety of his peripheral vision. It seemed like everyone working in the office was on the phone at that moment. He was grateful he'd never had to work in an office like this.

Alfredo stopped staring at the cubicles and noticed the portraits of past mayors to his left. The Daley family had a long reign in the city's top political position. While his father and grandfather never confirmed it, Alfredo was convinced that, at one point or another, they'd been in the mafia's pocket.

Once the office door was closed, Alfredo took off his fedora and hung it on the empty coatrack next to the door. He hoped removing the hat would relieve the building pressure in his head.

The mayor's office was sheer luxury, too extravagant for the office of a public servant. A mahogany desk took up most of the room from the center of the office and extended back to the wide window overlooking the street. Two leather-backed chairs sat in front of the desk, and there was a smaller oak table surrounded by more leather-backed chairs to his right. Various books on politics and the history of Chicago adorned bookshelves to the right of the desk.

Alfredo was so caught up in admiring the office—and contemplating an upgrade to his own study—that he didn't notice Caruso sit down.

"Would you care for a drink, Mr. Lewis? I can have Gertrude fetch something for you."

"Yeah, a coffee would be good. It'll keep me sharp enough to make sure you aren't fucking with me."

Caruso let out a small laugh and phoned the frumpish old broad that they'd passed on their way into the office. Alfredo would have to wear the ridiculous costume for a little while longer. Once Caruso hung up the phone, he turned his attention back to the boss.

"Alfredo, you know I would never do such a thing. I may not like it, but I know you're as much of an institution to the city of Chicago as deep-dish pizza. Your struggle is my struggle and your success is my success."

Alfredo wanted to knock the stupid smile off of Caruso's face. He wondered if the office was soundproof so he could rough Caruso up a bit. He wouldn't be able to get away with killing the poor bastard, but that could be arranged later.

"Cut the bullshit, Caruso. We both know you have a vendetta against us. You're still upset about what happened to your old gramps nearly thirty years ago. You mentioned us in your state of the city speech about cutting down on crime. And thanks to intel I've gathered from my associates, I know you know a little secret about me."

Caruso started to chuckle again but stopped when Gertrude knocked on the door and entered with a tray containing two steaming mugs of coffee. One mug had a picture of the Chicago skyline on it; the other was a mug for one of the mayor's programs for children. Alfredo hated kids, so he saved that one for the mayor.

"Thanks, Gertie," Caruso said as his elderly assistant exited the room. "She's great, isn't she?"

Alfredo grunted and took a seat across from the mayor while grabbing the mug with the skyline photo. "Oh yeah, she's a real treat to look at. I bet you can't resist the urge to have her blow you underneath the desk."

Alfredo took his mustache and wig off while the mayor leaned back in his chair and cackled. "For such a tight-ass, I didn't expect a joke like that, old boy."

Alfredo sipped the coffee and set the mug on the tray. It was overly bitter. He considered adding cream and sugar but didn't want to seem like a wuss in front of the mayor, so he held off.

"Can we get on track here? I have it on good authority you know something about my father's murder. I also know that men in your position love trading favors. I've come here to ask you, Mr. Mayor, what is it that you want to keep this from reaching you know who."

"Well, nothing would please me more than to tell the Commission about that hit you ordered on your father and have them take you, your son, Vinnie, and that hit man Boyle out. Just think of all the crimes we'd prevent. Just think about how good that would look for me. I can see it now. Mayor Ross Caruso, cleaning up crime one goombah at a time."

Alfredo exhaled audibly. His hands gripped the arms of his chair to avoid the urge to beat Caruso to a pulp. "You know as well as I do that, regardless of what happens to me, the Chicago mafia is here to stay. You'll never eliminate crime from this city. We're not even the worst of your problems. What about the black-on-black crime on the South Side? How are you gonna clean that up?"

Caruso seemed to consider this as he sipped more coffee. "Relax. Like I said, your struggles are my struggles and your success is my success. When you're struggling to do business, that's not a good thing for the local economy, is it?"

Alfredo shook his head. He had no idea where the mayor was going with this, but he wouldn't be able to wait much longer before he showed him who was boss.

"Superintendent Walker and I are well aware of the gang violence on the South Side, and I'd love to focus much more attention there. But for me to do that, we've got to come to certain agreements. You scratch my back, I scratch yours. I'm sure you get that?"

Alfredo knew that game all too well. He was used to

being the one in the threatening position and didn't like the feeling of being at the mercy of Caruso. What had been a dull headache upon entering the mayor's office was surging into an intense wave of pain heading for the center of his forehead.

"Tell me what the fuck you want."

Caruso drained the last of his coffee, stood from behind his desk, and began pacing the room. "Historically, political officials have been in the mafia's pocket. You bribe us, we look the other way when certain crimes are committed. But I think it's time for you to be in my pocket. Instead of relying on the police to clean up the city's crime, I can have you do some of the dirty work for me. Instead of killing for sport, you'll take out the most-wanted criminals and gang members in the city. You'll actually be doing good for once. We'll let bygones be bygones. The Commission will never find out about you ordering the hit on your father, and Walker and I will be sure to turn a blind eye toward your activities. What can be more of a win-win than that?"

Alfredo tapped his fingers on the armrests of his chair as he listened to Caruso. The whole thing smelled like dead fish. Caruso had a hidden agenda somewhere, and even if Alfredo agreed to help the mayor by having the mob serve as an enforcer of sorts, there was no guarantee Caruso would keep his promise.

"I'm assuming in exchange for your ignorance, you'll want a kick of our profits for yourself, am I right? It'll only serve to enhance your next campaign. Whether it be for mayor or something else."

Caruso walked back behind the desk and pointed at Alfredo while giving him a thumbs-up.

"Gosh, you're a smart guy. It would only be natural for

me to ask for a little token of appreciation for my silence. It only seems fair."

Alfredo was seething but restrained himself to save the violent reaction for later. He already knew what needed to be done. He simply needed to put a little more fear into Caruso to show him how powerful he still was.

"Alright, hotshot. You want my help to get your crime under control on the South Side? If that's what it takes, fine."

Alfredo paused, shot up from his chair toward the mayor, and grabbed Caruso's suit around the neck before shoving him against the window. The mayor hadn't expected such a quick reaction from the sixty-one-year-old.

"What the fuck are you doing?" Caruso asked, his voice rising in pitch. Alfredo could see the fear in his eyes as he held him against the glass.

Alfredo took his right hand off of Caruso's jacket, formed a fist, and punched him hard in the solar plexus. He was surprised at how firm the man's stomach was, but Caruso still yelped in pain. Alfredo knew he'd have to make it quick before anyone came into the office. He decked him again, and the mayor yelped louder. Alfredo pulled Caruso toward him and gave the mayor a forceful shove, this time into the bookshelf near the desk. He thought he heard something crack in the mayor's back.

"Is this how you're going to operate, Alfredo? By killing me in my own office?"

Alfredo sneered at the mayor before ramming him back into the wall and punching him in the stomach again. He pulled the mayor's face close to his and glowered at him. He could smell the coffee on the mayor's breath, and swore he felt something wet against his leg.

"If I were going to kill you, I would've blown your brains

out when you came to greet me. But know this—regardless of what I do for you, know that I'm in charge here and I'm someone you don't want to mess with. You better watch your back, Caruso, because next time you threaten me, my livelihood, or my family, I'll kill you."

Alfredo kneed Caruso in the stomach and let the sad excuse of a mayor crumple to the ground. He walked back to his chair, where he put on the wig and mustache and took the hat from the coat hook.

"By the way, Mayor, tell that ugly broad outside your office to learn how to make a fucking cup of coffee."

15

Cal and Maria lay in bed, exhausted after an afternoon of lovemaking. It'd been some of the best sex they'd ever had. Coupled with his recent promise to be more open about his personal life, Cal felt their relationship was better than ever.

"Can we lie like this forever? I feel perfectly content," Maria said.

Cal was cuddled behind her with one hand on her taut stomach and the other on her soft right breast. Everything was right with the world. He agreed with her desire to lie in bed forever. It would sure beat anything forthcoming with the mafia.

He knew Alfredo had gone to see the mayor earlier that afternoon. It would only be a matter of time before the boss called him in and ordered a hit on Caruso. But he also had his own life to worry about. What if Caruso acted on his threat to target him for the murders of Marco, Phillip, and MacErlean? He could claim he'd killed Marco in self-defense and doubted a case could be made for Phillip, but he had admitted to killing MacErlean in the hospital room.

Once they found the body, they could arrest him and put him on trial.

They were the only bodies even remotely tied to him. Over the years, he'd lost track of how many people he had killed. It was at least twenty, possibly closer to thirty. Given that he hadn't turned thirty years old yet, Cal wondered how many more he would kill if he kept this life up.

"Aren't you going to talk to me? Or are you going to lie there and fall asleep like you usually do?"

Cal yawned and reluctantly moved his hands off of his lover's body. "I'm not gonna fall asleep," he said in a half yawn. "Let's talk."

"Okay. I have an important question for you, then. Have you ever killed anyone?"

"Jesus! What a question to ask right after sex."

"I know, but you've never told me what you do for a living. In movies, it seems like everyone who is in the mob kills people."

Cal settled a hand back on Maria's stomach and placed another on her long black hair. He gently stroked it, almost in an effort to calm her as he prepared to tell her about his dark career.

"Promise me you won't repeat anything I tell you."

"I won't. I'm not a fool, Cal."

Cal sighed as he prepared the best way to broach the subject. "Technically, I'm not even in the mob. You have to have Italian heritage to be considered a made man, and I don't have it."

"Even with the Petrocellis adopting you?"

"Yes. I think Alfredo would love for it to happen, but the Chicago mafia answers to a higher power. All of the major cities' mafias do. It's a group of people called the Commission, made up of the mob bosses. They set the rules for everyone else."

"I see. What does that make you, then?"

"I guess you'd call me an associate. Sort of like a hired hand who does grunt work. I'm a mercenary in a way."

Maria turned her head toward him. Cal stopped stroking her hair. Even though her brows were furrowed and her lips curved into a frown, Maria still looked beautiful.

"You never answered my first question. Have you ever killed anyone?"

Cal's heart ached as he tried to form a response to Maria's question. He didn't want to tell his girlfriend the truth but knew he wouldn't be able to form the relationship he wanted with her if he kept any more secrets. He swallowed before finding the words to respond.

"Yes. I've killed many people. Far too many."

Maria lifted her head from the pillow in a jolt. "How many?"

"I'm honestly not sure." That was the truth. Admitting to her that he was a killer made his stomach twist in knots.

"Oh my God, you're a hit man?"

Maria bolted from the bed, her naked body glistening with sweat from the sex. Cal couldn't gaze upon her with admiration and lust like he usually did. Maria was clearly upset. She began to shiver, the chattering of her teeth growing louder the farther she moved away from him.

Cal rolled onto his back and scratched his three-day stubble, as if that would inspire his response.

"Are you?"

Maria stood over the bed with her arms crossed. Cal saw a sense of sadness and disappointment in her eyes. He hadn't meant to lead her on, but he realized that, in the period they had been dating, she'd never consented to dating a hit man. The revelation would've shocked most people. He couldn't blame her if she wanted to leave him.

"Yes."

The word took all of his strength to utter. His body sunk farther into the mattress. He instinctively reached for the sheets to cover his torso, as if he were covering up the sins of his profession by concealing his body's nakedness.

Maria searched Cal's dresser for clothes that she kept at his place. She eventually pulled out a pair of jeans and a T-shirt and slipped them on.

"I can't believe this. I'm dating a fucking murderer. What happened the other night at dinner? Did Alfredo ask you to go kill someone else for him while you left me there? To have some strange guy ogle me while he drove me home?"

"Isn't this what you wanted?" Cal shouted.

He felt a heat rising through his chest, similar to when they'd argued after eating the tamales. "You wanted me to be honest with you about who I am and what I do. You can't freak out when I try to talk to you."

"Oh, I can't?" She was shouting now. "Most people don't go a full year without telling their partner what it is they actually do for a living. And now that you've finally told me, don't you think I have a right to be more than a little shocked that you're a hit man for the Chicago mafia? Jesus Christ, Callahan.

"Do you know how much can happen in a year? People can fall in love. I fucking love you, Cal. How do I tell my parents that I'm dating a man who kills people for a living? How can I stay with you after you've admitted that?"

"Maria," Cal began. He tried to keep his voice calm. He couldn't respond with his usual defense mechanism of anger and shouting if he wanted to show her how much he was trying to change.

"After we fought the other night, I came to realize that I don't want this life anymore. I'd rather be with you and not have to kill people."

"Okay," Maria huffed, "then why don't you quit?"

"It's not that simple. I can't walk up to Alfredo and say I'm out. What else could I do? I'm not a college graduate. You think I can provide for you by bouncing for the rest of my life?"

"I don't know, but I know if you're going to keep doing this, I can't be with you." Maria walked backward, preparing to leave the room. Cal threw the covers off and stood, hoping he could convince her to stay.

"I understand it's a shock, but I'm trying, Maria. I'm going to try to make this right for you. Please don't go."

Maria shook her head and threw the bracelet he'd given her to the floor.

"I need some time, Callahan. I need to feel safe. I'm not sure how safe I am with you anymore."

Maria ran out of the bedroom, and Cal heard the locks unlatching as she exited the door to his apartment. He knew there would be no stopping her. He sat down on the bed and felt a tear forming for the first time in years.

lfredo Petrocelli sat in the booth end of a small table at Trattoria Dieci. Despite being angered by his meeting with the mayor, Alfredo was determined to enjoy a meal with his wife at one of his favorite restaurants in the city. He heard his cell phone vibrate atop the table for the third time during the dinner.

He made it a point not to answer his phone during dinner, but with Susan in the bathroom, he accepted the call.

"Hello?"

"Signore Petrocelli. How do you do?"

Alfredo couldn't identify the source of the sophisticated Italian voice.

"This is him. Do I know you?"

The man laughed a throaty chain-smoker's laugh.

"Yeah, you better know who the fuck I am. It's Leo Bertucci."

Shit.

Had the mayor squealed to Leo already? Alfredo cracked

his knuckles and wrinkled his forehead at the thought of Caruso going back on their agreement.

"Oh, Leo, I knew I recognized your voice. How the hell are you?"

"I'm doing alright. Better than you, from what I hear. Sounds like there's lot of police pressure on you guys right now."

"Yeah, that's certainly true. Hey, I hate to rush this, but I'm actually out to dinner with my wife. Do you think I could call you back later?" Alfredo winced as he spoke to Bertucci. Even for a confident and powerful man, Alfredo knew his clout paled in comparison to the head of the largest New York family and the leader of the organized crime Commission. Bertucci made sure the entire show ran without a hitch, and things were unraveling in Chicago.

"Alright, I need to make this quick anyway. I'm coming down to Chicago on Monday. The bosses from the other New York families are coming with me. Can you meet us in the lobby of the Palmer House Hilton at seven o'clock Monday night?"

Beads of sweat began forming on Alfredo's forehead. The temperature in the room felt like it'd been turned up to ninety degrees. He reached for the handkerchief he kept in his suit coat pocket and started to blot at his forehead.

Was the Commission about to have a scheduled meeting? In person? It would be the first in decades.

"Listen, Leo, I can assure you that I have everything under control with the cops. If you want to bust my balls, I'm sure we can find a time for that over the phone. You don't need to come all the way down here for that."

The deep, throaty laugh resumed. Alfredo wanted to laugh himself, if only to ease the tension in the pit of his stomach. He saw Susan walking toward the table and knew he'd have to end the conversation soon.

"This has nothing to do with the police. Someone else suggested I call this meeting. I'm merely calling to make sure you'll be there. Bring Vinnie and that bitch niece of yours along."

"Don't call Melissa a bitch!"

Susan stared at Alfredo like she'd seen a ghost as she sat back down, burying her face in her hands at her husband's outburst.

"Look, Leo, forget that I raised my voice. I'll make sure we're all there on Monday at seven."

"Good answer."

"Wait a second, Leo," Alfredo interjected. He wanted to find out who had called the meeting. If it was Caruso who'd tipped Bertucci off, the meeting would only have one purpose: his execution. "Who asked you to come down?"

"Enjoy the night with your wife, Alfredo. Good night."

Alfredo clicked the phone off and dropped it with a clang on the table. He continued to dab at his forehead with the handkerchief.

"Is everything alright?" Susan asked.

Alfredo couldn't answer. He swallowed and then drank an entire glass of water before he felt capable of breathing normally. If Caruso had gone against their agreement and spoken to the Commission, Alfredo knew it would be all over for him as boss of the Chicago mafia.

He wondered if Bertucci wanted Vinnie and Melissa dead too, which would leave Alfredo with no living relatives to take over. Otherwise, Bertucci would've had no reason to bring them up.

Either way, Caruso would have to be eliminated. Immediately. And someone else would have to take the fall.

17

C al awoke on Friday morning with a jolt. Vinnie called to invite him to a meeting, interrupting his nightmarish sleep where he dreamt of losing Maria forever. Cal didn't need to ask Vinnie what the meeting was about—he already knew what he'd be asked to do.

It wasn't often that Alfredo let his enemies linger for too long, allowing them to do serious damage. The reality of potential involvement by the Commission must have pushed the boss over the edge.

On the way to Alfredo's place, Cal considered the offer Caruso had laid out for him the other night. More of a bribe, really. If he refused the offer and his crimes were exposed, he knew his days with Maria would be over. She would never feel safe around him again. Plus, he would be facing a lengthy prison sentence.

Cal was tempted to accept the offer. Part of him couldn't care less about being exposed for his murders. He just wanted to escape. He wanted to escape the life of constantly being on the hunt for Alfredo's enemies. He didn't want to be known as a killer for life. Maybe he could talk Caruso out of being strictly a killer for him.

The thoughts spun around in his head like the merry-go-round he'd once ridden at a carnival in the city. His mother had taken him there as a young boy before she was murdered.

Murdered. He let that sink in. Was Alfredo really capable of ordering his mom's death? Had the car crash been staged? He had his own father killed after all; surely he'd be capable of such a thing.

The more he thought about it, the more it seemed that Caruso had the better offer. But what if Caruso asked him to be a killer too? Go with the devil you know or the devil you don't?

After what seemed like hours, Tony pulled up to the outside of Alfredo's building. He glanced toward the back where Cal and Fonzie were seated. They all looked at each other and nodded.

Time to go in.

They entered the building and took the elevator to the top floor, where Alfredo's penthouse was. Cal hadn't been there many times, but he remembered it was an awesome display of luxury. Upon entering, Cal saw impressive floor-to-ceiling tapestries, lush golden rugs atop cherry-stained hardwood floors, and leather furniture so stiff that even his jackknife blade would be unable to slice through. The unmistakable scent of freshly printed money filled the air.

Two soldiers in suits greeted Cal and Fonzie, not bothering to pat them down. It was a security measure he wouldn't have overlooked had he been in charge.

"You got a bathroom in this place? I've gotta piss."

The men looked at Fonzie as if he were crazy. The place probably had four bathrooms. The friendliest of the two men pointed Fonzie down a hall to their left before directing Cal through the foyer and into the great room.

"You boys made it," Vinnie called out from the kitchen. Cal had been distracted by Melissa on his way to the great room and hadn't had a chance to greet his adoptive brother.

"Dad will be out in a second. He's going over everything to make sure all is in order. I think you'll both find it to your satisfaction."

Vinnie walked over to the sofa and took a seat. "Did you talk to Melissa?"

"Not for too long, just a few pleasantries walking in. Everything working out with her?" Cal wanted to turn the tables. Melissa was a relatively new consigliera, and Cal knew she wasn't the most respected among the rest of the mob.

"She's doing great. Not that I wouldn't have been a better choice, but the old man has his reasons. She's a very smart woman."

"It helps that her husband brings home the bacon when needed."

"Enough."

Alfredo entered from his study, a look of disdain on his face. He walked to the sofa and sat down next to his son while motioning for Cal and Fonzie to join them. Once they were seated, Alfredo snapped his fingers and a man from the foyer brought a bottle of pinot noir and four glasses to the coffee table. He poured them drinks and returned to the entrance.

"Ahh, that's good stuff," Alfredo said after helping himself to a drink. "Now, let's address the reason you're both here. As you know, we have a royal pain in the ass to deal with in Mayor Caruso. I paid a visit to Mr. Caruso the other day. It was a very painful visit for him."

"Wait a minute," Fonzie interrupted. "You tellin' me that you fucked up the mayor?"

"You're goddamn right I am," Alfredo shouted. "Normally, I'd get pissed that you interrupted me like that, Fonzie, but I forgive you. That's how great I'm feeling about whooping the mayor's ass. He thinks he's won me over because I might have agreed to help him out with some of the gang problems on the South Side. He wants me to get rid of those thugs so he looks good when he runs for his next political office. Little does he know that, even if he thinks he has me backed into a corner, I'm still a powerful man.

"Caruso's trying to bribe us and have us in the coffers instead of the other way around. He's putting police pressure on our good business. It's pretty clear he's still sour over what happened to his granddaddy, and he wants his revenge. Well, as of today, I'm declaring that revenge is truly not sweet."

Alfredo focused directly on Cal and Fonzie, then continued. "This whole Caruso business is threatening everything we stand for, everything we've worked for. You are two of the most reliable men I've got, and I plan to reward you for that. I know you're not made men yet, but if you accomplish this for me, you'll be more than deserving of the honor. Even you, Cal. The Commission will back us up on this one hundred percent once they see how much of a squeeze the mayor is putting on us. Tell 'em, Vinnie."

Vinnie ran his hand through his ponytail and leaned forward on the couch. "It's simple. We're officially declaring a hit on Mayor Caruso. We'd prefer it happen as soon as possible, by whatever means necessary. After Dad met with Caruso the other day, there's no telling how long he'll hold off before he acts on the secret MacErlean shared with him."

Cal ground his teeth. He felt a sense of relaxation once the word "hit" had been uttered. He felt like a long-deprived junkie whose dealer was finally coming through with his precious fix. Only this time, Cal wasn't reaching deep into his pockets to pay up. He was starting to think about all the food he could buy with that drug money, and the thought of a temporary high didn't feel as good.

"Earth to Cal," Vinnie said, waving his hand in front of Cal's face. "Do you understand what we're asking? This is a pretty basic conversation."

Fonzie turned to Cal, the concern in his eyes all too clear. Cal couldn't hide his distaste for killing anymore. He had to tell Alfredo and Vinnie how he really felt. Or did he?

He knew he could always agree to go along with the hit. It would put him in a position of power to bargain for his way out of the mafia after taking care of perhaps the greatest threat to Alfredo Petrocelli's reign as boss of the Chicago mafia.

His heart was beating so hard he could hear it in his ears. He took a deep breath. Only after the last of his breath escaped his lungs did he dare give his answer.

"If I say yes to this hit, because I know what killing Caruso will do for us, I want your assurances that this is it."

Cal's breath caught in his throat like a fish being yanked out of water. All he noticed were the three pairs of wide-open eyes fixated on his face. Not breathing again seemed preferable to the perplexed gazes Fonzie and the Petrocellis gave him. Cal held his breath until he felt fuller than a hot-air balloon.

"Are you asking for a way out?" Alfredo asked.

"I'm not asking," Cal said. He found his inner strength, his ability to stand up for what he wanted. "I'm saying I'll do this because we're all in this together. I've done a lot of thinking about my life and my future. I don't think I can keep killing anymore, not after how messy my last few surveillance trips have been. You've all hinted at it in various ways. I'm slipping."

Vinnie rubbed his fingers over his chin. Fonzie stared at him, unblinking. Alfredo could only nod. The boss seemed to be calculating whether letting Cal walk away would be acceptable.

"Alright, Cal. If you need Vinnie and I to assure you that we'll let you walk away, in order for you to take down Caruso, then you've got my word. This is the most important kill you've ever been commissioned for. Make this one last kill and you'll be free to go."

Cal wanted to let out a sigh of relief. The tension in his stomach eased, and he imagined Maria jumping up and down with joy at the prospect of Cal's release from the mafia. Alfredo's reaction wasn't at all what he'd expected. Instead of snapping in anger, Alfredo had remained calm and collected.

Seeing Alfredo in this state was a rarity for Cal growing up. The boss was at his calmest when he knew things were going to go his way. Or when he'd already made up his mind that he was done with you.

Cal knew he couldn't afford any more slipups. Get this job done and Alfredo would have no reason to tie him down. Or take him out.

18

T he rest of the meeting was a breeze after Cal admitted his desire to leave the mafia. Even Vinnie's warning that he wouldn't have his usual amount of time to complete the hit—no chance to establish Caruso's patterns or get a feel for his tendencies—didn't worry Cal. With the Commission coming to meet Alfredo on Monday night, Cal only had three days to find Caruso and kill him.

Vinnie then rambled on about how handsomely he and Fonzie would be paid for their efforts, which Cal tuned out. He didn't care about money anymore. A six-figure sum for a hit wasn't anything new to him. What he wanted to do was leave it all behind him and then prove to Maria that he was a changed man, that he could move past a life of crime.

Tony picked them up from the penthouse and drove them to Lou's Tavern. The place had just opened. Fonzie selected a table instead of sitting at the long wooden bar. He patted his stomach and scrunched the muscles of his face in a tight contortion of discomfort.

"Tense meetings like that make me hungry. I don't know what it is, but when a brotha's gotta eat, a brotha's gotta eat."

Cal couldn't argue with that. The prospect of a tasty meal had his stomach grumbling too. A gum-smacking waitress took their orders, and the two men sat in silence.

"You're awfully quiet," Fonzie said once the waitress had brought their drinks. "You shaking in your boots about asking for an out? I can't believe you did it."

Cal sipped the beer and nodded. "I've occasionally thought about it, but it was something Maria said the other day that made me do it. She ran out after I told her I was a hit man. I'd kept it a secret for a year, and she no longer bought my cover story. She doesn't know if she can be safe with me."

Fonzie took a long swig of Bud Light. "You really like this girl, don't you?" He flashed Cal a smile and winked at him.

"Stop it. You're the only person outside of the leadership who knows about her. I'm worried what will happen now that Alfredo has met her."

"What do you mean?"

"He could use her existence as leverage, find a way to pull me back in just as I'm trying to force my way out. He could hurt her."

Fonzie nodded, and they both finished their first beer. Cal motioned to Gum Smacker, who was standing at the bar chatting with the overly muscled bartender. She brought another round for Cal and Fonzie, her eyebrows raised suspiciously.

"Let's think this through," Fonzie said once the waitress had left again. "We've got three days to find the mayor, get him alone, and then kill him?"

"Yeah, sounds right. If we're lucky, we might catch the

mayor on his way out of City Hall today. If we don't, we could have a problem. I'm not sure where he lives."

Fonzie flashed his trademark toothy grin. "Lucky for us, I do. Why do you think I stayed behind after he left the hospital? I followed his ass home."

Cal took another long gulp of beer as Fonzie debated whether they should follow the mayor home or try to take him by surprise elsewhere.

"If the mayor is smart, he'll stay at home all weekend," Cal said. "If he doesn't, he puts himself at a greater chance of harm if he's afraid Alfredo already knows the Commission is coming."

"Yeah, but what makes you think the mayor knows that? That's another thing I've been meaning to ask you. What is this secret that Alfredo doesn't want the mayor to know? The shit we killed MacErlean for?"

He knew Alfredo would probably have him executed on the spot if he revealed why Caruso was targeting him. But it was a chance Cal had to take. He told Fonzie the whole story around Louie Petrocelli's death and his own part in it before revealing he was finally cracking. Thinking back on the old mob boss's death was one of many links in the chain that was starting to rust, causing him to want out of the mafia before it was too late.

"Are we still gonna take Caruso out?" Fonzie asked after a long silence. "One last kill for old time's sake?"

Cal knew he had no other choice. He'd already committed to the kill and didn't see another way out. The Caruso offer seemed less appealing in his mind.

"Sure. But after this, I'm done. Now I'm gonna go take a piss, then we're gonna figure out how this will go down."

Cal drained another beer and rose from the table, heading for the restroom. A huge weight was lifted off of his chest, like a ship being unanchored. As long as everything worked out with the Caruso kill, he'd be done with this life in a few days and could begin a new chapter.

Cal opened the door and walked toward the urinals. A hand grabbed at his back.

"I bet you didn't expect to see me here, Boyle."

19

C al spun around and took a swing at the man but was blocked by a meaty forearm. He recognized the man as Bernie, the toughie with the falcon tattoo from the hospital.

Even though Bernie had his right arm restrained, Cal was able to fire at the rotund man with his left hand, knocking him back into the door with a loud thud. Cal jabbed him in the stomach, the bones of his hand sinking into the jellylike flesh of the mayor's enforcer.

Cal held him against the door with his forearm while he pulled his Beretta out of the back of his jeans, pointing the barrel of the weapon at Bernie's forehead. Instead of fighting back, Bernie bent forward, struggling to catch his breath.

"Tell me what the fuck you're doing here or I'll blow your brains all over this door and make Caruso come in here and clean it up," Cal whispered. Despite the quiet nature of the threat, it appeared to have its desired effect on Bernie, as he started blinking rapidly.

Cal held the gun steady and placed his finger on the trigger. He'd already switched the weapon from safety to fire while pulling the gun out of his pants. Bernie moved his hands toward his head, which was now pouring sweat. He looked more like an amateur than the seasoned pro Cal had mistaken him for at the hospital.

"Alright, Boyle, chill out. I didn't come here to kill you. I didn't even come here to hurt you. Caruso wanted me to give you a message."

"Oh yeah? I have a message for Caruso too. I'll let you go first."

Bernie stuttered as he prepared to explain his presence to Cal. Cal hoped he made it quick in case another male patron decided they needed to take a leak.

"Caruso's offer, it's still on the table. But I wanted to make your choice a bit easier for you. I've got some photos that I think you should see. Can I reach into my pants pocket?"

Cal looked at Bernie with disgust. What photos could this man possibly have? Cal nodded while lowering the gun to match the movement of Bernie's hand. The fat man pulled what appeared to be two black-and-white photographs from the pocket of his jeans.

With his right hand shaking, he handed the photos to Cal. Cal took them and lowered the gun, pointing it at Bernie's foot. The henchman must have taken this as a sign of Cal backing off. He straightened up a bit.

Cal saw that the photos appeared to be of a car accident. A smaller car was completely totaled as two SUVs crashed into it, one from each side. In the first picture, Cal saw police officers and other emergency personnel gathered at the scene, but he couldn't make out many other details. The car that had been hit was demolished; he wasn't sure what model it was.

He flipped to the second picture and saw a body being carried away on a stretcher. The sheet wasn't completely covering the victim's face. Cal's blood ran cold. He knew by the white streak in the jet-black hair that the victim was his mother. The photos were of his mother's car accident.

"Where the fuck did you get these? What does this have to do with anything?"

Cal felt a rage boiling inside of him like he had when he'd plunged the knife into MacErlean's heart and when he'd pushed the boy over the railing in the warehouse all those years ago. He raised his weapon at Bernie, determined to pump a round of bullets into his chest.

"Wait, wait a minute." Bernie was stammering again. Cal noticed a rather pungent odor as Bernie lifted his hands in surrender.

"Those are police photographs. The mayor got them. As far as the police were concerned, it was an open-and-shut case. Your mother runs a red light, and the SUVs are a little anxious to get going once the light turns green and smash into her. An unfortunate accident but nothing to suggest that it was more than an accident."

Cal scanned the photos and forced himself not to cry at the memory of losing his mother. Any inkling of tears quickly turned to rage. How could the police think this was an accident? It may have been one thing for a single car to hit his mother going through a red light, but two?

"It's funny the power the mafia used to have. They bought off the detectives assigned to the case; no one would suggest that Alfredo Petrocelli ordered his men to follow your mother and wait for the opportune moment to make her death look like an accident. Such a shame."

Cal noticed Bernie's mood change as he finished his story. Instead of sweating and quaking in fear, Bernie stood tall and puffed out his chest. The falcon tattoo above his chest appeared to be flying forward in triumph.

"These photographs are no proof." Cal knew Alfredo was capable of such things, but even with his desire to leave him and the mob behind, he refused to believe it. "What does this have to do with anything anyway? You're throwing something in my face that I can't change."

Bernie clicked the lock on the back of the restroom door shut, ensuring they wouldn't be disturbed. He wiped the palms of his hands together and moved closer to Cal. The gun remained pointed at him.

"It's not me you're mad at," Bernie said, eyeing the gun. "You're right that the photos don't prove anything and that you can't change the past, but you can change the present. Mayor Caruso is prepared to go to great lengths to ensure the downfall of Alfredo Petrocelli, even pretending to be a Mexican drug lord. Impersonating this drug lord, Caruso phoned straight to the Commission to engage in a partnership with the Chicago mafia, going over Petrocelli's own head. Only instead of being a Mexican drug lord, Caruso will show up as himself and tell the Commission everything, and the Petrocellis will be removed from power."

Cal snorted. The plan seemed foolish to him. "What makes you think the Commission will believe you?"

"That's where you come in." Bernie smiled. "Caruso needs you on his team. He's prepared to pay you double whatever the going rate is for your services. Maybe even triple. You'll be there at the meeting and confess to the killing. But you won't be hurt because you'll be the new underboss of the Chicago mafia, ordained by the Commission."

Cal raised a brow in confusion but refused to lower his guard. How could he be the underboss of the Chicago mafia? Beyond the fact that he wasn't a made man, the Commission would surely kill him if they knew he was involved in Louie Petrocelli's murder. After telling Bernie as much, the goon laughed again. It was surprisingly high-pitched for such a burly man.

"It's all part of the mayor's grand plan. This is how he finally gets back at the mafia after what they did to his poor grandfather and the first step in gaining the power he'll need to go all the way to the White House someday. You see, once the Commission has Alfredo and Vinnie executed, they'll install Caruso as the new boss of the mafia. Now, there will be a figurehead boss that I can't reveal yet, but the mayor will be making the decisions. It's what the mafia always wanted, a powerful political figure in their pocket. And the mayor can use the mafia for his own interests in cleaning up the crime in other areas of the city, helping his national profile."

Bernie smiled and straightened up further, seemingly no longer threatened by Cal. Cal had to admit, the plan seemed impressive.

It sounded like a secure future for him on the surface. Alfredo and Vinnie would be taken out, Caruso would see to his safety from the Commission, and he would likely be free from prosecution for his earlier crimes. But what would Caruso want him to do as part of his grand plan? Would Cal still be the killer that he didn't want to be? The killer that Alfredo seemed willing to have walk away once this job was done?

It was his turn to start playing the political cards that power-hungry mongrels like Alfredo and Caruso were used to playing.

"I'm intrigued by the mayor's proposal. If I accept, I'll need you to do a few things for me."

Bernie clapped his hands together. For a man who was so gruff the other day at the hospital, he appeared childlike. "Brilliant. What would you like?"

"I'd like a promise that, once the mayor's plan goes through, I'm free to go. I'm ready to put this life behind me. I'm tired of killing for others."

Bernie frowned and let out a loud grunt. The Bernie he had met at the hospital had returned. "Mr. Boyle, the mayor finds you too valuable to let go. You'll be sorely needed and extraordinarily compensated should you decide to join forces with us. But I'm sure the mayor will find a way to accommodate your request. Anything else?"

"Yeah. My friend out there, his name is Fonzie. We're supposed to be following the mayor over the next few days leading up to the meeting. I'm going to need your men to spot us and take us in, put us out of commission without killing us. Until the meeting on Monday."

Bernie let out another boisterous laugh. "Why is that, Mr. Boyle?"

Cal sighed and tucked his gun back in the waistband of his jeans. "Because I've been ordered to kill Mayor Caruso."

20

"Y ou alright?"

Fonzie shook Cal's shoulder, waking him from his dream. Cal tried to avoid flashbacks of past killings, but he'd fallen into the trap. Over the course of the night, as they took turns watching Caruso's house, he dreamt of his first contracted killing as a member of the mafia. It was a horrible, heinous killing and reminded him of why he wanted out of the business.

They staked the mayor out at City Hall after leaving Lou's Tavern the previous afternoon. After waiting for what seemed like hours, they watched the mayor get into his black Lincoln and followed him to his house in Old Town. They watched the mayor and a guard go in and waited the rest of the night to see what would happen.

Throughout the ordeal, Cal continued to question whose side he was on and whether he'd made the right decision informing Bernie of his orders to kill Caruso. Cal knew the big man with the falcon tattoo could pick them up any minute, but despite passing their car shortly after they parallel parked on the mayor's street, he hadn't made his move yet. Part of Cal felt like a sellout; another part of him felt like he was only doing what was in his best interest. Though his loyalty to the Petrocellis, and all they'd done for him, had him thinking he should go through with the hit after all.

Fonzie shook Cal when he didn't respond. "What the hell is wrong with you?"

"I don't know," Cal lied. "Just thinking."

"Well, stop it. A couple guys are leaving the mayor's house."

Cal rubbed the sleep from his eyes and saw Bernie and the guard walking down the front steps out to the garage. The door opened and Bernie got in as the thin guard scanned the street. If he'd spotted Fonzie's car, he didn't acknowledge it.

Cal saw a woman with shoulder-length black hair and a young boy of around twelve enter the black Lincoln parked inside. The guard ventured from the curb toward the garage and made his way to the driver's side of the car.

After a brief moment, the car backed away from the drive and out into the street. Cal saw four silhouettes in the car, meaning the guard, Bernie, Mrs. Caruso, and the boy were all inside.

Fonzie looked at Cal with a mischievous glance once the car had disappeared. "You thinkin' what I'm thinkin'?"

"Yeah. Unless we miscounted, Caruso ought to be all alone in the house right now. This is as good of a chance as we'll have to nail him before he goes out again."

"Yessir. I don't want to do any more surveillance than I have to. Let's take care of business."

Cal grabbed his gun and checked to see that his magazine was full. Fonzie did the same. They both had knives on them as well.

"The way I see it, one of us goes in the front, one goes in the back. We'll have to corner the mayor once we get inside, but that shouldn't be too difficult," Fonzie said.

"Yeah," Cal replied. "It would help to know what floor he's on once we get in, see if we can get an element of surprise going."

They exited the car and started walking toward the house. "It's been a while since we've done one of these together," Fonzie said. "You ready for it?"

"We whacked MacErlean not too long ago."

"Ah, forgot about that one already."

Fonzie strode to the front door. Cal headed toward the back. Picking a lock was child's play for the both of them, but Cal couldn't help but feel a sense of anticipation each time he broke into a home. By the time he reached the deck next to the back door and removed the tension wrench and pin that he needed to pick the lock, his heart was racing. Surely the mayor would hear him and Fonzie breaking into the house and have a weapon at the ready to start firing at them.

Within seconds, Cal was inside the house. The back door opened to a cozy kitchen with white walls above a red baseboard. The lights were all on and shone brightly from orange cones that hung from the ceiling. A white-legged table with a beechwood top and matching chairs was clustered tightly against the wall.

Cal was fortunate that the hardwood floors didn't creak as he crept to the hallway leading to the front room. The hall was clear, and Cal saw no signs of Fonzie through the visible front door. Perhaps he had ventured upstairs already.

Cal removed the gun from his jeans and held it close as

he tiptoed forward, preparing to fire. He felt a quake of nervousness course through his arms, tingling up to his fingers that held the gun. His left hand steadied his trigger hand.

A sharp tumble of a heavy object rattled his nerves further. He peered around the corner into the living room but saw nothing disturbed. He stepped around the corner and into the living room, with his gun at the ready. Cal scanned the stairs again and back to the hallway, at first questioning if the noise had come from behind the hall door. That couldn't have been it. He was sure the noise originated from above.

With his attention diverted to the hall, Cal heard another loud crash, and this time saw that Fonzie was the source of the noise. His friend rolled down the stairs and tumbled toward the bottom landing, his head smashing against the wall as he came to rest.

Cal raced toward him, keeping his gun pointed at the stairwell, ready to fire if someone had caused Fonzie to fall and dared reveal themselves. Two long legs emerged from the top of the stairs, and the rest of Ross Caruso's body came into view. His gaze was directly on Cal, Fonzie's gun aimed at him.

"Ah, Mr. Boyle," Caruso said. "I'm glad you were here to protect me from this brute who broke into my house. You arrived in the nick of time."

Cal looked at Fonzie and back at Caruso. Fonzie was out cold.

"What else did you do to him?"

"Don't worry about him." Caruso kept the gun pointed at Cal. "He's meaningless. Besides, this is exactly what you wanted, isn't it? You asked Bernie for a way to detain the two of you so you wouldn't have to execute Alfredo's order to kill me. The police will be on their way to take him away for breaking into my home. Everything will be taken care of."

A phony smile spread across Caruso's face. Cal's anger boiled as Fonzie lay motionless on the floor. Alfredo and Vinnie's orders filled his head once again. The only thought on his mind was killing Ross Caruso. He couldn't forgive what he had done to Fonzie.

Caruso stepped down to the lower landing, kicking Fonzie's legs out of the way as he made his way to the living room floor. He positioned himself solidly before the front door.

"I hope you're not having a change of heart. Because now you have no way out of here. I'm afraid what's done is done."

Caruso set Fonzie's gun down next to his unconscious body, his gloved hands not leaving any fingerprints on the weapon. It was the opportunity Cal had been seeking, though Cal was convinced something else was going on. Caruso seemed like a highly calculating man. He wouldn't leave chance in Cal's hands.

Anger welled up inside of him once again. He no longer doubted the decision he would make. Seeing his best friend lying in an unconscious heap at the foot of the stairs sent his rage to a tipping point. He pointed the gun at Caruso and fired.

Cal waited for the sound of the gun blast, the image of blood spurting out of Caruso's chest as he toppled to the ground, a victim of his own cockiness. Instead, all Cal heard was the click of his gun. He'd forgotten to take the safety off. It was an amateur move for a professional killer.

Caruso grabbed the door handle bent over in laughter.

"It looks like I'm in your head, Mr. Boyle. But don't you worry, Bernie leaving with my family was a setup for you and your friend. My men will be here to take care of you, and if they fail, the police won't. Good riddance."

Cal switched the safety off and fired his weapon again, the bullet meeting the door as Caruso dashed out of his house. He heard shouting outside and the sound of footsteps running across the street. Caruso must have escaped unscathed—it was *his* voice that was the loudest in barking orders to what presumably were more of his goons.

The sound of footsteps grew louder. Adrenaline pulsed through Cal's veins as he considered his next moves. He had two choices: fight or run. Fighting would be foolish, since he was outmanned and outgunned. He'd have no choice but to hope the back door was clear for a quick getaway.

Cal raced to the steps and grabbed Fonzie. He knew moving an injured man wasn't the wisest decision, but he had no choice if he wanted both of them to get out of Caruso's house alive. He draped him over his shoulder and ran from the living room into the hallway that led to the kitchen.

The front door kicked open with a start and gunshots rang out toward him. Fonzie, no longer unconscious, cried out in pain. He'd been shot.

Cal crashed to the floor once he reached the kitchen, ducking the bullets that shattered around them. He rolled Fonzie off of his back and spun to his feet, firing in the direction of the bullets while crouching near the doorway. He heard one man scream and another shooter fall to the ground. Two more men entered through the front door, and Cal continued to fire until he was out of bullets.

He knew he hit one of the men for sure but didn't have time to assess the fate of the others. Cal put his spent weapon back in his pants and looked at Fonzie, who was now writhing around on the floor. Blood poured from his shoulder, cascading down his arm and spreading through his shirt.

"Shit, Fonz, we've got to get out of here."

Cal grabbed a few kitchen towels hanging from the oven handle to treat Fonzie's shoulder once they got to safety. Fonzie grunted as Cal hoisted him off the ground and over his shoulder. Cal hoped no men were waiting for them at the back door. He hadn't expected an ambush and had left his spare ammunition back in the car.

Cal opened the back door and was relieved to see no one on the deck. He thought he heard more gunshots fire as his legs picked up steam and raced for the alley beyond the small backyard. He glanced over his shoulder to empty darkness. The load of Fonzie's body over his shoulder was weighing him down, but he knew he had to keep going. He ran for a couple of blocks, occasionally glancing behind him to make sure he wasn't being followed.

He stopped at a large rented storage unit that was in the process of being loaded up with goods. Squatting behind it, he gently set Fonzie on the ground. Fonzie's breathing was heavy and labored. Cal raced to dig the towels out of his pockets and wrapped them against his wounded shoulder.

"Shit, shit, shit. Work with me, Fonz."

The blood continued to pour out. Cal had to cut Fonzie's T-shirt with his jackknife to gain clear access to the wound. Even with the towels putting pressure on the wound, blood continued to pour through them. He feared that the brachial artery had been punctured due to the gunshot wound, which would mean surgery, if they could get him medical attention.

Cal kept pressure on the wound with one hand, and with the other, he called Tony. He needed the kid to pick them up and get them to Doc Parker. The mafia used the services of a retired surgeon when someone was hurt but couldn't go to a hospital for fear of police questioning.

"Tony, get your ass over to Old Town. Fonzie's been hit. It was Caruso's men. We need to get him help as soon as possible."

_____

21

The next morning, Cal debated whether he should leave Fonzie's side at Doc Parker's house and make another attempt at finding Caruso. He was sure that, despite all of the commotion at his house yesterday, Caruso and his family would attend Sunday Mass at St. Michael's. Al Meransky and his family also attended Mass there, and Cal remembered Meransky joking about Caruso's wife singing in the choir.

"When she gets ready to do her solo, make sure you get up to go to the bathroom or something. She doesn't get her voice from the angels."

Cal eyed the bed where Fonzie lay post-surgery. Cal had been right in thinking that Fonzie's brachial artery had been damaged. The doc had enough equipment to perform basic surgery in his basement, but without the proper diagnostic images, the best he could do was perform a ligation of the artery. In addition to the shoulder wound, Fonzie had suffered a concussion as a result of being thrown down the stairs. The doc suggested that Fonzie stay out of action for a few weeks until his wound healed up. He planned to keep Fonzie a few days to monitor him.

Fonzie was pissed they hadn't gotten Caruso the first time and was itching to get out of bed to join Cal on the chase. Cal had to force him to rest. He'd be of little use with a concussed brain.

After seeing what Caruso and his men had accomplished by nearly gunning down Fonzie, Cal felt relief at not joining forces with the mayor. He had to prove to Maria that he was committed to putting the mob lifestyle behind him, which he fully intended to do once Caruso was dead.

The buzz of his cell phone ringing in his pocket startled him, sending anxiety through his body.

"Hey."

A soft voice sounded on the other line. No other voice in the world could match the angelic quality present in it, despite the pain that was evident from the tone. Maria had finally called him back.

"Hi."

Cal didn't know what else to say. He hadn't expected her to return his calls.

"I'm sorry about the other day," Maria started. "It was such a shock to me, you know?"

"Yeah. I never wanted to tell you. Part of me wanted to keep living with my secrets."

Cal walked out of the room and into the upstairs hallway. He descended the carpeted staircase and brushed the fingers of his free hand against the peeling flowered wallpaper.

"I wanted to live with my secrets, but I realized I couldn't do that anymore. I love you too much for that. Before you, I never knew what love was. I do now."

Cal's face cringed as he muttered the words. While he

really loved Maria, he realized it sounded corny as he spoke. It was the kind of language Maria usually saw right through.

"I love you too, Cal, but it's hard for me to keep going like this. I don't think we can keep seeing each other unless I get a promise from you. I need to know that you're done with this, this killing life. I know it may take some time, but I truly need to see you get away from this.

"I don't care if you have to flip hamburgers at McDonald's to get out, but you need to do it. I've seen a tenderness in you that proves to me you're not the monster that Alfredo and the rest of them want you to be."

Cal paused at the bottom of the stairs, his chest stricken with a tightness that was the sudden outpouring of emotion that he'd kept hidden all these years. The feelings got in the way of what he did best, the profession that he planned to consider himself retired from after today.

"Believe me, I want to end this life too. Everything in me recognizes that. I promise I'll find a way out of this and be worthy of you."

Cal stopped himself from saying any more. As much as he wanted to leave this life behind, he knew he couldn't until he finished the job with Caruso. It was now or never. Still, Maria wasn't satisfied.

"But? There's something you're not telling me, Callahan. Don't tell me you have another hit you're pursuing."

Cal raised his brows, and his head fell into the wall in shame. There was no getting around it. He was going to have to tell her.

"Yes. It has to happen or it's the end of me. The man I have to kill would make sure my life and the Petrocellis' lives would all end. As much as I want to be free from them, I can't leave them like this. I have to see it through to the end. Once this is done, it's all over."

He heard Maria crying. He wasn't prepared for the shouting that followed.

"Oh, is it really over after this? Or will Alfredo offer you more money and a fancier apartment to keep the killings coming? Let someone else take care of this, Cal. Let's start living the life we were meant to live, free of all of this."

Cal's jaw clenched as he listened to his girlfriend's sobs. The sound of her sadness made him want to leave the mafia on the spot.

"Maria, I'm sorry. I can't do that yet. I'd like nothing more than to hold you and tell you it's all going to be alright. As soon as this is over, I will. I promise."

The intensity of her sobs was as loud as a jackhammer thundering into concrete. Maria eventually composed herself and was able to continue the conversation.

"Let me help make the decision a little bit harder, since you can't seem to see things from my point of view. I'm going shopping with my friend Reema from school. Lord knows I need a new dress to match the new purse I bought since the one you gave me was paid for with blood money. Then I've got a lunch date with another man."

Cal felt the tightness in his chest turn to a burning sensation. He hadn't expected to hear that.

"A what?"

"You heard me. I have a lunch date with another man, a man I met when I bought my new purse from Saks, actually. He's a very powerful man, and he's achieved a lot in his life. I'm pretty sure he didn't do that by killing people."

Cal scowled. How could Maria afford a purse from Saks? Was that a dig at him for not buying a purse from Saks in the first place? He hoped his annoyance wasn't audible over the phone.

"Who is this guy?"

"That's not important. He's a very successful public figure in the city. He means nothing to me right now, Cal, but he's the kind of man I could easily pull if you don't leave this life behind."

Public figure? If she was talking about that bastard Caruso, he'd be sure to kill him, even in public. He had to find out who it was and where she was headed.

"Where are you going? The person I'm being asked to handle is a public official. I don't want you to get caught up in this. Stay home where it's safe."

Maria laughed as if she didn't believe him.

"Please, no one will recognize me anyway. I'm doing this cultural experiment where I'm wearing one of Reema's hijabs to see what it's like to experience prejudice. I'm not getting all glammed up for this. When you're ready to stop being a criminal, Callahan, we'll talk again."

The hum of traffic and the honking of taxicabs signaled she was somewhere downtown. He wasn't sure where, but if she was going shopping, she'd likely be near Michigan Avenue and choose a restaurant or bar not too far from there.

"Maria, wait."

His voice was cut off.

"Goodbye, Callahan. Make sure you live up to your promise."

22

Vinnie was sitting in his familiar chair in his father's study, ready for Alfredo to conduct the business of the day. A big grin was plastered on his face.

Cal had failed. It wasn't something Vinnie had actively wanted to happen, especially with the Chicago mafia's future on the line, but it was refreshing that his childhood best friend wasn't able to get the job done the first time.

Despite all of Vinnie's success as a point guard on his high school's basketball team, Alfredo had cheered loudest when Cal hauled in a touchdown pass as tight end on the high school football team. Vinnie had the friends, the girls, and the grades in high school, and he had done well in college. Yet, it was Cal with his strength and calculated killing ability that seemed to be rewarded the most in his father's eyes.

Hearing Cal had failed to kill Caruso when he was firmly within his grasp gave Vinnie an idea. The idea that maybe he could be the one to solve his father's problems.

Melissa Ranieri entered the study and closed the door behind her before clasping her hands tightly together.

"Uncle," she started, then turned to meet Vinnie's gaze. "There's someone here to see you."

Vinnie's father didn't look up from the stack of papers he was reading.

"Who is it?"

Melissa unclasped her hands and smoothed the bottom of her short black skirt. Her swallow was audible even from the back corner of the room where Vinnie sat.

"It's Cal's driver, sir. His name is Tony, Tony Fregosi."

Vinnie stood up from his seat and looked at Alfredo and Melissa with both brows raised.

"What?"

Vinnie couldn't believe what he'd heard. Expressing his confusion in a one-word question was unlike him, but he was that surprised by the boy's request.

Why was a mere driver asking to speak with him and his father? What made him think he could get a visit with the boss of the Chicago mafia?

"I know, Vinnie. It's very unusual. But the boy is sitting out there. He was talking about Cal, how he's been off lately. He's worked with Cal for a while now, so I bet he would know his mood even better than we would. He wanted to see you both to talk about Caruso."

"Caruso?" Vinnie asked. "Mayor Ross Caruso?"

"Yes."

Vinnie laughed and looked at his father, pacing toward his desk.

"Isn't this crazy, Dad? No fucking way we let that kid in here."

Alfredo shifted his gaze between Vinnie and Melissa. He

let out a deep exhale and tapped his fingers on the desk. Vinnie wondered what was taking his father so long to send the kid packing. He was ready to give Melissa the orders himself.

"Bring him in."

Vinnie couldn't believe his ears. Some low-level driver was requesting a meeting with his father, and he was choosing to grant the request?

Melissa left the room before Vinnie could tell her it was a bad idea. Vinnie curled his hands into fists, ready to explode the way his father had so many times before.

"I know what you're thinking," Alfredo said, still looking at the wall opposite him. "And you're right. Just take a seat and let's see the set of balls this guy has on him."

Vinnie reluctantly returned to his chair just as Melissa opened the study door once again and escorted Tony Fregosi inside.

The kid looked like a nervous wreck. Vinnie wouldn't be surprised if he was about to shit his pants. Had he been in Tony's position, Vinnie would've felt the same way.

To put it in his father's words, Cal's driver must have had a huge set of balls on him if he dared to request a meeting with Alfredo, especially about Caruso.

Vinnie watched as Alfredo reached his large hand across the oak desk. Tony strode over and held his hand up to shake it. Vinnie could tell by the way Tony positioned his hand that he was trying to match the firmness of Alfredo's grip. He must have wanted to make a good impression.

"You must be Tony Fregosi," Alfredo said. "Melissa tells me you have something you want tell me about Ross Caruso. Vinnie says you bailed Fonzie out and got him to the doc in the nick of time. I appreciate that."

Tony scratched the back of his neck and nodded to acknowledge his contribution. The look on his face was one of uncertainty, as if he knew that the treasure was hidden beneath the dragon but he wanted no part of slaying it.

"Tony, when my father compliments you, you do more than nod," Vinnie said. "There's no need to be scared."

"Yes, sir. I'm sorry about that. I won't do that again. I appreciate the compliment very much, Mr. Petrocelli."

Alfredo nodded and poured a glass of brandy from the bottle on his desk. Instead of drinking it himself as Vinnie expected, he pushed the glass to the edge of the desk where Tony was seated.

"You ever had a real drink, son?"

"No. I need to stay sober and provide for my family. I don't drink."

Alfredo nodded and took the drink back. Even though Vinnie didn't care for brandy, he wished his father would've offered it to him.

"I respect that, kid, I really do. I hear you're doing great work for Cal. I really think he likes working with you."

"Thank you, sir."

Alfredo stood and walked around the desk and sat in the empty chair next to Tony. This is where his father would use the power play. He would show Tony just how small he was by comparison, even after complimenting him. Vinnie would find out how displeased his father was with Tony's request for the meeting.

"What do you really want, boy? You obviously know more than you're letting on. I'm sure you know that this stuff is kept pretty tight-lipped around here. Other than Cal, Fonzie, and the leadership, no one outside this room knows what we're up to with Caruso. I'm sure you can imagine what would happen if you were to tell anyone else about this."

Vinnie rolled his eyes. Why wasn't his father scorning

the boy and putting him in his place for the ridiculous ask? He felt like standing up and piling on his thoughts, but he thought he heard Tony's stomach quiver, like he needed to run to the toilet. He was nervous enough already.

"Yes, sir. I won't tell anyone."

Alfredo's face moved closer to Tony, who moved farther back in his chair in response.

Vinnie felt bad for the kid. He sensed his father was coming around to his own way of thinking, but he was finally being strategic about it, rather than letting his emotions burst out of control.

"I don't want to waste your time, sir, so I'll come right out and say it," Tony began. "I don't know why you want to kill Caruso, but I know time is of the essence. Cal said he needed to complete the hit by tomorrow, is that right?"

Vinnie glanced at his father. He hoped his old man wouldn't share too many details with Tony. The last thing they needed was the kid to get picked up by the police and for him to squeal and implicate the both of them.

"Yeah, that's right," Alfredo said, shooting his own daggers at Vinnie.

"I spend a lot of time with Cal. I've seen how he's acted lately. I know he's your best hit man, but I can't help but notice that something's off with him. I wonder if he's really the man for the job."

Vinnie raised his brow in Tony's direction. Was that the purpose for the meeting? Did an eighteen-year-old punk kid think he could walk in and ask Alfredo for the ultimate killing assignment?

"I know I don't have the skills that Cal does and that Caruso's a tough man to crack, but if I work with Cal now that Fonzie's laid up, I know I can pull the trigger. I shot one of the mayor's guys to save Cal. I'm ready to do more for you than drive. I know if I find Caruso that I can kill him."

Vinnie was fuming inside. Melissa's eyes appeared to bug out of her head. Vinnie wished he could see the expression on his father's face as he stood behind him. Would it be one of anger and fury, per his usual method, or one of amusement?

The answer to one of the most sensational questions that had ever been asked in the Petrocelli family study hung in the air like dust, waiting to settle on the most prominent piece of furniture it could find.

"We've got to find more guys like this kid, Vin." Alfredo got up from the chair, looked at Vinnie, and walked behind the desk, taking a powerful swig of his brandy before taking a seat.

Vinnie's own eyes grew wide. Alfredo was going for this? What the hell had gotten into his old man? If he was going to allow Tony Fregosi to help Cal take down Caruso, he feared he wouldn't be the only member of the Petrocelli family having a hit placed on his father.

"You know what, kid? You remind me of myself at your age, a real go-getter. I like your confidence. What do you think, Vinnie?"

Vinnie composed his facial expression. He couldn't let his anger overcome him. He stood and walked closer to Tony, leaning his arm on the chair next to him and setting his face a mere three feet away from Tony's.

As much as he hated the kid, he focused his eyes on the boy's forehead. He breathed deeply through his nose, letting his breath calm his maddening heart rate. When he felt in complete control of his thoughts, he turned to face his father.

"Are you crazy, Dad? There's no way we can let this kid

kill Caruso. Besides the fact that I'm sure he's never killed anyone in his life, we can't leave a hit like this to a kid. What if shit hits the fan like it did yesterday and Caruso's men come after him? We can't have the death of a kid on our hands. It would fuck us even more than the police interference right now."

Alfredo raised his large hand, stopping Vinnie in his tracks.

"I get it, this is a risky proposition for us." Alfredo turned back to Tony. Vinnie felt as if his concern was brushed aside, his opinion as underboss devalued in comparison to that of the complete amateur seated next to him.

"I want you to know that it's a risk for you too, kid. Even if you're successful, do you know what it feels like to kill a man? What that does to your life? You'll never be able to live the same way."

Melissa walked behind the boy, tapped his shoulder, and guided him out of the room. Vinnie was glad his cousin had taken the boy out of the room before he exploded. He couldn't believe his father was considering this.

He thought back to the faint idea he'd had before Tony was ushered into the room. It was the only way Vinnie could make this right for the mafia and himself.

He'd have to convince his father that he'd be the one to kill Ross Caruso.

23

Alfredo had a grin plastered on his face as Melissa escorted Tony out of the room. Seeing a kid with ambition was a breath of fresh air. It was a trait that was lacking throughout the rest of the organization.

Even though he'd warned the kid how his life might change if he decided to help Cal with the hit, Alfredo didn't give a shit. The more people he had going after Caruso, the better. Hell, he'd go after him himself if the mafia wasn't under tight police scrutiny.

Melissa reentered the study and slammed the door, causing the photos on top of the fireplace to shake. A few books from the shelves on the wall crashed to the floor.

"What the hell was that about?" Vinnie asked, storming toward Melissa in anger. "You sent this kid in here to ask if he could have the hit on Caruso?"

"What was I supposed to do? Do you think I had any idea he would come in here asking about *that*?"

Alfredo watched as the two cousins fought with each other. He was thrilled with the idea of sending as many men at Caruso as possible. Even though he wanted to keep the hit under wraps and leave Vinnie out of it for his son's own protection, sending Tony out there to help Cal would do no harm. They could easily cover up his involvement with the mafia if anything happened to him.

It was all looking like a win in Alfredo's mind. He poured another glass of brandy, leaned back in his chair, and watched Vinnie and Melissa argue. At some point, they both realized he hadn't chimed in and looked back at him.

"You wanna know what I think? I think we let the kid go. You both know we need Caruso dead. With Fonzie out of commission, Cal could use all the help he can get."

"No offense, Dad, but that kid didn't come in here looking like he was going to work *with* someone. I think he's hell-bent on earning the hit for himself. You said it yourself, he's motivated and probably thinks this will help him move up in our world."

Alfredo considered Vinnie's point and poured more brandy down his throat. The liquid burned and settled into a nice warmth at the top of his stomach. He couldn't remember how many glasses he'd had.

"If it is the kid that hits Caruso, I'll make sure he moves on up. Good soldiers are hard to find nowadays, Vinnie. Plus, he's got the Italian heritage. He could be made someday."

"You're thinking about that already? Who knows if this kid is even cut out for the mob long term?"

"Be that as it may, Melissa, right now I don't give a damn. I want you to go back out there and tell the boy that he has my blessing to join Cal in his pursuit and even to pull the trigger if he has to."

Melissa sighed and walked out of the room. Vinnie walked toward Alfredo's desk and took a seat across from his father.

"We're really going through with this? Trusting the biggest hit we've ever put on someone to a kid? Let me go out there, Dad. I'll get to Caruso before Cal or Tony come close."

Alfredo growled and slammed his hand down on the desk.

"I'm not putting my only son's life at risk for this endeavor. Let Cal and Tony take care of it. We have sacrificial lambs for a reason. Now is when we make use of them."

24

Five minutes after Tony left the house, Vinnie entered his gray 2014 Porsche Coupe and reversed out of the long driveway alongside the house, his foot hitting the gas pedal with such force that his car nearly propelled into the neighbor's front lawn across the street.

Vinnie floored it and headed south to the city. Cars filled with people going to and from church and brunch cramped the roads. It seemed like Chicago was the brunch capital of America. Even his mother preferred to take a morning off from cooking to drag the family to brunch after services.

His distaste for brunch wasn't the main source of his anger. He was pissed that his father had entrusted an eighteen-year-old kid with the murder of Ross Caruso. He resented his father for being overprotective of him. He never hesitated to put Cal in harm's way.

Vinnie slapped the thoughts away after nearly veering into a car in the next lane. He knew his father cared about him and didn't want to put him in danger, yet Vinnie speculated his father's concern had more to do with his worry that the Petrocelli family name wouldn't live on if Vinnie were killed, rather than the sadness he'd experience at the loss of another son.

Between the lack of interest in his business proposals for future mafia endeavors and not receiving his father's blessing to throw himself into the ring in the hit on Caruso, Vinnie felt an unmanageable anger. He rarely ranted and raved like his father, but Vinnie's grip on the steering wheel and the grinding of his teeth indicated his anger was more outwardly expressed than usual.

Vinnie drove toward North Ashland as he made his way down to the city. He had to switch his vantage point from an underboss to a hit man. What intel had Cal gathered on Caruso since they'd tried to kill him yesterday? Cal had only said he'd ridden with Fonzie to the doc's house on the West Side and stayed with him all night.

They knew where Caruso lived, but that did them little good—he likely wouldn't be hanging out at home until he was in the good graces of the Commission, leaving Alfredo, Vinnie, and Cal as hit targets themselves.

As the leading public official in Chicago, Caruso often mentioned his Catholic values. Vinnie decided to head for the churches in the Old Town neighborhood.

He knew Cal was likely staking out at least one of the Catholic churches as well. He didn't mind if Cal did the legwork in finding Caruso, but he swore to himself that he would be the one to make the kill.

He'd be the one to save his father from all the trouble Caruso was causing them and extinguish any threat of his father's awful secret hit being revealed to the Commission.

Maybe then he'd earn his due respect.

25

Cal watched from Doc Parker's Jeep Cherokee as the first wave of parishioners made their way out of St. Michael's following the conclusion of eleven-o'clock Mass. He was too busy scanning for Caruso to gaze up at the spectacular views of the cathedral that loomed over him.

The church was a historic landmark in the city, predating the infamous Chicago Fire of 1871. A good portion of the building had perished in the fire, but the walls were mostly intact and the church had been rebuilt using some of the existing structure. Cal had never been inside the church, though he had to admit the architecture of the building was impressive from what he could see.

Parishioners continued to spill out of the three large front doors and onto the sidewalk. Most of them gathered to chat around the trees perfectly centered across from each door.

At last, he saw the tall mayor and his beautiful raven-haired wife exit the church. His wife's hands were atop the shoulders of their middle-school-aged son. Caruso was talking excitedly to the priest, perhaps recapping the break-in at his home yesterday.

After a moment, the boy pointed to a group of kids hanging out by one of the trees. Mrs. Caruso patted him on the shoulder and watched him meander over to the other preteens while she waited for her husband's conversation with the priest to finish.

Cal's eyes followed the boy. He felt a pang of discomfort at what he was about to do. If Cal went through with killing Caruso to ensure his own safety and escape from the mob, he knew the boy would become fatherless. He was probably the same age Cal had been when he'd lost his own father.

What kind of impact would that have on the boy's life? Would Alfredo eventually ask Cal to kill the boy's mother for good measure and then adopt Caruso's son like he'd adopted Cal? Would he make him an emotionless killer in the mold of Cal? These questions clouded Cal's mind and filled him with doubt.

Caruso finally left the father's side and gestured for his boy to follow him and his wife to the black Lincoln that had pulled up to the curb. It was the same black Lincoln Cal had been in pursuit of the past few days.

Cal saw the trademark phony smile plastered on Caruso's face and thought back to his phone conversation with Maria. She was meeting a "very successful public figure" that afternoon for lunch. If Caruso was the bastard she was meeting, he'd be sure to end his life right in front of her and put any thoughts of the boy losing his father out of his mind.

Cal glanced at his cell phone lying on the passenger seat of the car. He'd called Tony at least ten times on his way to the church while waiting for Caruso. With Fonzie injured, he needed someone else to help with the surveillance.

He hated asking Tony to partake in the endeavor, especially with a mission as dangerous as this, but the kid had proven himself back in the alley, saving Cal's life and helping Cal eliminate one of the mayor's goons in the process. Cal hit the call button one more time.

"Pick up the damn phone, kid."

Cal watched Caruso and family enter the car and pull away from the curb. He was going to follow them as long as he could. He hoped the family left Caruso alone at some point. He didn't want to take them out too. If his hunch was correct, Caruso would be heading downtown to meet with Maria.

After getting Tony's voice mail again, Cal turned the Beretta back and forth in his hand and then extended the weapon as he would if he planned to fire, pointing it below the steering column. This time, he wouldn't be befuddled by the safety switch.

If he saw his lover and the mayor together for lunch, he'd make sure the only thing Caruso ate were his own brains.

He never saw the gray Porsche in the rearview mirror behind him.

26

C al followed the black Lincoln until he reached Polk Street, where the car idled in front of a small clinic. The two bodyguards Cal had seen earlier, when the driver had dropped off Caruso's wife and son at Ogilvie train station, got out of the car and entered the building. Presumably, that left only the driver and Caruso himself inside of the car.

Cal pulled ahead and entered the medical facility's employee parking lot, thinking the move would convince Caruso's driver that he hadn't been following them and had disappeared from sight.

If they'd recognized Cal following them in the Jeep Cherokee, they didn't seem too concerned about a possible hit on Caruso while he sat not far from where the car was parked. It would be a relatively easy job to walk up to the car and take out the driver and Caruso in one fell swoop—if Cal had someone with him to deal with the two bodyguards inside the clinic.

Cal shot a text to Tony, telling him that he thought Caruso would be staying put for a while. O'Dooley's Pub was up ahead, and Cal hoped Tony could come down to help out if Caruso stopped for drinks.

While Cal was waiting for Tony to respond, he fired off another text to Maria. His heart thumped with pain like a hammer driving a nail when she told him she had lunch plans with another man. The nail tore deeper when Cal suspected Caruso was the man she was seeing.

He wanted her to know that he cared about her and that he was ready to change. At the same time, he didn't want her to think he was stalking her and trying to intimidate her lunch date. If she was meeting Caruso, she'd probably have little incentive to forgive him. If Cal's anger resulted in murderous gunfire, any tenderness Maria had seen shining forth would be futile. He couldn't kill Caruso in front of her, not if he wanted to win back her love.

His jaw tightened as he pushed send on the text asking her where she was going. He hoped his mind would be at ease when she told him she was going to a different restaurant, a different bar.

Cal drummed the steering wheel, waiting for the bodyguards to return to the vehicle. The longer they took inside, the more Cal thought about crossing the street and blowing a bullet hole through the driver's window and following up with the shocked mayor inside. Instead, Cal opened the glove compartment to see if the doc had any useful weapons to add to his own collection.

He didn't see anything exciting inside, only the maintenance manual for the vehicle, a tire gauge, several expired auto insurance cards, and a fresh Gala apple tucked in the back corner. The doc must have been saving himself a snack.

Cal shrugged and promised he'd buy the doc another one before he returned the car. Peeling fruit calmed him.

His confidence that he could successfully take care of Caruso grew as he rubbed his thumb over the red apple skin.

He watched the street as he slowly peeled the apple with his jackknife, allowing the red skin to pool on his lap and the floor mat below him. He heard the phone on the passenger seat buzz, announcing a new text message. A quick glance at the screen told Cal it was Tony. He was on his way.

Cal blocked all other thoughts from his mind as he finished peeling the apple and prepared for his first bite. Tony and Fonzie often joked about Cal's peculiarity with fruit peeling and the explanation Cal gave for his behavior. The careful focus he displayed when peeling the fruit was just as precise as the details of each kill. Cal's meditative state continued as he neatly corralled the skin from his lap and the floor for disposal later.

Cal bit into the apple, savoring the rich sweetness of nature's candy while closing his eyes. He slowly chewed each bite, trying to burn the sensation of the taste into his tongue in case this was the last thing he ever ate. While he was certain it would all be over in a matter of minutes— there was no longer any time for games—he felt a deep sense of uncertainty over what he was about to do.

He'd rarely considered the impact of killing someone before he completed the job. Each mark was nothing more than assignments passed down from on high; he performed his duty as a hit man and made the kill. If he succeeded, his boss's problems were solved, and he walked away with the cash that enabled him to enjoy a luxurious lifestyle that he couldn't have dreamt of as a kid.

From the thought of Caruso's son growing up an orphan, to the expectation that he would extinguish yet another human life, Cal began to grasp what he really had become. Maria's fear and hesitation to keep seeing him began to make perfect sense. It was as if he hadn't been able to process simple emotions like uncertainty and doubt and the concepts of right and wrong. The recognition of his lack of self-knowledge scared him.

At long last, Caruso's men exited the clinic, scanned the area, and entered the vehicle. A few minutes passed, during which only a man in a fedora entered the nearby pub, before the bodyguards exited the vehicle again. This time, Ross Caruso got out with them. They were heading for the pub.

Cal disengaged the Beretta's safety switch and made sure the magazine was full. Judgment day had arrived for Mayor Caruso.

27

R oss Caruso smiled and took a hearty gulp from his Goose Island Pale Ale. His good friend State's Attorney Pete Rogers had just walked into O'Dooley's Pub.

The mayor hadn't expected to see Pete. He thought the attorney would be out on a date with the young Latina that he'd set him up with. Caruso would've loved to go on a date with the girl he'd met while shopping for a new handbag for his wife himself. Yet, the infidelity risk wasn't worth it, given all that was at stake.

He was all in on his political future, hoping his next move would take him to greater heights. He'd be mayor and mafia chieftain for a few years. After that, perhaps the family leaders would put him up for a US Senate bid. Then, maybe a decade from now, back him for the presidency.

Once he met with the Commission and told them how awful Alfredo Petrocelli was for ordering the murder of his father and the last boss of the Chicago family, the Commission would ensure both Alfredo and his kid were dead. If Callahan Boyle reformed his allegiance with his adopted family, Caruso would ensure he was implicated as the man who'd executed the evil deed.

Rogers walked up to the bar and removed his fedora. He was the second such man in the last five minutes to enter wearing a fedora. Caruso shot a quick glance at Bernie, who was keeping an eye on things nearby. While the second man wearing a fedora seemed suspicious, he ended up settling in at the bar like an Average Joe.

"Hey, Mayor, how are ya?"

Rogers had worked his way next to the mayor without him realizing it. He had to be more mindful of his surroundings in case Boyle or some other trained killer tried to knife him without warning.

"Pete, what happened with that young gal I told you about?"

Rogers chuckled. "This isn't exactly the classiest joint for a first date, huh? I figured it would be casual enough for a first meeting, to see what the girl is like, you know?"

Caruso nodded. He made a gesture to the bartender for a refill of his draft. Rogers ordered a pint of Coors Light, glanced back toward the door, and took the seat next to Caruso. Caruso nodded to Bernie that Rogers was alright.

"What brings you out today? I heard about the break-in at your house. That must have been quite a scare."

"It was. My wife and boy were pretty shocked by it. I've got them staying with her sister in the suburbs for now. I dropped them off at the train station after church."

"I see. So why are you out, then? Beer usually take the edge off for you?"

Caruso considered that. He wasn't sure why he'd decided to come out for drinks. He knew that there was nothing more important than getting to the meeting with the head of the Commission alive. He wanted one last moment of fun and relaxation before that fateful meeting occurred.

The very best of his security team was with him in the pub at that moment. Bernie and his associate Gorgi were the real top dogs, far more skilled than anyone Boyle and his posse had slain up to that point. Two more men, dressed as ordinary folks sitting in the back corner of the bar, were also on Caruso's payroll, constantly scoping out each person who came into the bar for any suspicious activity. There was no reason for the mayor to feel unsafe. Even the car that had tailed him from Old Town had pulled past the Lincoln when it'd stopped outside the clinic. That was one less thing to fear.

"Right now, I'm feeling pretty good. Sometimes, even in the darkest times, you want to keep riding the good times. That's what I'm trying to do."

"Here, here," Rogers said. Both men lifted their glasses and clinked them in a celebratory toast. Rogers only sipped at his beer while Caruso downed his quickly.

His drinking pace caught up to his bladder. Caruso rose from his chair and staggered down the narrow pathway between the barstools and the tables lining the wall, squeezing past a waitress carrying food to the front of the bar as he went.

When he got to the back where the bathrooms were situated, he noticed a line of four people all waiting outside of the women's restroom. There was an "Out of Order" sign on the door of the men's restroom.

"What's going on here?" Caruso barked.

One of the bartenders, a gruff, balding man with curly black hair and a matching beard, stepped from behind the bar and glared at the mayor as he walked back to the nearby kitchen.

"Some guy clogged the men's toilet," he said. "I called a plumber to come in and work on it. Until then, I'm afraid you'll have to wait."

"Christ Almighty," Caruso mumbled. He'd only been standing there for a few moments but was starting to become impatient. The mayor was used to everything going his way, each pawn on the chessboard easily maneuverable based on his desires. He didn't want to wait.

"You can go out back if you're desperate. I won't mind," the bartender said, meandering through the open doorway to the kitchen.

Caruso saw the exit leading out to what had to be an alley behind the bar. He glanced back at Bernie and over to the two men sitting at the back table and proceeded to walk into the kitchen.

"Wait, boss, you want one of us back there?" Bernie called out.

Caruso waved him off, the alcohol leaving him feeling more secure than he should have been. "I don't need someone to hold it for me. I'll be right back."

28

V innie recalled a time when he went off of caffeine for several months. The next sip of coffee he took had sent a jolt of adrenaline straight to his heart, caused him to sweat profusely, and made him think he was going to die if he took another drink. That was exactly how he was feeling at the moment, his heart aflutter with activity.

He was going to finally prove to his father that he could be more than just the brains of the Chicago mafia. Brawn and the ability to perform calculated kills weren't exactly his forte, but he would find a way to prove both momentarily. He'd set his bait. With a smattering of luck, Ross Caruso would walk right into the trap and squeal like a wounded rat knowing its last piece of cheese was right in front of it.

He'd arrived at O'Dooley's Pub with a purpose. Disguised under a fedora hat, Vinnie slipped into the pub, careful not to attract attention as he made his way to the end of the bar closest to the restrooms. He felt a few pairs of eyes watch him closely—eyes he assumed belonged to the mayor's men—before he settled onto the last stool and grabbed a beer.

After several minutes and a quick downing of the beer to give him the liquid courage he knew he'd need, he went into the men's restroom, opened the paper towel holder, and threw as many as he possibly could into the toilet. For good measure, he took some change he had in the bottom of his pocket and added it to the bowl. He attempted a flush and smiled in satisfaction when the toilet began to clog.

Returning to the bar, he told the bartender what had happened to the toilet, and suggested a sign be placed on the door indicating the restroom was out of order. The over-worked bartender obliged, and Vinnie slipped quietly out of the back door, hoping he wouldn't have to wait too long for Caruso to get desperate enough to urinate in the rear of the building rather than wait for the women's.

Vinnie had since removed his hat and clutched his gun, a Smith & Wesson 19, alongside his thigh. He stared intently at the door and waited, knowing that his plan would work. The clanging of someone inside the bar trying to open the door alerted him to the immediacy of his plan. It took several powerful pushes before it burst open, but it finally did.

Vinnie held his weapon high in his hands and hid behind the nearby green metal trash receptacle, allowing the individual exiting the bar to step outside.

The tall figure who exited the pub was none other than Mayor Caruso. Vinnie remained still; he didn't want the mayor to hear even the faint sound of his breath. He watched as Caruso took a few steps away from the bar and stared blankly ahead. After a shake of the head, he turned toward the building. Vinnie heard him unfastening his belt. His heart pounded as he knew what he needed to do.

Time to shine.

Vinnie jumped out from behind the dumpster with his gun pointed in front of him. The movement startled the mayor and sent his hands flying up in surrender. A trace of a smile faded quickly from the man's face.

"I wasn't expecting the boss to send his own son to kill me," Caruso said, his voice quivering.

"No one sent me. I came to take care of you on my own."

Caruso nodded. A stream of liquid ran down the inside of his khaki pant leg.

"You're scared shitless, aren't you?" Vinnie asked. "That's okay. I have mercy on all of my victims."

Caruso let out a loud laugh. Perhaps he was trying to attract his men to come outside and see what was going on.

Vinnie thought he saw a furtive movement out of the corner of his eye. He wanted to turn toward it and see what it was. Had Caruso been staring at something?

"You haven't done shit. That's why you and your dad drag in people like Boyle to clean up your mess for you. You've never had to kill anyone to rise to your ranking. Your old man's given you everything. Real men like me, we take our power."

Caruso was shaking, and the liquid stain had seeped farther down his pant leg, but his words suggested a confidence that his body could not match.

"Don't let him rattle you, Vinnie." Vinnie spun on his heels at the sound of the voice. It was the last person he wanted to see, that pipsqueak boy Tony Fregosi, ready to steal his moment of glory.

"We need to take care of business before his men come out."

"Yeah, listen to the boy. You better shoot me now if you want any chance of getting out of this alive. Even if you kill me, my message will be delivered to the Commission and you and your guido father will be long dead, and your mafia with it."

Caruso found the confidence to smile. Vinnie glimpsed at Tony and then back at Caruso. He noticed the boy had a Colt Rail Gun pointed at the mayor. He really was intent on going through with the kill, just like Vinnie was.

"Don't do it, kid. Make Vinnie earn his manhood by pulling the trigger himself. You've still got a reasonable future," Caruso said.

A loud banging startled Vinnie. The pub's back door burst open and collided with the white brick exterior. Two bearded men wearing Chicago Bears pullovers tried to squeeze past each other through the doorway.

"Everything alright back here?"

Before Caruso could answer, Vinnie fired at the two men. He struck the first man between the eyes, watching as he fell face-first into the concrete. The other man tried running back into the pub to escape but was gunned down by Vinnie in similar fashion in the doorway, with one bullet slicing into his shoulder blade and another ripping a hole into the back of his head.

The smile faded from Caruso's face. He stood motionless in the middle of the alley, hands clasped tightly behind his head. For whatever reason, his legs were still. Vinnie wasn't sure why he wasn't running.

Shouting could be heard from inside the pub. Vinnie couldn't rule out the possibility of more of Caruso's men being inside. He didn't wait for them to come. He pulled the trigger once again, aiming directly for Caruso's power-hungry heart.

Instead of the flash and bang of a bullet firing out of the

muzzle, a sharp clicking noise emanated from the weapon. His gun had malfunctioned.

Caruso smiled again. "I guess I have that kind of effect on people. Always jamming up the works. Goodbye, Vinnie."

Vinnie tapped the magazine and kept pressing against the trigger, willing for it to fire. Caruso used the opportunity to run down the alley in the opposite direction, searching for an escape. Vinnie reracked the gun and tapped on the magazine again, doing all he could to get the weapon in proper working condition. This was his one chance to vanquish his father's greatest enemy.

Caruso reached the end of the alley. Vinnie's finger grazed the trigger, confident his gun would fire this time. He noticed Tony positioning his own gun out in front of him, clasping his right hand around the barrel, supporting the weight of the gun in his left hand.

Vinnie ignored the boy, set his sights on the escaping Caruso, and fired.

The crimson explosion that followed was fierce and horrific. The back of Caruso's head shot blood like fireworks, splattering onto the pavement as fast as his lengthy body crashed to the ground.

"Holy shit, what a shot!" Vinnie couldn't help but shout in joy.

He wasn't completely sure that it had been his shot that had landed. A dozen golf balls could fit in the hole of shock left by Tony's mouth. It had to have been the boy's shot that killed Caruso.

Vinnie couldn't believe that the boy had beaten him to the punch. But his father's greatest enemy was defeated. The job was done. Their secret was safe from the Commission.

Another noise sounded from the back door. Someone

was struggling to open it again. The fallen bodies of the two men Vinnie had slain were blocking the door, making it difficult to get outside. He couldn't risk finding out if his gun was back in working order. He'd played the role he needed to play in ensuring Caruso's death. If he was lucky, he would still earn the credit for the takedown.

"Make sure my old man knows I made that kill, and I'll make sure you're duly rewarded in time."

Before the door could open, Vinnie ran past Tony and the slain Caruso, heading for the street. He couldn't care less if the boy survived.

The right man had been killed, and he wasn't going to be next.

29

Cal ran from the doc's Jeep as soon as the fourth gunshot rang out. He thought the first three noises he'd heard were gunshots, but they sounded too faint to be anything coming from O'Dooley's Pub. How wrong he'd been.

As soon as he turned the corner of the brick building, he saw the back of Bernie's doughy body fire at Tony. He'd clipped him in the back before the boy dove in front of a dumpster.

Cal's stomach fell, like he was racing down a never-ending roller coaster. He felt the hit man aggression return to his arms. He bit into his lip to fight the urge to scream Tony's name. The boy never should've been in this situation. There was only one way to help him now.

He fired two quick shots, one in the back of the head of Bernie's accomplice and another through the dense black Mohawk that sat atop Bernie's head. Both men fell to the ground, their weapons joining them in their descent into death.

Cal ran to the dumpster and reached out to the bleeding

boy at his feet. His heart was wracked with guilt. He should've handled the kill on his own and never dragged the boy into it with Fonzie out of action.

"Tony, stay with me." Cal squatted, his face inches away from Tony's. The color of the boy's skin appeared to be fading from a golden hue to a pale cream-like tone. Blood soaked through the back of his T-shirt. Cal watched as the wound continued gushing blood into the fabric.

The faint whirring of police sirens could be heard in the distance, not giving him much time to help the boy on his own.

He took his shirt off and tried to determine the best method for stopping Tony's bleeding. He settled on pressing the top of the T-shirt firmly against the wound, holding it with all of the strength he could muster in his hands and forearms.

As much as he hated Tony's life being in danger, he couldn't believe someone had beat him to the punch on the Caruso kill. There had to be another shooter with Tony, based on all of the carnage strewn about the alley. It seemed like too much for one man, especially for someone with next to no training.

When the bleeding hardly slowed, Cal started to worry. He had an inkling to call 911 himself, just to make sure Tony wasn't in mortal danger. But as the sirens drew closer, he knew that if he didn't get out of there, he'd be tied to these murders.

Cal's thoughts were disrupted when he felt a sudden tap on his shoulder. He spun around to face a balding man with a curly black beard wearing a white chef's apron. The hair that was left on his head matched the beard.

"Hey, pal, you're alright. You saved that boy's life. I saw those two pigs shooting at him. They were hanging out with the mayor in the bar earlier, but they looked like scum." The man paused and scanned down the alley, his eyes falling on Caruso's brains splattered on the pavement. "Jesus Christ, is that the mayor?"

Cal grabbed his gun and thrust it at the man. The sirens were even closer. The man must've called the police after all of his patrons escaped the murderous chaos at the bar.

"Don't call me 'pal.' I saw absolutely nothing that happened except for what you saw—those men trying to kill this boy. I want you to stay with him and make sure he gets good medical attention. Tell the police everything you saw with those two men hanging out with the mayor."

Cal glared at the man, hoping to force his message across. "You will not mention one word about my presence here or I will come back and make sure worse happens to you than what happened here today. You got that?"

The man nodded, clearly frightened. Cal could still play the role of psychotic hit man when he wanted, but it was a role he no longer desired. Guilt strangled his heart as he decided he would have to leave Tony behind to face the risk of interrogation and police charges. Even though Tony was only a driver, Cal was confident the mafia would get lawyers for him and make sure he wasn't tied to this mess. They'd have no choice.

Cal got to his feet and ran past Caruso's dead body, wondering how the scene surrounding him had unfolded. Had Tony really killed Caruso? Or was another gunman present? Something was off about this entire operation.

His world felt less real than it had twenty minutes ago, when he was only preparing for what he hoped was his final kill. Now he had to find new courage. He'd have to explain to Alfredo that the Caruso kill had gone bad.

30

C al ran harder and faster than he had in months, trying to put as much distance between him and O'Dooley's Pub as possible before the police arrived. He ran for the parking garage exit of a dilapidated warehouse building across the street, hoping he could hide out for a while before moving on to a safer location.

He was shirtless, having used his shirt as a bandage for Tony. He hoped the boy would pull through, though he didn't understand what Tony was doing in the alley with a gun in the first place. As far as Cal knew, Tony had never fired a weapon until he'd been forced to save Cal's life in the alley across from City Hall. The kid had made a lucky shot. Cal figured he could've gotten the gun from home, unless someone in the mafia had given it to him.

Cal wondered again if someone else had been back there with Tony. The police would be able to answer that question soon enough once they examined how the men on the scene were killed.

Cal caught his breath while he crouched behind one of only a few cars in the garage. He assumed no one was working on a Sunday, save a few workaholics who used their jobs as an excuse to escape their lives.

"This is ridiculous," he whispered to himself. "Why am I hiding?"

Cal stood up as he heard the sirens continue to strum their death sound across the street. He needed to get out of there and make his way home. He had to find a plausible alibi for his whereabouts in the unlikely event that someone in the family was questioned and threw him to the wolves. Alfredo wouldn't risk the chance of his secret getting out.

Cal knew that his knowledge of Alfredo's secret and being the actual perpetrator of the hit against Louie Petrocelli put him in a compromising position. He didn't think Alfredo would purposefully lose his best hit man and take him out over one secret. Though that hadn't stopped Alfredo from ordering the murder of Cal's widowed mother.

While dead men couldn't talk, Cal wanted to ensure his own safety now that he was planning to leave the mob once and for all. Caruso's death meant there were no more men on his hit list. He'd find a way to go back to the Petrocelli compound when it was safe, when the police wouldn't be questioning Alfredo as one of Caruso's chief rivals.

Cal was determined to reach Maria despite her failure to answer any of his previous calls. He hoped she wasn't enamored with her date, if it wasn't Caruso himself.

The moment he reached for his phone, it vibrated with an incoming call. Much to his surprise, it was Maria, the last person he expected to hear from.

"Hey," Cal said apprehensively. He wasn't sure if she was still angry with him.

"I'm sorry I didn't answer before," Maria said. She was holding back tears as she spoke.

"What's wrong, babe? Did something happen at lunch?"

Maria hiccupped. She cursed under her breath and sniffled before answering him. "Oh no. I decided not to go."

Cal was surprised. Maria had seemed so insistent on going to lunch with whichever public official she was meeting. It wasn't like her to threaten Cal and back down at the last minute.

"You didn't?"

"The whole thing made me feel like I've been a little unreasonable with you, that's all. I've missed you."

Cal placed his hand over his heart to quell the pounding in his chest. He rarely experienced the emotion of concern that was present in him now. Anger was something he always felt strongly, as if he was drawn to it by Cupid's arrow. Hearing his girlfriend say that she missed him convinced Cal that, even with all of his wrongs, he had at least done something right to win a love like hers.

"Unreasonable? How were you being unreasonable? I was focused too much on me. Like I always have been."

Maria chuckled. "You'll finally admit that now?" Whatever had gotten her down wouldn't keep her in defeat. That was one of the many things he loved about her.

"Yes. There's many things I haven't admitted to you. The whole mafia business is a start, but there's a lot more you don't know about me that I've got to get off my chest. Next time I see you, I'll start with one little thing. Then the next day, it will be something different. I feel like we have to make up for so much lost time."

Maria sighed. It was nice to hear her breath again. He loved hearing, feeling, smelling it on his ear, especially after they made love. Over the phone it wasn't the same.

"Well, we'll have plenty of time. I want to see you soon. How about tonight?"

"You're sure? You're not angry with me?"

"Yes, I'm still angry, Cal. But I love you too much to let that linger. I'll come to your place."

Cal paused. He was ready to tell her he loved her again, only the second time in their yearlong love affair. He was still having a tough time accepting this side of his humanity.

"Maria, before you go, there's something I have to say. I'm done."

"Done? Done with what? Done with me?"

It was Cal's turn to sigh. "I'm not done with you. I'm done with the mob. Forever. I don't want to kill another man again. Something happened today. You'll hear about it on the news. I didn't kill the man, Maria. It was my kill to perform, but I didn't do it. As soon as this blows over, I'm telling Alfredo that I'm done. I'm willing to leave it all behind, if that's what it takes."

He expected Maria to scream sweet shouts of joy. She stayed silent, though Cal could feel her smile through the phone. Somehow, knowing it was there was enough.

"I love the sound of that. I gotta go, but I'll see you soon. Love you."

Cal said the three magic words but heard nothing in response. She hadn't even given him the chance to choke under the pressure of living up to the expectations of a normal loving couple.

He had a lot of work to do.

31

A lfredo sat in his living room, curled up on the couch with his wife, Susan, beneath his arm, clutching a bottle of Budweiser in his right hand. Susan wasn't much of a television watcher, but he'd convinced her to sit down for a few minutes and watch one of his favorite films, *The Godfather*.

He heard his cell phone vibrate against the table behind the sofa, rattling against the family picture frames that decorated the cherry oak table. Alfredo dashed to his feet, doing his best to avoid letting his wife fall completely into the couch. He didn't bother noticing who had called. He was desperate for any information.

"Yeah, what is it?"

"Alfredo, Captain Joe Blutarski of the Chicago Police Department speaking. I would've called you at home, but I assumed your cell phone would be the best place to reach you."

"Jesus Christ, Blutarski. You're giving me a heart attack. What's going on?"

Alfredo's heart pounded in his chest. Blutarski had long

been on the mafia's payroll, and he was a good source of intel on a lot of the gang violence in the city. A call from the cop usually meant something bad had happened.

"We've got a kid in the slammer here. Actually, he'll be in the slammer once he's released from the hospital. I have no way to tell if he's affiliated with you other than the fact that he was at a major crime scene this afternoon."

"What crime scene? This isn't in the press, is it?"

"Oh yeah, it's in the fucking press. I sure as hell hope none of your guys are connected with this, because the mayor of Chicago's fucking brains are splattered behind O'Dooley's Pub. Lots of other bodies at the scene too. The owner of the place says some thugs were trying to kill the boy we've got. Two more Joes got plugged, but he didn't know if they were involved with the mayor or not. We have no clue if the boy killed any of these guys yet, but we've got to investigate as if he did."

"Jesus."

"Yeah, it's pretty gruesome. More shootings, just what we need. I want to help you here, Alfredo. You've been good to me and my family over the years, and I respect you a lot. You know what I'm sayin'?"

Alfredo nodded. Even though he was hearing from Blutarski, a cop that he trusted, he was puzzled that he hadn't heard anything from any of his men. Neither Frankie nor Cal had contacted him.

"What makes you think this kid has anything to do with me? Who is he? Is he talking?"

Blutarski let out a puff of air. Alfredo pictured him enjoying one of the nice, fat cigars that he sent to all the cops on the payroll for their birthdays each year. If he remembered correctly, Blutarski's birthday was in July.

"Not yet, he's not. But you know how some of these cops

are, Alfredo. They know you and Caruso didn't exactly see eye to eye. A lot of heat's been on you guys from all over the force, especially with my old buddies in Narcotics. Anyway, the kid's name is Tony Fregosi. Young kid from the South Side. Doesn't seem like the guy that you would send after someone like Ross Caruso, especially with these thugs that he hired."

Alfredo had feared that Tony was at the scene. Had he been the one to fire the bullet that killed Caruso? If he had and was able to get out of this, Alfredo would take note to give him a more meaningful job.

"Yeah, yeah. You're saying these guys are gonna be the ones asking the kid questions when he comes to at the hospital?"

"You're damned right. And they're going to go at him hard. They're probably gonna come up to Evanston and ask you questions too."

Alfredo fumed at the mention of being questioned. He'd been very careful to ensure he and his top people weren't connected to the killings of Caruso or his men. It was the primary reason, other than his top hit man's usually swift and calculated killings, that he'd assigned Cal to execute the Caruso hit.

"I'm not involved in this garbage in any way, shape, or form. I don't even know this Fregosi character. I don't know what the hell I got to do to get your cops off my back, but they have no reason to show up here while I'm enjoying a relaxing Sunday afternoon with my wife."

Alfredo's voice had risen to Lewis Black–like shouting levels. Susan looked at her husband disapprovingly, causing Alfredo to reconsider his next words.

"Alfredo, I want to help you," Blutarski said. "Superintendent Walker's thumbprint is all over this case. You know how close he was with the mayor. Whatever vendetta they had against you, he was in charge just as much as Caruso. He saw this Fregosi kid taken to the hospital and swore he saw him at City Hall a while back coming out of the mayor's office. He says two of the mayor's guys were killed right after that. Someone's gonna have to answer for those murders, and my money is they're gonna think it was one of your guys."

Inside, Alfredo was raging. He prepared to yell at Blutarski again but thought better of it. The front door opened and closed with a loud bang. Alfredo ran with the phone in his hand toward the foyer to see a perspiring Vinnie rush into the house.

"What's going on, Dad?"

Alfredo waved his son away, toward the living room. He had no answers on who had killed Caruso, but he needed to get to Tony before Superintendent Walker or any cop with malicious intentions against the mafia interrogated him. The boy wasn't well versed in the laws of omertà, and his youth would be used against him when the police threatened him with a life sentence. Alfredo was beginning to regret involving the boy in the whole affair.

"Alright, keep tabs on it. Try to interrogate the kid yourself or get someone you trust with the lives of your children to do it. When do you think he'll be out of the hospital?"

"Tough to say. Kid's back was shot pretty bad. He was unconscious when they first picked him up and he's lost a lot of blood. I'll try to make sure no one with sticky fingers gets down there before we take him in for questioning. We have nothing to charge him with anyway, since we don't know facts. He could've been shot by the mayor's thugs and not fired a weapon at all."

"Yeah, alright. Look, I have some business to take care of,

but you promise you'll call me when you find something out?"

"Sure thing, Mr. Petrocelli. You've been good to me my whole career. But if I were you, I'd make sure you have a good lawyer for this kid in case things go south. Maybe two of 'em, if you know what I mean."

Alfredo responded in the affirmative and bid goodbye to Captain Blutarski. Susan fetched a towel from the kitchen and was using it to wipe Vinnie's sweaty forehead. Even though Vinnie was almost thirty years old, Susan had a habit of babying her son. It made Alfredo sick, especially given Vinnie's rank within the family business.

Susan saw that Alfredo had hung up the phone. She removed the cloth from Vinnie's face and her expression of concern for her son was replaced with a stern look for her husband.

"Who was that?"

"No one important. Some cops have this harebrained idea that because Mayor Caruso was murdered this afternoon, I'm behind it."

Susan's mouth formed into an O and her hand made its way to her cheek in surprise. Alfredo shifted his gaze to his son. Vinnie flinched slightly at the hardness of the look.

"That's ridiculous," Susan said. "Why the hell would you want something like that? Mayors can be very useful in your line of work."

Alfredo ignored her and asked Vinnie to follow him into the study. He had a lot of questions for his son. He hoped that he somehow hadn't gotten involved in Caruso's murder. Once he entered the study, another call came in. It was Blutarski again.

"Mr. Petrocelli, I'm sorry for calling again so soon, but I forgot to mention something else that you might need to know when you're thinking about how to make this look clean."

Alfredo was even more annoyed now. He couldn't even celebrate Caruso's death given the mess surrounding it.

"What the hell is that?"

"They found another body. A couple blocks from the crime scene. Big fat guy. I don't have to tell you who it is, do I?"

Alfredo's heart jumped. He rarely felt emotion for any of his associates, even those he'd known for years. But he'd never worked with anyone as pleasant as Frankie Ramone. They'd grown up in the business together, and Alfredo had figured they'd grow old and powerful alongside each other. He was devastated at the news.

"Yeah, I got it. I want to call his wife. Has anyone contacted her yet?"

"Not that I know of. I'll be in touch soon."

Alfredo hung up and turned toward his son.

"Sit down, drink up. We need to talk."

32

V innie's voice quivered. The look in his father's eyes was as sharp as a jagged edge of stone. Caruso was dead. Such news should've been cause for a joyous celebration. But Vinnie knew something was off.

Instead of his usual vodka soda, Vinnie helped himself to a glass of his father's favorite brandy. Alfredo had polished off one glass and started on another before he finally spoke.

"I took some interesting phone calls. Just when it seemed all of our problems were solved, we've got more shit to deal with."

The boss's voice rose with each word. When Vinnie didn't react to his father's sudden burst of hostility, Alfredo picked up his drink, shot it down his throat, and threw the glass into the open fireplace, breaking it into pieces.

"You listen to me, you son of a bitch. I want you to explain everything. You left this house in a rush, and I knew you were pissed off. I sent Frankie out to make sure you didn't do anything stupid, and what do you know? A cop on our payroll calls telling me Caruso is finally knocked off and says poor Frankie is dead. You want to explain that one?"

Alfredo rose out of his chair and stared at Vinnie like a priest gazing disdainfully upon his sinful congregation. His knuckles turned ghostly white as the blood rushed down to his fingers, which formed tightly into fists on top of the desk. The scare tactics may have worked on others, but Vinnie had seen them too many times to take them seriously.

"I don't know anything about Frankie. I never saw him."

"You never saw him?" Alfredo leaned forward on his knuckles, spit flying from his lips and landing on Vinnie's forehead as he moved in closer.

"No, I didn't," Vinnie lied. He had to find a way to divert his father's attention back to Caruso's death. That was the real triumph and Vinnie planned to be rewarded with his father's favor once he took credit for the mayor's downfall.

Alfredo removed his fists from the desk and studied them, as if expecting damage.

"Alright, what happened? Where'd you go after you left the house?"

"I went to my apartment. I needed to cool off for a while. Frankie called me and asked where I was. When I told him I was at my place, he told me to meet him on Polk Street for a drink. He wasn't at the bar but I did see Caruso there. I was armed, and I figured it was a risk, but he didn't know what I looked like thanks to this disguise I had on. I shut the bathroom down and figured he'd drink enough that he'd have to take a piss eventually. When he refused to wait in line for the women's, I waited out back, knowing he would take a piss outside. I was ready and waiting for him."

Alfredo wrinkled his nose and his eyebrows squeezed closer together in a sign of confusion. "Wait a minute. You're telling me it's a mere coincidence that Frankie picked the same bar that the mayor was at? You didn't happen to find the mayor and follow him down there?"

Vinnie started to think he wouldn't be able to outsmart his father. Lying had never been his strong suit. He blamed his mother for bringing him up as a strict Catholic boy and not letting him spend enough time with his tough father early on in life.

"You want to talk about Frankie first? I can tell you're upset that he's gone. I'm not too happy to hear about it either."

Alfredo sat back down at the mention of the former capo. He grabbed a fresh glass from the bar cart, poured some brandy in the glass, and slowly poured it out onto the wood floor beneath his feet. Vinnie followed suit with his own glass of shitty brandy. It was a subtle gesture to memorialize their fallen comrade.

"Frankie meant a lot to me," Alfredo mused. Vinnie could tell his father was doing his best to hold back the tears that were clouding his eyes. "We grew up in this business together. He was a family cook back in the day when I was still going to school and living at home with my own pops. But my old man saw a lot of potential in Frankie. We were the ones that roughed people up when they wouldn't pay protection money or wouldn't settle their debts. We fought and killed many men together. Soldiers in the trenches of war, we were."

Alfredo wiped a tear from his eye and looked at the ceiling. Vinnie was surprised his father didn't pour another drink. Vinnie had heard the stories several times growing up but didn't mind hearing them again. If he could get his father to calm down a bit, perhaps he would be less upset if Vinnie admitted to killing his longtime friend.

"Frankie was indeed a great man," Vinnie found himself saying. "He was always someone we could trust. He did good work for us. It'll be awfully tough to replace him, especially with the way the police are cracking down on our drug operations on the South Side. Frankie could strong-arm a lot of guys down there."

Alfredo nodded and paused for a moment before peering into Vinnie's eyes. "What made you kill him?"

Alfredo placed his arms on the table and folded them. Vinnie was shocked at his father's assertion. He had to keep the lie going.

"Like I said, I never saw Frankie. If I had, I would've told him that any business I was prepared to conduct was my own, with no disrespect to you, of course."

Vinnie glanced at his father for a sign of approval. Seeing none, he continued.

"Back at the alley, I was waiting outside for the bastard Caruso to come out. Eventually he did, but that's when I saw I had company. Someone else was there to kill Caruso."

He could see Alfredo thinking along with a squinting expression on his face. It would be tough to crack the wise mob boss with a false story.

"Who got him? You or this 'someone else'?"

Vinnie didn't laugh, though he felt like it. "We originally sent Cal on this mission, but he's been very flaky lately. Did it cross your mind that your golden boy killer could be involved?"

Alfredo snarled but did not shout at his son. "We'll talk about Callahan later. Besides, this was too big of a mess for the kill to be Cal's, even if he's been acting odd lately and wants out. I think he might know what's coming."

Vinnie sat taller in his seat and uncrossed his legs. "What are you getting at?"

"Never mind what I'm getting at. I want you to tell me what happened. I've already heard everything from the cop. Caruso and two of his goons are dead. Two other John Does were killed too. If you were in the alley and someone else was there, surely they weren't after you too?"

"Alright, Dad, you've got me." It was time to end the charade. He didn't care if Alfredo was angry about how the kill unfolded. The point was that Vinnie had taken out the greatest threat to the Chicago mafia's power. Shouldn't he be commended for that?

"I had some help, but I was the one who killed Caruso. I'm not some useless figurehead who only takes and gives orders. I can solve big problems. Big fucking problems. Meeting with the Commission tomorrow night will be smoother than a baby's bottom.

"The 'someone else,' that little shit Tony, came rushing in and nearly shit his pants when he had to fire his gun once the mayor's men came out. We were able to get rid of them and then I hightailed it straight here. I figured you'd hear about it before then, but I wanted to see your reaction. I wanted to see if you were proud of me."

The small child inside of Vinnie gave him a high-five for finally asking for appreciation from his father. Alfredo took another drink of brandy and settled his arms in his lap. Vinnie could see he was finally starting to relax.

"You're right, son, I should be prouder of you than I have been. That fucker Caruso is gone and we get to build our empire to new heights. You can bet your ass you're going to have a big future in that. But let's cut the bullshit. Blutarski, the cop I've been talking to, says Chicago PD is gonna come out here and ask questions, so we don't have much time to get our story straight. I already know that you killed Frankie. I'm not happy about it, but you did what you had to do. You're the underboss, and if you felt Frankie was overstepping his bounds by reining you in, I'll support it."

Vinnie breathed a loud sigh of relief. He was surprised that his father had been able to admit his admiration. He couldn't even enjoy the moment since it was so unexpected of him. He took a deep breath and then it was back to business with his father, like a loyal employee helping their boss figure out how to increase the profits after a rough quarter.

"Alright, here's the real story. I killed Frankie. Tony was back there behind the alley and we both had Caruso at gunpoint. The two John Does were walking out, and I shot both of them. They were dead in the doorway and that's what started the commotion. I went to shoot Caruso, but my damn gun jammed. That's when he tried to run away and Tony shot him. It seemed like two other guys were trying to move the John Does out of the way to come out and take care of business.

"My gun was in bad shape. I hightailed it out of there and came straight here. Kind of a cowardly move looking back on it, but that was the only way I was getting out of there alive. There'd be no guarantee that kid could have shot those two guys."

"Jesus," Alfredo said. His voice was loud once again. "When ballistics see the bullets that killed the John Does and the one that killed Caruso, they'll see completely different guns. Then there's those two guys you were talking about. Blutarski said they were dead too, didn't say how. Sounds like there may be a third gun involved here. Where's your gun?"

Vinnie patted at his hip. His gun rested in a holster clipped on his belt.

"Get rid of it," Alfredo ordered. "I don't care if it's untraceable or not, chuck it somewhere before the police get here. Go back to your apartment. Tell your mother you were stopping by to help me with something on my computer, I don't know."

"What about you? You're going to talk to the police all by yourself?"

"If I have to. Melissa will be here, she'll get one of my lawyers over. Besides, the police probably aren't going to talk to me until they can talk to Tony, if he makes it out of the hospital."

Vinnie stood, prepared to leave. "They've got the kid? We're going to have to take care of him, aren't we? He could talk."

"If he knows what's good for him, he won't. He's got a good relationship with Cal, maybe he can talk some sense into him. If there was a third person on the scene, my money is on Cal. If you hadn't admitted to killing Frankie earlier, I might have pegged him for it."

"What a shame," Vinnie joked. He wondered how his father had known that he'd killed Frankie. Maybe he hadn't known after all. "I'm assuming you'll want to talk to Cal, maybe have him take care of the boy?"

Alfredo nodded. "I know Tony's his driver, but Cal's made tough kills for us before, including the one that nearly got us all killed. Thankfully we don't have to worry about Caruso anymore, but we do have to keep the police at bay and take care of this kid. Then there's only one other person who could possibly speak out against us to the Commission and damage our interests."

Vinnie nodded in acknowledgment. Now that one tough kill was in the books, he knew there would have to be another. He walked toward the door and brushed the thought from his mind.

"You think Cal will go for it? Killing the kid if that's what it takes to make sure he doesn't talk?"

"Absolutely. In the words of the immortal Marlon Brando, 'I'm gonna make him an offer he can't refuse.'"

33

From the moment Maria walked through Cal's apartment door, the evening's mood had been nothing short of sensual. Maria's arms immediately found themselves around Cal's waist. Any words they had for each other were stilted by the movement of their intertwining tongues, slipping their bodies into a euphoric state of passion.

Arms and hands joined the movement of their tongues as Cal caressed every inch of Maria's body through her clothing. He only stopped when Maria backed away and removed her T-shirt. The way she hung the gray garment from her shoulder and pouted as she walked into Cal's bedroom had him instantly turned on.

They made love for over an hour. It was the best kind of makeup sex imaginable and put Cal's mind into such a soothing state, he forgot about killing Caruso's goons earlier in the day. He forgot about Tony fighting for his life in the hospital, or Fonzie lying injured at Doc Parker's house. He didn't even notice the large cut he'd suffered across his chest when he escaped the parking garage.

Instead of a postcoital nap, Cal sprung from his bed and into the kitchen. He felt like whipping up a gourmet meal for his girlfriend, to be enjoyed with wine and good conversation. He planned to tell her all the painful stories he'd hidden from her, to show her how much he wanted to change and how much their relationship meant to him.

Cal prepared a wooden cutting board and one of his sharpest knives to slice carrots, celery, and onion for a minestrone soup. Shortcuts like food processors weren't allowed in his kitchen. Chopping each vegetable allowed him to focus on the importance of each ingredient.

Once the vegetables were chopped, he put them in a pan to heat before adding garlic, canned tomatoes, yellow potatoes, fennel, parsley, and basil. He took some presoaked fava beans, chickpeas, and cranberry beans from the refrigerator and added them to the pot before covering the vegetables and beans in water to cook.

He'd first learned how to make the minestrone from Frankie Ramone during a Sunday dinner at the Petrocellis'. Frankie regularly boasted of his cooking prowess and how he'd taught Susan many of the recipes she was famously credited for.

While Cal waited for the soup to cook, he went back to the refrigerator and grabbed a cold Dos Equis. Cal thought of Frankie again and wondered why he hadn't responded to his calls following his escape from O'Dooley's Pub. Surely the Petrocellis received word that Mayor Caruso was dead by now. But why hadn't Frankie checked in with him?

Cal's thoughts shifted to what he would do now that Caruso was dead. Maria was correct that Cal wouldn't be able to afford his current lifestyle without the Petrocellis paying him a handsome sum of money. He'd have to move to a cheaper place. He still had no clue what he would do in order to earn a living, but he wanted it to be honest work and something that Maria could be proud of.

Cal downed the rest of his Dos Equis and opened another beer as he sat in the living room and allowed Maria to sleep. The minestrone had simmered for an hour and a half by that point, so Cal added some couscous and salt to the dish and let it cook for another twenty minutes. He put fresh bread in the oven to warm and pulled a bottle of cabernet out of the wine fridge to warm to a proper serving temperature.

Cal made his way to the bedroom to find his Latina beauty queen had already awoken and was slowly putting on her T-shirt, covering up her supple breasts.

Maria's shirt fell softly around her slender torso. She smiled as she ruffled her long black hair behind her and gathered it into a ponytail. Her smile was infectious. Cal wanted to press her body back down onto the mattress and ravage her one more time. Only his hunger for the minestrone, its delicious smell wafting through the apartment, stopped him.

"Did you have a nice nap? I've got dinner waiting."

Maria smiled and smoothed out her shirt after finishing with her hair tie. Only a thin cotton triangle covered her lower half.

"It was lovely. I can't remember the last time I had a proper nap."

"That's because you study too hard. C'mon, let's eat."

Cal grabbed her hand and led her to the kitchen, where he'd already filled two bowls full of the delicious soup. He set separate dishes of freshly chopped Italian parsley and Romano cheese out for them to garnish the soup with. Helping herself to only the cheese, Maria headed straight for the refrigerator and pulled out cilantro.

"You know it doesn't taste right if you substitute cilantro for the parsley?" Cal said. He actually preferred cilantro, but the bitterness of the parsley balanced the slightly nutty flavors of the beans and the richness of the tomatoes. He thought adding cilantro caused the soup to resemble salsa.

"You obviously don't know me that well." Maria stuck out her tongue for Cal's benefit. "I love my cilantro over any kind of parsley."

"If you wanted hot salsa, you could have said so," Cal replied with a laugh.

Maria broke a piece of the bread off into her soup. Cal was already halfway through a glass of the wine and had a feeling he would need to prepare a second bottle with the way the night was shaping up.

The ambiance of the food, his girlfriend sans pants, the lushness of the fruity wine, and the allure of having time to make love to Maria all night long would be a cause for celebration for most men. It should've been for Cal. Yet a hint of nervousness made his heart queasy. He'd heard nothing further about Tony's condition and hadn't been in contact with anyone from the mafia ever since Caruso's murder.

The hit man in him had to wonder. What was next? Was he out just like that? Was it that easy?

"Alright, mister, what do you want to share with me first?" Maria asked. "I thought you were prepared to tell all."

Cal swallowed a spoonful of the hot soup, savoring the feeling of the warm cranberry beans as they slid down his throat. They were cooked just perfectly—not too long that they were rubbery, but just enough to give them a meaty texture.

"Padre, I promised to give my confession. Let me drink some more wine first."

Maria rolled her eyes and didn't laugh.

"C'mon, I'm serious. Tell me something I don't know about you. Not some throwaway story either. I want to go deep into the mind of Callahan Boyle. What scares you? What gives you nightmares?"

Cal recalled one of the most painful memories from his youth. He saw a flash of anger and heard the grinding of his father's teeth. It was a scene that often repeated itself through his childhood and became progressively worse as the years marched closer to his father's death. One evening, his parents were in a deep argument about how often Cal's mother went shopping.

Cal told the story of his father, half drunk after only an hour at home from his workday at the warehouse, yelling at Cal's mother at the top of his lungs. His mother took the verbal abuse for what seemed like hours before taking Cal to the pantry in the kitchen and telling him to be quiet. She promised to retrieve him later when his father had calmed down.

Cal's father became extremely violent. Cal heard the crash of a beer bottle outside the pantry door. He heard his mother's screams only a few feet farther away. His father growled and Cal heard a loud *clap* before something was shoved against the wall.

His mother's loud wail forced young Cal to open the pantry door, exposing him to his crazed father. He couldn't believe his father was acting this way toward his mother. Cal wondered if it was something he'd done that caused his parents to fight. He remembered his arms trembling in fear, wondering if his mother would die at the hands of his father.

"Whatcha doin' in there, boy? I saw you lookin' at what I been doin' to your momma. You don't listen to me, that's whatcha gonna get. You hear me?"

Cal heard his father loud and clear. Something told him that his father would get drunker and the assault on his mother would intensify. He may have only been eleven years old at the time, but he felt his courage spring him into action to stand up to his drunk father. His abuse had persisted long enough.

Cal stepped out of the pantry and walked toward his father. His mother saw the blank, faraway look in Cal's eyes, the same look she often saw in her husband before he struck her night after night. She was still crying, her arm streaked in blood. It looked like her face was starting to bruise.

"You tryin' to get tough with me, kid? I'm your father. You will respect me, damnit."

Cal's father staggered toward him as his mother screamed out and cowered farther down the wall, collapsing to the floor.

"Cal, don't. Run, Cal, run."

"Shut up, whore," his father yelled. He pointed a grimy, stubby finger back toward his fallen wife.

Cal's mother tried to get to her feet, only to fall again. A deep heat spread throughout his chest. Sweat trickled down the side of his face. His body shook uncontrollably.

Violence was not a part of his plan. His only intention was to stand up to his abusive father. They stood in front of each other, separated only by the invisible fog of their breath.

"You got somethin' you wanna say to me?"

His dad leaned down and growled at him. Fear joined the anger that was coursing through Cal's body. Without thinking, he blurted out words that would change his appearance forever.

"Real men don't hurt women like that. If you want to hit someone, hit me."

"No, Cal, don't. Get out of here!"

Cal heard the growl emanate from his father's jowls but couldn't brace himself for the impact of the punch that landed against his cheek, sending three teeth flying out of his mouth. The force of the blow was so strong that Cal nearly teetered back far enough to fall on the ground where his mother lay.

Despite the pain, he regained his position and stayed on his feet. His father rocked back his fist, ready to deliver another blow. Cal flinched and saw his father reach instead for something buried in his pocket. It was a jackknife, the same jackknife Cal would later use as a hit man.

"What are you doing, Tom? What are you doing? Put it away, Tom. Put it away!"

Tom looked at his wife with utter disgust. "Keep it zipped. I'm gonna teach your son a real lesson."

Without warning, he opened the blade and staggered toward Cal. For some reason, Cal didn't think to run. He was paralyzed by fear but ready to show his father that his mother shouldn't be pushed around. Serving as a sacrificial lamb to prevent her suffering was worth it to him in that moment.

"Cal, run!"

Immediately after his mother screamed, Cal felt the blade slice beneath his right ear. Pretending to be tough wasn't enough as the pain from the wound became unbearable. He wailed as the pain from the punch and his father's cut blended into a cocktail of agony.

His father's eyes signaled no remorse. He dropped the knife and stormed out of the house, presumably to walk the few blocks to the neighborhood bar. Cal remembered the frightened expression on his mother's face as they tried to heal each other's wounds. He begged her to call the police, but she refused, saying that it wouldn't be right to ruin their marriage and that deep down his father was a good guy.

Had the beatings continued for much longer, Cal would have grown up resenting both of his parents. Six months later, his father was killed.

Maria's eyes were glazed in sadness as Cal finished telling her about his traumatic childhood experience. Her body shook and Cal could almost see her heart thumping out of her chest as her breasts rose and fell quickly beneath her shirt.

"So that's how you got that scar."

Cal nodded and touched the red scar that ran two inches across his right cheekbone, just below his ear. The scar had barely faded in the eighteen years since the incident.

"I rarely think about it these days. I try to put it behind me, in the past."

Maria got up from her seat, walked to Cal, and embraced him. Cal was surprised at the emotional display and wrapped his arms around her, if only to reassure her that he was alright.

"I can't believe your father would do something so terrible. I guess I can see why telling Alfredo you're leaving his family business behind is really hard for you. He gave you a home, he was a much better influence than your own father."

Cal rubbed her back and realized she was right. He wanted to make her happy and leave the mafia behind, yet he felt some apprehension at the thought of disappointing a man he respected. Despite Alfredo's faults, he'd always treated Cal well. Vinnie had been his best friend growing up, and the two were still close. Susan was practically his mother. It would be tough for him to disappoint them and actually leave the mafia behind.

"I know, but letting go is for the best. Even if they're the only real family I have."

34

The next morning, Cal sat on a sticky vinyl-covered seat at the Walker Brothers Pancake House. He was looking forward to some delicious apple-cinnamon pancakes, though his stomach was twisted in so many knots that he wasn't sure he'd be able to enjoy the food.

He'd received a call from Alfredo to meet him and Vinnie for breakfast at the restaurant in Wilmette, the next suburb over from Evanston. It was the first time Cal had heard from anyone in the mafia since the Caruso murder the previous day. The worst news of all was that Frankie had been found murdered near the scene. Cal wasn't an emotional man, but hearing the news was a major blow.

"I'm glad you finally got here," Alfredo started. "I'm absolutely starving. Susan usually has breakfast on the table at seven thirty. This is really late for me."

Cal didn't smile, but he could relate. He remembered his days as a starving teenager, back when he and Vinnie could both eat Susan's homemade pancake stacks up to ten cakes high, with plenty of room for sausage and bacon on the side. It made getting up early for Sunday-morning Mass worth it.

"Cal, I want you to tell me everything that happened yesterday, every little detail. This is a father and his two boys getting together for a Monday-morning breakfast. Nothing more, nothing less. We'll never discuss what we spoke about here again. Capisce?"

Cal and Vinnie glanced at each other and nodded at Alfredo.

"Can I get you gentlemen anything to drink?" asked a nondescript waitress.

Alfredo rolled his eyes and slammed his fist on the table in anger. Cal assumed he wanted to get right to his food order.

"Yeah, I'll have a black coffee, decaf. You think we can order our food too? I'm starving."

Vinnie sent Cal a knowing glance. They'd shared many meals where Alfredo exhibited worse patience toward the waitstaff.

They finished ordering. Cal wondered how long it would take for his pancakes to arrive. The sooner they were all eating, the happier Alfredo would be. It would also save Cal from talking too much.

Alfredo again asked Cal to recount the circumstances of the events yesterday. Cal started with mentioning following Caruso to church. He'd gotten lucky that he'd picked the right church and Mass time, thanks to Al Meransky's hunch that the mayor's wife sang in the choir at St. Michael's. From there, he'd followed Caruso to the pub, where he explained he'd stayed in his car in the parking lot across the street until he heard gunshots.

Throughout his explanation, Cal couldn't help but notice Vinnie stare at his fingers as if they were overly dirty and needed to be washed. His complete lack of interest in the events of the day was uncharacteristic of someone in his position. It signaled to Cal that Vinnie was already well aware of what had happened.

Alfredo took a sip of his steaming-hot decaf.

"What did you see once you got back there?"

Cal didn't want to waste any unnecessary words in the restaurant. He thought Alfredo was speaking a little too loudly given the information they were discussing.

"I saw two of Caruso's guys shooting at Tony. I had no clue he was there. They shot him in the back before I took them out. I stayed with him until the owner of the bar came out. Then I left."

Alfredo nodded and held the coffee mug in a death grip, yet his face indicated he was pleased with what Cal had said. Cal still had more he wanted to know.

"Are you gonna tell me who fired the shots at Caruso and the two dudes in the back doorway?" Cal didn't believe Tony was responsible for all of the deaths.

"It was Tony," Vinnie said. "It was all Tony. The cop we got on our payroll says the bullets in the two men and Caruso were most likely from the same gun, the weapon the boy left at the scene. It's only the two guys you whacked that are different."

Cal stared hard at Vinnie and searched for the hint of a lie written on his face. He sensed a slight shaking of his facial muscles, his eyebrows quivering slightly. As he spoke, his forehead wrinkled inward. Cal knew a liar when he saw one and could tell something else was going on.

"If the cops already know that, then it's only a matter of time before they try to get him to talk and charge him."

Alfredo nodded. "I talked to our cop an hour ago. Says the kid's starting to regain consciousness. That's bad news, because he doesn't think he can hold off some of these cops from asking the kid questions. A lot of guys on the force are pretty upset that Caruso is dead. He and Walker had a lot planned to clean up the city."

"Yeah, and clean our clocks," Vinnie said. "I'm glad we got rid of that fucker."

"We have to get to Tony before he talks to any cops," Alfredo continued. "At one point, I thought he might be a valuable asset for us. Now we've got no choice but to take him out. He's too young to appreciate the power of omertà."

"Wait a minute," Cal said. His voice was rising higher than he wanted it to. He couldn't let Tony be killed. The kid had a bright future if he stayed away from the wrong people.

"I know Tony. I can get through to him and make sure he doesn't implicate anyone else. He doesn't know I was involved. As long as no one else was at the scene, there's no reason to think he'll blab that it was a mob hit, and it won't get tied back to anyone."

Alfredo and Vinnie turned toward each other. Alfredo was ready to speak again when the waitress returned to the table with several large plates of food.

"Look at that, Dad. We can finally eat," Vinnie said.

"Amen to that."

They dug in to their food. Cal struggled to enjoy the sugary sweetness of his pancakes while he wondered how Alfredo would proceed with Tony. He hoped the mob boss would show mercy and let Cal talk to the boy before he placed a hit on him.

After a long glance out of the window, Alfredo spoke again.

"Cal, I know you're close with the boy. But we can't take any chances whatsoever. I'm sure if I sweet-talk Captain Blutarski enough, he'll let the boy have visitors at the hospital. You'll have to kill him, Cal. You're the only one who can do it discreetly enough. You're the best killer I've got."

Alfredo's gaze was firm on Cal. He was sure the boss experienced no discomfort in asking him to make this kill, despite Cal's earlier ask to leave the mafia once Caruso was dead. Cal took a deep breath and felt his heart pound in his chest. He couldn't snuff out Tony's life like this.

"Alfredo, you know I've been very loyal to you. I've done a lot of things that, had my parents not died, I may never have done. I'm grateful for everything you've done for me in my life. I told you I was walking away once Caruso was killed. I'm willing to talk to Tony and convince him to keep his mouth shut, but I can't kill him."

Cal's eyes fell from Alfredo and Vinnie to his plate. His heart hammered like a pianist's fingers playing a staccato melody. He didn't want to provide any further explanation for why he wanted to leave the crime life behind. He also wanted to avoid mentioning that things were getting serious with Maria. That could put both of their lives in danger.

Vinnie maintained his bored look and picked at his half-eaten hash browns with his fork. Alfredo cracked his knuckles and leaned back against the booth. The lines on his forehead were deep set in calm as opposed to the usual fury he could unleash.

"You're right, Cal. I promised after Caruso was dead that I'd let you leave. I'll meet with the Commission tonight and smooth this all over, but I can't let you go yet. We need to tie up this Caruso business and make sure we're all in the clear with the law before you can leave."

Cal felt his own efforts to be calm failing him. He couldn't control the rising heat in his chest, the temperament that was more akin to his father's violent outbursts.

"I'm not asking to leave. I'm telling you that it's over for me."

Vinnie interrupted him.

"How dare you talk to my father like that!"

Vinnie had spoken a little too loudly. Other patrons of the restaurant began glancing in their direction. If they'd overheard any of the conversation and reported it to the media or shared it with the police, they would have had a field day with it. It was a good thing they weren't as recognizable this far north of Chicago.

"Easy now, easy," Alfredo said. "Cal, you step out of line like that again and you'll be the one with a hit on your head. I know it's hard for you to hear this after your mind has been made up. I'm going to give you a great offer to change your mind. Are you ready to listen?"

Cal was ready to maintain his stance and fight for his decision until Vinnie once again spoke up.

"Forget it, Dad. Cal's doing this all for his girl. You saw her at the house. She didn't look too pleased to be around us. She's got to know what we're all about. Cal's leaving for her. Things must be getting pretty serious."

Cal's insides were roaring with the fire of the hottest of kilns. If he weren't in such public surroundings, it would be inextinguishable.

"Is that true, Cal? You want to go legit, maybe start a life with this girl?" Alfredo asked.

Cal choked back his anger and nodded. They had found his weakest point. He was now in his most vulnerable position. He hadn't felt this exposed since his mother was killed and Alfredo had adopted him.

"That's cute. But let me remind you what you're giving up. There's the pay, for one thing. I don't know anywhere else you can get paid ten grand for a night's worth of work.

You have no education or trade skills of any kind. How the hell are you gonna support yourself? You're also giving up our protection if the police want to go after you for any crimes.

"You're still welcome at home for dinner and you can always call us family, but it'll be a much different relationship. Are you ready for that?"

Cal wanted to say yes. He was ready to do whatever it took to leave the mafia behind, even if it meant exile from the family that had raised him to be the man he was today. He wanted to please Maria; still, he felt the need to please Alfredo. The mob boss had that magical power.

"Cal, if it's your girl you're worried about, we can fix her," Vinnie said. "She's probably dead broke forking over tuition for her PhD program. We can cover her tuition. We can make sure she has nice clothes, nice jewelry. Maybe we can move her to one of those high-end apartments you're living in. You'll still be close together, but she can have her space to study. It'll be a great little setup."

Cal couldn't believe that the Petrocellis would offer that much of an incentive to keep him around. At the same time, the Chicago mafia was having a hard time finding skilled killers who could do their dirty work. Retaining Cal's services would be well worth it for them.

Even if they could guarantee Maria wouldn't be bothered by Cal's decision to stay, given all they planned for her, Cal couldn't take the risk. He didn't have anything else to fall back on, and he might have to work in the warehouse like his drunk father before him, but he wouldn't let his anger overcome him and compel him to damage another boy's life.

"I don't think she'll go for it," Cal said. "Besides, it's not her decision, it's mine. I want a chance to prove myself on my own and be in control of my future."

Alfredo rubbed his chin between his large index finger and thumb. Cal wondered what type of sales pitch Alfredo had up his sleeve.

"Cal seems pretty serious about this," Alfredo finally said to Vinnie. "I tell you what, Cal. When I get the word that Tony can talk, I'll have Blutarski send you and another guy in to play the kid's lawyers. You'll go in there and talk some sense into the kid. If he listens, you can let him walk and talk to the cops knowing he won't say jack squat. If not, you'll have to take him out. But I'm counting on you to be convincing. After all, if he talks, it's not just his ass that's at risk of getting killed, it's all of ours.

"We'll all be back in the same position we were when Caruso threatened us before. How would Susan, who has always loved you like a mother, feel if all of us were tied to this and thrown in jail? Or even worse, what if the Commission decides they don't like this funny business and have us all killed?"

Alfredo eyes slanted sharply at Cal, and a sudden wave of pressure fell upon him. Cal hadn't considered the possibility that, just because Caruso was dead, he and the Petrocellis wouldn't be out of the woods yet. Maria was right. Cal still cared about them, even as much as he wanted to get away.

Would he lie to Maria? If he decided to go through with Alfredo's order, would he have another obligation to fulfill? Would he ever find a way to escape?

Cal took a deep breath and sighed. "Shit, I guess you're right. If I can guarantee Tony won't say anything that incriminates us to the cops, and if you can guarantee that if he sees any jail time that his family will be taken care of, you won't require me to kill him. Is that acceptable?"

Both Alfredo and Vinnie nodded.

"It's going to be a tough ask," Vinnie said. "Kids that young threatened with long jail sentences break down pretty easily. You're gonna have your work cut out for you, Cal."

"It's a good thing I'm gonna send someone else with you," Alfredo said. "Remember, if you have any sense the kid's going to talk, you're gonna have to kill him. You'll have to hope it doesn't come down to that."

Cal had hardly touched his pancakes since they'd started talking. He no longer desired the inevitable sugar rush that would come from finishing the delicious meal.

"If I do this one last thing for you, am I free to go after that? Once this is over, hopefully Tony will focus on school and move far away from Chicago so he won't be influenced by this mess."

Alfredo swallowed the last of his omelet and nodded. He held his empty coffee mug and swirled it in the air.

"Let's hope we get to that point, Cal, for all of our sakes."

35

Two days passed before Cal heard from the Petrocellis. During that time, he felt a dull emptiness instead of the sense of bliss he'd expected after thinking he'd be able to walk away from his hit man career. Maria excitedly asked him if he'd told the Petrocellis of his intentions.

When he responded in the affirmative, Maria assumed it was over and they could move on with their lives together, free from worry. But Cal knew it wouldn't be that easy. He didn't bother telling Maria that he would have to stick around until the Caruso business was cleared up.

The Commission still came to visit Monday night, as planned. Only, no one from Caruso's contingent met with them to discuss Alfredo's secret. Cal and the Petrocellis were in the clear.

On Tuesday, the police sent several men to the Petrocelli house to question Alfredo and Vinnie about their involvement in Caruso's death. They denied any responsibility or knowledge of how Caruso was killed and the events leading up to his death.

When the police provided a description of the two men who'd broken into Caruso's home and engaged in a shootout with his hired thugs, the Petrocellis gave no indication they knew the men who matched Cal's and Fonzie's descriptions. Even though they had one high-ranking officer on the payroll involved in the case, he wasn't able to completely keep his colleagues off the mafia's tail.

Any evidence the police had was circumstantial at best, but Alfredo took no chances. They had Al Meransky, who was acting as Frankie Ramone's replacement as South Side capo until he could be replaced by a suitable leader, call Cal Wednesday morning.

"Cal, how are you?"

"I'm hanging in there, Al. It's been a pretty quiet past few days."

"Well, it looks like you've avoided the worst of it, then. I'm sure you know it's been crazy up at the house. We moved some people to the city to throw the police off and get them away from here. Hopefully it'll die down now."

"The police mention anything more about the break-in at the house? They might figure out the bullets are similar to the two guys I got in the alley."

"They might, Cal. I don't know how fast their ballistics team works. But I don't think they're too ready to act on it right now anyway. With some of the press we've got out about Caruso having his own ties to the criminal underworld, the police don't really want to give any credence to his involvement with some of these tough guys that were taken out. It seems like most people thought the mayor was a real prick anyway. Not exactly the hero that he wanted himself to be."

Cal sighed. He wanted Meransky to get the point. He knew an order was coming, and he didn't want to waste any more time before getting down to business. It was odd to have an abundance of free time the last few days. He didn't miss killing, by any means, but he missed the hunt, the pursuit of a target. He hadn't considered anything else he could do to entertain this adventurous side of him while earning a legitimate living.

"Listen. I've got a job for you. You're gonna have to get dressed up for it. You even own a suit, Boyle?"

"Of course I own a suit," Cal said. "Do you think living with a man like Alfredo for half of my life that I didn't learn a thing or two about style?"

Al chuckled. "Thought I'd check. Make sure it's a nice suit. Something an attorney would wear, not something your grandpa would don at a funeral. You won't be able to carry your piece on you anyway, so don't worry about concealment. Maybe a knife, nothing more. We'll find a way to get that through the metal detectors."

"You're sending me to the police station?"

"That's right. They moved Tony there early this morning. The same guys that were at the house the last few days have been champing at the bit to question the kid. Blutarski's kept them at bay at the hospital, but he may not be able to hold them off much longer. You're gonna arrive as the kid's counsel before they send in those dicks for questioning. I'm assuming you know what the outcome of that meeting must be."

Cal's temple pounded at the thought of the worst of the two possible outcomes. He didn't want to have to kill the boy. He hoped he would be able to convince him to keep his mouth shut, even if the evidence pointed to Tony spending the rest of his life in jail for Caruso's murder.

"It won't come to that, Al. I'll make sure he pleads the fifth. We can stay with him for questioning. At the restaurant, Alfredo told me he wanted two of us down there. Who else is playing Tony's attorney?"

Meransky cleared his throat. "I can't tell you that. It's gotta be a complete surprise. But don't worry, as long as you play the part well enough, you'll be fine. The cops don't even know what you look like. There's no worry about them tying you to any of this stuff over the past few days."

"Are you sure about that? Shouldn't I wear a wig or something?"

"That might not hurt your case. Your new identity is Rich Larson, a big-shot attorney from Texas who recently started taking private clients in Chicago. Fregosi is a pro bono case since you knew the kid's mother growing up. The other guy is Joseph Fletcher. He's a fresh law-school graduate getting his feet wet in public defense. You got that?"

Cal felt his headache grow stronger. Too many details were pouring in. He had to know whom he'd be working with to try to save Tony's hide. It was important to know the whole situation going in, especially since he wasn't completely sure of his own safety.

"Is Rich Larson a real person? How do you know he grew up with Tony's mom?"

"Yes, Larson's a real guy. He's too new to have any relationships with any of these guys. Melissa's working on him. Fletcher's not real, but who cares? We'll get Larson on the payroll if the boy can actually keep his mouth shut. Larson's a big, strong guy like you, a real native Texan. Tony's mother was from Texas too."

"I still don't like this. You know I don't like to go into these things cold. Why can't you tell me who I'm working with?"

"Don't worry about it. I don't want to bother you with that now. Get ready. We're sending a driver for you in a half hour. Captain Blutarski is expecting you around eleven. A minute past, and there may be nothing we can do for the boy. I know you'd rather not kill him after he's squealed."

"Right. See you later."

"Take care of yourself, Boyle. We'd hate to lose you."

Cal put the phone down and stared at it in disbelief. He didn't like the situation one bit. It smelled like a setup, a no-way-out situation where he'd be asked to kill Tony regardless of the outcome. To think he'd been so close to escaping the mafia and putting this life behind him.

He heard Maria's voice echo in his head. She was telling him to leave now. They could go anywhere. She could pick up her studies somewhere else, somewhere warm and remote, where no one could touch them. Cal pictured Mexico City, but he didn't care where they went as long as Maria was happy and they were together.

He stepped back from the bedroom window that over-looked the empty streets below. Everyone had gone off to work or settled in at a nearby coffee shop. He felt enraged thinking of the helplessness of the situation. He couldn't control his reaction this time. He didn't feel the hatred for his target the way Alfredo and the others had convinced him to feel so many times before.

He'd felt it with MacErlean. He'd felt it with Caruso. He'd felt it with the little boy who spoke poorly of his awful father. He couldn't arouse the same sense of anger with Tony. His rage reached the clenched knuckles of his stone-hard fists as he turned sharply to his left and landed a sharp hook against the solid plaster wall.

His fist screamed in agony as it forced its way through. He was lucky it went straight through the drywall and that his hand wasn't broken. He shook his hand violently after he pulled it free from the wall.

Cal found that delivering the punch wasn't as satisfying as he'd expected. He shook his head and changed out of his shorts and T-shirt into his brown suit. His hand shined bright red in contrast with the tan leather shoes, brown slacks, and brown tweed jacket. He wore a cream-colored button-up underneath and threw on a maroon tie for good measure.

A text from the driver let him know it was time. He needed to control his anger better than he had when he'd punched through the wall. If he punched Tony like that, it would mean death.

36

C al sat in the back of the old taxicab, which had been confiscated by the late Frankie Ramone, that picked him up at his apartment. He felt out of place in his suit, like an office worker heading to his cubicle job. It was something he'd never anticipated experiencing.

Cal played with his cell phone while the car was stuck at a red light. He considered texting Maria to ask her how her first day of teaching had gone. He knew she was nervous as hell in preparation for her lecture. In all of the silence of the last few days, one of the constants he appreciated were the joyous moments they spent together.

The car moved again, and Cal rested his right forearm against his leg, feeling the bulge of the jackknife in his pocket. He wasn't sure how he was going to get into Tony's holding cell with the jackknife, given the metal detectors and the likely searches from investigating police officers. Surely, real attorneys had tried to pull this stunt to help their clients escape. Maybe the other "attorney" he was working with was taking care of that.

Cal was tired of thinking. He wished he didn't have to go

through with this, that he didn't have to scare the living shit out of Tony. Hell, the kid was probably beyond scared already.

It still bothered Cal that Tony was blamed for all of the deaths that had occurred outside of O'Dooley's Pub, excluding the two men he killed himself trying to save the boy. Cal remembered that crease in Vinnie's forehead, his tendency to look away from Cal as he spoke to him. The expressions indicated Vinnie was lying. Somehow Vinnie had to have been involved.

It didn't matter, though. Neither Vinnie, Alfredo, nor anyone else would say otherwise. Tony was going to be the fall man even if he didn't rat out the mafia when questioned by the police. Cal hoped he could be convincing enough, not only to dissuade Tony from explaining what had really happened but also to convince Alfredo to have mercy on the boy if he got out of police custody scot-free. Then he had to convince Alfredo to let him leave the mafia once and for all. It seemed Alfredo would always find more loose ends to be tied up.

The car slowed a few blocks from the police station. Meransky hadn't indicated whether the person would ride with Cal or meet him there. Cal's mind raced with idea of the whole operation being a setup, and he imagined a man entering the car and blowing him away.

The car stopped and someone knocked on the door. Cal placed his hand on the jackknife inside of his pocket, ready to fend off a potential attacker. He felt like he couldn't trust anyone, especially on this mission.

A man, shorter than Cal, ducked into the car. He wore a fedora and his Caucasian face had a rubbery texture to it. A charcoal-gray suit with a white button-down dress shirt, black tie, and polished black shoes completed the outfit.

Other than his unusual skin texture, the man was well kept. Cal didn't notice the white gloves on the man's hands at first, then thought it was odd for them to be worn at this time of year.

"Rich Larson," Cal offered, staying in character. He didn't want to give too much away in case Alfredo had chosen someone not in the mafia to play the other attorney. "I'm Mr. Fregosi's chief counsel. You are?"

The man turned to him. A smile formed on his face and Cal felt like he recognized him, despite the odd complexion. Yet the person he pictured didn't resemble the man that was sitting next to him.

"Joseph Fletcher. Make sure you call me Joseph, not that Joe shit. Especially not Joey."

Cal nodded, the voice matching who he assumed was playing Fletcher. Still, he didn't want to break from character to acknowledge it. The car started up again, pulling away from the curb. It would only be a few minutes before they arrived at the Cook County Department of Corrections, where Tony was being held for questioning.

Once they'd driven for a while, Cal turned toward Fletcher and whispered, "Is that a mask, or did you just get a piss-poor plastic surgeon?"

The man looked Cal up and down and snorted. "Speak for yourself, Rich. I thought you were supposed to be some kind of hotshot Texan. Don't Texans usually have a real thick drawl?"

Cal cleared his throat and tried his best attempt at a Southern accent. What came out of his mouth was too twangy, causing Fletcher to laugh.

"Nice try, Mr. Larson. You better be able to convince those motherfuckin' police officers that accent ain't fake."

It's when Fletcher added the "motherfuckin'" that Cal

knew for sure it was Fonzie behind the mask. He'd only been shot five days ago and was still at the doc's place as far as Cal knew. Why was he here? And why the mask?

Fonzie's eyes met his in acknowledgment. He had to know that Cal saw right through the mask.

"I'm as shocked as you are, good sir. Mr. Al called me and told me he wanted me to be a lawyer. Momma said I was too dumb to do anything with my life other than be an actor like her or a gangbanger like my daddy. But here I am, ready to fight for the life of my client. Our client, Mr. Larson."

The driver, a man Al Meransky trusted to the highest degree but someone who Cal hadn't interacted with previously, rolled his eyes and laughed from the front seat.

"Boy oh boy. You both have a lot of work to do."

"Shut the hell up, white boy," Fonzie said. Realizing he was impersonating a white attorney, Fonzie cleared his throat and dropped the profanity. "You know what, sir, you're absolutely right. Thanks for pointing that out."

Cal laughed at Fonzie's attempt at playing lawyer. He was glad he wasn't the only one confused by the cover stories. It helped him ease his mind a little before they arrived.

Cal felt the buzz of his cell phone in his pocket as they pulled up outside the main gate of the division V section of the jail. He saw "No Caller ID" flash across the screen and assumed it was Meransky from an untraceable phone with last-minute instructions.

"Excuse me, is this Cal?" The voice was authoritative. Not something Meransky was known for.

"Why don't you tell me who you are first," Cal replied. Still in character, he spoke in the accent he imagined Rich Larson would use.

"This is Sergeant Luis Rodriguez of the Chicago Police Department. I'm calling about Maria Espinoza. You were listed as her emergency contact in her phone. I'm sorry to report that she's had an accident and needs immediate medical attention."

Fonzie opened his door and stared at Cal. Cal's body went numb at the officer's words.

"Are you hearing me, sir? Miss Espinoza needs immediate medical attention. Are you—"

Cal cut him off and found the nerve to speak. "Yes, medical attention. Yes, you need to give her immediate medical attention. What happened?"

Fonzie stepped out of the vehicle, and the driver had a furious look on his face.

"You gonna get out or what? I can't dillydally here; these guys will think something's up."

Still distraught over the situation and waiting for the sergeant to respond, Cal found he was unable to move from the seat. One of two officers standing at attention outside the door walked toward the car and yelled at the driver.

"She took a stumble on the sidewalk, hit her head against the concrete. She said someone may have been chasing her. We've called an ambulance to run some tests and make sure she doesn't have a concussion, but she should be okay."

Cal's heartbeat drummed faster inside his chest. At least it wasn't as serious as he'd feared. Hearing that Maria thought someone was following her held his attention.

Who could have been chasing her? Was it someone from the mafia? Maybe it was one of Caruso's thugs, seeking revenge for their boss's murder. None of them knew about Maria, did they? It would be hard to concentrate on the meeting ahead with Tony.

He finally forced himself out of the car and onto the street, with the phone still held up to his ear.

"You make sure she gets to the hospital, you hear? Tell her that I'll be on my way as soon as I can," Cal ordered in his Texan accent.

"Yes, Mr. Cal. I'll give you a call if anything else comes up."

Cal hung up and put the phone back in his pocket, walking behind the car as it pulled away from the gate. An officer shook Fonzie's still-gloved right hand. In his other hand, Fonzie held a briefcase that Cal hadn't noticed before.

"Mr. Larson," the officer said to Cal, shaking his hand. "I'm Captain Joe Blutarski. I'll be escorting you to see your client, Mr. Fregosi. A pleasure to meet you and your associate Mr. Fletcher."

The name "Blutarski" sounded familiar to Cal. He may have been an officer on the family's payroll.

Cal wondered why he was the man greeting them at the door. He wondered what Alfredo had up his sleeve. He couldn't worry about it too much, because Tony's life was on the line. On top of that, he was worried sick about Maria. What exactly had happened to her? There wasn't time to worry about himself.

"Pleasure to meet you as well, Captain. How's the boy doin'?"

Fonzie added, "We'd know ourselves, but we've only talked to one of your detectives and the boy's father. The guy seemed real eager to question the boy without us being here."

Cal was unsure how Fonzie knew this much information. Maybe Meransky had given him different instructions.

They arrived at the entrance of the gate. The other

officer nodded as he saw Blutarski walk to the door and badge everyone in.

"The boy's doing fine. Nothing to worry about. Don't worry about Detective Thomas either, he's a ballbuster. He's got no real authority on this case."

Blutarksi led them into a small foyer with a metal detector straight ahead.

"I'm sorry, boys. I know you're both law-abiding citizens, but we've got to send you through these."

"Even the briefcase?" Fonzie asked.

"Yes, Mr. Fletcher, even the briefcase." Fonzie stepped forward to the metal detector and smiled at the officer manning the x-ray machine. The female officer's eyes locked on Fonzie, scanning his face, perhaps wondering why his appearance was so rubbery and wrinkly looking. Blutarski eased closer to Cal and prepared to whisper in his ear.

Whatever he had to say, Cal knew there was no going back. If Blutarski wasn't on the payroll, Cal would be in serious trouble for bringing a weapon into a penitentiary like this one. He'd just have to trust him.

37

"Give me your knife. If you need a weapon, there'll be one given to you in the boy's cell. You're in good hands here, Mr. Larson."

Cal nodded and slipped Blutarski the knife. He hated his prized weapon being in someone else's custody.

"Don't worry, you'll get it back when you leave," Blutarski said, sensing Cal's unease. "I'll be in the area if you need to make a quick escape."

Blutarski walked outside to stand at the guard post, leaving an uncomfortable Cal frozen in the foyer. Whatever was in Fonzie's briefcase passed through the metal detector without incident.

Cal cleared his throat, put on a Southern gentleman smile for the female officer, and proceeded through the metal detector. It beeped back at him loudly.

"Be sure to pull out your pockets, sir. Most of you hotshot lawyers forget to take out your fancy cell phones, iPads, Rolexes. It's all got to go through the x-ray machine."

Fonzie laughed from across the detector. His fedora was

nearly touching his nose from Cal's vantage point. How he'd escaped the officer's scrutiny was beyond him.

Cal placed his phone in front of the x-ray machine and waited for it to enter before going proceeding through the metal detector. Relieved that it didn't beep back a second time, Cal smiled again at the officer and picked up his phone.

"Did that big dumb cop tell you where the hell we were supposed to go?" Fonzie asked.

"He sure didn't," Cal said, scratching his ear beneath the blond wig that fit too tightly against his head. "Wouldn't someone tell us where the hell Tony's cell is?"

They looked farther down the hallway, only seeing a row of offices to their left. Cal felt a sudden nudge on his shoulder and jumped around, facing a short man dressed in a blue-and-black flannel shirt and a pair of dark-blue jeans. He donned a pair of brown leather cowboy boots and a brass stud with an American flag emblem at the front of his belt.

"Howdy, gentlemen. M'name's Detective Bobby Thomas. The captain asked me to direct you to Mr. Fregosi's cell. Right this way."

Cal and Fonzie looked at each other and followed Detective Thomas, expecting a relatively silent trip before they could brief Tony in whatever holding cell he was in.

"How long have you known Mr. Fregosi? The kid doesn't have much of a legal record. Can't imagine he could really be involved with somethin' like this. World's a crazy place nowadays, though."

"I grew up with his momma," Cal lied. "She was a real nice gal, both of us bein' from the same town near San Antonio. It was a darn shame she passed away a few years ago from the cancer. I figured it was the least I could do when I heard from his daddy that they needed an attorney. I've got a new practice and figured it could be my first pro bono case."

"That a fact?" Thomas said in an even thicker drawl than Cal was using. "I'm from Texas myself. Don't know why I ever came up to this crappy state. The things you'll do for a good job, though, am I right?"

They walked past four empty holding cells and arrived at a fifth cell near the end of the hallway. Steel walls with secured doors led to the jail cells for short-term inmates behind the wall, with an expanse of even more division V prisoners in the jail beyond.

"Well, this is it, boys." Thomas fixed his gaze on Fonzie and nodded his head toward the door. "You might want to go in first, young fella. I need to have a word with the big guy for a minute."

Fonzie shrugged as Detective Thomas opened the door and allowed him to step inside. Disguised as Joseph Fletcher, Tony wouldn't be spooked by Fonzie's sudden presence.

Cal diverted his gaze from the cell and back to Bobby Thomas. The detective was looking for something deep in Cal's eyes. Cal swallowed hard, uncertain as to the man's intentions. Thomas leaned closer to Cal, as if he were a new lover deciding whether to pursue a first kiss.

"I expect the captain told you about your weapon," Thomas said. He reached around to the back of his belt and pulled out a jackknife that looked exactly like the one Cal had surrendered moments before in the entryway. Thomas handed it to Cal and patted him on the shoulder.

"My momma always said that sometimes in life, you gotta do what you gotta do. This is in case you gotta do that. Try not to make it too noisy. I can keep other cops outta the area, but we don't want any of the other folks hearin' anything about this."

Cal shook his head and entered the holding cell, closing the door behind him. He looked at Tony for the first time since he'd gazed upon the unconscious boy in the alley behind the pub.

He was seated in a wheelchair behind a metal gray table, his skin as white as the walls surrounding them. His eyes were as far away and empty as a 1950s Chevy that ran out of gas in Havana. Cal figured Tony's back had been shot up bad, but unless there was damage to his spine, he wasn't sure of the need for the wheelchair.

Fonzie was seated in one of the two chairs across from Tony. He had his hands folded and was leaning forward over the table, his fedora masking his face.

Tony's eyes settled on Cal's as the hit man sat next to Fonzie. Tony's face didn't flash recognition or relief, which was exactly the reaction Cal had hoped for upon entering.

"Howdy, young feller. I'm Rich Larson. I'm the attorney your father hired to talk to you before the police ask you any questions. You do exactly as I say, you're gonna get out of this, you hear?"

Tony stared blankly ahead, unblinking, his arms firmly clasped to the armrests of his wheelchair.

"My father can't afford to hire a lawyer. You're one of the public defenders, aren't you?"

"No, young man, I'm a legitimate attorney. Opened up my own firm here in the city a few months ago. I knew your momma from way back. We grew up together in Texas. I'm taking this case on as a favor to your father, pro bono."

Tony cocked his brow. "Who's the other guy?"

Cal glanced to his left and shrugged his shoulders at

Fonzie. It was a gesture he anticipated a snobbish lawyer would make.

"Oh, him? That's Joseph Fletcher. He's fresh out of law school, but he's one of the sharpest young men I've met. We'll be prepping you for the questioning and stay with you when the cops come in and ask questions."

Cal hoped he wouldn't have to stick around for the actual questioning if he convinced Tony to keep quiet. He didn't want to get close enough to the cops for them to realize who he was. While he had never been specifically identified by the police, he was still a suspect for several crimes.

"I'm sure you're very scared," Cal continued. "To be clear, the police aren't charging you with murder. They have no evidence that says you killed anyone. At least not that I've been made aware of. What we want to do today is clear you of any wrongdoing. But before we do that, I'll need you to tell me what happened."

Fonzie stood from his chair and walked about the room, stopping to inspect each wall and corner of the room before settling in front of the two-way mirror. After looking for a few seconds, he shook his head and stood next to Tony, placing his hand on the boy's shoulder. Tony's eyes shifted upward to meet his, the boy's expression signaling fear instead of reassurance.

"Tony, I can't help you unless you talk to me."

Cal saw Tony's Adam's apple jump up and then accelerate down into the base of his throat. His hands twitched against the armrest. Beads of sweat poured from his forehead like a dripping faucet.

"I heard my father and this cop talking when I was in and out of sleep at the hospital. The cop knows about some of the work I did. I worked for some dangerous people that I wanted to please. I wanted to show I could be helpful to them."

"When you say you worked for dangerous people, who might these people be?"

Tony shook his head.

"Tony, you won't be saying any of this to the police yet, only us," Fonzie said. "They've got no cameras in here. They can't tell what's going on. You can tell us anything."

Cal felt a vibration in his pocket and saw the "No Caller ID" flash across the screen once again. For a split second, he broke character and fear passed across his face as he realized he'd have to let this one go.

"Alright," Tony started. "I'm a driver for these guys. They're with the mafia. I don't even know how I got started in it, but my dad works two jobs and we're still really poor, so I figured I could chip in with some driving gigs along with my construction job to make us extra money. This guy I drive around has been following somebody for the last few weeks. I guess the mafia wanted him dead."

Fonzie cut him off. "You're saying way too much, kid. Way too much."

"Leave him be, Joseph," Cal said. "Go on, kid."

Tony told them the rest of the story, many pieces of which Cal knew little of. He hadn't known that Tony had met with the Petrocellis and asked to help with the hit. He hadn't known that Tony had intended to find Caruso on his own and kill him in order to get a stake of the hit money.

He'd fallen into the same trap that Cal had fallen into with the mafia. More money, more opportunity, more respect could all be earned when you worked for such a powerful organization. Tony didn't know what Cal knew, that it all came with a hefty price tag. Cal grit his teeth and nearly lost control of his temper when Tony told him there was another man in the alley with him, and the description fit Vinnie to the letter.

When Tony mentioned he shot Caruso as he was getting away and Vinnie escaped after the other men tried to burst out of the pub, Cal lost all respect for his childhood best friend. Only a true coward would run away from a fight like that and let a young kid get slaughtered, even if his gun was jammed.

Even more striking than that was the fact that Tony was now a murderer. He had killed for the mob and wiped out Alfredo Petrocelli's greatest foe. Had he not been shot and now taken in for police questioning, he'd be celebrated instead of vilified by Alfredo.

"I'm really struggling with this one, Mr. Larson," Fonzie said. "Based on the kid's story I think he's gonna have a tough time telling this to the police. They'll probably ask much tougher questions than we will."

Cal wracked his brain for any way he could trust Tony to sway the police that both he and the mafia had little involvement. He could convince Tony to not cooperate and save the real problems for a trial. But not cooperating would likely lead to an arrest, which would implicate the Petrocellis even further.

Cal and Fonzie openly debated how they would play this in front of the police. Cal suggested they play the self-defense angle until Fonzie reminded him that Caruso was found running away from the crime scene. Anything they thought of seemed to get them nowhere. Fonzie glanced at Tony before looking back at Cal and shrugging his shoulders.

"Let's face it, this kid's fucked."

The carefully guarded identify of Joseph Fletcher was starting to lose its luster for Fonzie. He tugged at his mask, loosening the rubber flesh from his face. The look on Tony's face was one of horror.

"Well, you've gotta give me something to say." Tony's corpse-looking form awakened in protest. The color slowly returned to his pale flesh. Every movement of his body signaled that he knew what was coming. The sheen of sweat was visible on his forehead, and his fingers fidgeted against the armrest.

"Cal, it's you, isn't it? Why are you here? Is Fletcher a fake lawyer too? You've gotta help me."

Cal took off the wig and threw it to the floor. He nodded to Fonzie, who removed the fedora and rubber mask. Tony's breathing quickened when he saw it was Fonzie.

"Oh God. You're here to do it, aren't you? You're here to keep my mouth shut. That's it?"

The sweat poured down Tony's forehead and onto his neck. His arms moved frantically as he attempted to rise from the wheelchair.

"I never had any intention to hurt you, Tony. I liked you a lot, thought you had a good future. But I hoped you'd find a way out. You could've done anything other than this, getting involved with the mob. I know you're poor, but your family would've survived without that hit money," Cal said.

Tears streamed down Tony's face as he shook in fear.

"It wasn't only about the money. It was to show I'm worth a damn. To show that I have potential. I want to be important like you, Cal. Give me that chance. I won't say a fucking word to those cops."

"It doesn't matter," Fonzie chimed in. He stood behind Tony and set his briefcase at his feet. "They'll have the evidence to put you away and will make a pretty sweet deal to get you to talk. You don't want to be in prison your whole life. You're only eighteen. But, if they say you might be out at sixty with parole, or some shit like that, maybe you make a deal. We can't have that happen."

Tony's eyes grew wide. He struggled against the seat. His mouth opened as if to scream, but Fonzie wrapped his hand over Tony's mouth, stifling any noise.

Cal took the knife Detective Thomas had given him out of his pocket, opened it, and stared into Tony's eyes as the blade shone in the dim light of the cell.

Tony's feet furiously kicked against the table. His muffled screams made Cal flinch and caused him to shed his own tears. He didn't want to do this to the boy. He *couldn't* do this. Yet, he stood over the table and brought the knife forward, as if his brain were on autopilot.

His phone buzzed yet again. No doubt it was the police with an update on Maria. A familiar wave of anger coursed throughout his chest. The longer he spent in here, the worse things would get for Maria.

Cal saw her pretty face and remembered the promise he had made to her. The promise of leaving the mafia and his hit man lifestyle behind. Starting a new life with her. Tony was the reason that had all changed. If he hadn't tried to kill Caruso on his own and let Cal do his job, then the Caruso kill would've been Cal's last-ever assignment and he could be free from all this.

In his effort of pleading with Alfredo and Vinnie to let Tony live, he'd ignored their own lives and his own, not thinking they would be at risk if the boy was allowed to walk away safely. How stupid he'd been.

Fonzie's grip on the boy was starting to slip. His eyes were set on Cal, urging him to do what they had come to do.

Cal felt the heat of his anger spread throughout his chest, like he had when he was about to plunge his jackknife into George MacErlean's heart. His brain had shut off and his body made the choice to move forward with his arm, to jab the knife into Tony's heart.

His attention was diverted by a flicker of light from the ceiling lamp overhead. Something was going on with the power. It was that brief action, small but noticeable, that caused Cal to freeze.

"What are you waiting for?" Fonzie asked.

Cal looked up and saw an expression of confusion blended with anger on his best friend's face. Tony stopped trying to fight Fonzie off and glanced at Cal in surprise. The prospect of sudden salvation alarmed him.

Cal shook his head and withdrew the knife, still only inches away from Tony's chest. This was his chance to overcome his anger. He'd find a way to help Maria later. How would she be able to look at him, knowing he'd been responsible for the death of such a young boy, especially when he was so close to escaping?

"There's another way to do this."

"Oh really? 'Cuz the last time I checked, your knife's the only weapon we got."

Cal shook his head again, walked behind the table, and bent down to the floor, picking up Fonzie's discarded mask from the ground. He walked back to the front of the table and held the mask in front of them.

"See this mask? This is how we're going to keep Tony's mouth shut. Not by killing him."

38

"You kidding me? You think Alfredo will go for that?"

Fonzie's defiance bothered Cal. For someone who often called the mob boss "Fredo" behind his back, Fonzie's use of Alfredo's proper name indicated Fonzie may have been under different orders than Cal. Had Meransky told him to ensure Tony's death regardless of their conversation? Alfredo said that if Cal could convince Tony to keep his mouth shut that he could live. Now was the time to pursue that strategy.

"Tony, we're going to put this mask on you. Fonzie, take off your hat and your clothes. Tony and I are going to sneak out of here. Hopefully, they won't know it's Tony until after we've already left."

Fonzie moved within inches of Cal's face. Cal sensed his friend's anger boiling inside. It was something he was all too familiar with but hadn't expected to see in his affable friend.

"What the hell am I supposed to do?"

"You'll have to find a way out. Blutarski, Thomas, they're both in on it. Tell them what Alfredo told me. Tony can live if he doesn't talk. I'll find a place to keep the kid and figure out how to sort this out with Alfredo and Vinnie. You're a good talker. Use those skills to find your way out of here."

Fonzie exhaled and released the squint he'd formed with his eyes. He let out a cough and covered his mouth with a trembling hand.

"I don't like it one bit. But if it means we can save the kid's life, then so be it."

Another exhale echoed through the room, and Cal turned to see Tony, tears still streaming down his face.

"Thank you, thank you so much, Cal. You won't regret this. I won't say a word to anyone."

"Let's hope you can keep that promise, boy. For your own sake," Fonzie said.

Fonzie stripped out of his clothes and helped Cal get them on the injured boy. Tony could barely walk on his own in his weakened condition. Cal would have to support him down the hall and through the gate. He hoped they wouldn't be stopped and the taxi would be waiting for them out front. He gave it five minutes before Blutarski and Thomas came to the cell, expecting to find Tony or his corpse, only to see Fonzie.

Cal donned his blond wig and prepared to use the South Texas accent of Rich Larson once again as he opened the door of the holding cell and guided Tony into the hall.

"What am I supposed to say if they ask me a question?" Tony whispered.

"Quiet," Cal said in the drawl. "Joseph Fletcher is a very quiet man. They said nothin' to him on the way in."

They barely walked ten feet from the cell when Detective Thomas and two other officers marched toward them.

"Ah, Mr. Larson and Mr. Fletcher. I trust everything went well with your client."

"Yessir," Cal said. "When are you going to question the boy? We may need to make other arrangements for providing the boy counsel. My schedule's packed with meetings today."

Thomas eyed Cal and then Tony, perhaps trying to decipher the meaning behind Cal's words. Cal wasn't sure what Thomas expected the outcome of their meeting to be.

"I'm sure we can arrange that, Mr. Larson. These boys won't be doing the questioning anyway. They're just here to perform a little cleanup. Is there a mess to clean up? We know your client was having issues keeping everything together."

Thomas flashed Cal a wink. That's when Cal knew the purpose of the muscled police officers. He didn't want Thomas to think Tony was dead only to see Fonzie alive in the cell. He figured if he hinted to Thomas that Tony was alive that he would save his officers the trouble of going to the cell as well as increase their own chances of escape.

"There ain't no problem at all with my client, Detective Thomas. You give me a call when your boys are ready to question him. Let's not keep him here too long. I'm thinkin' that boy is innocent."

"Yes, sir. You'll be hearin' from us soon."

Cal and Tony walked past the officers and back toward the foyer where Cal had entered. They didn't need to go through the metal detectors on their way out. Cal gave a half-hearted wave toward the female officer at the x-ray machine before reaching the door leading to the outside world, and Tony's freedom.

Cal opened the door and collided with an officer outside. He made sure Tony had made it outside before offering an apology.

"Mr. Larson. Everything go alright?"

Cal had collided with Captain Blutarski. Why he was still outside was anyone's guess.

"Everything went great, sir. Not a problem at all. Detective Thomas is gonna give me a call to come back when you're questioning my boy. If you ask me, he's an innocent man."

"Wait a minute," Blutarski said before turning to his right and noticing the other officer standing at the door. "You're telling me your client is—"

Cal cut him off. "I'm awfully sorry about this, Captain, but I've got a busy day ahead, and Mr. Fletcher and I need to get back to the office. Good day."

With as much energy as he was sure Tony could muster, Cal and the boy jogged down the stairs and out to the waiting taxi. He knew Blutarski was onto him, but he didn't care. All that mattered now was keeping the boy safe, and Cal knew exactly how to do that.

39

Cal walked away from the Megabus stop on Polk Street, feeling a sense of unease at being so close to the scene of the Caruso murder. His footsteps moved too slow for a run but faster than any of the other pedestrians around him. He had to find a way to talk to Alfredo. He knew there would be a lot of explaining to do for breaking Tony out of jail instead of killing him. He had to convince Alfredo that his decision to put Tony on a bus to visit a childhood friend in Indianapolis had been the right one.

He pulled out his phone, ready to call Alfredo, only to see he had several missed calls. One of them was from the number without caller ID, and the rest were from Al Meransky.

That's when he remembered Maria. He'd been so caught up in anger at not being able to get to her when he was only moments away from fulfilling Alfredo's order to kill Tony. His change of heart and decision to spare Tony had cost him the ability to be by Maria's side when she needed him most.

He knew he had to do better by her to be the man she deserved.

He brought up his voice mail, hoping the officer that had been in contact with him had left a message updating him on her condition. Just as he was ready to click play on the message, he noticed an incoming call from Meransky.

"Hello."

"Cal, you finally answered, where the hell have you been?"

"Al, it's a long story. Can you meet? I'd rather see Alfredo, but I'm sure he's not gonna let me talk to him."

"You're right, asshole. With all this scrutiny around us, we can't chance it. Where are you? If you're downtown, I can meet you anywhere in twenty minutes."

"I can meet you at Murphy's on Wacker."

Meransky seemed to hesitate. Perhaps he had another venue in mind and wanted to control the meeting. If that were the case, maybe he had an agenda and a plan to ensure Cal was taken out, but Cal knew he could be putting the cart before the horse.

"Perfect. See you soon."

Cal clicked off the phone and quickened his pace even further. He knew it would only take about fifteen minutes to arrive at Murphy's, but he wanted to get there before Meransky to stake the place out.

As Cal hustled to the restaurant, he brought up his voice mail once again and was able to hear the message that Officer Luis Rodriguez had left for him about Maria. Maria had suffered a minor concussion as a result of her fall. Officer Rodriguez also said Maria was convinced someone was following her and that she believed she'd been shot. There was no evidence of anyone unusual on the scene, and the cop assured Cal that Maria hadn't been shot. Cal's heartbeat drummed faster and faster, but he knew there was nothing he could do right now.

He hoped the meeting with Meransky would be quick and fruitful. He needed to stop by the hospital to see Maria and make sure she was alright. If someone really had been following her, he had to know. The last thing he could handle was someone trying to hurt the only woman he'd ever loved.

Cal arrived at the bar a tick after three o'clock. He scanned the bar, the tables, and the booths that encircled the tables on the outside. No sign of Meransky. Only a few people were eating, but there was a decent crowd at the bar for a Wednesday afternoon.

Cal had purposefully picked the bar because it was the epitome of class, just the way Al Meransky tried to portray himself. The restaurant featured dark wood framed paintings and photos of all varieties along the walls. Solid wooden booths were covered in brown leather above hardwood floors. The ceiling consisted of light-brown wood planks, like that of a barn. The main bar vied for attention at the center of the restaurant, shouldering its way into the surrounding dining areas.

Cal told the hostess that he would take a seat at the bar and order a drink. Cal wasn't a man who often needed liquid courage, but he hoped a nice cocktail would loosen him up.

Cal sipped his drink as he waited for Meransky. Ten minutes passed. Then fifteen. It was unlike Al Meransky to be late. What was going on?

Finally, Cal saw Meransky enter through the front door. Cal got up from his barstool and moved toward an empty booth in the back.

Cal sat and waited for Meransky to approach the booth.

He could tell from the look plastered on the North Side capo's face that he wasn't happy.

Meransky slid into the booth with unprecedented speed. He glowered at Cal before gazing at Cal's drink and then to his lap. Something was definitely going on.

"What are you drinking?"

Meransky's eyes continued to dart all over the restaurant. First, he looked at the picture of a woman in a black cocktail dress on the wall next to them, then at the bar, before returning his gaze to Cal's drink.

Cal told him he was drinking a NorCal margarita. A waiter came to the table and Meransky ordered the same.

"Such a bizarre drink," Meransky said. "I've never heard of such a thing before."

Cal cleared his throat, determined to break the silence. He knew he had to explain his position, and he needed to do it fast.

"I'm sure you want to talk about Tony."

Meransky took a sip of his drink, made a sour face, and set the glass down on the table in disdain. He pushed the glass toward the wall with the back of his fingers.

"That's why we're here," Meransky said. He paused and leaned toward Cal. Even though no patrons were seated close enough to eavesdrop on their conversation, Al positioned his lips in a whisper. His eyes lit up like a flash of lightning, so quick was his rage.

"Why the hell didn't you execute the hit on Tony like you were asked? As far as I know, the order was to have him killed. That's the only way we know he'll keep his mouth shut. Anything less than that and—"

"Al, you need to listen to what I'm about to say."

Cal didn't have time to hear a lecture from Meransky. If Al had wanted a better outcome, he would have had real attorneys in there with the boy to make sure he didn't say anything that would incriminate the mafia. That's not what they wanted. They wanted Tony to die because it was the safest—and most typical—option. Death was always the preferred outcome in the mafia; your enemies couldn't speak when they were dead. Yet another reason for Cal to get out of the mafia as soon as this mess was sorted out.

"You're talking about me killing an eighteen-year-old kid. A kid who did exactly what Alfredo wanted. Ross Caruso is dead thanks to that boy. Alfredo should be grateful for what he did."

"Oh, believe me, Alfredo is more than grateful for the service the boy performed."

"Good. But Alfredo's main concern was keeping the boy's mouth shut, right? Alfredo told me I wouldn't have to kill Tony if I could keep his mouth shut. That's exactly what I did. Thanks to that mask you gave Fonzie, I busted Tony out of jail by giving him Fonzie's gear. I told Fonzie to settle up the story with the police. Tony's on a bus as we speak, heading way out of town where he won't tell a soul what happened."

Al raised his brows and slammed his fists on the table. He was acting in a manner that Alfredo Petrocelli would've been proud of. Spittle formed around the edges of Al's mouth and his forehead was creased with the tremors of anger, like the earthquake that was Alfredo's temperament.

Cal knew the only way he could get what he wanted—Tony's safety and his peaceful exit from the mafia—was to not let his own anger overcome him in the way it was overcoming Al.

"What the hell makes you say that? Alfredo talked to the police on the scene. He relayed their message to me. They're in a hell of a spot, Cal. It's not every day that a potential murder suspect is brought in for questioning and then disappears. That doesn't look good on any cop's watch."

Cal sighed and leaned back in the booth. He was going to have to package his solution in a way that alleviated both Alfredo's and Meransky's concerns. That it was the best outcome for everyone.

"My problem wasn't dealing with the police. Blutarski seemed like a smart guy. I'm sure he can figure out a way to pin the blame on someone else. As long as that someone else isn't Fonzie."

Cal paused and glared at Meransky. "Did he make it out?"

"Oh yeah, as much as Blutarski wanted to kill you and that little shit for the mess you caused, they let Fonzie walk. Detective Thomas will be the fall guy. He'll get an all-expenses-paid trip back home to West Texas, one way.

"It doesn't matter what Alfredo said anyway. What matters is what was done. Fregosi shouldn't have walked out of there. You fucked up."

Cal felt a twinge of guilt at hearing what would happen to Detective Thomas.

"I couldn't kill a kid that young. He's got big dreams, he's very ambitious. He wanted to prove how valuable he could be by going after Caruso. But someone else was there, someone else made this a mess and killed the two guys in the doorway. I bet Blutarski can confirm that."

"Bullshit. Tony killed both of those men. Then he killed Caruso. The kid's a murderer, and he would've had his ass owned by a good prosecutor. He would've given us all up had the police offered to cut him a deal. He should've died."

Cal shook his head and felt anger welling up inside him, rising to the top of his head. Meransky wasn't getting it. How could he not see the lack of humanity in the decision Alfredo had made?

"He was scared shitless, Al. You should've seen him. He's not going to say a word to anyone because I got him the hell out of town. The police may look for him eventually, once ballistics shows for sure he killed Caruso, but it will be a wild-goose chase. He'll be a fugitive on the run. It'll take more work on our part to keep him hidden, but it's been done for much worse guys."

Al shook his head and threw up his hands. He apparently wasn't in a fighting mood, but his manner looked unconvinced, like he wasn't going to have a nice time sharing the story with Alfredo.

"Where is Tony exactly? Who's he hiding out with?"

Cal finished his drink and set the glass at the edge of the table. There wasn't much more he could say. He'd made his case. It was Alfredo's choice to live with it and determine if Cal's case for leaving the mafia was a strong one.

"Don't worry about it, Al. A good attorney doesn't make the case easier for his opponents. See you around."

40

Alfredo sat at the desk in his study for the first time in weeks. Ever since the Caruso murder and Tony Fregosi's disappearance, police had poured into the Evanston house with nonstop questions, forcing the mafia boss to hole up in his Gold Coast penthouse. His nerves were so shot, he couldn't even summon the desire to pour himself a glass of brandy.

"What's next? I think we've managed to fend off the police. It seems like the first day we've had them out of our hair for a while now."

Alfredo cracked his knuckles and nodded at his son. There were so many things to straighten out. The business that they'd lost while under the mayor's scrutiny, for one. It was important they got every segment of their operation up to full speed. Alfredo couldn't be seen as weak in the eyes of the Commission, after convincing them everything was as right as rain.

"You should meet with Frankie's lieutenants down in the South Side, figure out how to get things up and running again. I'm sure Walker would love nothing more than to keep his guys glued to us, but they'll have to give up that charade eventually."

Vinnie nodded and leaned forward in his seat. Alfredo thought of the other item that had been irking him for the last few weeks, having Tony Fregosi free to roam, able to tell anyone about the Caruso murder.

"Another thing," Alfredo said. "We've got to find the Fregosi boy. As much as we yelled at Cal for letting him go, I did tell him he had that option. I want you to find some other guys to round up and hunt him down. See if he has family around here that knows where he is. Get them to talk."

"Alright. Sounds like that will be a fun hunt. Anything else?"

Alfredo raised his brow, wondering if his son was confused at just how important his original instructions were. The phone rang loudly on the desk, startling him.

Alfredo picked it up and answered. "Hello?"

"Alfredo, I've got a development on the case. You ready for it?"

Alfredo hadn't expected Blutarski to call. Right when he and Vinnie thought they were done hearing from the police, they had to listen to the crooked cop yap. He decided to put the cop on speaker. Vinnie needed to be in the loop on the investigation, especially since he had a chance of being implicated if things went south.

"Shit. Are you sending more of your cronies to question my ass?" The boss's voice was rising, ready to snap. "Well, I've got news for you, I—"

"Relax," Blutarski shouted. "We finally got some security footage from the building next door. It was a shame we couldn't see in the alley, but we got a good shot of Clinton Street. We saw someone, a Middle Eastern woman, walking near the scene. She saw the whole thing. We've got it right in the photos."

"Jesus Christ, Blutarski. You're saying you have a potential witness to one of the biggest crime scenes in the city's history, and it's taken you two weeks to find out about it?"

Vinnie stared at Alfredo. The mob boss wondered if it was his son's attempt to calm him down.

"My apologies, sir. I only recently got access to these. Our investigation hadn't considered a witness possibility until very recently."

Alfredo let out a loud sigh. "You're absolutely sure she saw it? Did she see the murder or just randomly pass by?"

"Dead sure, boss. She was there at the exact time our forensics team says Caruso's murder took place. You want to know what else? She threw her hands up in the air when she was facing the alley. That bastard kid who got Caruso probably would've killed her had he not been shot at the scene."

"Jesus. Have you got any way of identifying this witness?"

"Not yet, but I can get some guys to work on it. This will be public evidence to the investigation one way or another. I wanted to tell you before anyone else saw it."

"I appreciate that, Joe. Let me know as soon as you find out who this Middle Eastern woman might be. I'll send my best to take care of her, I can promise you that."

Alfredo hung up and shook his head, his skin turning a deep shade of red. The stress of looking for and taking out a witness was the last thing he needed right now.

"Looks like we have a new priority," Vinnie said. "You

said you'd send your best after this woman. Who did you have in mind?"

Alfredo raised his brow at his son.

"Don't be getting any ideas. We saw what happened when you took matters into your own hands to go after Caruso. I'll call in Al, tell him we've got a final job for Cal if he wants his freedom."

41

On the morning of September 23, Cal woke up and found the space next to him empty. He was surprised to see the morning sunlight fight through the blinds of his bedroom window. He yawned and managed to lift his body from the bed and stumble to the window, where his tired eyes squinted at the street below.

Traffic was picking up, and multiple cars were exiting from their parking places along Hyde Park Boulevard. Everyone was heading out to work for the day, while Cal was able to take his time looking at the vehicles and beyond to Harold Washington Playlot Park, where he and Maria planned to enjoy a nice breakfast outdoors.

In the two weeks since the Caruso murder and helping Tony escape from the clutches of the corrupt Captain Blutarski, Cal and Maria had been the happiest they'd been in their relationship. Without the daily grind of hunting down Alfredo's next victim, Cal found himself spending nearly every day with Maria, listening to her discuss her psychology research and giving her a nonacademic point of view into her insights.

They cooked together, with Maria finally teaching Cal her tamale recipe and Cal making some of his childhood favorites, including shepherd's pie and his mother's famous beef stew. Cal told Maria more about his past, and some of the brighter times he enjoyed in the Petrocelli household as a youth, including his high school football career. The sex was more passionate than ever. Things were really starting to shape up for both of them.

Receiving the official go-ahead from Alfredo was something he pined for every day. Until he got the call, he'd contemplate his next steps. Much like at the family dinner he'd taken Maria to and the night at the hospital where he saw the woman and her newborn baby smile at him, Cal pictured the day where he and Maria would have children of their own. He would make sure they were loved and cared for and that they never felt an ounce of rage in their bodies that would turn them to killing like him.

Maria's thin arms wrapped around his waist and she kissed him with her moist lips. He wondered at how he was lucky enough to have a girlfriend like her.

As much has he wanted to stay in her loving embrace and forget about the realities of life, he'd have to find a way to tell her the truth, that he was still on the mafia payroll.

After struggling to convince Meransky that Tony's mouth could be kept shut outside of the city and nearly getting into a physical argument with Alfredo after sharing the news, Cal managed to stifle their concerns while the news headlines were dominated by police incompetence and Mayor Caruso's suspected involvement with organized crime.

Cal knew that the police searches would come up empty. He hadn't told Tony's father a word about his son's whereabouts and had urged the boy to consider leaving his old friend if he couldn't be trusted to keep him safe. Eventually, the FBI would get involved to find Tony, but no action had been taken yet.

Despite cleaning up the mess surrounding the Caruso murder, Alfredo hadn't granted Cal's wish to leave the mafia yet. The boss wanted to ensure they had a plan for Tony when he eventually returned to the city.

"Are you ready for an epic breakfast of milkshakes that pretend to be coffee and overpriced egg and sausage muffins?"

Maria's voice sounded as sweet as her minty-flavored kiss. Cal realized his own breath was rather rank.

"You bet I am. As a bonus, we should have the entire park to ourselves."

Hand in hand, they left the apartment and walked to the closest coffee shop. Cal ordered a large black coffee. He didn't want to mess with any funky syrups or flavorings. He more than made up for the healthy coffee option by grabbing two giant blueberry muffins. Maria settled on a frozen coffee filled with an inordinate amount of sugar, syrups, and whipped cream, and an egg-and-sausage breakfast sandwich.

Cal sipped the coffee and Maria slurped her coffee milk-shake as they made their way to the park, appreciating the sights of the trees at the park's outer edge. The formerly green leaves were slowly turning to various shades of red, gold, and brown as fall approached. A gentle breeze swayed the leaves to the cool hymns of the wind. A lone wet red leaf managed to blow into Maria's hair, where it stayed for a moment before landing onto the sidewalk.

They reached a paved path beyond the trees and walked for a while, talking. A few morning joggers ran past, most of them older and retired. Some of them had large dogs of different breeds and colors, obediently trotting alongside their masters. Cal wasn't a huge fan of animals but would acquiesce to getting one if it would make Maria happy. He'd do anything to make her happy.

After a lap around the park, they settled on a park bench, eating their chosen pastries. Cal knew this is where he would have to tell her that he hadn't left the mafia as she believed. He started to speak, struggling to form the words he needed to share. At that moment, his phone rang with a call from Al Meransky.

"I gotta take this. I'll be right back."

Cal walked out into the green space, leaving Maria at the bench. He hoped the call wouldn't take too long. He needed to get back to her and say what he needed to say before he wavered on his promise.

"Cal, it's Al."

"Yeah, Al, we've got these things called caller IDs now. I know it's you."

"Don't be such a smart-ass, Boyle. I've got another job for you. I know you'll want to turn me down, but you've really got no choice on this one. The way we see it, this is the knot that ties up all of the loose ends in this Caruso case. As long as your boy Tony stays hidden, there's nothing they can do that can prove any of us guilty, so you're free as a spring chicken after this. Sound good?"

Cal didn't believe it. Not for a second. He didn't like that he was dealing with Meransky and not Alfredo or Vinnie directly. They'd asked him to treat them as family, even in his discontent and desire to leave the mafia, yet they were worried about establishing any connection to Cal that they still had to go through channels like Meransky to communicate their messages.

Dead Frankie Ramone would've been better to talk with than Meransky. Cal didn't trust Meransky.

"Alright." Cal would play along for now, see what he had to say. "What's the deal?"

"We got a tip from our cop downtown. He told us that there was a witness walking down Clinton Street at the time of the Caruso murder and that she saw the whole thing. Some Middle Eastern girl. We're pretty sure the kid would've shot her, too, if he had the chance."

If Tony was the only one in the alley as Vinnie had claimed, they wouldn't care if the witness had seen anything since Tony was in hiding outside the city. There was a chance the witness hadn't seen the Caruso murder at all but instead witnessed Vinnie killing the two guys in the doorway. That was their real concern, keeping the boss's son protected.

When Cal asked Meransky if his concern was because of someone else being in the alley, Al claimed ignorance.

"I don't know what you're talking about. But it's important to the boss that this girl be taken out. We want you to do it."

Meransky's words didn't even hit Cal hard. He knew what would be asked of him as soon as the word "witness" was mentioned. He didn't want to do it, even if it was his last kill. That's what Alfredo kept telling him. Caruso was supposed to have been his last kill, then Tony. Who else would they ask him to kill after this witness was taken care of?

"Can you guarantee it's over after this? No more hits, no more killings?"

Meransky took a deep breath and sighed. "That's my understanding. You'll be able to speak with the boss in person very soon. He's making a special trip out to the city today."

"I'm surprised Alfredo is actually taking an interest in me all of a sudden. Why wouldn't he have you come down for that?"

Cal knew Meransky wouldn't chide him for speaking out of line. Being Alfredo's adopted son gave Cal more privileges to speak his mind than other associates.

"Go over to his place in the Gold Coast around two. We should have more details on the woman by then. We've got a guy working around the clock to find out who she is. Once we know her whereabouts, I want you on surveillance at all times. Find the best opportunity to get her when she's out alone, get the job done, and you're a free man."

Cal nodded to himself and voiced his agreement. He wanted this to be the last time he'd have to talk to the North Side capo for a while.

Cal walked back to the bench and sat down next to his love. Maria was shivering from the autumn-morning breeze and the cold beverage. Cal put his arm around her, moving it up and down to try to warm her up.

"Who was that?"

Cal looked up at the sky, wanting to enjoy the brightness and beauty of the day before he answered her question. He basked in the warmth that he felt on his face.

"You cold?" Cal asked Maria.

"A little bit. Who were you talking to?"

There was no use in skirting around the issue anymore.

"Al Meransky."

"Who's he? Was he one of the men at dinner when we ate with Alfredo and Susan?"

Cal nodded. He hoped Maria's reaction would be one of

understanding and not of fury. Out of the corner of his eye, he thought he saw her jaw clench.

"I thought you were done with all that, Cal. What's going on?"

Cal cleared his throat and took a sip of what was left of his coffee. The black liquid was cold and overly bitter. He threw his cup to the ground in disgust and heard a *tsk* sound from a nearby jogger displaying her frustrations about Cal's littering. He glared at her before realizing the harshness of his reaction.

"I *am* done with it, babe. But they need me to be available in case anything happens with them regarding the mayor."

"But you didn't kill him, right? Why do you need to be involved?"

"Because I was supposed to kill him. There's a lot of loose ends to tie up. There were a couple of guys on the scene they need to make sure keep their mouths shut and don't blab to the police. They're still trying to figure out who did it."

Cal felt like he couldn't reveal the complete truth. He didn't even know the truth himself. While he suspected Vinnie had been the other shooter, he had no way to prove it. He also had his suspicions that the mafia was going to make a play on Tony and try to lure him out of hiding. This potential hit was just the latest roadblock to Cal's freedom from the mafia.

Maria wrapped her arms close to her chest. She was shivering again, but Cal gathered it wasn't from the chill of the frozen coffee drink.

"I know you're the psychology expert, but I see something's bothering you too. What is it?"

Maria shrugged her shoulders before leaning her head on his shoulder.

"Let's get out of here, huh? Spend the rest of the day in bed?"

Cal turned to face her and gave a cheeky grin. "Now that sounds like the perfect prescription, Dr. Espinoza."

They rose from the bench and headed back to the walking path. Maria still had a worried look on her face and shivered against him.

She stopped suddenly and grasped Cal's hand, the strength of her grip nearly crushing his bones. A stride ahead of her, Cal glanced back and saw tears form on her face. Her cheeks reddened against her terra-cotta skin and shook along with the rest of her body.

Cal expected her to say she was breaking up with him. That would be just his luck. Commit to leaving his criminal past behind, only to lose the woman he loved in the process.

"I saw the whole thing, Cal. I can't believe I'm just now telling you this when I had a feeling you could've been involved, but it's true. This has bothered me a lot these past few weeks, but I know you had nothing to do with Caruso's death."

Cal's heart sank. The *thump-thump* pattern quickened again in his chest. Instead of anger, he felt fear. Fear that the mafia would harm Maria if they found out.

"What are you talking about?"

Maria blinked. The tears cascaded down her cheeks like a gently flowing waterfall.

"I saw Ross Caruso's murder."

Cal felt his heart stop and wished he could take over the suffering his girlfriend felt at the moment. He would let her explain everything later. There was only one more question left to ask.

"Was that the only murder you saw that day? Was anyone else there besides Tony?"

Tears flooded down Maria's cheeks and she let out several sniffles as she nodded.

"Yes, another man killed two customers coming out of the restaurant. I'm pretty sure it was your brother, Vinnie."

42

As soon as Maria told Cal she'd witnessed the murders of the two bar patrons and Ross Caruso, he knew his life wouldn't be the same. He knew Vinnie was back there in the alley with Tony, and that he'd been right all along. All of the happy memories he'd shared with his adoptive brother were erased from his mind.

His plan to leave the mafia would be much bumpier than he could've imagined. He didn't dare tell Maria that he was asked by Al Meransky to find the witness and take her down. It would bring her into the only part of Cal's life that she despised. That was an avalanche he had to dig his own way out of.

Telling her she was a target, like so many other victims he'd been asked to pursue in his lifetime, would destroy their relationship. He couldn't blow this; he'd grown to love her entirely too much for that. They'd become so intertwined that he figured it was impossible for his heart to beat without hers. He had to spare her the pain, and he had to find an answer.

Cal considered the situation. He wondered if having

Maria go to the authorities to expose what she saw would ultimately be the best outcome for the both of them. How vindicated he would feel to see Vinnie locked away for his crimes and the Petrocelli empire fall into chaos.

Ultimately, he knew it wasn't the right idea. It would put a lifelong target on Maria's back, not to mention his own. He needed to do with Maria what he'd already done with Tony. Get her out of Chicago and make sure no one ever found out that she was the witness.

They returned to her student apartment, and Cal watched as she packed a small suitcase with a few changes of clothes and other essentials. She was going to spend some time with a second cousin that lived in the northern suburb of Fox River Grove until Cal could figure out what to do.

Regardless of what he did, Cal knew time wasn't on his side. Maria's decision to wear her friend's hijab that day and keep it on for her planned date at the pub may have saved her life. Cal knew that, eventually, with the combination of the crooked cop Blutarski and the mafia's own resources, they would discover that Maria was the girl wearing the outfit. He wasn't sure how they could trace it back to her, but he knew from his time living in the Petrocelli household that if Alfredo wanted to find someone, he would. Especially if it prevented a potential witness from speaking out against his son.

"My professors will never believe me when I tell them the mafia is trying to kill me," she said.

"What makes you think they're trying to kill you?" Cal asked. "They might be able to buy you off."

"That's not funny," Maria said. Her lips and eyes grew tense, not giving Cal a single hint that she was pleased at his poor joke. She didn't blink as her voice rose in a harsh whistle.

"I know from your stories that the mafia doesn't like witnesses. You don't have to tell me that they're not trying to kill me. I already know they are."

Cal held his hands up and stepped back, choosing to drop the subject. Yet he was somewhat relieved that Maria was fully aware of the dire circumstances she was in. Other than her desire to stay near Chicago for her studies, she would go along with Cal's plan all the way.

Her new "home" would be with the closest relative she had in the area, her cousin Julia, whom she hadn't seen in years. Julia was more than willing to take Maria in for what she called "a short while." Cal didn't like that option either, since he wouldn't be able to watch her like a hawk in Fox River Grove.

Cal cursed himself for not having anyone he could trust in the organization to hide Maria with. He never hung around with any of the other associates, aside from Fonzie and a few other guys, mostly drivers like Tony. His involvement with the bigwigs of the mafia was unusual, and accessible to him only because of his family ties as Alfredo's adopted son.

He thought of poor old Frankie Ramone, whose killer still hadn't been identified. That he'd died so close to the Caruso murder scene gave Cal a reason to think Vinnie was responsible for his death as well. While the fat man's loyalty to Alfredo was unquestioned, if he knew Cal's lover was the witness, he would find a way to let her live without anyone else having to pursue her. Now that Frankie was gone, Cal would have to find a way to protect Maria by himself.

Once Maria finished packing her suitcase, Cal picked it

up and carried it downstairs where he would wait with her outside for her cousin Julia to arrive.

"Well, this is it, huh?" Maria asked. "I really don't want to go, but I know it's for the best. Promise me I'll get to come back home someday without feeling like there's a target on my back. You'll straighten this out, right?"

"Don't worry, I'll fix it."

The truth was that Cal didn't know how to fix it. He wasn't sure when the mafia would have enough information to give him an actual witness to target. That's when an idea hit him.

Would it be possible to create a fake witness?

The only information he had was exactly what Meransky had told him, that a woman in a hijab had seen the murder. But Maria had told Cal about her planned shopping trip that day prior to the Caruso date. He could easily come up with a way to put Reema at the scene instead of Maria, who would never have had an excuse to wear a hijab aside from her social experiment. He knew Maria wouldn't like his plan, so he didn't bring it up.

"How are you going to stop this? I want to know."

The frustration in his girlfriend's voice was understandable but annoying. It was hard for him to think under these conditions. He knew he should tell her that he would target her friend Reema, whom she went shopping with that day, and make it seem like she was the witness instead of Maria. The only problem was that he couldn't bring up how he knew about Reema. He would have to get creative with his explanation.

"I'll have to go straight to Alfredo and find out what they know, see if I can convince them to not go hard after the witness. Who knows how long it will take them to find out it was you anyway? I'm sure you did a pretty good job rocking that outfit."

The playful jab was received with a piercing glare from Maria. "The goal isn't to look good wearing a hijab, it's to conceal beauty and display modesty."

"Well, I'm not being very modest in saying that no matter what you're wearing, you look very beautiful."

Cal moved to kiss Maria. He felt nothing more than warm air on his lips as his girlfriend moved away from him. Her eyes were slanted, not open to his flirtatiousness in such a serious moment.

"That's Julia's car," she said, pointing to a gray Audi pulling up to the curb outside her apartment.

"Let me help you with that suitcase. We don't want you getting injured in case you have to kick some lowlife's ass up there in the burbs."

"Cut out the humor, Cal, okay? I'm so nervous I could shit bricks right now."

Cal set his jaw as he dragged the suitcase toward the car. Julia didn't bother getting out and greeting either of them, only letting the passenger door open so Maria could crawl inside.

Maria peered into the car before pulling Cal into a tight embrace, squeezing the air out of his lungs. She was holding on so tight that Cal wondered if she would ever let go. Considering the nature of the last few weeks, Cal would've loved for her to hold on forever.

"I'll call you once everything's clear. Don't leave the house unless you have to."

Maria stepped into the car and strapped on her belt. Her lips formed a faint smile, showing off her playful side that Cal was sure had abandoned her.

"Anything else, Warden?"

Cal leaned into the car and laughed, getting a good look at Julia. The overly tan blonde was too busy talking on her cell phone to do anything other than wave. Cal already couldn't stand her.

"Be careful, Maria. I love you. I'm gonna get us out of this. Then we can be together without any worries. Okay?"

Maria nodded, blew him a kiss, and shut the door.

Cal smiled and waved as she left, a sense of relief that Maria would be safe with Julia flooding his insides. Walking back toward the bus stop to catch a lift toward his apartment, he prepared to call Alfredo. He'd have to pull out all the big guns to ensure Maria's safety. He just wasn't sure which card he'd play first.

He didn't see the short man with the briefcase, standing directly inside the doorway of Maria's building, watching his every move.

43

V innie and Alfredo were seated in Alfredo's office of his penthouse apartment in Gold Coast. They decided to plan their next move in the city and didn't want the odd chance of some low-level soldier overhearing their conversations. Their decisions over the coming days would determine their fate as much as the murder of Ross Caruso had saved them from the Commission's wrath.

Vinnie watched as Alfredo rose from his desk and walked toward the open door of his office. Aside from a hired maid, who was busy cleaning other areas of the apartment, no one else was at the residence. Alfredo lingered at the door, his eyes glancing at both sides of the great room, then he shut the solid oak doors.

"We need to keep this under wraps," Alfredo said, walking toward Vinnie's chair. "We've briefly discussed it before, but it's time to put the plan into action, especially now that Blutarski has told us about this witness."

"You really think she saw me kill those guys? What if all she saw was Tony take out Caruso? If anything, we need to get Cal to go after *him* first, before we worry about this witness. Don't you think?"

"Don't question my decisions! Those Middle Eastern types may be silent in most cases, but think of how many Caruso sympathizers there are out there, particularly Superintendent Walker. He'd love to see us rotting behind bars, especially if it was your ass in the slammer."

"I can't believe Cal didn't kill the kid. I wasn't sure he'd have the guts to do it, since the kid was his driver and all, but that's never stopped him before."

"It's got to be that girl he's with. He's changed because of her."

Alfredo put his hand over his eyes, scrunching his face behind his palm. "Why do you think he doesn't want anything to do with us anymore?"

Vinnie considered this and tapped his thumb and index finger on his father's desk. He wished his father had something else to drink besides brandy.

"I can see why he'd want to do something else. At some point people move on. Even some of our best, who have a chance to get made, take off at times. You know the Commission wouldn't have Cal made. His options for growth in the organization are limited."

Alfredo grumbled as he walked back to the desk. Much to Vinnie's surprise, his father didn't reach for his usual glass of brandy. Instead, Alfredo drank from a cooling mug of coffee. The boss removed a cigar from the breast pocket of his jacket, offered it to Vinnie, and lit it, before following the same process with his own cigar.

The father and son sat in the office, smoking for a short time. Sharing a moment together, in silence, was something so rare that Vinnie made sure to appreciate it, filing it away in his brain for a time when he didn't have a positive view of his father. With a puff of the cigar, he was able let his worldly cares escape from his mind.

"Now," Alfredo began, bringing Vinnie back to reality. "This witness business is one thing. Al Meransky called Cal to take care of it. There should be no mess-ups this time, Cal knows what's on the line. Hopefully Blutarski can get some leads on who this woman is so it won't take too long. Then we have to prepare for what's next with Cal."

Vinnie set his cigar down in the ashtray in front of him and leaned forward, his head hanging over the desk.

"What's next for him? Aren't we going to let him leave after all this is taken care of?"

Vinnie certainly hoped his father would let Cal take a hike. As great of a killer as Cal was, it was Vinnie's turn to prove he could be the most valuable asset in the mafia. He wouldn't mess up during such a critical mission the way Cal had failed to take out Caruso and then Tony to boot.

Alfredo puffed on his cigar and let the ashes fall down onto the desk. Vinnie rolled his eyes as his father reached for his bottle of brandy and poured himself a glass.

"That's what I told him, wasn't it?" Alfredo asked before taking a swig of the brandy. "But in this business, son, you can't always keep your promises."

"What do you mean? Are you saying we need to worry about Cal too?"

Even with the disgust he felt toward Cal, Vinnie was prepared to outshine his adopted brother on his own merit. It wouldn't sit well with him if his father wanted something bad to happen to Cal. He didn't want responsibility for any of the action either; his mother would never forgive him for it. She'd taken to Cal as her own son after his younger brother, Luca, died as a boy.

"Think about it, Vinnie. MacErlean somehow found out

about our secret. Caruso knew about it. He was going to tell the Commission. You know what that would have done to us, right?"

Vinnie nodded. He shouldn't have even asked. He knew where this was going. Now he had to listen to his father lecture him some more.

"We went to all these lengths for a reason, Vinnie. You know who else knows this secret we worked so hard to protect?"

"I take it not many people know other than Cal."

"Exactly. You and Melissa are the only ones who know. Frankie never knew. Meransky doesn't know. You and Melissa are family, real family. It was never in your best interests to blab to the Commission because your lives would be at stake being tied to me. Cal on the other hand, isn't family. As much as we've loved having him in our lives for years, he isn't family. He can blab. He can still hurt us in the same way Caruso could."

"Okay, but why would Cal go to the Commission? Cal wants to be free from all of this, he isn't out to cause trouble. Besides, you may have ordered the hit, but he's the guy who actually killed a boss. His own life would be in danger too. This isn't like Caruso telling them about it. It's completely different."

Alfredo leaned back in his chair and took another drag of the cigar. Vinnie mirrored his father's action by retro-haling his own cigar smoke. The elder Petrocelli's face began to contort in an expression of rage before settling back into a more peaceful profile.

"Son, you'll make an excellent peacetime boss. I'm sure of it. All your ideas for our future are peaceful and soft. No more selling drugs, no more hits, no more gambling, no more beating people up for not paying their loans on time.

Our entire enterprise is very risky. Lots of people I've been close to have died or been locked up over the years. But there's a reason we do this, son. We'd never get this type of power with a regular working gig."

Vinnie held his gaze firm on his father. A small pile of ash was piled above the breast pocket of Alfredo's jacket, just above the wine-colored handkerchief that sat inside the pocket. Vinnie wanted to flick the ash off. The mere presence of the dirt bothered him as much as his father's insistence that he was smart and weak as opposed to menacing and strong. The speech made his jaw tense and caused him to wonder if his father thought he was less of a man, that he couldn't handle his own problems. He wanted to stomp the ground in protest.

"This is a time of war," Alfredo continued. "Think of all the enemies we have, even with the Commission off our back. We have this witness to get rid of, and we're still being questioned about the mayor, even though ballistics shows the boy did it and they have no way to connect him to us. We've got all the mayor's thugs that we're being tied to. All these murders are going to come screaming back to us at some point."

"You're saying Cal has to be the fall guy," Vinnie said. "He answers for the MacErlean murder, the murder of all the mayor's guys, maybe we throw the police a bone for a few others if we're creative enough. It's a risk. You think our lawyers can keep our noses out of it?"

Vinnie pulled at his bangs that nearly reached his eyebrows and ran his hands through his freshly cut hair. He didn't like the idea of Cal going down for all of this, but it was better that his adoptive brother take the fall than him. Vinnie had a future of running the mafia and keeping it powerful, while all Cal had if he left the mafia was a future of being a poor warehouse worker like his father.

Vinnie smiled at those thoughts. He no longer relished the early memories of their childhood friendship. Instead, he welled with pride that he'd finally won out over Cal and that his father felt that the hit man was no longer worth keeping around.

"I pay these lawyers a lot of money. They know what to do. Besides, there's no evidence we committed any of these murders, especially now that you got rid of that gun after making such a rookie mistake. You did get rid of it, didn't you?"

"Yeah, yeah, I got rid of it." Vinnie couldn't believe his father. Did he think he was a complete amateur like the posers who stood out on the front lawn? He pulled hard on a clump of hair near his ears, wishing he were causing the discomfort to his father.

He wanted to ask his father the question that he had been circulating as fact in his brain the entire meeting. "So, we're going to get rid of Cal? For sure?"

"We have no choice. I've worked too hard to keep this family in power, and I'm not going to risk any more damage. Cal did what we needed him to do. He was a tough killer who got the job done. It won't be easy to replace a guy with skills like that. Just like it won't be easy to replace Frankie. But we'll find a way."

"You want me to find someone?"

"Make a list of guys and get it to me as soon as you can. Hopefully, we figure out who this witness is and Cal can take care of her pretty quick. After that, we move fast. Hit him when he least expects it."

Vinnie felt a need to play an assertive role in this. He needed to show his father that he was capable of running the family, and having Cal taken out would prove a lot. If Alfredo was determined Cal had to go, then Vinnie would make sure it was a clean, swift kill that his friend never saw coming. Cal didn't deserve the long, torturous death that he often inflicted on the mafia's victims. His excellent service warranted something quick and painless. It would be a way to thank him for all of his hard work. A sudden idea formed in his mind.

"You know, Pops, I understand there was some chemistry involved in Grandpa's death."

Alfredo looked at him quizzically and set his cigar on the ashtray below his wrist.

"There was."

"Let's have a big send-off dinner after the witness is killed. We'll have Mom cook Cal's favorite meal, let him invite his girlfriend and his buddies over. All we'll need to do is slip whatever we slipped in Gramps's pills into his food."

Alfredo shook his head and his face reddened in fury. It wasn't the way Alfredo would've wanted to eliminate a hardened killer like Cal. He would've wanted to bury the muzzle of his gun into Cal's temple and pull the trigger. The shaking of his head and the reddening of his face softened into a gentle shaking of laughter. He was coming around to the idea.

"You sure are a passive-aggressive fucker. Not the way I'd have him go, but I like it. It keeps it simple and keeps it between us. That's exactly how we'll do it."

Vinnie bid his father goodbye, left the office, and prepared to head down the elevator to his own luxury suite, smiling at his creative ingenuity and his ability to please his father.

44

C al couldn't help but notice a sinking feeling in the pit of his stomach as he watched Maria leave in her cousin Julia's gray Audi. Helplessness washed over him like a cloud of moving fog. He hated not being there to watch over her.

What he couldn't tell Maria was that her friend Reema made an ideal replacement as a witness he could present to Meransky and Alfredo. Aside from the fact that she was Middle Eastern and was likely wearing a hijab with Maria that day, she was considered a loner. Other than Maria, she didn't have a lot of friends. No one would notice, or even care, if she went missing for a length of time.

After a light lunch of cold sockeye salmon, avocado, and some almonds, Cal felt the crisp fall air slap his face like a cold-hearted ex-lover as he ventured out. He knew Reema's apartment wasn't too far away from Maria's. He boarded the Number 28 bus for the apartment complex, Beretta and jackknife in tow. If Reema cooperated as he hoped, he wouldn't have to threaten her with them.

Cal sent a text to Fonzie asking him to fetch a car and

meet him in the vicinity of the University of Chicago campus. If he found Reema at the apartment complex, they would pick her up, stuff her in the car, and take her down to the same place they'd killed MacErlean. Fonzie would find a more permanent location to store her if they needed to.

Getting Reema on board to sign her own death warrant was going to be a challenge. Cal felt increasingly awful that it had come to this. He knew Maria would hate him if she found out that her friend was sacrificed for her own safety.

It was a choice he had to make. If he wanted the woman he'd grown to love more than himself to remain alive, he would have to sacrifice the life of another. It made him feel terrible, even though he wouldn't have cared about this a few months ago, when he didn't give a damn about who lived and who died.

Fonzie answered his text, saying he was busy but would try to get a car in a few hours. Cal's shoulders tensed as he exited the bus and walked the familiar path to Maria's building. He wasn't sure which building Reema lived in but knew it wasn't too far away. He considered asking a few girls walking past with stacks of books underneath their arms but decided against it. The last thing he needed was one of the girls calling the police saying a large man was asking questions about a girl. Despite wearing an oversize University of Chicago sweatshirt, Cal stood out like a sore thumb.

He saw a bench nearby and sat on it. He would pass the time people watching, hoping one of them was Reema. It would be much easier to formulate a plan for interrogating her once he knew exactly where she lived.

Half an hour passed before Cal saw a tawny-colored woman approaching from his left, turning to the building directly across from him. Though the girl wore a dark-red hijab, he wasn't sure if it was Reema. He'd only seen one photo of the girl on Maria's phone.

Cal watched as the woman entered the apartment building through the front doors. A few other tenants entered and exited the building and loitered near the trees surrounding his bench. A wrinkly maintenance man passed from one building to the next.

He saw an opportunity and hoped he could still take advantage of it. Through the main upstairs window, Cal could see the woman had reached the landing of the second floor. She began a turn to the right. Acting fast, Cal transformed his voice into one that was higher pitched than his usual baritone and shouted her name, hoping it would carry through the open window.

The girl turned around with a flash just as her silhouetted face passed the window. His plan had worked as intended, confirming she was the girl he was after. She crawled closer to the window and searched for the voice that had called her name.

Cal waited until he was confident Reema had entered her apartment, then took two steps to his right to see if she would open a window, giving him direct knowledge of which second-floor apartment she lived in. After what seemed like hours, he saw her hands appear behind a lacy white curtain, unlatch the window from the inside, and lift it open.

Cal now had two pieces of valuable information. He knew the girl in the hijab was indeed Reema, and he knew exactly which unit she lived in. If she was as much of a recluse as Maria said she was, she'd find little reason to leave the apartment. Cal had to act fast.

He smiled and thought a career as a private investigator could be in the works once he was finally free of the mafia.

He had the toughness for the job and might even have enough street smarts for the work.

Cal figured the building's main door was locked but knew he wouldn't have a tough time attempting to break in. He had a few small tools in his front pocket, beneath his wallet. His jackknife, resting in the rear pocket of his jeans, could also come in handy.

He entered a gate leading to the small garden entryway of the apartment building. Once he got to the door, he tried it, only to find it locked. He dug out his tools. A quick glance behind him revealed no one else walking about. He had the tools in his hand and was prepared to pick the lock when a resident opened the door to the left, startling him.

"Forget your key, man? Go ahead."

Cal nodded at the stranger, his heart pounding with relief that he wasn't busted. He found the stairwell and marched up to the second floor. It didn't take long for him to find the last apartment on the right, which is where he'd seen Reema open the window.

Cal reached the door. A sense of calm washed over him as he rapped on the door. He'd been in this position so many times before, he was numb to any bodily reaction. When he needed to extract information from someone, especially to save the life of a person he cared about, he wasn't concerned with how much pain that someone had to go through. He blocked all such considerations from his mind and focused on the task at hand.

His right hand reached for the Beretta tucked in its holster. He was surprised at the speed with which Reema opened the door, and that she had an infant in her hands. The presence of the infant startled Cal; he couldn't manage to bring the gun from his holster. His hand stayed frozen at his side, his mind quivering at the idea of bringing harm to a baby.

Regardless of why the child was there, it completely changed Cal's plan. He'd have to go through the friendly routine after all.

"Can I help you with something?"

Reema's soothing voice calmed Cal's nerves, despite his shock at the baby's presence. The child kicked its little legs out, squirming in Reema's arms.

"Hi. I'm Maria's boyfriend, Callahan Boyle."

Cal wasn't sure what else to say. He'd have to improvise.

"I'm sorry to disturb you and your baby, but can I come in for a second? Something's happened to Maria."

It was the best tactic he could come up with. Cal hoped the mention of her best friend being in trouble would play on Reema's good nature to let him inside.

"Oh no, this isn't my baby. It is my sister's girl. Her husband is a bad man. I watch the baby sometimes so my sister can be in peace and quiet. Let me set her down and we can talk."

Cal sighed in relief while Reema went to a room in the rear of the apartment to set down the child. He was relieved it wasn't hers. He'd be able to do the work he'd come to do.

His hand reached for the Beretta as he stepped through the threshold and into the apartment, gently closing the door behind him. He held the barrel down in his hand, behind his back, while he waited for the young woman to return. The beating of his heart steady, he gazed into the woman's eyes as she approached him.

In a flash, Cal raised his gun and lunged forward, ready to get this over with.

"Oh my God, don't shoot!"

Reema threw her hands in the air and took a step back.

Cal held the gun in front of him and closed the gap. He was ready to get on with the show. He was going to explain that she was the witness who had seen the murder. He would ingrain it in her brain with as much force as he could muster.

The phone in his pocket vibrated. *Perfect.*

Fonzie must have arrived and was ready to take the woman to the spot. The spot where Cal would make her confess her crimes to Alfredo so he and Maria could be free. Together.

Cal clicked the phone on, ready to answer. Reema saw this as her opportunity, breaking into a run to get to the door. Cal jumped to his right to block her attempt. They collided, and Cal's brute strength sent Reema careening to the floor.

Cal thought the screams that filled his ears were Reema's. He was ready to shoot the bitch if he needed to. Only upon closer inspection, he realized the screams were coming from the phone. They were the screams that filled his nightmares.

Cal knew that voice. It was the voice that whispered sweet nothings into his ear. The voice was in trouble. Not safe. In pain.

Maria.

45

C al's head shook with the ferocity of an earthquake as he heard his girlfriend scream on the phone. He wanted to unleash a roar of anger himself. Thousands of questions ran through his mind.

Did she not make it to Julia's? Was Julia a rat? Who had her? Were they hurting her?

Cal squeezed his left fist tightly while holding the gun at a dazed Reema, who was sobbing on the floor. Perhaps she'd heard Maria's screams too.

After what Cal was sure was hours of screaming, a masculine voice came on the phone. It was accented in heavy Italian.

"We've got your girlfriend, Mr. Boyle. We know what she saw a few weeks ago. And in twenty-four hours, we are going to kill her. Unless you come to us and give us what we want."

Cal growled. He wasn't sure who this man was, but he was sure the kidnapping had the approval of Alfredo Petrocelli. He wondered how Alfredo had found out about Maria's presence at the shootings. Surely the police couldn't have fed him information that fast.

That didn't matter now. What mattered was finding a way to get her back. But what did they want?

He asked, still pointing the gun at Reema, despite his shame. Since he could no longer use her for leverage, he felt disgusted for being there.

"That's for us to discuss once you get here. Come alone —no guns, no funny business. You fuck up, your lady dies. You got it?"

Cal was even more certain that Alfredo was behind this now. He'd even heard the voice before. It had to be one of the boss's low-level flunkies who stood outside the compound, watching the cars come in and out. Bruno came to mind at first, since he was the most recent to get the job, but it could have easily been someone else.

"Where is she? Tell me where she is."

The man laughed before blowing his evil breath into the phone.

"I'm afraid you aren't in a position of power here, Mr. Boyle. We are. Just know your lady is safe and sound, and she'll stay that way as long as you come to us. We'll be in touch with instructions."

Cal thought the man was going to hang up. He wanted to shout at him, tell him he would tear him limb from limb if that's what it took to get Maria back. Maybe his yells would give Maria some encouragement that she would be saved. Her knight in shining armor would be there to rescue her. Instead, the man spoke again.

"Speaking of touching, your girlfriend is sexy as hell. I think I'll take advantage of the situation and play with her a bit."

That was the last straw.

"You motherfucker! I'll—"

Cal's yells fell on deaf ears as he realized the call was

disconnected. He took a glance at the screen before throwing the phone across the room, where it bounced hard off of the wall, separating the phone and case that enclosed it.

Reema's gentle sobs turned into high-pitched wails. Cal was sure neighbors would come pouring in at any minute. He had to clean up the situation as fast as he could, then he would find Maria.

He shifted his gun toward the ground to show he no longer meant harm, then put the gun back in the holster and extended a hand to Reema to help her off the floor.

Reema slapped Cal's hand away and scuttled to her feet.

"Get away from me!"

The young woman staggered toward the bedroom at the back of the apartment, where her sister's baby joined Reema's cries. Cal would have to recover fast if he wanted to avoid spending the rest of the night in jail instead of finding Maria.

"Reema, I'm sorry. I shouldn't have barged in here the way I did," Cal called out. "Maria's in trouble and I over-reacted."

Cal followed her into the bedroom. Despite the fear written on Reema's face, she made no effort to shoo him away again. She coddled the baby girl and rocked her gently, whispering reassurances into her ear.

"Reema, did you hear me? Maria's in trouble."

Her eyes snapped up at him like the crack of a whip slashing across a bare back.

"Yes, I heard you. What can I do? Maria's my best friend, but if a bunch of guys have her, I don't know what to do. Call the police."

"It's more complicated than that."

Cal couldn't tell her why it was more complicated. He

didn't want to bring up his occupation now any more than he'd wanted to tell Maria what he did for a living when she'd confronted him a few weeks prior.

"Well if you don't call the police, I will," Reema hissed. She walked past him and back into the living room, the baby safe in her arms. "I'm going to call them right now if you don't leave my apartment."

"Hold on. Calm down for a second." Cal rushed to keep up with the woman before she reached the door.

"I need to ask you a few questions about your shopping trip with Maria the other day. Did anyone follow you around? Was she meeting anyone after your trip?"

Reema made a loud *tsk* noise and shook her head as she reached for the door. Cal put his hand over hers, hoping she wouldn't scream at the intrusion. Her gaze resembled pure rage. She was anything but the passive woman he'd first encountered when he'd entered her apartment.

"Listen, mister. If Maria wanted you to know about what we did, she would've told you herself. You should probably know that she wasn't too fond of your behavior lately and that you upset her quite a bit. I can see why, since you're nothing more than a rude, invasive man. You're no better than the man who married my sister."

"She told me about it," Cal interrupted. He knew he wasn't winning any points with the woman, but he didn't care at this point. He had to see if she knew anything more than what Maria had already told him. Was there something that Maria had left out that could tell him exactly who was behind this?

"Maria said she was meeting some public figure for lunch. Who was she was really meeting? You have to know that Mayor Caruso was murdered there around the same time. You're sure she couldn't have been meeting someone else?"

Reema's face was firm and unchanging. It seemed that she was finding her strength in Cal's desperation.

"Yes, I'm sure. She showed me the guy's picture. He was cute. Cuter than you."

Cal shook his head. "Was anyone following you on Michigan? Has she talked to you since then and mentioned anyone following her home from the pub?"

"No, no, no. None of that. No one was following her." Reema paused. "But you know what? She told me she thought someone was following her home from class one day. She was going to the bus stop when she tripped. She said someone had a gun and was going to shoot her."

Cal remembered it well. The phone calls from the police officer while he was with Fonzie in the holding cell, deciding to spare Tony's life. He remembered the constant calls and his feeling of hopelessness as he let his girlfriend suffer while he saved his young friend's life.

"I was there in the hospital with her after it happened. The cops insisted it was nothing and she'd only hit her head. She seemed unsure of it when I was there with her. Did she tell you anything different?"

Reema laughed. "Of course she didn't want to tell you. You're her big, scary boyfriend who would've gone after revenge if she confirmed it was true. I'll tell you what she told me a few days ago when I talked to her. It was true. There really was a man there."

"Did she say what he looked like? C'mon, Reema, this is a matter of life or death."

Reema frowned and shook her head. "No, she couldn't remember. First, she described a Hispanic man; the next time she described a black guy. It's hard for her to remember, she was hurt pretty bad."

Cal knew he wasn't going to get any more information out of Reema. She'd been helpful enough, given the trouble he'd caused her. There was only one way he knew he could find answers. He'd have to use everything he could from his hit man bag of tricks.

"Thank you, Reema. I'll leave now."

Cal removed his hand from hers and allowed her to open the door. His mind raced with hundreds of thoughts, but he only had one destination in mind. There was only one place he could go to find out who had taken Maria. Only then could he get her back.

46

C al had to get answers. From the moment he'd found an unlocked car parked near Reema's apartment, to the instant he'd highjacked it and made his way to the Petrocelli compound in Evanston, Cal knew he'd have to do whatever it took to get Maria back.

He was certain Alfredo, Susan, and Vinnie would be home. It was a Saturday evening, which was usually reserved for family dinners. Only close friends of the family were ever invited to the dinners. Now that Frankie Ramone had been killed, only the likes of Al Meransky and other higher-level associates in the mob would be invited. It would make it easy for Cal to get the answers he needed.

Cal remained astonishingly calm as he rehearsed his plan in his head on the drive over. There was no question that his days with the mafia were over. If he threatened Alfredo, or fired on any of the associates guarding the property, he knew he'd no longer be viewed as a cherished member of the family. Instead, he'd become public enemy number one. That status meant certain death. Even Mayor

Caruso's security team hadn't been able to prevent his assassination. Cal knew he couldn't avoid a similar fate.

That didn't stop him from wanting to try, to prove to Maria that he could be a changed man and live a legitimate life, one that allowed both of them to be happy.

Cal pulled up to the street where the house was located. Darkness had enveloped the entire neighborhood and only a few street lights lit the space.

The exterior lights of the Petrocelli compound were on. Cal could see three men in dark jackets and matching slacks standing on the front lawn, right behind the circular drive where dinner guests would park.

With only one car parked in the drive, Cal realized there weren't many guests at all. He'd never considered the possibility that Alfredo wasn't home. As long as someone opened their lips to tell him where Maria was, he would take the information.

Cal parked on the street, not bothering with the driveway. One of the men gazed at him and motioned to the others. Bruno stared back at him, the man whose voice Cal suspected he'd heard on the phone telling him Maria had been taken.

Cal had his hand atop his holster from the outside of his sweatshirt. He didn't plan to go in with guns blazing; rather, firing the weapon would be a last resort. When Cal saw the two men flanking Bruno reach for their belts and shout orders, Cal knew it wasn't time for games. He would have to fight.

"Boyle, you made a mistake showing up here," Bruno said while motioning for the men to hold back their reach toward the guns. "You're not going to find what you're looking for."

Cal walked closer, not concerned that he was outnumbered as he reached the spot where the curb and the circle drive met. While Bruno was relatively new, he had experience helping guys at Fonzie's level out on the streets, except his forte was gambling and working with a family bookie. The two guys standing behind Bruno were so fresh that Cal had never seen them before. They didn't appear very confident, being approached by a known hit man such as Cal.

"You and your boys aren't going to do shit, Bruno. I'm going to go inside and say hello to my mother. I want nothing to do with Alfredo."

"Mother," Bruno joked. "Since when did you start calling Susan your mother? Didn't your mother get cooked in some car crash? Probably got made uglier than she already was."

Bruno turned back to the men and let out a loud laugh. His two companions responded with nervous laughter of their own, one of them pulling down on his long brown hair.

Cal felt the blood boil inside his veins. The muscles in his arms and legs tremored. He didn't have time for games. Bruno had made a big mistake disparaging his mother.

He used Bruno's diverted attention to his advantage, whipping out the Beretta from his holster and holding it firm in both hands in front of the three men. He knew if he shot them, a flurry of men would come running outside and it would be that much trickier to get Alfredo to tell him where Maria was.

It took all of his willpower to not fire the gun. The smile on Bruno's face vanished immediately once he turned back to Cal. The nervous men behind him couldn't decide if they should reach for their guns or run off. Long Hair took off, heading for the street.

Cal trained his gun on the escapee before deciding it wasn't worth wasting bullets on him. As close to the mafia's power structure as he was, he knew men like Long Hair would leave and never come back. Most of them didn't have the guts to face the violent nature of the profession.

Bruno appeared less confident now that one of his men had deserted him. The man to his right kept acting fidgety, and Cal noticed that he had withdrawn his gun.

He fired at the man's hand, leaving him howling in pain. Bruno reached inside his jacket pocket. Cal pulled the trigger of the Beretta once again, sending a sharp bullet exploding into Bruno's heart, jets of crimson pouring through his shirt.

Bruno's face slackened and he slumped to the ground before his head landed on the cement. Cal's eyes darted to the front door of the house, expecting more men to flood the yard, but there was no movement.

Smart decision. Anyone coming out of the house would be easy pickings for a master marksman like Cal. He would have to go to them.

The first man Cal shot was slumped on the ground, howling in pain from the gunshot wound to his hand. The shot was fired at such range that the hand was practically smoking and covered with blood. Cal walked over to the man and removed his gun from his holster.

"Let's make this easy because I'm pretty sure you know damned well who I am. Tell me if Alfredo is in there."

"Fuck you," the man spat, turning his back to Cal and making his best effort to crouch against the tall pine in the center of the yard.

Cal walked to him and pressed the barrel of his gun against the young man's temple. His anger was driving his decisions now. He couldn't care less if anyone heard the shots.

"I'll kill you if you don't answer me," Cal warned. "There's a woman's life at stake. More importantly, there's your own. Don't make the mistakes I did, kid. You've got your whole life ahead of you. You get that shit bandaged up, get a good job, and you can walk away with your integrity intact. You got it?"

The man muttered something under his breath before putting his damaged hand into his tie, doing his best to construct a makeshift bandage to stop the bleeding.

"I've got no clue if the boss is in there. I ain't never seen him before. I know Meransky's in there. He knows where your lady is."

Cal kept holding the gun against the young man's head before deciding he would have to trust the information. He would let him go, confident he would make the right decision for his future while Cal's own efforts to leave the mob proved to be too late.

"Get out of here, kid. Don't come back."

Cal kept one eye on him as he stormed toward the front door. The kid ran off in the same direction as his long-haired friend before him. Cal focused his attention on whomever might be at the door. It was locked, but that was no problem for him. Using a copy of the house key he had on his key chain, he opened the door, stepping back as he did so in case a volley of gunshots came spewing from the entry.

The hit man stepped inside, glancing to his left, then his right, and to the stairwell in front of him. Each direction was empty. The only sound of movement in the house was the sound of Cal's boots against the floor. It was eerily quiet for a Saturday night at the Petrocelli household. Too quiet.

Cal walked through the foyer and into the sitting room directly off of Alfredo's study. Still no movement.

He glanced from the sitting room to the large living room immediately to the right, then to the door of the chef's kitchen straight ahead. No sound emanated from any of the rooms.

Cal contemplated the best possible way for them to set him up, if he was being set up at all. Someone had to be in the house waiting to confront him. Someone had to have heard the multiple gunshots outside. Yet the house was uncomfortably tranquil.

Cal nudged the Beretta forward and opened the study door, expecting a horde of men to have assault-grade weapons pointed at him, finally ready to gun him down before ordering Maria's death too. Instead, only one man sat in the room, at Alfredo's desk. From the back of the man's head, Cal could tell it was Al Meransky. Given the sound of the ass-kissing performance Meransky was giving on the phone, it wasn't likely he'd heard Cal come in.

"Absolutely, sir. The instructions have been given... Yes, sir, I'm certain he'll show up tomorrow once we tell him where she is... Okay, sir. Good night."

Al removed the phone from his ear and spun around in the chair to hang it up. The moment his eyes fell upon Cal, the phone dropped with a clang on top of the desk.

"Not expecting me, Al?"

The capo's eyes widened. Cal thought he heard a mumbled "shit" come out of the man's mouth. Perhaps Meransky really hadn't heard the commotion outside.

"Alfredo would be really mad to see you sitting in that chair," Cal said. The way he saw it, he had plenty of privacy for interrogation. There was no one else in the house to stop him.

"What are you doing here, Cal?" Al asked, the bouncing of his knee giving away his nerves. There was no question that the entire mafia was behind Maria's kidnapping.

"Next time, put some better men outside."

Meransky raised his brow and stammered a response. "You waste them all?"

"Maybe I showed some mercy for once."

Cal walked toward the desk, glancing intently at Meransky to see if the capo had any sign of a weapon on his person. Meransky's hands were resting neatly on the desk. No bulges under his shirt. If he made any effort to reach below his waist, Cal would blow him away.

"I never wanted this to happen, Cal, any of it. You know the saying 'it's not personal, it's just business'?"

"I'm only going to ask once," Cal threatened, his eyes cutting through Meransky like glass. "Where is Maria? I heard everything you said on the phone. I'm not waiting until tomorrow. You can call Alfredo and tell him I'm going to get her back now."

Al sighed and shook his head. "You don't get it, do you? The whole Caruso thing? It wasn't only about Caruso. But I'm sure you know that."

In that moment, it all made sense. Cal silenced Alfredo's secrets only to later be punished for knowing himself. It was nothing more than a fucking death trap.

Cal pointed the gun at Meransky's head, prepared to shoot. He would ask one more time.

"Where is she, Al? I know you have kids. They'd hate to see their dad's brains all over his face at the funeral."

"How thoughtful," Al quipped. "But it's not my business to say. My loyalty is to the familia first, even before my own family. That's the way it is. You seem to have forgotten that."

"Only one problem with that, Al. I'm not made. Last chance. Where is she?"

Meransky chuckled as Cal clicked the trigger. He saw a furtive movement in the capo's eyes. He was delaying for a reason. Cal saw a presence in his peripheral vision. He wouldn't have time to startle the person by turning around with the gun. That would set up Al for an easy chance to blast Cal if he indeed had a gun below the belt.

The only chance Cal had was if he used the jackknife. Reaching into his pocket, he grabbed the knife and in a swift motion, threw it diagonally over his shoulder.

A click of a trigger and the ripping of flesh rang in the air at once. Meransky had risen from the chair and was preparing to fire. Only Cal's trigger clicked first, sending a bullet careening into the capo's skull.

The clunk of two bodies falling was the next thing Cal heard. Meransky had fallen back into Alfredo's chair. Cal had to turn to see Long Hair, who'd decided to return to the house. His body slid down the doorframe, the blade of Cal's jackknife firmly lodged in his throat.

Cal walked over to Meransky. The man he'd known for so long was breathing jagged breaths in Alfredo's precious seat. He needed the dying man to give him something, anything, to help him find Maria.

"Make sure you don't die in vain, Al. You can save Maria's life. Tell me where she is. Please tell me where she is."

Al's eyes blinked once before rolling into the back of his head.

Cal shook his head in disbelief. He'd come to the house for a single purpose—to find out where Maria was being held. Instead, he'd killed three men and seriously injured another, with no information to show for it. He wasn't any closer to saving his girlfriend's life.

Turning away from Meransky, a tiny piece of paper on Alfredo's desk caught his eye. On it was an address. The old warehouse where his father had worked. It appeared it would all end in the same place the killing had started for Cal.

47

C al stormed out of his childhood home, Meransky's piece of paper in hand. The young man with the wounded hand had left the property, but Bruno's dead carcass was still evidence that there had been a disturbance at the house. Porch lights glowed across the street, and Cal thought he heard nearby whispers, perhaps wondering if their mafia neighbors were up to no good again.

He considered moving Bruno behind a tree but didn't want to give anyone watching across the street the idea that he was moving a dead body. He saw an old man walking his dog approaching the Petrocelli compound from just down the road, which caused his heart to thump. It was best he kept on the move before anyone asked questions.

He got into the stolen car, fired it up, and headed back to the city and his apartment in Hyde Park. It was time to gear up to get Maria back. He placed a final call to Fonzie to see if he could count on his old friend for help.

"Cal, what's up? I was waiting at that chick's apartment, and you weren't there."

"I know. A lot of shit's gone down. I'm not sure if you want to hear about this."

"Hear about what? If shit's going down, I want to be there. I've always had your back, man."

Cal sighed. Things had gotten so bad that he didn't know who to trust. Fonzie was his best friend, but now that his family had turned on him and taken his love away, he wasn't sure if he could stomach Fonzie getting caught up in this mess too. He wondered if it was his battle to fight alone.

"Maria's been kidnapped. Somehow they think she was the witness I was supposed to go after. I have no idea how."

An audible gasp sounded across the other line. When Fonzie didn't follow with a comment, Cal pushed the pedal closer to the floor, not caring how fast he was driving.

"It doesn't matter now," Cal said. "I have to go and find her. They said they'd kill her tomorrow if I didn't give them something they wanted. They didn't say what."

Fonzie remained quiet. That meant he was thinking. A thinking Fonzie was a dangerous Fonzie. Whatever gears were churning in his brain, Cal wanted them to be the right ones.

"I don't know, Cal. It sounds like it could be a death trap," he said finally. A trap it surely was. Cal didn't give a shit about much in life, but he gave a lot of shits about Maria. He was going to do anything he could to get her back, whether Fonzie would help him or not.

"Yeah, but I don't give a damn. I've got a lead, and I'm going after her. You may not hear from me again, Fonz, depending on how this all goes."

"Whoa, whoa, hold up. I'm not gonna let your big ass walk with a knife into a gunfight. Count me in, I'll help your ass out."

Cal paused to consider Fonzie's offer. Part of him wanted

nothing more than to have Fonzie's help. He didn't know how many people Alfredo had at the warehouse guarding Maria. Another part of him wanted to do this alone, to ensure that no one else got hurt because of him.

"I think they've got her at the old warehouse where my father used to work. That's what the paper on Alfredo's desk said anyway."

"Paper on Alfredo's desk? You went home?"

"It was the only way I could find out where Maria is." Cal's chest tightened, and he pushed the pedal even farther to the floor on the last stretch of road he could before hitting city traffic. "Now are you going to help me or not?"

"Fuck yeah, I'll help. Where you want to meet?"

"We need a game plan. As much as I want to go in there and rip their heads off, I've got to think this through. Come over to my place. We'll talk it over."

"Alright. You think we need anybody else? Knowin' Alfredo, he's gonna have a lot of guys in there."

"Not any more than we can take down. See you soon."

Cal hung up. He couldn't help but feel that they were walking into a death trap that they would never walk out of.

48

C al waited a half hour for Fonzie to arrive at his place. In addition to the Beretta and the jackknife, Cal had prepared a duffel bag filled with larger firepower to blast his way to Maria. He had no idea how many men he'd be up against.

The largest weapon he had wouldn't be easy to carry or conceal while weighed down with other equipment. Cal unearthed a sawed-off double-barrel shotgun buried under a loose floorboard in the bedroom closet. It wasn't a weapon he turned to often, but he kept it just in case.

He'd left the door open for Fonzie and wasn't startled when he heard his friend's soft footsteps greet him in the bedroom. Cal was busy tucking the shotgun into a duffel bag, which was just long enough to encase the entirety of the weapon.

"What you got that big fuckin' shotgun for? Ain't no way you'll be able to shoot anybody that quick with that slow thing."

"It may be slow," Cal said after a long silence, "but what it lacks in speed, it makes up for in power. Those bastards who took Maria will regret the day they were born when they feel the wrath of this gun."

Fonzie let out a nervous laugh and squatted beside Cal.

"Alright, what else you got?"

Fonzie bit onto his index finger as Cal showed him a few more weapons he had for the occasion, though Cal doubted he would use most of them. One of the weapons was a small spring-action knife that he planned to strap to the inside of a long pair of socks, in case his other weapons were confiscated or he was otherwise compromised. He was heading into what Fonzie had perfectly described as a death trap, and the more weapons he had at his disposal, the better.

The other weapon he planned to feature was a seldom-used pistol that he'd obtained from Alfredo when he was first starting out in the mafia, a Glock 22. While the gun was fine, Cal preferred the Beretta and thus hadn't used the Glock in many years. If Fonzie was going to help him, he could at least use the gun, which would give him two at his disposal.

Fonzie looked at the Glock, compared it with his own, and nodded in approval.

"This should do. But if these guys are wantin' to talk to you so you can give them what they want, what makes you think they won't just take their chances and shoot Maria once they see you have weapons?"

"I figured we'd load up on weapons, find our way in, and take out as many guys as we can. Hopefully I'll get to her before they do. It's not like Alfredo or Vinnie will actually be there to give orders. It sounded like Meransky was running the show anyway. He won't be giving the orders anymore."

"Why is that?"

Cal hadn't told Fonzie that Meransky had perished when Cal had stormed the Petrocelli compound earlier that evening. Upon mention of Meransky's demise, he saw his friend's jaw drop.

"Damn. If you weren't a marked man before, you sure are now."

Cal nodded. "You think a stealth operation will be better?"

Fonzie shrugged his good shoulder. "Let's say you go in alone. You blast a few guys, and I sneak in the back door somehow. Maybe I can get a read over how many guys they have around Maria and can tip you off if things are getting dangerous, or I can try to take them out if you can't get to her."

Cal considered this. He maintained a good mental image of the interior of the warehouse based on all the time he'd spent there as a kid, but he wasn't sure if anything had been updated over the years. He doubted it. He'd overheard both Alfredo and Vinnie mention that it was more of a dilapidated property and that not many drugs were being stored there or funneled out anymore. The police had caught on, and the mafia had moved the operation elsewhere.

If his intimate knowledge of the warehouse was correct, he anticipated Maria would be kept somewhere on the first floor, probably in the back of the warehouse, where many of the machines were. It would give anyone guarding her many more places to hide. Most importantly, it would force Cal out into the open middle of the shop floor, where he would be a sitting duck. If he could somehow get to the second-floor catwalk, he could fire on them from above, but he would be helpless to save Maria if someone attacked from below and his bullets were trained elsewhere.

Cal could only hope that Fonzie's suggestion of sneaking in through the back would work in keeping the mafia soldiers at bay. It wasn't perfect, but it was the best Cal could think of. It would have to do.

"Head for the back. Once you hear the bullets are done spraying and I get into some negotiating, you barge in and blow the rest of them away. They shouldn't see you coming from behind. Let's hope that, if there are guards outside, you can take them out too."

"I like that," Fonzie said, his toothy grin growing wider. "If we can all make it out of there alive."

"I'm sure we will," Cal said with no hesitation in his voice. "We'll just have to find a way."

49

Alfredo watched from the warehouse catwalk as Maria struggled against her restraints, trying everything to free herself from the rope that bound her wrists and ankles against the metal pole that extended from floor to ceiling in the dusty warehouse. He felt like laughing, seeing her struggle the way she was. It took a great deal of effort, but he was able to hold off.

In the faint sliver of moonlight that crept through the foggy upstairs windows of the warehouse, a sheen of sweat was visible on her forehead. Her hair had been ruffled and lay messily atop her shoulders thanks to her captors shoving her in the back of a van and likely having their way with her before tying her up.

He couldn't believe his luck. Thanks to the savvy work of one of Frankie Ramone's junior mob associates, they'd been able to identify and follow Maria throughout the preceding weeks. Rather than being furious when the young man came clean about the knowledge of her identify and where-abouts, Alfredo had celebrated the fact that one of the men lower in his operation had been resourceful enough to find her. It made the moment he was witnessing all the more special.

The more Alfredo thought about it, the more he realized how necessary her harsh treatment had been. He felt like getting in on the action by slapping her around a bit. Maybe that would turn her into less of a loudmouth.

She'd been the bad apple that had poisoned his prized hit man. She'd slowly peeled away Cal's primal instinct to kill, to hunt down the Chicago mafia's gravest enemies. Her love for Cal made him want to leave the mafia and walk away from everything Alfredo had ever given him.

Fuck the bitch. Now they'll both die.

Alfredo watched as Captain Joe Blutarski stalked toward Maria from the rear of the warehouse. Alfredo felt giddy with delight, wondering if the cop would frighten the already-scared young woman.

Maria attempted to turn to face Blutarski but whimpered in pain. The ropes around her wrists had been tied extremely tight. Alfredo hoped they burned into her flesh further with each move she made. Blutarski finally made his way to Maria's side, and Alfredo could see the look of horror on her face.

He took that as his cue to descend the stairs from the catwalk, the same stairs he'd rushed Cal down seventeen years ago after Cal had pushed that young boy to the floor. Alfredo's eyes remained trained on Blutarski. The officer was holding something in his hands and looking at it. Perhaps it was a photo from the crime scene. Regardless of whether Blutarski could match Maria to the photo of the girl, she was as good as dead. Everything Cal loved had to die.

"Miss Maria, it's nice of you to join us," Alfredo said. "I see you've met a good friend of mine. A man so loyal and dear to me, and very smart to boot, Captain Joe Blutarski. Mr. Blutarski, does Maria resemble the woman at the scene of the crime?"

Blutarski nodded. "It's clearly her, Mr. Petrocelli. I don't know how your inside man realized it was her so quickly. This kind of work would've taken us weeks."

"Don't concern yourself too much over that, Blutarski. You've done very well here. If you don't mind, I'd like you to stick around. Now that we know Maria is our witness, we can butter her up really quick. Prepare her for what she's going to say to the jury."

Maria's face was beet red. Alfredo could feel anger radiating off of her body. He couldn't help but loosen his collar in response.

"Is that what you want with me? You want to make sure I don't tell the police about your son blowing away those two innocent civilians walking out of the bar? Is that it?"

Alfredo laughed, holding his stomach with his large hands and bending over in a raucous roar of hilarity.

"That's a good one, Maria. Those men weren't innocent civilians. They were criminals working for the mayor, going undercover to protect his sadistic interests. Thanks to my son, the young boy you saw kill Mayor Caruso, and your disloyal lover, we've been able to vanquish our most heinous enemies, and the family I've worked my whole life building up will remain strong. Isn't it great?"

Maria shook her head and stared at the ground. She looked defeated. Alfredo smiled and nodded at Blutarski, pleased that his tactics were working.

A minute later, Maria finally lifted her head. Her eyes were wide and her arms tensed as she tried to pull herself farther from the pole she was tied to. Even though the ropes were tight and had to be digging into her skin, she kept trying to move forward, her gaze sharp on Alfredo.

"Fuck you, Alfredo. Your family is nothing but a power-hungry sham that gets off on ruining the lives of other people. I'm not gonna say a word to anybody. I've learned from the best. He's done such a great job of keeping your secrets."

Alfredo's heart pounded like a bass drum. How dare she criticize him and his family. He walked toward her slowly until his face was only inches from hers.

"I never would've imagined Cal dating someone so mouthy. What would you know about family greatness? Your family's probably never built anything worth a damn. Maybe a tunnel to cross the border?"

Maria clenched her jaw and the veins in her forehead were bulging in hate. Alfredo smiled once again; he was back in the driver's seat. He lifted his hand and brought it behind his head before slowly moving it toward Maria. He wanted her to think that he would smack her across the face. Maria closed her eyes before the tips of his fingers grazed her cheek.

"Ahhhh!"

Her screams filled the warehouse like the call of a rooster signaling the rising sun. A pair of hands tugged at her hair from behind, pulling it toward the pole that held her.

Alfredo's face lit up in laughter upon seeing the pain the man was causing her. He backed away from Maria, still laughing, joining the policeman and a third man, the man who had yanked her hair like it was an unsightly weed in a bed of flowers.

"Hello, Maria."

It was Vinnie.

"I hope my father has treated you with the utmost hospitality."

Vinnie ran his hands through his hair, letting it fly messily behind his head before pacing the room. Alfredo wondered what he was going to do next. He didn't mind if his son wanted to get in on the action. Nothing would piss Cal off more if he found out.

"Your stay with us will be rather brief, I'm afraid. We've called Cal to come get you, so you have a chance of getting out of here alive. If he does exactly what we tell him and you promise to keep your mouth shut, we just might let you live. After all, it would be a shame to lose a pretty face like yours."

Vinnie's laughter carried through the room. He continued to pace in front of Maria, as if moving slower would strike more fear into her heart.

"What are you going to have Cal do? I know he won't listen to you. He'll kill you and save me before he gives in to anything. He's a changed man; you all mean nothing to him anymore."

"Is that so?" Alfredo asked. "Cal's a very loyal man. I took him in when the kid had no right to live. He owes everything he's achieved in life to me. He'll do what is right."

"What if he doesn't?"

"Then I'll kill him. No questions asked. Some secrets, Miss Maria, can only remain so in death."

50

Fonzie parked the borrowed car a block away from the warehouse. In Cal's estimation, the warehouse hadn't been operational in years. He remembered a large employee parking lot as the first point of contact from the road into the facility. Parking there would make them visible to anyone Alfredo stationed outside. For this reason, they decided to make their approach on foot.

Cal draped the duffel bag over his shoulder as they exited the vehicle. Inside the bag was the shotgun and a few boxes of ammunition, along with some basic first-aid supplies, in case Maria had been injured by her captors. That he or Fonzie may not make it out of the building alive wasn't a consideration.

He knew in his bones he would find a way to get Maria out of there. That there would be no going back. The lure of the Petrocellis, the only family he'd had since he was twelve years old, no longer controlled him. Not after Maria's kidnapping.

It was beyond personal; the kidnapping was a repulsive

act. Even if they had no intention of killing him, kidnapping an innocent woman to get whatever they wanted from him removed Cal's blinders, revealing just how cruel Alfredo was.

Almost as bad was how Vinnie had followed his father's destructive path by desiring the Caruso kill for himself and running away from the murder scene, leaving Tony to face two of the mayor's thugs alone. Cal had no doubt Vinnie was also responsible for Frankie Ramone's death. Cal's blood boiled at the thought.

"We gonna get the fuck out of here? I'm ready to kill some motherfuckers."

Fonzie's remark focused Cal on the immediate task. He blinked away any thoughts of anger toward the mob and set his eyes on the warehouse, preparing his plan of attack. His hit man instincts were kicking in.

"You realize you're probably going up against some of your buddies on the street, right?" Cal asked. "This isn't a normal 'let's kill the bad guys' thing. In Alfredo's eyes, *we* are the bad guys now. I'm surprised it's taken me this long to realize I've always been one of the bad guys."

"Don't sweat it, man. I know what I'm getting into. I've got my own reasons for being here. I'm trying to get away from all this too."

Cal was surprised by Fonzie's admission. He remembered Fonzie suggesting doing something else on occasion, but they hadn't seriously discussed it. At the same time, it didn't surprise him.

"What are you going to do?"

Cal was curious about Fonzie's plan. He had no idea what his next step was after he rescued Maria and they were allowed to live the life they wanted together.

"I've been getting some singing gigs. Guess you were right that day back at the house. I got talent after all."

Cal turned to him in surprise, a genuine smile forming on his face, forcing his thoughts away from Maria for a brief period.

"Wow, that's great. How'd you get them?"

"Forget about that shit. Let's save your girl."

They walked down to the end of the street they'd parked on, which intersected the main road leading to the warehouse. The warehouse was set deep at the end of the street, beyond a rusty fence and spacious parking lot, with a row of office buildings dotting the sides of the street ending in front of the gate. The metallic siding of the warehouse looked downright dingy in comparison to the maroon brick buildings.

Cal and Fonzie huddled behind a thick evergreen bush, pausing to glance at the front entrance of the building, which was barely visible through the cluster of parked cars near the doors. The chill of the midnight air tickled Cal's skin like a bad dream dancing in his brain.

Cal couldn't discern the details of any of the cars, nor could he tell if anyone was out front.

"Jesus H. Fuck," Fonzie whispered.

"What?"

"Take a look for yourself. I've got some binoculars here."

"You brought binoculars?"

"Yessir. You never know when there'll be a cute girl in some window that you want to take a peek at."

Fonzie laughed and handed the binoculars off to Cal. Cal put them on and saw why Fonzie was surprised. Alfredo's car was parked among the cluster of cars huddled near the entrance.

"I wonder what Fredo is doing here."

Cal wondered the same thing. That's when the realization hit him that he'd have to kill his adoptive father to save Maria. He'd grown to hate Alfredo's guts but had never desired to kill him and cause distress to the family he'd considered his own. He thought of Susan, how heartbroken she would be to see her husband slain by a man she'd considered her son.

He hoped Vinnie wasn't inside the warehouse too. The pain Susan would feel at Cal killing her husband would be nothing compared to the devastation she would feel if Cal had to take Vinnie out.

"He must really want to make this personal. If he wants to kill me, he has to make sure it's actually done and that no one fumbles it. Seems right."

"I guess if it's that important to him. You see anyone standing out by the front?"

Cal scanned the area again and couldn't see anyone outside. He shook his head and handed Fonzie the binoculars.

"How about the back?" Cal wanted to make sure both entrances were clear.

"Sure don't look like it. But if we go in together and you cover me, maybe I can sneak around to the back."

Cal shook his head. "You can't go in with me. You're the element of surprise. If we both go in together and they see you, they might get scared and do something drastic with Maria. I'll go in. You can go to the back on your own."

Before Fonzie could argue, Cal lurked toward the warehouse, doing all he could to avoid detection. His senses told him someone was outside the warehouse looking for him, ready to hunt him down.

Going past the front gate, he stopped at the first light post he found toward the rear of the parking lot. The beat of his heart pounded like a bass drum vibrating through his body. He set the duffel bag on the ground and considered whether or not to bring the bag closer to the door with him. Even with the five cars in the parking lot, he doubted more than a dozen men were inside with Maria.

He glanced around once again and proceeded to the row of parked cars, deciding the duffel bag was too important to leave behind. Crouching behind the cars was his last stop before he entered the warehouse.

Cal sat behind Alfredo's prized Cadillac; the license plate read "BIGSHT1." Alfredo explained it meant "big shot," but Vinnie often joked with Cal that it actually read "big shit."

The humorous thought did nothing to calm Cal's nerves. He tried to slow his breathing and lower his heart rate. Thinking about it caused his heart to beat faster and his breath to become more laborious. Never had he felt this nervous when he knew he had to kill someone. Never had the stakes been this high. If he failed tonight, not only would he likely not make it out of the warehouse alive but Maria would die along with him.

Cal shook his head as he took one final glance at Alfredo's license plate. He had to be the big shot now and take Alfredo down before the mob boss ruined any more lives.

After catching his breath and listening for any sign of movement, Cal knew it was time to attack.

He bolted from behind Alfredo's car, duffel bag in tow, and rounded the other two cars parked beside it, forgetting how quiet he needed to be as he dashed toward the warehouse's front door. Looking up, his eyes met those of a bearded man who'd just emerged from the front of the warehouse, his face forming the expression of a scream as the door closed behind him.

Before the man could call for help, Cal removed the Beretta from his holster and blasted a bullet into the man's screaming mouth. The lower half of his face exploded in a smear of flesh and blood before the rest of his body collapsed on the ground.

Cal moved to the front of the last car and waited. He peered around the corner, his gun at the ready. There was no movement.

Confident he could proceed, Cal marched to the door, avoiding the massive pool of blood spreading on the pavement beneath him. More blood would be shed before the night was through.

Cal tried to pull the door open but groaned as it stayed shut.

Fuck.

He preferred not to break the door down; that would be far too noisy and would attract more attention than he wanted. He peered over his shoulder toward the bush where Fonzie was hiding, to see if his friend could provide any inspiration to solve his problem. He gave up when he realized he couldn't see him. Fonzie was too dark to stick out against the black night and the dark green of the bush. The door opened and Cal snapped to attention, ready for conflict.

"Shit!"

On instinct, Cal grabbed the man's neck and pulled him outside, squeezing hard as he tried to gain leverage on the man while shutting him up. The man's leg was jammed inside the door, preventing Cal from dragging him completely out. While he had a pretty good grip on the man's throat, he couldn't prevent the man's kicks against the door.

He went to twist the man's neck but was jolted back by a

sharp punch to the gut from his combatant, causing him to lose his grip. It wasn't the pain that startled him; rather, it was the quickness of the punch.

The man turned back toward the open door and yelled for backup. He was clearly an amateur and not prepared to deal with someone like Cal. His hesitation allowed Cal to recover.

Cal shoved the barrel of his gun directly into the man's stomach, and pulled the trigger, feeling the heat of the man's blood splatter against his jacket as he fell to the ground.

He opened the door fully and stepped around the dead body, more than prepared for the multiple footsteps he heard running toward him. A narrow hallway greeted him, with a reception desk and a row of offices and cubicles to his right. The doors directly in front of him led to the loading dock, while the doors to the left led to the shop floor. He wasn't sure where the boots were coming from, but he knew they would reach him in a matter of seconds.

Without further delay, he leapt over the barrier in front of the reception desk and huddled beneath it, bracing for the impact of the bulky shotgun still encased in the duffel bag as he crashed to the floor.

Several footsteps entered the room. It would only be a matter of time before they searched under the reception desk and the nearby offices.

"Fuck! Look at poor Nicky."

Cal heard the boots of one of the men rushing toward the front door where Nicky's stomach had to have been bleeding out.

"Don't worry about that shit now. Some fucker's trying to get in here and we've got to find 'im."

"You think it's another family?" A third voice had

entered the conversation. "A gang maybe? Trying to use this place to store drugs, guns, that sort of thing?"

"Hell no. It's Boyle. He's coming to save his girl."

"Who?"

"Jesus Christ. Callahan Boyle? Alfredo's adopted boy. The toughest hit man around."

"I ain't ever heard of him."

"You kidding? Let's split up, see if we can find him."

The man who had rushed out to see bleeding Nicky raced back inside to join his two comrades. "Holy shit, they got Bruno too."

"Bruno? That ain't Bruno. Bruno was back at the house. You mean Mikey?"

"Oh right. Half of Mikey's face is gone. We better find this guy before he finds us."

There was a pause as the men considered what to do. Cal heard a pair of boots march closer to the desk. He slowly lifted the shotgun out of the duffel bag, his fingers itching for the trigger. Once he got past these lowlifes, he knew he would be that much closer to saving Maria. He couldn't waste time.

"He couldn't have got to the shop floor, we woulda heard him. He's gotta be in the offices."

"Good call. Let's take a look."

Cal had to make a choice as he heard the men draw closer. He could remain hidden beneath the desk and hope they wouldn't find him or act fast and attempt to blow them all away.

He settled for the latter, ever confident in his abilities after killing the two men out front and taking care of business at the Petrocelli house earlier in the evening. He wanted to use the shotgun to blast each of them away, but it fired too slowly to protect him. Cal watched as the men's boots walked past the reception desk and toward the first row of cubicles.

When the last man had passed, Cal set the shotgun down, prepped the Beretta, and tried to inch his way out of the underbelly of the desk.

"Hey, wait a minute," one of the men said. The last man in the group doubled back and looked directly at Cal. Before his hand could move to his weapon, Cal sprung up from the desk and fired two quick bullets into the man's chest.

He knew the other men would come running but hoped the silencer deterred any other visitors.

"Shit!"

Instead of running toward him, Cal heard the other two men scatter back to the offices. They wanted no part in engaging with him. He would have to hunt them down.

Finding the two men and putting them out of their misery was part of the game of being a hit man that excited Cal. He leaned back against the cubicle wall at the back of the reception area and glanced over his shoulder to see if he could spot either of them. A bullet grazed his right shoulder before he could react, causing him to shout in pain.

A rapid succession of bullets rang out at him from one of the offices. The man shooting at him had an automatic weapon. They were bringing out the big guns now. Cal stayed static behind the cubicle wall, cursing in pain. Given he was at least partially hidden, he grabbed the shotgun and placed the quicker-firing Beretta inside its holster.

He waited until the automatic ceased firing and then lifted the shotgun, the stock buried into his left shoulder. Emerging from behind the cubicle wall, Cal waited for the man to step out of the office. Just as he stepped forward to shoot, he felt a thumping pain at the back of his head.

Someone had hit him with something. A hard something. His vision became blurry and his entire surroundings started turning black. He fought to remain standing, to hold the bulky shotgun and fire upon Alfredo's goons. The blurry vision rolled into his brain like the spread of a hazy fog.

As he slumped toward unconsciousness, he hoped he hadn't lost Maria.

51

T he first thing Cal noticed when he came to was a sharp pain radiating through his head. His jacket had been removed and his shoulder bandaged with gauze. He tried to lift his head to see what was in front of him, but all his eyes could register was a hazy fog of stars.

Cal knew he was seated in a metal folding chair and that his arms were tied behind him to a railing. His feet felt the grating of a metal floor. When he heard sounds from below, he knew exactly where he was. He was on the catwalk above the shop floor of the warehouse.

"Who would've thought I'd be able to catch Callahan Boyle? They're gonna be making me a made man any day now."

Cal recognized the voice. It was the leader of the pack of three he'd encountered in the lobby. He wasn't sure if it had been him or someone else who had knocked him out. The last thing Cal remembered was dropping the shotgun. He had no way of knowing whether he'd been able to get off a shot.

Cal's vision cleared enough for him to see there was

another man next to the ringleader. He sensed a familiar scowl plastered on the tall man's face, which was becoming clearer by the second.

"Remember me, Mr. Larson?" It was Captain Blutarski. The tough bastard's face shifted into a smile.

Blutarski walked toward Cal holding a baton. He brought the weapon forward in a swinging motion, aiming for Cal's head. Cal crumpled lower in the chair in anticipation of the painful blow. With the baton just inches from his face, Blutarski stopped his motion at the sound of a throat clearing. Blutarski and the ringleader immediately fell in line.

Alfredo Petrocelli, the man Cal had long considered the father he'd never had, rose from the stairs and entered Cal's view with a tight grin on his face. Everything else about his appearance signaled he was at ease with the events of the evening. His thick mane of hair was neatly combed back; intermingled with his brown locks were a scattering of gray hairs, representing the souls of the people who'd been killed under his watch.

"I hate to do this to you, Cal, but I have no choice. I couldn't have you killing all of my soldiers in one night. You came by a lot earlier than I expected, but I know you're a fighter and you want to get your girl back. I respect that. Only that's not the way things are going to happen."

Alfredo smiled at Cal and walked closer. He put his large palm on Cal's face and pinched his cheek.

"You thought you were invincible, didn't you? You thought I'd let you leave this all behind and go away with your girlfriend to find more freedom than you could ever imagine? No, sir."

The heat from Cal's wounded shoulder raced to his face in a blood-filled flash of rage. He was disgusted that he'd let himself get in this position. Being touched in such a condescending manner pissed him off even more.

Blutarski and the other man pointed and laughed. The once-powerful hit man was relegated to nothing more than a whipping boy.

"You recognize where you're at right now?" Alfredo asked, pacing away from Cal on the catwalk before circling back. "You're in the very spot where you pushed that little boy over the railing seventeen years ago."

The smirks on the men's faces opposite him turned sour, the soldiers surprised by Alfredo's revelation. "Yes, boys, that's how the legendary Callahan Boyle got started killing. He pushed an innocent little boy over the edge of the railing. All because his feelings were hurt that I shot his asshole daddy."

Cal felt the sudden urge to yell, like vomit that was rocketing up his esophagus, ready to be unleashed. It hadn't been an angry coworker who'd killed his father as the police and his mother had suspected. Alfredo had killed him, just like Cal had killed Alfredo's father.

Anger consumed Cal to the point of speechlessness. He tried to strain against the ropes that held his wrists to the railing, wishing he could break free. Instead, a stinging sensation sliced against his right wrist, almost as sharp as a knife.

"Fuck!"

Alfredo laughed. "You see it now, Cal? You kept a secret for me for so many years, but you have no idea about all the secrets I've kept from you. Shooting your father was an accident, but it opened up a great opportunity for me. I saw the anger inside of you. I saw what you could become. It was such a convenience that you and Vinnie were good buddies. He wanted me to help you since your mom was struggling.

It didn't take much effort to set up her death either. All so I could bring you in and train you to be the killer you've become today. And look where we are now? I'm the chess master, you are my pawn. Only the brightest among us can control where each piece on the board moves, and I'm about to sacrifice some of my pieces for the grand strategy of winning the game."

Cal's teeth clenched together, his jaw hardening in anger. What MacErlean had said to him before his death was true. Alfredo had sent men to T-bone his mother's car only months after his father's death. It had all been for Alfredo's gain.

Cal's entire life was nothing more than helping a sadistic ruler build his empire. He couldn't despise anyone more than he despised Alfredo. He'd become a worse man than Cal's father had ever been. Not only was Alfredo angry and violent like his old man, he was ruthless. His cunning and the ease at which he could get away with his crimes made Cal feel like a small boy again in the pantry closet. A helpless victim. There was nothing more Cal wanted to do than tear him apart.

"All this time I knew you were only interested in yourself and keeping your precious power. I should've been the one to go to the Commission. If only I'd joined up with Caruso, you'd be dead right now."

"Is that a fact? You killed someone dear to me too. The way I see it, we're even."

Alfredo turned to the stairway leading up the catwalk, then faced Cal with a smile.

"Vinnie, bring her up."

Cal spun to his left. He felt faint at the sharp movement of his head, his skull hammering from the blow he'd received in the lobby. The twist caused the sharp metal piece from the railing to pierce his right wrist again.

Cal let out another yelp of pain. He had no idea what was taking Fonzie so long. Unless there was an army of men outside, he should've found his way through the back door by now.

"That's right, Cal. Scream for her," mocked the ringleader.

While Cal couldn't see the "her" that Alfredo was referring to, he knew he was talking about Maria. He couldn't stand the thought that she was suffering at the hands of Alfredo's men.

He remembered the wailing scream he'd let out as a boy when he'd found out his mother was killed in that car accident. The bitter acid tears that he'd forced back upon seeing the pictures from the crime scene were finding their way back to the surface. He felt like crying and screaming for Maria, wishing the force behind his sorrow would take the place of any suffering she had been dealt.

Yet, being tied up, there was nothing he could do about it. Alfredo would try to take her away like he had both of his parents.

Cal felt the pain in his wrist once again. He figured the piece of metal from the railing would be sharp enough to break his right wrist free from the ropes.

He'd still have to find a way to free his left hand. Surrounded by three men, plus the oncoming Vinnie, it would be nearly impossible for him to take them all out alone. He had to believe Fonzie heard the chaos and would barge in soon.

Before he could think of breaking free, Cal saw Maria and wondered how much she'd been hurt. Her hair was disheveled, her cheeks red and puffy, and there were deep scratches on her arms. He scanned down her body and noticed the bottom of her shirt was torn.

What the fuck have they done to her?

Cal let out a low growl, fearing they had violated her. There was nothing more that he wanted than to end his hit man career by ripping everyone in the warehouse to shreds.

Vinnie walked toward him, holding Maria's arms behind her. A familiar cheesy grin made his face glow. Cal couldn't care less about their childhood friendship; he wanted to pulverize Vinnie's smiling face. First he had to break free.

He needed to create a distraction. He'd found the right point to slash the rope on one of his wrists to give him a shot at breaking free. But if he moved his arm too fast, they would sense what he was up to. The maneuver would require stealth. More importantly, he had to reassure Maria they would make it out alive.

"Oh, Cal," Maria cried upon seeing him. "I figured it was you when I heard the commotion. I was worried they'd killed you."

A loud smack echoed against the walls of the warehouse. Maria's face fell forward. Vinnie had struck her with his open hand, his smile growing ever wider.

"You like that? You should've seen me with her earlier. The only smacking you could hear was me against her cunt."

This time Cal's growl was audible. He was a lion returning from the hunt only to see his cubs in danger. His heart pounded in a combination of fear and fury, and the only way to make it stop was to pummel Vinnie and save Maria.

He jerked his right wrist against the sharp metal. The rope severed and his hand was free. Fortunately, no one seemed to notice as Cal kept his wrist against the railing.

Now that one of his hands were free, he needed to get a weapon.

"Enough," Alfredo ordered. "It's time to get to the point of why we're all here, don't you think?"

Maria whimpered, her body sagging as if she was struggling to stay upright. Daggers pierced Cal's heart at hearing her in such pain, and he imagined her enduring the type of torture he'd seen these men deal out to others. Alfredo moved away from Cal and toward Maria. His hands gripped the side of her face just like they had Cal's moments earlier. The sight of the mob boss putting his hands on Maria, the shining light in Cal's future, infuriated him.

"By now it's pretty apparent to everyone why you need to die, Cal. The same reason your girlfriend needs to die. You killed my father and yet you walked free, able to tell the Commission at any time that I'd ordered a hit on a living mob boss, the cardinal sin of the mafia. I trusted you all these years. Then you came to me wanting to abandon the family, wanting to stop killing. I knew then you couldn't be trusted, you had to go. The same with your girlfriend here. She can rat to the police. Police who aren't as forgiving as Blutarski over there. I can't have either one of you breaking the law of omertà. It's time for you both to die."

With his right hand free, Cal knew he could reach for the spring-loaded knife taped to his right sock, cut his left hand free, and plunge the knife into Alfredo's heart. None of the men had guns pointed on him; he'd at least have a chance.

"Dad, someone else heard our secret just now. What do you suppose we do with him?"

"You're right, Vin." Alfredo nodded toward Blutarski.

Blutarski removed his police-issued Colt gun from his holster, pointed it at the ringleader from the lobby, and fired into the man's skull. The blast from the gunshot reverberated throughout the warehouse.

Maria's subsequent scream provided the cover Cal needed. With Blutarski as the only man to his left, Cal could eliminate one more threat. He didn't think he could take down Blutarski and the Petrocellis at the same time.

Where the hell was Fonzie when he needed him? He couldn't afford him to take his sweet-ass time.

Cal moved his right hand to his ankle, ripped at the tape, and grabbed the knife, springing the blade into action. Blutarski was putting his weapon back in his holster when Cal cut the rope from his left hand and charged at him.

He heard the cries of the Petrocellis and Maria. Blutarski saw him charging and went to draw his gun again. Cal quickly reached him and plunged the knife into the nearest body part he could reach as he tackled Blutarski to the floor.

Cal heard footsteps running behind him. One of his hands held on to the knife as the other struggled to push aside Blutarski's fighting arms so he could resume stabbing the corrupt policeman.

Cal felt a pulling sensation on his shoulders. He figured Vinnie was coming for him. Cal spun around with the knife's blade extended and buried it into the first piece of flesh he could manage.

Vinnie let out a wild yell and staggered back. Cal saw the fear in Alfredo's eyes at the realization of what he had done to his son. The blade of the knife was buried just above Vinnie's knee.

Once it was clear Vinnie was surrendering, Cal removed the blade and focused his attention on the cop pinned underneath him. The distraction had provided Blutarski the opportunity to regain control. He threw a couple of hard right hooks to the side of Cal's head, dazing his tender skull even further. The force sent him falling back onto the floor, his knife sliding away from him.

He wanted to lie there and give in to the pain, but he couldn't. He had to fight his way out of this to save Maria. After all they'd been through, the progress they'd made, he couldn't lose her.

In all the commotion of fighting Vinnie and Blutarski, he wasn't sure what had become of Maria. Cal looked up and saw Blutarski work his way to his feet. The cop reached for his belt to draw his gun. Cal had to get up and fight or he would be shot.

He wanted to spring to his feet and take Blutarski down, but the pain in his head rooted him to the ground. As much as he knew he needed to move, it was like an anchor was weighing down his brain to the metal floor.

Alfredo was shouting behind him, warning Vinnie not to get involved. That was how it was going to be, then. Blutarski would pull out his Colt and shoot Cal in front of Maria.

A glimmer of light caught Cal's eye. The knife he'd dropped wasn't too far away. Neither Blutarski nor Vinnie had spotted it. This was his chance, if he could only find the strength to crawl toward it.

As Blutarski began to draw his gun out of his holster, Cal shook away the pain and reached for the knife. It would be a race to see who could take the other down first.

Cal had the knife in his grasp and heard Vinnie's footsteps lumbering toward him. Blutarski had his gun drawn and brought it forward, ready to fire at Cal.

Knife in hand, Cal found the strength to rise to his feet. He managed to spring his leg up to kick the Colt out of Blutarski's hand just as the officer fired the weapon. Blutarski was left defenseless. Cal turned back toward the approaching Vinnie, planted his feet, clenched his fist, and gave him a hard uppercut to his jaw, sending him flying back to the ground.

Cal saw Maria out of the corner of his eye. She began to run toward Cal as if her presence would help Cal fend off his attackers. Alfredo scooped her up in his large arms before she could get closer.

Cal readied the knife to attack Blutarski. His first lunge hit nothing but air as the cop stepped aside. Blutarski swung at Cal with another right hook. Cal dodged the punch, and the move left Blutarski open for another attack.

This time, Cal used all his strength to lunge the knife forward, the blade heading straight for Blutarski's throat. The cop began gurgling for air as he tried to remove the sharp blade from his throat. Blood from his jugular vein erupted everywhere, showering Cal in the process. Blutarski sank to his knees and collapsed to the ground.

The only people who now stood between Cal and the woman he intended to spend the rest of his life with were the Petrocellis themselves.

52

B efore Cal had a chance to catch his breath, Vinnie was back on his feet, ready to attack. His eyes darted from Cal toward the ground. Cal kept one eye trained on Vinnie and the other on the ground. Blutarski's discarded gun was only feet in front of both of them. Cal decided not to go for it. He'd wait for Vinnie to make the move. Then he could overtake his adoptive brother, giving himself the position of bargaining power he'd need to get Maria out of Alfredo's clutches.

Vinnie did exactly as Cal expected and dove toward the ground for the gun. Cal was on him, landing a hard blow to the side of Vinnie's face. Vinnie absorbed the blow and his next action surprised Cal; he kicked the gun backward—in the direction of his father.

Cal watched as the weapon skidded toward Alfredo, who bent to the ground to pick it up while holding Maria firmly in the clutches of his right arm. With Cal's attention on the gun, Vinnie punched Cal hard in the jaw. Cal fought back with a punch of his own before reaching back to Blutarski's slain body and pulling the knife from the cop's neck.

Holding the weapon, Cal made a stab at Vinnie as his adoptive brother attempted to counter with a punch. Cal slashed into Vinnie's hand, sending spurts of blood in the air from Vinnie's fingers. Cal saw the anger on Alfredo's face, and the mob boss raised Blutarski's gun to Maria's temple.

"You hurt him again and I'll blow her brains all over this warehouse!"

Cal reached out and grabbed Vinnie, holding his arm around his neck and pointing the knife at Vinnie's throat. If Alfredo made one move against Maria, Cal would take out his only heir.

"Let her go or he dies," Cal threatened. "I know how important Vinnie is to you. Maria is just as important to me. Let her go and we can both walk away from here with our loved ones."

Alfredo laughed and pressed the barrel of Blutarski's Colt harder against Maria's head. "You wouldn't do such a thing to Vinnie. Real friendship runs deep. Hell, the two of you are brothers. I think I have all the leverage here, Cal. There's no room for peacemaking."

Despite his life being in Cal's hands, Vinnie smiled with one corner of his mouth. Cal was amazed at how much Alfredo underestimated his love for Maria. He knew if anyone threatened to even touch Susan, Alfredo wouldn't think twice about killing them. In fact, he'd enjoy every minute of it.

"What makes you think I won't kill him?" Cal took the blade and ran it against Vinnie's skin. It was just enough to create a thick scraping sound, as if he were shaving him.

Vinnie flinched with the movement but Alfredo held steady; this was only another part of the game the two enemies were engaged in.

"Because I know what you've become, Cal. You're not the ruthless killer I raised you to be. You used to not give a shit about killing anyone. If we asked you to take somebody out, it was never a problem. But this bitch here changed you. I guess I should've known the moment you were willing to introduce her to the family."

Alfredo gazed at Maria with a false sense of adoration while she shot daggers at him.

"Think how much better your life would be without her in it," Alfredo said. "If she's gone, I just might give you the chance to live. Think about that. You can get what you wanted, a life away from the mob."

Cal didn't trust one word of Alfredo's lies. Still, he needed to bargain for Maria's release. The only way to do that was to let the boss keep talking.

"You want to know how I can promise that? Because I hold the entire key to your future. Either I kill your girlfriend tonight before I take you out or I let you walk away from here with the knowledge that you'll be the most wanted man in Chicago in the morning."

Alfredo smiled and laughed. Vinnie's smile grew wider under Cal's hold. Cal wasn't worried about Vinnie trying to escape his grasp. There was no way he could break Cal's hold despite the pain reverberating through Cal's body. Yet Cal was worried about what Alfredo was saying. How could he be the most wanted man in Chicago?

"What do you mean?"

"Well, Cal, I'm so glad you asked. Somewhere in this building I hold your Beretta M9, the very weapon you used to kill so many people for me over the years. You may spend your life in jail, but you'll be free. You won't have to kill for me anymore. Isn't that what you wanted?"

Cal growled at Alfredo. He knew they'd taken his gun

after knocking him out. At first he'd thought he only had two choices—accept his fate of death or be resigned to life in prison. But there was a third choice.

"How about I kill you and walk out of here with Maria? I like the sound of that better."

Alfredo laughed again and rolled his eyes. Maria exhaled deeply, seeming relieved that Cal was about to do something to help her.

"Since when have you grown so bold? It's a shame that you're finally standing up for yourself at the moment where you'll no longer be of use to me."

Cal couldn't waste any more time with words. He had to take action. He figured Vinnie had to have a holster on his belt somewhere. Since his arms were preoccupied, Cal moved his hips closer to Vinnie's waist and felt the bulge of a gun on his right hip. That's when he realized the plan for getting Maria back. It was risky, but he knew that Alfredo had the leverage and that he'd have no chance at saving Maria without taking a risk.

Alfredo could shoot Cal and later find a way to kill Maria. Cal was perplexed over why the boss hadn't tried the maneuver already. Maybe he really was concerned that Cal would kill Vinnie.

"You know what? After all this talking, I think I've had a change of heart."

Alfredo cocked his brow and smiled. "Really? It was that easy, huh?"

"You bet. In fact, I'm going to send Vinnie back over to you."

Maria started bawling as soon as Cal spoke. She must have been convinced that Cal was abandoning her, that he hadn't really changed and become the man he'd promised to be.

"In fact, here's Vinnie right now."

In a swift move, Cal dropped the knife to the ground and grabbed Vinnie's back. He reached for Vinnie's hip holster and shoved him forward just as he withdrew the pistol.

The look of shock on Alfredo's face was exactly what Cal had hoped for. He raised the pistol and fired right for Alfredo's cold heart.

The shot from Vinnie's weapon rang out like a firework. The bullet struck Alfredo square in the chest. The mob boss's face slackened. He glanced down to his chest wound. Cal wondered when the man would fall and drop his weapon. Could his power-hungry ways extend to his moment of death?

Vinnie had finally slowed down from Cal's shove. He looked at his wounded father before turning to Cal. Cal saw his eyes fill with a rage that he was all too familiar with. Their once sincere friendship and brotherhood had now fallen apart.

Cal knew he had no choice but to kill Vinnie. He knew this was how it worked with the Petrocellis. Kill or be killed.

Cal didn't hesitate when Vinnie reached inside his jacket. Perhaps he had another weapon. Cal shook his head. A lone tear rolled from his eye as he pulled the trigger. Vinnie was down in an instant, his wound appearing more fatal than the impressive wound Alfredo had sustained.

Alfredo fell to the ground, his attempts to stand strong in the face of death failing. He dropped Blutarski's weapon. That's when Cal knew he would make it out of the warehouse with Maria alive.

Maria must have sensed the same thing as she looked back at Alfredo before rushing forward toward Cal. Cal dropped Vinnie's gun and opened his arms, ready to hold her close, take in the lavender scent of her hair, kiss her lips.

He saw Alfredo move toward his coat pocket. Cal remembered Alfredo saying he had his Beretta in the building. The same Beretta that Alfredo finished pulling out of his pocket.

"Maria, no!"

Alfredo took the shot, hitting Maria in the back.

Maria fell to the ground midstride. Cal reached for Vinnie's gun in retaliation but Alfredo had given up, falling back to the ground in what Cal assumed would be his final act. He raced to Maria, praying that her wound was not fatal.

A loud bang sounded from the warehouse floor below. Cal heard the shouts of several men rushing in. They had to be reinforcements. If he was going to be thwarted, he would ensure Alfredo's death in the process. He went back for Vinnie's gun and ran toward Alfredo, determined to shoot the bastard in the head and send him to his death.

A set of footsteps sounded, marching up the stairs to the catwalk. Just as Cal reached Alfredo, he pointed the gun upward at the intruder.

"Wait a minute, Cal, it's just me," Fonzie said, holding his hands up in the air. "There's more of 'em coming. We've got to get you and Maria out of here."

Cal lowered the gun and focused his attention back on Alfredo.

Fonzie ran toward Cal, holding him back before he could fire. Why was his friend betraying him in a moment like this? And why the hell had it taken him so long to get inside?

"Save it, Cal. He's dying. Look at his face and you'll see that he's dying. Think of Maria. We have to get her out of here. We have to save her."

Cal's insides quaked in anger, but he knew Fonzie was right. He looked back to his girlfriend and realized her safety was more important. Alfredo had to be dying. The shot he had taken was right below the heart. Surely he'd die.

Cal and Fonzie walked over to Maria. Her body was cold and shaking, but she was alive. Fonzie put his jacket around her and pressed the material against her back.

Seeing the only person he'd ever truly loved in pain crushed Cal. Tears of fear and guilt stung his eyes. It was all his fault. If he'd done the proper thing and kept the weapon in his hand, Maria wouldn't be fighting for her life.

"Baby, I'm so sorry, I never should have put that weapon down. We're gonna get you out of here, okay?"

Maria whimpered while gazing into Cal's eyes. Cal wished he'd been the one Alfredo had shot at. It was exactly in Alfredo's nature to leave someone in complete misery, even if he couldn't control the outcome from beyond the grave.

"Cal, I can't feel anything. I'm not in pain, but I can't feel anything."

53

Fonzie sped away from the warehouse, exceeding the speed limit by a good fifteen miles an hour, until they were a safe distance away. He said nothing about heading for the hospital, but Cal assumed that's where he was headed.

Their escape from the warehouse was even more dangerous than Cal's entry into the facility. They were greeted by a swarm of freshly arrived mafia soldiers, each one vying to make the kill that would make them a made man. For they knew if they managed to kill Cal when even Alfredo and Vinnie couldn't, they'd be seen as the next big thing by the higher-ups. That was something worth putting your life on the line for.

At least that's what Cal had believed for the many years he'd been brainwashed under Alfredo's rule. As he and Fonzie returned volley after volley of bullets, all while trying to keep Maria safe and calm, there was nothing Cal would rather risk his life for than ensuring Maria got to live hers.

Cal rubbed Maria's shoulders to comfort her, fighting his

own pain as he watched Fonzie drive. "Where are we headed? We need to get Maria to a hospital."

"You crazy? You see all the bullet holes in us? As soon as we walk in there, our asses are thrown in jail, and Maria still might be in trouble."

Maria groaned upon hearing Fonzie's words. Cal couldn't even imagine how much pain she was in. He'd been shot many times but never to the point where he was in danger of losing all feeling. He knew if they didn't get medical attention soon, that any shot doctors had of helping her could be for naught.

"What do you suggest we do then? Keep driving?"

"No, I don't suggest we keep driving. I'm gonna take her ass to Doc Parker's and tell him what's going on. If he can't treat her, he and his wife will take her to the hospital. Say she was a random girl that got shot. It's not like they live in the safest neighborhood. Then we'll get our asses out of Dodge. Shit's hittin' the fan. I can't do no jail time, and neither can you."

"Maria's life is more important than worrying about going to jail."

Fonzie sighed and turned to face Cal as he kept driving. "You really want to go to jail now? After taking Vinnie and Alfredo out and earning the freedom you wanted? You want out now?"

"If it keeps Maria alive, then yes."

Out of the corner of his eye, Cal saw Maria attempt a smile as she leaned against his lap. How she could manage to smile and look so beautiful after such a traumatic event told Cal how special she truly was. He regretted not listening to her sooner about how bad the mob life was.

"You're something, Cal, you know that? Doc Parker's a good doctor. He'll take care of her."

"He's not a spine surgeon. I've known him long enough to know exactly what kind of medicine he's fit to practice. They have a better chance of helping her at the hospital. Besides, we don't know if he's even on our side. If he hears about Alfredo and Vinnie, he'll probably kill us himself."

"Take me to the hospital," Maria cried. "Please, just take me to the hospital."

Fonzie shook his head and kept driving, speeding through a red light on Cicero Avenue and turning onto Sixty-Seventh Street.

"I can't do that, sister. I'm not getting arrested. Not today."

Fonzie drove, peering over the steering wheel to follow the lights that pierced the early-morning darkness. He pulled into a parking lot that looked awfully similar to the lot of the warehouse they'd just left.

"What the hell are you doing? Keep driving or call an ambulance." Cal realized his cell phone hadn't been taken when he was tied up at the warehouse, and he searched his pocket for it. If Fonzie was having second thoughts about taking Maria to the hospital, Cal would take the fall. He'd let his friend get out of there to cover his own ass if he had to.

"Hold up!"

Fonzie shouted in a voice that was louder than Cal had ever heard him use before. It was a voice of power, a voice of authority. Cal wouldn't have been shocked if Alfredo had shouted like that, but it sounded off coming from fun-loving Fonzie.

Cal watched as Fonzie turned off the ignition and sat in the darkness of the car. The outside air was chilly, causing goose bumps to crawl up Cal's arms. He wasn't sure if the cold was entirely to blame. It could've easily been his worry over what would happen to Maria if they waited too long to get help.

Fonzie stayed silent and breathed deeply in the driver's seat. Cal wanted answers. He started to lean forward in his seat, ready to shake Fonzie into action if that's what it took.

After what seemed to be ten minutes of silence, Fonzie spoke. "Cal, you remember when we used to talk about getting away from all this? A day when we didn't have to work for the mafia if we didn't want to? Doesn't it feel good now that it's happened?"

"We're out now, aren't we? We need to get moving. Quit dicking around."

Fonzie didn't say a word. Why had he pulled into a random parking lot? They couldn't waste any more precious time.

Cal leaned forward, his face right next to Fonzie's. It was time for him to take a stance he'd never taken before with his friend. He would treat him like one of his victims and take full control, rough him up a bit. It was only a sharp poke in his side that caused him to stop.

When Cal looked down, he saw the blood-stained barrel of Fonzie's gun—Cal's old Glock—pointed at him. A realization washed over him. Fonzie had no intention of helping Maria, he only wanted her to suffer. But did he intend for Cal to suffer too?

"Cal, Cal, Cal. Did you really think I would get you and Maria to the doc and let you escape? I always knew you were one tough son of a bitch. That's why I went along with you this whole time. Someone had to be there to take you out, even if you managed to escape."

Cal could only swallow and blink at the man who had transformed from friend to foe. He never would've suspected Fonzie would turn on him. Hearing the words come out of his mouth sounded exactly as if Alfredo Petro-celli had said the words himself.

"But why? Why not kill me on the way to the ware-house? Why not take your shot earlier?"

Fonzie shrugged and looked up at the car ceiling.

"Maybe I helped you because I had a little vengeance of my own to seek out by killing all those guys at the ware-house. I really meant it when I said I wanted to get out of this life and use my talents for good. Sometimes you've got to get in the good graces of the right people for that to happen."

"You mean get in the good graces of this person who's getting you these singing gigs?"

Fonzie nodded while jabbing the Glock harder into Cal's ribs. "That's right."

"Who is it? Who's so powerful that they can get you these gigs? Is it Alfredo?"

Fonzie sighed but kept the gun firmly lodged in Cal's side. "Hell no. This is bigger than old Fredo. This goes all the way to the top of the chain."

Top of the chain. *The Commission.*

Fonzie chuckled when he saw the gears turning in Cal's head, putting the pieces of the puzzle together.

"How long? Does this go back to when we started staking out Caruso? MacErlean?"

"Nah. I legitimately wanted to help you kill that egotis-tical prick of a mayor. Who gives a shit that we had to use MacErlean as a scapegoat to set things in motion."

Cal couldn't believe it. The whole series of events that had unfolded over the last several weeks had nearly cost him, Tony, and maybe now Maria their lives.

"If MacErlean didn't actually know, how did you find out about the secret?"

Fonzie sighed. "Don't worry about that, Cal. It doesn't matter anyway. You already made it easy for me, killing Vinnie and Fredo back in the warehouse. All I've got to do is kill you and I've fulfilled my promise. Bertucci and the Commission keep getting me singing gigs and life is good."

Cal didn't know what to do. He could try to make a move against Fonzie, but he sensed a determination in his old friend that he hadn't seen before. He had a feeling that Fonzie really would shoot him if he tried anything.

He had to make the ultimate sacrifice if he wanted Maria to survive. Cal swallowed, his throat feeling like he was forcing down sawdust.

"Fine. Kill me if you have to. But let Maria live. Drop her off at a hospital, then you can speed away and do whatever you have to do to me."

"No!"

Maria shouted and kicked her leg forward in a flash of movement. Cal peered over his shoulder in shock at his girlfriend's sudden movement. He was startled by Fonzie's gun flying in the air and exploding a shot of gunfire.

Maria screamed. Cal immediately feared the worst. It could have just as easily have been the rear window shattering or the close proximity of the gun blast that had scared her.

He looked back to Maria and saw a torrent of blood pouring through the side of her shirt. He couldn't tell where Maria had been shot, but there was no doubt she'd been hit again. Her screams of pain were far louder than when she had been shot by Alfredo at the warehouse.

Cal ignored the threat of Fonzie behind him. The bastard couldn't kill Cal with his bare hands if he tried. He placed his hand against the side of Maria's shirt but only felt a small amount of fresh, wet blood. Perhaps the rest of the blood had been from her original wound. Cal lifted her shirt and examined her wound near her right rib cage. Not necessarily enough to be fatal by itself, but if it punctured the vital organs or led to enough blood loss, coupled with her back wound, it had a chance to be a killer shot.

Cal scanned the floor of the Cavalier for something to press against Maria's wound, to keep the blood loss to a minimum until she got to a hospital. He noticed Fonzie reaching next to him toward the floor mat, grasping for Cal's old Glock that had fired moments ago.

Cal delivered a hard blow with his left elbow to the back of Fonzie's head, sending him cursing and falling back into the front seat. He climbed over the front console and landed a few hard blows to the side of Fonzie's head, hoping he could take his former friend out quickly so he could get back to Maria. Somehow, Fonzie had managed to grab hold of the gun.

Cal took hold of Fonzie's right hand and pointed the weapon toward the windshield. Fonzie shot twice more, his arm unable to straighten and point the gun at Cal.

The men continued to struggle, with Fonzie trying his best to keep the gun in his control. Cal couldn't keep hold of Fonzie with both hands and find a way to take away the weapon. He let go, reached back, and fired a right hook into Fonzie's jaw, causing the gun to fall out of his hand.

Cal winced in pain after the punch, his right shoulder radiating in fresh agony from delivering the blow. He ignored the ache and dove on top of Fonzie, determined to end the fight. In that moment, he saw his friend as a traitor, someone who was so obsessed with his own escape that he had forgotten the loyalties he had to his important friendships by agreeing to kill Cal.

Fonzie delivered a sharp kick to Cal's abdomen, causing

Cal to shout and fall on top of Fonzie. The kick was followed with several sharp right hooks to the face. Cal felt a popping sensation below his eye. He suspected his orbital bone may have been shattered.

Cal didn't have time to collect himself as Fonzie pulled a knife from his pocket and jabbed Cal in his injured right shoulder.

Cal screamed and rolled off of Fonzie and into the passenger seat, clutching at the freshly opened wound. What had been a numb feeling in the shoulder intensified into a searing surge of pain as Cal tried to stop the bleeding with his free hand, all while reeling from the effects of the punch above his cheekbone and the dizzying sensation of the concussion he'd sustained earlier.

Fonzie was up again from his seat and came at Cal with the knife. Cal reached for the door handle and stumbled backward out of the car, landing with a sharp thud on the ground.

Cal struggled to his feet as Fonzie pursued him. He had no choice but to fight through the pain if he wanted to live. As much guilt as he felt for the crimes he'd committed since entering the mob, he knew he would become a different man. He would use his skills to save others from the evil of men like Alfredo, if only he could escape the fight with his life.

Fonzie lunged at Cal once again with the knife. Cal sidestepped the attempt and sent a roundhouse kick to the back of Fonzie's leg, using every ounce of energy he had to deliver the blow, sending Fonzie crashing to the ground.

Cal leaned over him, stealing the knife from his former buddy's grasp. It was time to convince him to give up.

"End this charade, Fonzie. You don't need to do this. The mob never treated you right anyway. Go back to Hollywood, land on your feet, and start your career there. You don't need the Commission to make it with your singing. You need to end this now."

Fonzie shook his head. "You don't understand. I'm in this too deep already. I need to deliver on this or I'm dead too. We can't both win, you understand?"

Cal knew Fonzie was right. The Commission would ensure someone came after Fonzie if Cal didn't end up dead. That was why Cal would have to kill him first, just like he'd killed Vinnie and Alfredo in the warehouse.

Fonzie tried to land a blow from beneath Cal, but Cal was able to block him with his forearm. Cal held the knife in his right hand and attempted to plunge down with all of his strength, to take care of Fonzie and be able to help Maria before it was too late.

"Why can't you just die?" Fonzie asked, his hands gripping at Cal's wrist, doing everything he could to not give up the fight.

"Because," Cal panted. "I have to live for something more than myself. I'm more than a hit man."

A loud yell and a thrust of the hands later, and Cal had sunk the blade into Fonzie's pectoral muscle. His old friend sank down into the concrete, bleeding profusely, his head rolling to the side.

Cal hoped he hadn't killed Fonzie but couldn't waste any time discovering if he had.

54

Cal raced back to the car. He had to get Maria to the hospital before anything else happened.

He wanted to help Fonzie too, despite his betrayal, especially as Fonzie grunted and writhed on the ground in pain. Maybe he would call 911 later and let them know Fonzie was hurt. Though his friend was misguided, he wasn't the one who wanted Cal dead. That was the mob's desire.

Cal entered the back seat and looked Maria over. She was shaking, perhaps growing cold from the loss of blood. Cal placed his hand on her face and brushed her hair aside, feeling how cold and clammy her skin had become. He looked back at her side and saw that the blood staining her shirt continued to spread. He had to find a way to temper the blood loss from both her side wound and her back before she got to the hospital. He was thinking it would be a better idea if he called an ambulance.

"Baby, I'm going to get you the hospital. Nothing's in our way now. I took care of Fonzie. Hang in there. You're gonna make it, I promise."

Cal wasn't sure if he believed the last part. Maria had lost an inordinate amount of blood, and he had no idea how badly her spinal cord had been damaged from Alfredo's shot at the warehouse. He didn't know if any of her vital organs had been hit from the shot in the car. Things certainly didn't look good.

"Cal, it's no use," Maria said. Her voice was like a soft whisper in the wind, barely audible. "I'm dying, Cal. Can't you see? I can't feel anything below my waist. Just when I thought I could feel something and I tried to save you, I ended up getting shot. Funny how that works, isn't it?"

Cal wasn't laughing. He shook his head in shame that Maria had to lose her life, one full of promise and hope, as opposed to his own life of crime and murder.

"No. I'm going to call the ambulance. Even if I spend the rest of my life in jail because of what happened tonight and everything else that I've done, I can't lose you. You have to live."

Maria sighed and tears fell from her eyes. Instead of being scared, she appeared to be open to the death she was facing. Too open.

"You're changing for the better, Cal. I saw the sacrifices you tried to make for me tonight. I was right in thinking you could turn it around so we could spend the rest of our lives together. You rejected your father's evil. You saw the light."

Cal cringed at the suggestion that Alfredo Petrocelli was remotely close to a father figure, but he didn't press the issue. He had to take action. Maria may have been slipping into death, but he had to give her a shot at life. He pulled out his phone to make the call.

Maria's arm brushed against his own. Though it was a gentle touch, the feeling of her fingertips sent shivers running up and down his spine. He moved his phone back toward his pocket, tantalized by her beauty, even in death.

"I feel it. I'm going to die. Kiss me one last time, Cal. Let me think this was worth it."

"No, don't say that, Maria. Let me call the hospital."

How could he have come so far only to lose her?

"Cal, do it. This will be the last memory I have. Don't you want it to be happy, instead of seeing how miserable I look?"

While her skin was cold, she was covered in blood, and her breath was beyond ragged, Cal couldn't say she looked terrible. He would love her and fight for her no matter what. But he could also see that she was going to die. He'd seen enough of his victims over the years meet a similar fate. Even if an ambulance got there within seconds, they wouldn't be able to save her.

He bent down and placed a kiss on Maria's lips. There was no intertwining of their tongues, no passion. There was a sense of love, even a sense of mourning, in the kiss. A final reminder of what they meant to each other, two lives in chaotic harmony.

Cal broke the kiss and stared into Maria's eyes for the last time. She smiled and blinked twice before looking toward the sky as she breathed her last breath.

A river of tears poured down Cal's face. He let out a loud, bellowing scream, confident anyone in the surrounding neighborhood would hear him, as if calling Maria's name would bring her back to him.

The fall of a steady rain could be heard outside the car. Pitter-patters of water made their way onto the windshield and through the open cracks and bullet holes in the damaged glass. The sadness the world was pouring on him compared little to the pain that weighed on Cal's heart. Pain that he was responsible for. Because he had failed.

He buried his face into his hands and cried the last of his tears, until he couldn't take the pain anymore and his tear ducts had run dry. The only thing he could do now was escape. He felt he should pay for Maria's death by waiting until the police found him so he could rot in jail for his crimes.

Cal's hand vibrated and he remembered he'd pulled out his phone to call the ambulance. He had no idea who would be calling or why he thought to answer. Part of him wished it was Maria, as if the voice on the other side would be a message from an angel.

"Callahan."

Cal sat up in shock as he heard the voice. He thought he'd heard the last of Alfredo Petrocelli. Somehow, he was alive.

His calm voice was the opposite of his usual temper. It was stern and controlled, with a hint of heavy breathing. Cal knew Alfredo wanted to scream at him for what had been done to his son, just as Cal wanted to lay into Alfredo for his role in Maria's death.

"I take it Alfonso failed to finish you off. Whatever he wanted to call himself, Little Fonzie or Fonz Man, or whatever, he was worthless. No matter who the Commission picked to take us out, I knew they couldn't get the job done. There's no one as good as you."

Cal remained silent on the other line. Only Alfredo could offer scant praise when the meaning was worthless, given the death that had been strewn about both of their lives. Anything he had to say to Cal meant nothing to him. The words were empty.

"But I want you to know that, no matter what hole you

manage to land in, I will find you. No more second-rate soldiers will be going after you. I'm gonna have to go to the hospital, tell some bullshit story to the police, then go home to Susan, who loved you like a mother, and tell her that you killed our boy. I'm going to have to bury our son, our only heir. You know how much that hurts?"

Alfredo coughed and caught his breath. How he'd managed to survive the shot to the chest was beyond Cal's comprehension. How could a man so evil survive a perfect shot, while a young woman so loving and full of life could be killed by a random, poorly aimed one?

"There'll never be another male Petrocelli to run our empire. You were the direct cause of it. Once Vinnie is buried, there'll be no more games. You'll be lucky if the police manage to find you before I do. You left your precious Beretta behind. That weapon is the key to all of your other murders. All the men you killed tonight, the mayor's men, all the hits you've been given over the years, they'll finally be revealed."

Cal's stomach boiled. He took a deep breath and let the anger subside. There was no point in getting riled up about this. He knew Alfredo would come after him. He would want a piece of him before the police got involved, so the legal threat was only a partially veiled one. Now that he was a possible fugitive, his need to escape was much more urgent.

"You know what, Alfredo?" Cal said after a long silence. "It's men like you who make the world a terrible place to live. You try to manipulate and control other people to get what you want and make sure you stay in a position of power. And for what reason? To have a sense of self-importance? I can't believe I put up with that bullshit."

Alfredo chuckled, only his laugh was unconvincing.

"Don't worry, you won't have to put up with it much longer. I'll be sure of that. I'll be self-important while you're portrayed as one of the most violent hit men in history once your story gets out. How does that sound?"

"You caused this, Alfredo. Maria's death, your son's death, thousands of deaths are on your hands. I want you to know that I'll be coming too. I'll be back to end your reign of terror over this city and to squash the rest of the mob with it."

Cal hung up the phone, not concerned with what Alfredo would say next. He could spit in anger if he wanted. Cal was going to find a way, as hard as it would be, to move forward. He would no longer be anyone's puppet. He was going to live the life he wanted to live. He was battered, he'd lost the few people he loved, but he was finally free.

He kissed Maria's cheek, exited the Cavalier, and ran off, his physical wounds nothing compared to the painstaking devastation at losing his girlfriend. He envisioned Maria's sweet face as he drew up his escape plan, vowing for revenge.

GET YOUR FREE BOOK!

A HIT MAN IS BORN IN THIS RIVETING PREQUEL THRILLER

The wrong man is killed in a hit gone bad. A burgeoning drug war between the mafia and a rival gang has reached a tipping point. There's only one way this can end.

Callahan Boyle is new to his role as top hit man in the Chicago mafia and has a tough target in front of him. After following his mark for weeks, it turns out that when the deed is done that Cal has killed the wrong man. His victim? The seventeen year old brother of a rival gang leader battling with the mafia over drug territory in Chicago's South Side. On his quest to become a "made" man as a mafia outsider, Cal is caught between a power hungry mafia leadership and a warmongering drug gang. When the mafia and rival gang collide, all bets are off and all lives are at stake. Will Cal get his wish to become made and help the mafia win the drug territory they feel is rightfully theirs? Or does Cal fall victim to the most personal revenge ploy Chicago has ever seen?

Marked For Murder is a prequel novella that showcases Callahan Boyle early in his hit man career. If you like explosive shootouts, high speed car chases, and a never ending set of enemies, you've gotta grab Spenser Warren's latest Cal Boyle thriller.

Claim your FREE copy of the Cal Boyle prequel novella, *Marked For Murder*, by joining Spenser Warren's "hit list" today!

Visit the link below to get your free book and join the list.

spenserwarren.com/freebook

Enjoy this book? Make a difference with your review.

Reviews are a powerful tool in helping readers like you discover their new favorite reads. Your honest review of *One Last Kill* can make a huge difference in my career as a new author and introduce other readers that will love this book to my work.

If you've enjoyed this book, would you please take five minutes and leave a short review of *One Last Kill* on the book's Amazon page?

Thank you for your support. It means everything.

Spenser

ACKNOWLEDGMENTS

There are so many people to thank for the parts they played in the creation and publication of *One Last Kill*. This book started as nothing more than a faint idea in my mind when I decided I wanted to start writing again back in 2015. Over the course of the past three years, it transformed into something I'm truly proud of, thanks to the help of some truly awesome and dedicated publishing professionals.

My sincerest thanks to Shelly Stinchomb for her developmental edit. Shelly is a first class editor who helped me take my writing to the next level. I've learned so much from you, Shelly, and I owe the emotional strength of my characters to your quality guidance. I'd also like to thank Michelle Hope for her superb copyedit and ensuring I didn't repeat the same words over and over again, which I have a tendency to do! Beth Attwood was a life-saver with her proofreads and Dane Low provided an outstanding cover that I know will make *One Last Kill* stand out amongst the ever-crowded virtual shelves.

I'd also like to thank my support system throughout this book's journey including Mom, Dad, Alex, Diane, and many more of my family, friends, and co-workers for believing in me on this journey. Your encouragement and support kept me going, even when my writer's block was at its' toughest and I felt like giving up. For everything you've done for me during this writer's journey, thank you.

Lastly, I'd like to thank you, adventurous reader, for taking a chance on a brand-new author. If you've found this book enjoyable or entertaining, then I know the journey was worth it. Thank you, and I hope we cross paths again.

READ ON FOR AN EXCERPT*

from

ERA OF EVIL

Book Two of the Callahan Boyle Series

COMING SPRING 2019

*This excerpt has been set for this book only and may not reflect the final content of the forthcoming novel.

ERA OF EVIL EXCERPT

Callahan Boyle slowed his jog along Pacific Beach in America's Finest City. He never imagined he'd be living in San Diego at any point in his life, yet here he was. With both Christmas and his thirtieth birthday approaching, he wasn't sure if he should be grateful he was avoiding another Chicago winter or relieved that he had Uncle Judd as the only family member he could turn to following his escape from the mob. Either way, his mood couldn't be described as merry or happy.

The gentle waves of the Pacific Ocean crashed against the sand. Families in wetsuits were laughing and enjoying the high fifty degree weather, glad they were able to surf and paddleboard so close to the holidays if they were locals, or excited to avoid the snow and icy roads of their less temperate homes if they were visiting.

Cal sighed as he spotted a group of college girls in jean shorts and bikini tops walking from the beach toward him. Even though the weather wasn't frigid, Cal couldn't understand how the young women were comfortable in the tiny clothing. He would normally wear a winter coat and perhaps long johns underneath his jeans at this time of year. Despite being away from Chicago's hellish winters, Cal was still clothed in one of his uncle's blue multicolored drug rugs and a pair of tan cargo pants.

One of the girls, a blonde with windswept wet hair and a seashell necklace, smiled at him. Normally, Cal would've smiled back. He was an attractive man and stood a tall six feet three inches, with brown hair and calming but fierce brown eyes. His only blemish was a scar just below his right ear from where his drunken father slashed him in a fit of rage when Cal was just a boy. But this time, Cal had no desire to flirt with the girl, attractive as she was. He felt dead inside and was still awash in grief at the loss of Maria.

Cal wasn't the romantic type, and it had taken him nearly a year into their relationship to tell Maria that he loved her, but he realized now that she was his one true love. She was passionate, she was comforting, she was independent, but most importantly, she was patient. Despite Cal's mountain of faults, she'd stuck with him until the end. The end that was brought about when he was unable to save her.

He couldn't believe he put down Vinnie's gun after he thought he'd finally vanquished his adoptive father and mafia boss, Alfredo Petrocelli. Had he done exactly what he'd been trained to do as a hit man - not putting the gun down until he knew his foe was eliminated - he and Maria would still be together and Alfredo would be dead. He'd likely be on the run, but he'd have his love by his side.

Cal wondered what else he could've done, what other avenues he could've pursued to ensure Maria lived that night, but he'd already exhausted all of the possibilities. The only thing he could've done differently was to leave the mob way before the Caruso business started, way before he met her.

Maria had been one of the reasons, perhaps the biggest reason aside from finding the truth about his mother's death, that Cal chose to leave the mafia in the first place. Yes, he realized his desire to stop killing for pay, but he never would've found the courage to ask Alfredo to leave when he did had it not been for her.

Cal's heart remained stricken with grief, and his burden didn't feel any lighter as he looked out onto the beach. The morning clouds had yet to part, meaning the typical Southern California sunshine had yet to appear over the sand. Cal's gaze settled on the group of girls and he noticed that they'd stopped their approach. A beer-bellied man around Cal's height in a white tank top and open red button-down shirt was talking to the girls. He was paying particular attention to the blonde that had smiled at Cal.

Cal focused his entire attention on the man and the group of girls. He could tell from the frowning of their lips and wideness of their eyes that they weren't pleased that the man was talking to them. The two girls flanking the blonde seemed unsure if they should make a run for it or if they should stay and support their friend.

Cal stepped forward, his eyes trained on the uneasy young women. He hoped that their gazes would meet, and they would see in his eyes that he sensed their pain and was ready to help.

One of them, a black girl in an orange bikini top and faded denim shorts, looked at Cal with hesitation and turned toward her friend, who seemed on the verge of exasperation talking to the man. Even from a hundred feet away, Cal could decipher from the man's slurred speech that he was already drunk. It wasn't even ten in the morning.

"Hold on pretty little lady, I'm just trying to talk to you," the man shouted.

The girls darted toward Cal. The man stumbled after them. Now that the man was drawing closer, Cal realized the drunken beach-goer had a striking resemblance to the man he hated the most, Alfredo Petrocelli.

"Get back here, ma'am."

The girls broke into a full-on sprint. The drunk continued his pursuit and wheezed as his feet swept through the sand in effort to catch up. He reached out and caught the blonde's right arm. She pumped her legs, struggling to escape his grip, but the man had both hands around her wrist and his feet set in the sand. There was little stopping him.

The girl screamed as her friends kept running, scampering past Cal. His eyes hardened as he turned back to look at them. They were too scared to ask for help. Cal knew he had to act fast. But what approach would he take? He'd promised Maria to continue down the path of good, leaving his previously violent instincts off the table. He could shout at the man to stop, hoping that when combined with the girl's screams, it would motivate the other beach goers into action.

It was the drunk's striking resemblance to Alfredo that caused his blood to boil and his mindset to default to violence. He knew that the man in front of him wasn't his adoptive father, yet his eyes saw a different story. He saw the same brown hair with gray streaks, the same bulging arms and shoulders, and the same devilish smile with wide white teeth that Alfredo featured. Cal felt a rage build from his feet, through his legs, into his chest, and radiate into his arms. The tension built up to a boiling point at the top of his head. Even though the man holding the girl wasn't Alfredo, Cal was desperate to do anything to inflict damage on his adoptive father.

Almost as if on autopilot, Cal's protector instincts kicked into gear. He was off, racing toward the girl, ready to save her. There was no time for words, no time for diplomacy. Cal was determined to beat the shit out of the drunken man, to have at him as if he were pummeling Alfredo.

As Cal charged, and his eyes met the drunk's, he noticed that the morning boozer refused to loosen his grip on the girl; a costly mistake. Cal had covered the slightly less than one hundred feet distance between them in rapid fashion, the pile of sand he ran through not even fazing him. His first was raised, ready to strike. A blend of confusion and terror was written on the blonde girl's face. He just hoped her reflexes were quicker than that of the drunken man.

"Duck!"

In a flash, the girl dived for the sand below, the drunken man loosened his grip, and Cal's fist collided with the left side of the man's jaw. He was down on the ground in an instant and Cal was on top of him.

Cal's fist slammed into the man's head again. This time the man cried out in pain and Cal swore he heard the crunching of bone beneath his punches. Seeing Alfredo's face beneath him, Cal showed no mercy. His knuckle clenched hands flew back and forth across his victim's face. The other beach goers ran over to watch the action. Out of the corner of his eye, Cal saw the girl stand from the sand and collect herself, a smile shining across her face.

Cal grabbed the man by his shirt collar and looked into his slits for eyes, which became smaller by the second as his cheeks swelled.

"You thought you could get away with it? You thought you could take Maria from me and not expect to face me? Well, you were wrong."

Cal stopped his punches and realized every set of eyes

on the beach were glued to him. The drunk slipped from Cal's grip, and his head collapsed into the sand. Cal knew that he had to get out of there before the cops found out what happened. He'd done his part in saving the girl, but he couldn't take the fall for beating up the bad guy. One major slip up and he knew he would be in serious trouble.

Cal rose to his feet, brushed off the sand from his pants, and smiled at the girl. She winked at him, perhaps ready to resume what Cal had thought of as her attempt to flirt with him earlier. Cal could only nod, running off in the direction in which he'd came, ignoring the cries—some of support—of the beach goers behind him.

Cal kept running as fast as he could through the sand and up to the rock leading to the beach's parking lot. He was ready to do whatever it took to get off of the beach without facing prosecution. He took one last look over his shoulder and saw that the commotion had stopped. He turned to face the other direction, but before he saw what it was, he knew he had hit something hard.

He'd struck the muscled pectorals of a San Diego police officer.

ABOUT THE AUTHOR

Spenser Warren is the author of *One Last Kill,* the first novel in the Callahan Boyle series. When he isn't busy at work on his next novel, Spenser is often reading, catching a comedy or improv show, and desperately rooting for a doomed Chicago White Sox rebuild. You can get in touch with Spenser at his website, spenserwarren.com, or by connecting with him on social media. Spenser lives in Chicago.

Lightning Source UK Ltd.
Milton Keynes UK
UKHW042138050319
338545UK00003B/55/P